W9-BJZ-587

THOMAS CRANE PUBLIC LIBRARY
QUINCY MA

CITY APPROPRIATION

ASK BOB

ASK BOB

a novel

PETER GETHERS

HENRY HOLT AND COMPANY NEW YORK

Henry Holt and Company, LLC
Publishers since 1866
175 Fifth Avenue
New York, New York 10010
www.henryholt.com

Henry Holt® and ® are registered trademarks of
Henry Holt and Company, LLC.

Library of Congress Cataloging-in-Publication Data
Gethers, Peter.
  Ask Bob : a novel / Peter Gethers. — First edition.
      pages   cm
  ISBN 978-0-8050-9331-5
  1. Veterinarians—Fiction. 2. Human-animal relationships—Fiction. 3. New York
(N.Y.)—Fiction. 4. Domestic fiction. I. Title.
  PS3557.E84A93 2013
  813'.54—dc23   2012050501

Henry Holt books are available for special promotions and
premiums. For details contact: Director, Special Markets.

First Edition 2013

Photographs by Warren Photographic
Designed by Kelly S. Too

Printed in the United States of America
1 3 5 7 9 10 8 6 4 2

I haven't dedicated a book to my mom in thirty years.
And she deserves it. So . . .

For your strength, sense of humor, toughness, stubbornness,
willingness to hold a grudge, support, love, and, most of all,
your extraordinary resilience and perspective. You are an
inspiration to all your children, the two real ones and the
many you've accumulated over the years.

ASK BOB

PART ONE

ANNA

From the *New York Daily Examiner:*

Dr. Robert Heller is one of New York's leading veterinarians. Dr. Bob takes care of cats, dogs, birds, turtles, frogs, and many varieties of rodents. You can write to him c/o the *New York Daily Examiner* at 642 W. 46th Street, NY NY 10036 or e-mail him at DrBob@NYDE.com and ask him any question you need to have answered about the animal you love. His column runs every Tuesday in NYC's most popular newspaper.

Dear Dr. Bob:

Our son just went off to college and my wife and I are suffering a bit from Empty Nest Syndrome. I want to get a dog to help ease the blow. I'm a serious bike rider and love the idea of a little four-legged guy running along beside me on my Saturday bike jaunts. The problem is, my wife is dead set against it. She feels the responsibility of taking care of him will fall on her. I keep explaining that it's not a responsibility—having a dog is a labor of love, and once he's a member of the household, she'll be thrilled to take him for walks during the day and have romps with him in the park. She says I'm crazy. I'm thinking of getting one anyway, taking the gamble that he'll grow on her. Got an opinion?

—A Hoped-to-Be Pet Owner in the Near Future

Dear Hoped-to-Be:

Yup, I sure do have an opinion. I'm with your wife: You're crazy. Ask yourself this: Suppose he *doesn't* grow on her? Then what? I remember a wise man once telling a friend of mine who was having a baby, "Having a child is not like having a dog." Well, that wise elder was only wrong about one thing: Having a *dog* is not like having a dog—it's like having a child! The exact same rules apply. At least they should. It's a responsibility, and unless you're prepared to sacrifice and keep sacrificing, you shouldn't be taking the plunge. You sound as if you want all of the fun without taking any of the responsibility, and that's a formula for pet disaster. Not to mention divorce. When you're ready to go to your wife and say, "I don't just want a dog to make my bike rides more fun, I want a dog I can take care of and feed and pet and play with, a dog I'll come home from work for so I can take him on a good walk in the park at lunchtime," then maybe you'll be ready to fight the good fight. Right now it sounds as if you think having a dog is like owning some kind of cool toy. And if it breaks, you can just toss it. We're not talking some kind of Wii version of a family canine. Being a dog owner is not something you can start and stop at will. There's no magic button that makes everything end up the way you want it to end up. Trust me on this, though, Hoped-to-Be: When you get a dog, you're entering into a relationship. You have to be ready for that relationship. And you have to want to commit to that relationship. Until you're ready to commit to a serious, deeply caring, and loving one, stick to biking with your buds and leave our canine friends out of it.

—Dr. Bob

CHAPTER 1

I fell in love with Anna because of her laugh.

Well, that's not entirely accurate. What really happened was that when I met her, I heard the laugh—gentle but not delicate, more than a giggle, less than a guffaw, and it came with a smile, one that caught me by surprise and opened a quick glimpse into a world of delicious absurdity and wonder—and then she turned around and said something that made my heart ache. In the few moments before the laughter and heartache, I wanted to kill her. It was a brutal combination.

I was twenty-four years old, on a summer break from my second year of graduate school, midway to becoming a VMD, which is Latin for DVM, which is Doctor of Veterinary Medicine. I was traveling through Europe, taking trains from one place to another for the most part, hooking up with friends and acquaintances in various exotic places (or at least places that seemed exotic to me), spending much of my time alone drinking cheap wine, smoking excellent pot, reading dark thrillers or spare Scandinavian treatises on death and despair, and staring out windows while doing my best to ponder the essential questions of life. Occasionally, I sent postcards back home hinting at a vague cultural awakening, but actually I spent most of my energy trying unsuccessfully to pick up women in museums and cafés.

My only success came, a little bit to my shame, in the Anne Frank

House in Amsterdam. I was standing in the middle of the famous attic, trying to figure out how it was possible that the Nazis hadn't simply looked up from the street, seen the top part of the house, and thought, "Hey, that seems like a good place to hide some Jews," something I never did come to grips with, when I saw a girl wearing jeans and a tank top. Her back was to me at first; then she shifted her feet so she was turned sideways. While pretending that I was looking at some yellowed photos of Mr. Dussel and the Van Daans, I studied her more closely. She wasn't beautiful by any means, but there was something I found very attractive. Her face was round and soft-looking, sensual in its fleshiness; her skin was smooth and cried out for touching. All that was extremely appealing. But mostly what attracted me was that no cool, good-looking guy with a backpack and a wire-chain tattoo on his bicep came up and put his arm around her while I was gawking. So I took a deep breath, strolled over, and started to say something about how I was alone and she seemed to be alone and that I wasn't very good at this whole introducing-myself-to-women thing, when I saw that she was crying. That stopped me cold.

"I've made women cringe before," I said. "And occasionally roll their eyes."

She stared at me and it crossed my mind that she didn't speak English, but I kept going. I figured it couldn't get any worse. Not speaking English might actually turn out to be a plus in this instance.

"I even made one vomit once. Although, no matter what my friend Phil says, it was really the tequila. I was only peripherally involved."

The crying seemed to slow down, so I sped up.

"But I've never made anyone cry before," I told her. "At least, not this quickly. And not without running over her foot with a shopping cart."

She looked like she was trying to smile. Or at least trying to stop the tears, so I thought the hell with it, skipped the semi-clever banter, and went for sincerity. I said to her, "Are you all right?"

"Yes," she said, her first actual word. Then she added, "No, not really." She sniffled a little bit more. "I'm just so moved by what I'm seeing and feeling."

Her response was touching and also encouraging, because not only did I now know that she spoke English, but when she said things like "not really" she said them with some kind of a German accent (it turned out to be Norwegian), which makes everything, even when you're sniffling about Nazi-related devastation, sound sexy. I wound up taking her out for a drink, and we talked for hours. During that time our mutual attraction grew. She started to look lovelier to me and she decided I was sensitive because I was going to work with animals when I got out of school, and then we went back to her hotel room and spent the night together. We didn't actually have sex—instant passion with a Norwegian stranger was definitely not my lot in life—but we did sleep in the same bed and cuddled. The first night she wore a T-shirt and nothing else. The second night she wore nothing at all but still insisted on the whole cuddle thing. Even without the sex, being in bed with a very attractive woman with a cool accent within twenty-four hours of meeting her was thrilling for me and way more exotic than most of the places I'd been visiting. Then, on the third night, when we made love, it moved from thrilling to spectacular.

Immediately after that it moved to something else entirely because we wound up spending the next four days and nights together, during which time I realized that Joly—short for something long in Norway-speak that either meant Son of Joe or Forged from the Steel of Thor's Loins—didn't just cry at museums for Holocaust victims. She cried when she saw mothers yell at their children on the street, and at magazine covers that showed rehabbing celebrities, and when I turned away from her too soon after having sex rather than cuddling, and even when walking among ancient ruins in Rome (they prompted visions of the people who had once lived and played and worked there, which in turn made her unbearably sad because they had all shuffled off their mortal coil and couldn't see that a two-thousand-year-old column they'd once leaned against had managed to outlast them). I also realized that all this crying wasn't really so touching. It was pretty annoying.

Once that realization set in, I did my best to go my separate way. But I was lonely by that point in my travels, and I wasn't very good at going my separate way, especially with someone who was so vulnerable that she teared up when the sun went down. Finally I wound up going with her to her friend's parents' vacation house on a small island off the coast of Sicily, which seemed more fun than making her cry yet again and traveling somewhere by myself. Besides, I only had a week left before I *had* to untangle myself from the relationship and return to the States and my last year of veterinary school. It turned out to be the right call. Because of Joly—neurotic, tearstained descendent of the Thunder God—my entire life changed.

The island off Sicily was called Favignana, and it was known for two things. One was its famed tuna hunt, written about as far back as the *Iliad*. People came from far and wide to watch the fun-filled spectacle of Favignanian fishermen herding thousands of tunas toward the island and then brutally slaughtering them. Even then, as a veterinarian-in-waiting, I could barely stand to see animals in pain. I especially did not like to see pain inflicted upon them by humans. But also, even then, I was learning to distance myself from the pain, so I could study it (some might say so I could stand it and cope with it) and possibly do something about it. In this case, however, there was nothing to be done. Inflicting pain on large fish was what kept the place thriving. So I did my best to accept the fact that I was visiting an island where a lot of people in boats felt very Hemingwayesque when it came to killing creatures of the sea, and where, as a tourist, one could buy an astonishing variety of dried tuna, tuna roe, canned tuna, tuna refrigerator magnets, and probably tuna-flavored toothpaste and rolls of toilet paper emblazoned with little silhouettes of tuna.

The other thing the island was known for was tufa—an ancient stone that had been excavated there for centuries. Every house seemed to be made of the stuff, which not only gave the island a distinctly medieval feel, it made every single dwelling look exactly like every other dwelling. As an outsider, I discovered that finding a specific home on the island was like looking for your suitcase at an airport baggage claim and realizing that everyone has the same Samsonite bag. The house that Joly's friend Marcella's parents owned was three or four hundred years old and built on a cliff overlooking the water. The walls were thick, which kept the house cool despite the staggering heat outside, and it was furnished, incongruously, with brightly colored couches and wall hangings from New Mexico. It was like staying in some weird cross between a Crusader castle and Graceland. I'd never seen anything remotely like it; growing up in a small town in upstate New York, I had never even imagined anything like it.

All in all, that house was my idea of perfection, except for the fact that Marcella was even more annoying than Joly. Unlike my depressed Norwegian, Marcella didn't cry at the drop of a hat; she scowled. At everything. I'd compliment her on the breakfast she'd made, and she'd glare at me as if I'd taunted her. I'd make her lunch, trying to be a good houseguest, and her lip would curl up as if I'd insulted her cooking. Between the tears and the scowls, I had to escape, even just for a little while, so the third day we were there I went for a jog. When I announced my intention at eleven that morning, I could see Joly's eyes go moist and Marcella's jaw start to harden. I got out of there as quickly as I could, running a little bit faster and harder than I normally would have.

I was about twenty yards from the house when I realized that my chances of finding it again were, at best, fifty-fifty. Not only did every house on the island look exactly the same, I also had possibly the worst sense of direction of any person who actually had all five senses functioning normally. So I did something clever. On a road leading up a hill, I saw a sign for a little trattoria. The sign said, BAR INGRESSO, and now I knew that no matter how lost I got, all I had to do was ask someone where the restaurant-bar named Ingresso was and eventually I'd find my way back. As an extra precaution, I did my best to memorize my jogging route. The whole time I was running, I would say to myself, "Okay, I just passed one street on the left," then, "That's a second street going off to the right," and "Street number three, winding up into the hills." I did that for about twenty minutes, which I thought was plenty, since I would of course have to spend another twenty minutes jogging back and by now the temperature felt like it had risen to about a hundred and fifty degrees.

I turned around and began backtracking. Fairly soon it occurred to me that my route looked completely different running in this direction. Within minutes I was a lot farther away from the sea than I thought I should be. But because I didn't trust my sense of direction I just kept going, figuring that in another ten or fifteen minutes I'd recognize something—with a little luck, the Ingresso bar. After twenty minutes or so, I still hadn't recognized anything. And I was now even farther away from the water: I couldn't even see the shore anymore, although I was certain I'd been running parallel to it the whole time.

By this point I'd been running ten or fifteen minutes longer than I'd planned and had absolutely no idea where I was. Bar Ingresso was nowhere in sight. I also realized that because I'd made such a hasty exit from the house, I didn't have any money on me. I didn't know Marcella's phone number. I didn't know her address, or even what street she lived on. Or if her street actually had a name. Then it occurred to me that I had no idea what Marcella's name was, other than Marcella. The other nice touch was that I didn't speak a word of Italian other than *grazie, ciao,* and *carbonara.*

So I did the only thing I could think of: I kept running. Eventually I had to see the house where I was staying. Didn't I?

When I hit the hour mark, the answer was starting to seem like a resounding no.

At an hour and fifteen minutes, I saw my first person. A car was coming toward me. I flagged it down, waving my hands, doing my best not to look like a lunatic. The driver slowed and cautiously rolled his window down. I politely said, "Speak English?" When he shook his head no, I spoke in your basic, sophisticated Chico Marx accent, saying something that was very close to "Excusa mio . . . Bar Ingresso? Knowa Bar Ingresso?" At first he looked puzzled—hard to blame him—but when I mentioned Bar Ingresso he nodded and pointed in the direction I was headed. I hoped the look in my eyes and the raised eyebrow somehow communicated the words "How far?" They seemed to do that because he said, *"Due chilometri."* I said *"grazie"* seven or eight times and resumed my jog, this time happily. In about two kilometers, I did indeed get to a bar. But it wasn't Bar Ingresso. It was also closed, and it looked like it had been closed since the last dinner party thrown by the Medicis. Deflated, I decided to keep going and quickly resumed my running. Moving seemed like a better alternative than simply lying down on the side of the road and getting parboiled.

I'll spare you an account of the next two hours of my life except to say that it was pretty much the same as the previous hour and a half, only a lot hotter. Along the way I encountered three different people, none on foot, each of whom confidently sent me to a different bar, none of which turned out to be Bar Ingresso. When I encountered a fourth person—actually a small group of people—I went back to Chico Marx and did my best to say the following: "I'm a really stupid American, I don't know where I'm staying or who I'm staying with, and I don't have money, but could you please send me to Bar Ingresso?" When they stared blankly at me, I asked if they knew anyone named Marcella who lived on the sea. They beat a hasty retreat.

Somewhere around three P.M., I decided that Joly and Marcella would come looking for me. So I began to walk slowly—and "walk" is a slight exaggeration here; I was by now struggling to put one foot in front of the other—but whenever a car appeared in the distance, I'd raise my head, puff up my chest, and start jogging, so if my two hostesses really had formed a search party, I could tell them that I'd simply been running and had forgotten all about the time. Being a macho athletic machine seemed a lot more appealing than coming across as a total and pathetic loser on the verge of sunstroke.

At three-thirty I passed a small fire station and a park, which I was reasonably sure I'd passed an hour or so before. As far as I knew I'd been going in one direction, so I wasn't quite sure how I could have passed something twice. But by this point I had stopped trusting anything that was emanating from my brain. And my trudging was on the verge of becoming something closer to a crawl, the hands-and-knees kind. Then, somehow, I found myself on a small, white-stone beach. (There's no sand in Favignana, just white pebbles and crushed shells, a fact I discovered when I sat down, exhausted, and discovered that lying down on the lovely landscape was like leaping onto a red-hot table topped with crushed glass.) Since I knew Marcella lived on the water and I was now on the water myself, I took this little white beach as a very good sign that I was on the verge of finding my way home.

And here was another good sign: On that pebble-and-shell beach was one of the most stunning women I'd ever seen in my life, lying serenely on a towel a few feet from me, impervious to the pain of the shells and pebbles. She was wearing cut-off jeans and a bathing suit top. Her legs were long and flawlessly tapered. Her hair was medium-dark brown, streaked lighter from the sun and layered as it made its way down to her perfectly shaped shoulders. Her eyes were brown and oval and hypnotic. I honestly don't think I'd ever seen anyone who was so beautiful in a nonintimidating way. She was so intoxicating that I didn't give all that much thought to the fact that I was sweating more than Shaquille O'Neal after quadruple overtime, or that my skin was starting to blister in a way that made me look vaguely leprous. I just stumbled over to her and went into my new Vito Scotti imper-sonation, the by now almost rote I'm-a-dumb-American-no-money-no-idea-of-anything-except-I-have-to-find-Bar-Ingresso.

She looked at me strangely. I'd gotten extremely odd looks through-out the day, but this one had that special extra subtext of "Are you a *dangerous* lunatic or just a tragic, helpless lunatic?" But when she didn't say anything, I finally said, "Do you speak English?"

She hesitated, then said, "A leetle."

If I thought the Scandinavian accent was appealing, this Italian accent almost made my head spin, which wasn't much of an accom-plishment at that point. Still, it was pretty intoxicating.

"You want Bar Ingresso?" she now said.

I nodded.

"Nothing more?"

"Well," I said, "I'd also like to find my friend or maybe even a hos-pital with an oxygen tank and a burn unit, but Bar Ingresso would be a good start."

She looked at me blankly, obviously not understanding a word I'd said. Determined to help my cause, I said, "See, I was jogging, but I have a terrible sense of direction, so I memorized the name of a bar, Bar Ingresso, that was close to where I'm staying and . . . and . . . well, I've been running around the island . . . and . . ."

I degenerated into "and"s and "well"s because I perceptively realized I wasn't actually helping my cause. I was making a case for commitment to a mental institution. But she must have seen something that touched her because she mercifully interrupted my blathering and said, "You want you should walk with me?" Then she shook her head fiercely, annoyed at herself. "You want I should walk with you?"

All I could think of was how beautiful her hair looked when she shook it that way, but I just said, "Bar Ingresso is close?"

"Close," she mimicked, nodding. "Sì. At end of . . . how you say . . . bitch?"

"Beach."

"Ah yes. Beee-eeech. At end of beach."

"Then yes," I said, hoping I didn't burst into tears of relief and giddy joy. "I would very much want I should walk with you."

She smiled now, just a little slip of one, but it was more than enough for me. We began walking to the far end of the beach.

After a few steps, the beautiful, saintlike Italian woman said, "You look . . ."

She trailed off, shrugged in frustration, not coming up with the English word.

"Tired?" I said. "Burned? Frustrated? Stupid? Insane? Ridiculous?"

"No," she said. "But okay. All of them."

We walked across the beach, then up to a road, talking the whole way, me in my imbecilic nonlanguage, her in her poor English with the beautiful Italian lilt. Somehow we understood each other. We didn't talk about anything important, but it was all very easy and comfortable. I learned that her name was Annabella and that she wasn't from the island, just visiting a friend for a few days. I told her my name was Bob, Robert; she called me Roberto, and the way she said it made me loathe the flat, one-syllable version I'd used my entire life. I told her I was studying to work with animals, and she liked that. I asked if she was a model, and that made her laugh. When she laughed, the sunlight caught her hair and made it glow and my heart skipped a tiny beat.

As she led me down the road, I forgot about being lost and my Lawrence of Arabia–like past few hours and having no idea how I'd ever get my money or my passport. I certainly forgot all about Joly and Marcella, at least until they drove right by us.

Marcella stopped short, her tires screeching. She and Joly both jumped out of the car, Joly crying hysterically, saying she thought I'd had a heart attack and fallen and drowned, and I went, *What?* because even for her that seemed a tad melodramatic. Marcella scowled harder than ever and muttered ominously in Italian. Joly, as it sank in that I wasn't dead, got angrier and angrier and then, noticing Annabella, angrier still. She started screaming at Annabella in English, who shrugged and tried to say she didn't understand, so Marcella started yelling at her in Italian. She must have said something really awful because Annabella turned around and started walking away, without saying a word. And then, in remarkably short order, Joly took my suitcase out of the car and threw it on the road, and she and Marcella drove off. My first thought wasn't that they'd just left me in some godforsaken spot, basically on my own; my first thought was to wonder why they'd bothered to put my suitcase in the car. I figured they must have expected to discover that I was floating in whatever sea Favignana was in the middle of, and they were either going to ship my belongings back to my parents or give everything away to the Home for Unslaughtered Tunas. At which point I began to wonder what the hell I was going to do now.

I bent down, rummaged through my suitcase, and found my money and passport—they'd done a very tidy and complete packing job. Suddenly I remembered Annabella; turning, I found her staring at me in total bewilderment. Happily, she'd made her way back to me after the two crazy women had left.

"Your girlfriend," she said in halting English. "She's very angry."

"Not my girlfriend," I said. And for some reason, I began to pour out the whole story. My first trip to Europe, and how I wanted it to change everything, only it hadn't; traveling alone, which was exhilarating but lonely and isolating; going to the Anne Frank House and all the crying and scowling and how I was going to be a vet and only had a few days before I had to go back to reality. And how reality was starting to scare the shit out of me now, and I wasn't exactly sure why, except that I felt as if I was on the verge of understanding something after my summer in Europe, even if I didn't know what that something was. I told her everything I'd been thinking but hadn't acknowledged, realizing I hadn't even fully known what I'd been thinking until I spoke the words.

Finally I stopped babbling and said, "Oh shit, you don't even understand anything I'm saying."

"*Sì,*" she said. "I understand."

"You do?"

"*Sì.*"

"Well, I'm glad. But I don't see how, because *I* could barely understand what I was saying."

She nodded and said, "There's something I'd better tell you."

I nodded back and said, "Okay." And then said, "What happened to your Italian accent?" Because it had disappeared.

A look of deep embarrassment crossed her face. "Don't kill me," she said.

"Seriously. What happened to your accent?"

"I don't have one."

"I don't understand."

"I'm American."

I said the following, I think without taking a breath: "*What?* No, you're not! You're Italian! You're American? *What the hell do you mean?*"

Now she was fidgeting. Even so, she projected a certain confidence as she confessed, as if she knew she'd do it all again if given a chance. "Well . . . you seemed so confused, and there was no one around, and I thought it'd be funny if I pretended to be Italian, just to see how long I could keep you going. I didn't realize quite what a mess you were, and by the time I did I thought maybe you'd get angry so I just kept it going, figuring I'm never going to see you again anyway, so what difference does it make. And then when those two crazy girls came by, I didn't want them to talk to me."

"What was Marcella screaming at you in Italian?"

"I don't know," she said. "That's why I didn't want them to talk to me. I don't speak Italian."

"What!"

"Well, that's not totally true. I speak a tiny little bit. Enough to know why you couldn't find your Bar Ingresso."

"Why not?"

"Because *ingresso* means 'entrance.' "

I said, "What?" for probably the hundredth time, but I wasn't capable of coming up with anything more incisive.

She nodded, and that's when I got the smile—the killer one, not just the little subtle one. "You've been going up to people saying that you're lost and don't have any money and all you need to do is find the entrance to the nearest bar."

"Oh shit," I said.

She nodded in agreement. "Yeah." And with that "yeah" there was also a raised eyebrow and an even bigger smile. She didn't bother to attempt to suppress it.

I was about to get really angry. At the fact that I was so hot and thirsty that I was on the verge of collapsing. At how humiliated and lost I felt. At my own stupidity. And mostly at her for making me feel even stupider than I already was.

That's when she burst out laughing. She couldn't keep it inside any longer; the smile was no longer enough to convey the sense of the day's absurdity. It was an unusual laugh. Not violent in any way. More seductive than a giggle, and more grown-up. I could tell she wasn't laughing at me. Well, yes, she was. But she was also laughing at the whole world, at all the craziness everywhere. It was a laugh that made you appreciate that craziness even though you wanted to run away from it. You wanted to run right into the arms of the person laughing at it.

Then I started to laugh, too. I couldn't help it. It was impossible not to.

"You're not angry?" she said.

"I don't know," I told her. "Just tell me your name is really Annabella."

"Nope," she said. "Just Anna. I needed something that sounded more Italian, so I added the 'bella.'"

"Oh my god."

"I know," she said. "I'm sorry."

"No, you're not."

"But I know that I *should* be, if that makes you feel any better."

She led me a few hundred feet away, and we got in her car. She didn't invite me; it simply seemed the thing to do. And as she began driving—it was her friend's car, the one she was visiting—the laughter turned into a remarkably comfortable silence. Remarkable because both things—comfort and silence—shouldn't have been remotely possible at this point. It wasn't broken until she asked me a question. She had a real talent for being able to veer from laughter to comfort to serious probing without making it seem anything but natural.

"The angry girl. Joly. What did you see in her? I mean, what possibly made you think it was a good idea to spend a week with her other than breasts the size of mutant watermelons?"

"I don't know," I said. I went quiet again, although this was a different kind of silence, because when Anna asked a question she asked it in a way that made you want to think about it so you could give her a worthy answer. "Actually, I do know," I finally said. "It's because everything seemed so sad to her. She took everything so hard. I thought she needed someone to be nice to her."

"You *were* nice. But you could have left. You didn't have to *keep* being nice."

I shrugged. "It just didn't seem right."

"Is that why you want to be a vet?"

"What's the connection?"

"Because you feel this compunction to make everything feel better?"

I thought about this. Shook my head and said, "No."

"So what is it? Why are you so nice to small little animals and big-breasted women?"

"I don't know," I said. "I guess it's because I've always been better with animals than with people. And because I think the world's a fairly fucked-up place. So sometimes it's important to be kind. I find it a lot easier to be kind to animals. Well, that's not quite right. I find that animals respond a lot better to my kindness. They don't . . ."

I wasn't sure how to finish my sentence. Anna finished it for me.

". . . shit all over you? Like Watermelon Breasts?"

When I nodded, she cocked her head at me in such a curious way I felt compelled to ask, "Is that so weird?"

"No," she said. "I think about this a lot. I mean the fucked-upness part. Sometimes I try to separate all the bad stuff from the good stuff, put the bad people in a different place from the good ones, you know? Think about what the difference is."

"And?"

"And I think if you get rid of all the shit and all the bad stuff and just try to keep what we're supposed to keep and strip everything else away . . ."

She hesitated. I told her I couldn't stand the suspense.

"Well," she said, "then I think all we have left is our kindness."

I realized it later. Or, rather, acknowledged it later. The truth is, I knew it even then. My heart ached with an emotion I barely recognized. But I was sure I knew what it was. That's the moment I fell in love with Anna.

I don't know exactly when she fell in love with me—probably a few months after that—but the important thing is that eventually she did. So a little less than a year later we got married and set about trying to be kind to each other for the rest of our lives.

From the *New York Daily Examiner:*

Dr. Robert Heller, one of New York's leading veterinarians, is the author of *They Have Nothing but Their Kindness,* a book about how to care for your pet. Dr. Bob takes care of cats, dogs, horses, birds, snakes, turtles, frogs, small pigs, and many varieties of rodents. You can e-mail him at DrBob@NYDE.com and ask him any question about the animal you love. His column runs every Tuesday in NYC's most popular newspaper.

Dear Doc Bob:

I just bought my first kitten, a lovely little girl I've named Lulu. I've had Lulu for a week now, and the problem is that she seems so mournful. She's not a happy cat. She doesn't want to play most of the time. She's not eating well. I guess I'm probably anthropomorphizing, but she seems to be moping. When I bought her from the breeder, I saw that she came from a large litter and had five or six brothers and sisters. I'm wondering if the moping is because she misses her siblings and her mother. Should I go back to the breeder and try to reunite Lulu with one of her family members? Do you think that would solve the problem? I can't stand seeing this sweet little girl unhappy.

Sincerely,
Struggling with a Broken Family

Dear Struggling:

Might Lulu be better off being reunited with a sibling? Sure. But is that a foolproof solution to her (and your) problem? Let me put it this way: Family reunions can be awfully nice. Or they can be your basic nightmare. It all depends on the family. I don't think that parents and siblings a family make. At least, to quote George Gershwin's cat, Rhythm, who once said to George, after he accused her of scratching a few piano keys: "It ain't necessarily so." Families can be a source of comfort, but the crucial thing is how one defines the word "family." I'm not a big believer in using bloodlines as the defining factor. A family is, or should be, any group that provides love and support. Groups I'd define as happy families include Snow White and her very loyal seven dwarfs, the 1969 Knicks, and the von Trapps. Note that not all of them were actually related. In my book, unhappy families would include Willy and the rest of the Lomans, the Manson clan, and Cinderella and her charming stepsisters and stepmother. In case I haven't made my point clear: Would it be a bad thing for you to go out and bring one of Lulu's bros or sisters home? No, of course not. I'm all for adding as many animals as possible to a happy home. But it's no longer Lulu's biological family's responsibility to be there for Lulu. You and she need to be there for each other. Lulu is now your family, and you are hers. It can take time to create that kind of bond and that kind of trust. But that's what you need to do: get Lulu to love and trust you the way she trusted her cat mom. Give her the same kind of comfort she got from her cat siblings. Once you both learn to love and trust each other, most of your family problems will be solved. At least until Lulu becomes a teenager and starts dating.

—Dr. Bob

CHAPTER 2

I would never say that I am an expert on human nature—far from it. I'm on much surer footing when it comes to analyzing the symptoms of Cushing's disease in cats (I will wager my knowledge of the feline adrenal cortex against anyone's) or the reasons many Yorkshire terriers lose half their teeth by the age of two. (In case you're interested, it's because our desire to breed perfect show dogs, hunting dogs, and just plain cute dogs, particularly when it comes to toy breeds, has led to the distortion of the Yorkie's natural jawline; in other words, humans have created adorable little dogs that now have jaws too small to accommodate all their teeth.) However, I don't only pay attention to the animals that are brought to me; I try to focus a bit on their owners as well. So while my powers of observation may be somewhat limited, I have come to trust in their accuracy.

One thing that constantly astonishes me is the human refusal to absorb knowledge. Pets are different. Granted, dogs and cats have a narrower range of things they need to pick up on in order to live happily ever after. For them it's mostly: *Where do you usually put my food bowl? How do I let you know when I need to relieve myself? Which places are unsafe when I'm wandering outside?* And: *What's the most effective way to make you scratch my ears?* But they sure do learn those things quickly. And once they learn them, they don't forget them.

We humans are capable of taking in important information, of course. But we also tend to reject any fact we'd rather not know. Instead, we prefer to listen to someone who either reinforces what we already believe or shows us the easiest possible path to (a) money, (b) happiness, or (c) immortality. I don't think that necessarily makes us inferior to our four-legged friends, because they have something of the same tendency. It's just that in their case, instead of piling on the greed and lusting for eternal life, they tend to go for food and pats of affection. I must admit that I find both of the latter desires a little more palatable.

I can say this with great certainty as well: The older we get—and this applies to humans, cats, dogs, and giraffes—the more like ourselves we become. If someone is fearful at age thirty, by eighty he or she will be cowering under the bed at the faintest creak in the floorboard. If nervous when young, fingernails will be chewed down to the bone by coffintime. Crankiness will turn into downright meanness. Masochists become more self-flagellating, and sadists become more de Sade–like. Relationships become warmer or more abusive. Age doesn't change us. It simply reinforces what and who we are before it decides to take everything away.

The third and final thing I will stake my rep on is something that took me a long time to understand. All the great writers and thinkers tend to bring everything back to history. Shakespeare, Faulkner, Euripides, all the South Korean factory workers who write the James Patterson novels—if they agree on anything, it's that the past casts an inescapable shadow over our present and future. I don't think it's quite that simple, however. It's not history that makes us what we are. I'm not who I am because of some vague link to Henry the Eighth or de Soto or some thirteenth-century rabbinical scholar. I think the past we're linked to is much more immediate than that. It's family. It's our own flesh and blood that shapes what we think and what we feel and who we are. That's what shackles us to the past. It's our family we can never quite get away from.

The further I move into adulthood, the more I see that life often becomes about three choices: re-creating one's family, running away completely from the idea of family, or reinventing and creating a totally new kind of family.

When I met Anna, though, I wasn't doing any of those things. I was mostly in a state of puzzlement and indecision about my parents and my brother. By the time it was appropriate to introduce them to Anna, I was a little less indecisive. In fact, I was dreading the sit-down because I'd recently come to a conclusion about them.

My family was completely crazy.

Okay, that's a slight exaggeration. Almost all families are crazy, something I first realized when I was still in grad school and interning at a local animal clinic. A woman brought in her dog—a three-legged boxer—to be put to sleep. She was nervous, and probably guilty and definitely sad, already feeling the loneliness that was sure to overwhelm her once the dog was gone. So she started talking to me. Because she and the dog had been together for so long, almost twenty years, he was part of her family, so that's what we talked about: her family.

She was a lovely woman, soft-spoken and gracious, although she told her story very quickly, probably because she was so anxious about her dog. She said she had recently turned sixty, and on her birthday she'd made a big decision. She'd been estranged from her brothers and sisters for decades. Most of them had adjusted to the situation—it had become more a question of benign neglect than outright hostility. But one brother, eight years younger than she, never let go of the anger he felt toward her. They hadn't spoken in over twenty-five years, yet she still sent him a Christmas present every year. He never sent her a thank-you note, never responded in any way. When she turned sixty, she decided that enough was enough. She was old enough to do what she wanted—and what she wanted was to stop sending a yearly present to her wretched, spiteful younger brother. So the Christmas before I saw her and her dog, she hadn't sent him anything. And two weeks after the holiday, she received the first note from him she'd ever gotten. She said she could quote it word for word, and she did. The letter said:

Dear Jennifer:
Every year I throw your Christmas present to me in the
garbage. But fuck you for not sending me one this year.
                                   Your brother, Daniel.

When she finished, she shook her head, hugged her dog to her chest, and burst into tears. I told her it was okay to cry, in fact it was a good thing, and then I put the boxer to sleep.

My family was probably no crazier than most. It's just that their insanity was, so to speak, closer to home.

The odd thing about them wasn't really that they were so screwed up. What I couldn't figure out was how it had all gone so wrong, because at one time we all seemed like such a happy group. We were what a family was supposed to be. But by the time Anna was about to step inside the ring, that image had proved to be, like so many images from childhood, far more illusion than reality.

My father rarely spoke—at least to me—about anything in his past. His military experiences, his education, his girlfriends before he met my mom. I could probably dredge up a few tidbits and images and maybe even a full anecdote or two about my father's past, but that's about it. And he *never* spoke about his own family. His mother died when he was fourteen years old and that is, literally, all I know about her. I don't even know my grandmother's first name. He never mentioned it. Of course, just to prove that I, too, can show an utter, all-too-human lack of interest in information gathering, I have to admit that I never asked.

I do know that my father's father owned a small canning factory on the Massachusetts side of the New York–Massachusetts border. I remember my grandfather as regal, elegant, and patrician, with white hair and a white mustache and a throaty, commanding voice. According to the few things my father told me, and a few more details courtesy of my mother, my memories are accurate as far as they go. But the elegance was affectation, as was the regal demeanor—in fact, my grandfather was a German Jewish immigrant who hadn't gotten much past the sixth grade. And the throaty voice came from all the cigarettes he chain-smoked. He also, according to my dad, was arrogant, selfish, and controlling. For the last fifteen years of my grandfather's life, he and my father didn't speak because my dad didn't want to go into the canning business. Instead, he wanted to be an actor, which is what he did.

And that's another thing I don't know: Why did my dad want to become an actor? Did he need a way to express himself? Did he crave attention? Was he trying to bury his identity under layers of pretending? I could speculate, but that's all it would be. I know only two things for certain: That at one point he wanted to be Marlon Brando but settled for being the real-life equivalent of the older-actor-soap-opera-guy in *Tootsie*. And that my grandfather disapproved of acting, the big city, and all forms of rebellion, so he never spoke to his oldest son again once he fled the family business.

My grandfather did reach out to my mother when first my brother and then I was born. When we were kids, my mother would drive us up north to visit him. For some reason she thought it was important that we get to know a really mean old guy who disapproved of and looked down on our father. (Families are like quicksand: It's very, very hard to drag yourself out of the mire.) But those visits became scarcer when my grandfather became ill. And they stopped altogether when, due to his five-pack-a-day habit, he died of throat cancer when he was fifty-nine years old. I was eight, my brother was fourteen, and my dad was thirty-seven.

My grandfather's name was Hymie Getzelman. When my dad graduated from the American Academy of Dramatic Arts and started making the rounds as a young actor, he didn't think that "Sol Getzelman" had that appropriate Cary Grant ring to it, so he reversed his father's initials and changed his name to Greg Heller. He switched to Heller because he thought that this momentous deciscion represented an escape from the hell of his family. And it wasn't just Hymie from whom my dad was running—it was also his younger siblings, Ruth and Fred. However my father and grandfather felt about each other, they must have shared a measure of mutual respect, as well as an abiding contempt for the two youngest Getzelmans. When my grandfather died, he left a third of the factory to each of his children, along with a private letter to my dad requesting that he look after Hymie's second wife, Eloise. The reason he made the request of my dad, Hymie wrote, was because he didn't think his other two children would give a shit. He was right about that. They soon proved themselves to be a little less than stellar when it came to family ties.

Within a year of my grandfather's death, Ruth and Fred convinced my dad that he should sell his share to them, since he had no physical or emotional connection to the business. As young as I was, I clearly remember the dinner at our house to celebrate the sale: the slightly melancholy severance, as well as the joy of a rare happy extended-family moment. In this group, severance seemed directly connected to pleasure.

I recall my Aunt Faith—married to my father's brother, with two sisters named Hope and Charity—toasting the entire family that evening. "I hope this leads us to become a closer family," she said. "Because nothing is more important than what we're sharing here today."

My Uncle Ben, husband to my dad's sister, also raised his glass and said, "I'll go further than that. What we have here today . . . family, people we love, people we can trust . . . that's all we have. Nothing else matters."

Even I was allowed to join the celebration by having a tiny sip of wine, and everyone made a big fuss out of that. I remember the flush of happiness that started at the back of my neck and ran down my spine, making me shiver with pleasure.

Ruth and Fred bought my dad out for a relatively small sum, and at first it was all lovely and fair and very amicable. But what my dad's siblings failed to mention was that they had already lined up another buyer for the place—a buyer who had made it clear how valuable the factory was. Mere weeks after my father sold them his share, Uncle Fred and Aunt Faith and Aunt Ruth and Uncle Ben closed their pre-negotiated deal for the factory and became multimillionaires.

That pretty much ended any hope of regular family reunions. But it didn't end our connection to my dad's family; growing up, I watched his rebellion gradually come to an end. Ultimately he returned to his roots, drawn back as if magnetized to a somewhat insipid past. Though he remained an actor for his entire life, he managed to turn that potentially glamorous and ambitious career into something that, as closely as possible, resembled a life spent in a factory that shaped and manufactured tin cans. When he was in his early twenties, he landed a role on a daytime soap opera. It was a good job and a fine start to a career. Except it wasn't really the start; it was also the end, because he never left. He played the same part for thirty-five years, preferring a steady paycheck to risk or the potential for artistic growth. He also decided, much like his dad, that he didn't really like or trust the city, so after only a few years of toil in a TV studio on West Sixty-third Street in Manhattan, he moved his wife and two sons to a small town in upstate New York—just opposite the small town on the Massachusetts border in which Uncle Fred and Aunt Ruth lived. He spent four days a week in Manhattan and three days a week plus seven weeks of the summer with us. He also became the creative director of our local summer-stock theater. In over thirty years in that job, I don't think he ever did an original play, just revivals. He directed and starred in *Our Town* eight times and *The Odd Couple* five times; he also played Oliver Warbucks in *Annie* four times during his reign.

Life was good when I was a boy. I had plenty of friends and got to ride my bike to their houses. I was an excellent student and liked my teachers. I never really noticed the odd marital and familial arrangement. My mom was always around, and although my dad was gone half the time, whenever I realized I was missing him I talked to him on the phone in New York. And when he was home he was *really* home, day and night—available for fatherly conversations and to hand over an extra buck or two for my allowance and to look disappointed when I didn't live up to his standards.

My mom didn't work; she managed the household and took good care of her two sons. She cooked and cleaned and paid the bills, but she also threw the football around with me in the backyard and took me bowling and helped me with my homework. When I was six and seven and ten, it all seemed kind of perfect. Everyone got along. Everyone was happy. Everything was exactly how it was supposed to be.

The best part was Teddy. Six years older than I, he was the perfect brother. Handsomer than I was, stronger, and a better athlete, he had girls falling all over him. He tortured me the way an older brother is supposed to; his favorite game was to push me to the ground, kneel on my chest, grab one of my hands, and force me to slap myself in the face, the whole time saying, "What are you hitting yourself for? Are you crazy? Stop hitting yourself," while I'd be simultaneously crying in frustration and laughing at the absurdity of the whole thing.

But Ted also liked me enough to take me along on some of his dates. When he was sixteen and I was ten, he'd take me to movies with his girlfriend, Sandy. Ted would buy me popcorn and candy and talk to me like I really belonged. Sandy talked to me the same way, so suddenly I became part of a new world of teenagers who were far more sophisticated than I was. Sometimes I'd wander off, maybe to some remote part of a movie theater lobby, occasionally half a block away, just to see how protective my brother would be; he'd always find me instantly and, without making a fuss, guide me back to join the date. He also let me play sports with his peers. (I always had to be the center in football and the catcher in baseball, but I didn't care; I simply couldn't believe my luck in getting to join in with the big boys.) He taught me how to play chess because he wanted someone to practice with. And because he read the sports pages religiously, I did, too. Eventually, I even leaped ahead of him with my knowledge of stats and strategy.

What I didn't realize then was how sometimes leaping ahead isn't such a great thing, and how roles can change. And how being a hero to your little brother at age sixteen is no guarantee that everything will work out later on. I particularly didn't realize how my dad's absence affected Ted.

Whereas I felt special when my dad came back upstate each weekend—his homecoming on Thursday night always seemed like a celebratory event—Ted grew increasingly resentful at the absences and less and less interested in our father's return. It might have been the age difference. At sixteen he knew a lot more about the world than I did at ten. I remember Ted asking me once if I thought Dad saw other women when he was in New York. I was shocked; he might as well have asked me if I thought our father was actually from Jupiter, had a pod at the back of his neck, and munched on small children in the middle of the night. I shook my head vehemently, to emphasize how crazy that was, and Ted told me that there was at least one other woman he knew of. I started to cry, not loud sobs, but hard tears that suddenly poured out of me, until Ted slapped me playfully and said, "Hey, I was just kidding. How the hell would I know what he's doin' in New York?" I looked at him suspiciously, but his smile only grew wider and he said, "Besides, who the hell would go out with Dad?" I stopped crying and life went on and I never did find out if Teddy was inventing the other woman or knew some deep, dark secret. Over the ensuing years, he told me at various times that both sides of that equation were true. Sometimes I was positive he was telling me the truth; other times I thought he was lying. Eventually, I was certain he no longer knew what the truth was, if in fact he ever did.

By the time he was fifteen, Ted had stopped listening to our mom and seemed to delight in torturing her as only a teenager can torture a parent. He got drunk a few times, and the manner in which he ignored her attempts to discipline him was his way of saying, "You're not my father, you're not strong enough to tell me what to do." He left pot lying around, knowing it would upset her but also knowing that she wouldn't tell our dad, because it would cause an explosion that would blow the roof off our house. Two or three times I came home from school and found my mom crying. I would ask her what happened and she would only say, "Nothing," and then hug me tightly.

I was the good child; the more Ted became the bad child, the easier it was for me to look better, and the more I wanted to act better. It soon became obvious that Teddy couldn't ever get the approval from my parents that I could. By the time he went away to college, he wasn't inviting me into his life and looking out for me quite as much. Now in junior high school, I still looked up to him. He had all sorts of talents, none of which he valued. He was an athlete and a terrific musician; he was movie-star handsome and could charm anything that moved. But I was the smart one, which is what he wanted to be more than anything. And so, due to a combination of all sorts of things, some coming from within, some pushed upon us by outside forces, some just the natural erosion of all things simple and innocent that comes about with age, my brother and I began to grow apart.

Here's another human truism: Most of us want to be exactly what we aren't.

Nonhuman animals are capable of doing all sorts of things that aren't so great. I have not treated any large zoo animals—no lions, tigers, or gorillas—so I have never dealt directly with an animal capable of ripping apart human flesh or doing serious damage to our musculo-skeletal system. I have, however, dealt with a pit bull who once took out a small child's eye, as well as an otherwise lovely Chesapeake Bay retriever who picked up a small wirehaired fox terrier and broke its neck. I have treated a cat gone mad, who suddenly began to leap upon and claw the humans it had lived with for nearly ten years in bliss and contentment. I have seen animals fight to the death, and I have been bitten, scratched, growled at, and hissed at countless times. But I have never seen an animal be anything but true to its own nature. Animals do not lie. I cannot say the same thing for people. Not people I've observed or talked to or even loved. Or maybe it's just that lying is, in fact, a deep-rooted part of human nature.

I don't know when Ted began to make things up. I don't know when he became disenchanted with who he was. But I'm fairly certain that the former followed soon after the latter.

Once, when he was home from college, we were in his room, talking about things. We'd always been confidants, although I was usually the one confiding; Teddy tended to absorb information rather than reveal it, using what he learned, at some point, to get something or just wreak havoc. He was nervous during this conversation, jumpy, but then Teddy had become perpetually nervous and twitchy—he always seemed to be breathing harder than the situation called for, as if something dangerous was lurking nearby. At one point he told me a story about some restaurant he liked to go to near the University of Wisconsin campus.

"It's great," he said. "I go in there for breakfast, like, almost every day, and I don't even have to order. As soon as I walk in, they just bring me a bacon, egg, and cheese sandwich on an English muffin."

Somehow I knew he was lying. He looked uncomfortable, and his eyes were flitting around the room as he talked. I don't know how I knew, because it seemed like such an inconsequential thing to lie about, but I did. So I asked him a couple of questions.

"But what if you don't want the sandwich that day? They'll just bring you something else?"

His shoulders twitched a bit and he said, "Oh, yeah, yeah, they don't care."

"So you know the waitress?"

"Yeah, I see her, like, every day."

"What's her name?"

He took a couple of breaths that were even deeper than usual and said, "Andrea."

"And what makes the sandwiches so good?"

"They use Canadian bacon. Cook it perfectly. And they put jalapeños on it. I mean, they do for me, not for everybody."

I was certain that none of these answers were true, but the details he provided were both trivial and vivid, which is probably why the conversation stayed with me. When Teddy graduated from Wisconsin, I went out there for a couple of days to be with him; the first morning, I asked him to take me to the restaurant that made the great egg sandwiches. He looked at me like I was crazy, and then maybe something deep in his brain remembered. Or didn't. Maybe he just knew I was questioning him about something he'd made up, without knowing exactly what it was. So he looked at me blankly and then, distracted, said, "Oh, it closed a few months ago."

It's not hard to create an alternate reality. You start by telling small falsehoods. *I went out with Cindy last night—she let me get to second base.* Or: *I did fifty push-ups.* And then they get a little bigger: *I went to Harvard . . . I was in the Gulf War . . . I'm running for president and I never cheated on my wife.* If they hear it often enough, people will accept almost anything as fact. If you can convince other people that you're one thing, it's awfully difficult for them to ever accept you as something else. But this also explains why family ties can be so binding and restrictive and scary. It's almost impossible to convince your family that you're someone other than who you really are.

In college, Teddy got into trouble almost from day one. Nothing serious, nothing criminal. Just a series of fuckups, followed by a string of lies to try to avoid punishment for the fuckups. But he always got caught. He wasn't allowed to buy a car; he bought one anyway and the insurance company called our dad to verify some information. Busted. My father told him it was a mistake to live with his girlfriend, so Ted told him he wouldn't. Then my dad came to visit and, of course, realized Ted was living with the girlfriend. Busted again. Each time he got caught, his relationship with my father got worse. Each time he uncovered a lie, my father lost more faith in what Ted said, and Ted became less likely to tell the truth.

When it came to Ted, my father grew more and more controlling and increasingly unforgiving. Their relationship turned into an epic battle of wills, but in the end my father had a much stronger will, at least in the two-man war in which they engaged.

Euthanizing a small animal in its owner's arms is painful, but watching two human beings spend their adult lives doing their utmost to dominate and destroy each other is tragic.

The more my brother's life—and, I suppose, my father's—went in uncontrollable directions, the more controlling my father became with everyone in the family. It never got physical, not even close; there was no melodrama and nothing overtly traumatic. But my dad's anger became a nearly constant presence in our lives. I escaped the brunt of it, partly because Ted was there to absorb it. But I also never took my dad's temper all that seriously, maybe because I never really cared about being accepted the way Ted did. I didn't argue with my dad; his neurosis seemed amusing to me, and distancing, so I didn't pay much attention to him when he tried to dominate. My brother couldn't do that. He had to resist, and then he had to capitulate.

The insurmountable barrier that ultimately sprang up between them came when my brother quit his job as a grade school teacher to become an actor. Oddly enough, Ted was a fantastic teacher. He related to the kids; he loved their enthusiasm and the way they looked up to him. I think what he thrilled to the most was being perceived, for the first time in his life, as the most adult person in his surroundings. But after his third year of teaching, one day he simply walked away from it. He'd never taken an acting class in his life. He'd never even shown much interest in anything related to acting—I don't think he watched TV or went to more than two or three movies a year, and I'm not sure if he'd ever seen a Broadway show in his entire life. Nonetheless, he moved to New York and decided he was now an actor. Ted's sudden career change drove my dad crazy—like all parents, he hated to see his child repeat his own mistakes. Even so, he tried to help Ted as much as possible. But every time he offered his help, the war grew more intense. Ted wouldn't deign to appear on my dad's soap opera; he was only interested in theater or what he called "quality film work." My dad offered him a part at his upstate summer theater, but Ted rejected the job; he said the role wasn't big enough.

Ted got a few small parts in off-off-Broadway shows. I remember one in which his character killed his father and left him to die in a heap of garbage—very inspiring, and I think that was the only play he actually invited the whole family to come see. But that was it. He started going out to L.A. periodically, usually for "pilot season," but nothing seemed to come of it, except now, he told me in a phone conversation, he knew the woman who ran a great breakfast stand at the Farmer's Market, and she would put jalapeños in his egg sandwich without his having to ask.

Ted never studied acting, never showed any interest in the process or the actual work, and never discussed acting or actors or films when we'd get together and talk. We talked about restaurants where the staff knew him and women who wanted to fuck him; we talked about the great grass he was getting and his new best friend. But every six months or so he'd have a newer best friend who I'd never heard of. When I'd ask him about his previous best friend, he'd always say, "Oh, he turned out to be a real asshole." I'd rarely find out why except in the vaguest terms: The guy had gotten pissed off at something Teddy had done, or he hadn't done something Teddy wanted him to do, or the guy's girlfriend or wife had gotten pissed at something Teddy had or hadn't done. They always disappeared from Ted's life as quickly as they entered it.

Teddy also got cruder. It was as if he lost any kind of self-censor. He told inappropriate jokes. He would tell embarrassing stories about other people—often in front of them.

One weekend when I was in college I came into the city to see him. Well, I was really there to see this woman named Robin, who'd been dating a friend of my parents'. I was nineteen and she was around twenty-seven, and the guy she was dating was probably fifty. But a month or so before, she'd come to my college town in Vermont—she produced TV commercials and they were shooting something set on a small college campus—and we'd hung out for a week. After a few days of having fun, we went to bed together. She was my first older woman (and, now that I think about it, my last; I was not exactly a Don Juan) and I felt incredibly sophisticated and excited. At that time, having sex with *anyone* would have made me feel incredibly sophisticated and excited, but because Robin was seeing a friend of my dad's and our affair was illicit, it was particularly exhilarating. Naturally, she asked me not to tell anyone. Naturally, I told Teddy at the first opportunity. What was the point of doing something thrilling and illicit at age nineteen if you couldn't share it with your older brother?

Before coming down to New York to see Ted that weekend, I invited Robin to dinner with us, assuring her that my brother knew absolutely nothing about our little fling. Right before she arrived, I reminded him that mum was the word.

Actually, I got so nervous that all I could say was "Look, you're not gonna say anything, right?" When he didn't answer right away, I said, "I mean, you promised."

He looked at me, annoyed, as if I'd insulted him big-time. But I had to get this out.

"I'm serious, Ted. It's important to me."

His face softened. "I know. Don't worry."

When I still looked worried, he punched my arm, playfully, but just enough to hurt and let me know he was still my older brother.

I apologized. Robin joined us—she'd met Ted before, as the date of our parents' friend—and sat down, and before we ordered, while she was studying the menu, Ted said, "So, you fucked my little brother's brains out, huh?"

It was not a good moment. She was embarrassed and hurt and angry, and she left halfway through the meal. I was livid. When I confronted Ted, he just said, "Fuck her if she can't take a joke." And then: "Oh yeah. You already did."

I didn't speak to him for a few weeks after that. But Ted had a talent for making you forgive him. He also had this amazing knack for making you believe that almost anything that went wrong was your own fault. In this instance, he convinced me that I'd made a serious error—and violated Robin's confidence—by telling him about my two-night stand. The fact that he had violated *my* confidence was irrelevant. In time, it became a story he'd tell to show off his willingness to stretch any normal limit. He also used the story to subtly prove some kind of weakness on my part: My trusting him became part of the joke, as did my inability to find the whole thing zany and crazy and hypocrisy-puncturing. From my perspective, I was just a kid who'd lucked into a wonderful and wild thing that Ted had destroyed for his own amusement. In Teddy's version, he had simply used the truth to seize the high ground: I was having an illicit affair; I was lying; I was cheating and so was Robin. All he'd done was call us on it. If we couldn't deal with it, too bad for us.

There was enough truth in his version to stop me cold.

When I was twenty and Ted was twenty-six, he got married.

It was all very sudden and, of course, my father thought it was a big mistake, which is probably what helped to make it so sudden. My father said Ted should slow down, so my brother rushed right into it.

The surprising thing was that Karen, Ted's bride-to-be, was absolutely wonderful. Actually, most of the women Teddy attracted were pretty wonderful: beautiful and smart and caring. They all shared certain traits. They would shake their heads at Ted's wildness and unpredictability—they knew there was something off about his insistence on always blowing things up—but at the same time they were attracted to it. I think it's because they all believed they could tame him. The look on their lips and in their eyes always said, "Oh, well, that's Ted, what can you do?" But on a deeper level that look also said, "Well, I *am* going to do something—I'm the one who's going to change him."

Much of the time, Ted had a kind of puppy-dog, sappy, "I'm in love" expression when he was around his girlfriends. I always thought it was fake and kind of awful—as if true love and devotion weren't enough on their own and he had to demonstrate them as visibly and publicly as possible. But the recipients always seemed to eat it up with a spoon. When that look disappeared, though, it sometimes got scary; his puppy-dog demeanor could instantly turn into a pit bull's rage. I once saw him throw a punch at his college girlfriend while they were having an argument. She'd caught him in a lie and wasn't backing down as he tossed out his excuses. She was standing against the wall, demanding an explanation, and his fist suddenly flew through the air, a short, violent jab. It missed her face, as it was intended to, and rammed into the wall, cracking the plaster. It must have hurt like hell, although Teddy was so wired he didn't let on. Her face showed real fear; she didn't know the punch was going to go awry when it was launched. But I also saw her next expression, one that manifested itself instantly: *I'm sorry. It must have been my fault.* Teddy calmed down and whispered to her and, within minutes, they were making love in the bedroom while I was standing in the living room next to the cracked plaster wall, not knowing what to do and feeling like a total schmuck.

Karen fit the pattern, and I couldn't understand it. She was a very special person: sweet, observant, and clever. Not an intellectual; her looks and interests had taken her in a different direction. But she was smart, and in my eyes she was rich. Though she was only twenty-six, she was a senior publicist for a big record company. She raked in the bucks and the perks, and she and Ted lived very well. They got a gorgeous apartment—at least by my college standards, which were admittedly pretty low—on Manhattan's Upper West Side. They had a refrigerator with an ice machine built into it, which I thought only millionaires could afford. And Karen used a salad spinner to dry her lettuce, which seemed the height of luxury. (Not that I ever actually made a salad, but if I had I would have washed it in the sink and dried it with a paper towel—if I'd ever thought to dry it, which I wouldn't have.) Sometimes she traveled to Europe and South America for work, and her friends were models, photographers, songwriters, musicians, and filmmakers. They were all successful, which meant that Teddy was always the slight outsider in this group, always on the verge of success rather than actually riding a wave of success. Always up for a part, always ready to make it when he finally landed the big job. But somehow never actually working. His role in this new crowd was to shake things up, to make the outrageous statement, to point out hypocrisy, to raise his middle finger to authority. To be the wild man.

But that role can grow old quickly, especially as we gradually turn into the people we've always rebelled against, which is what happens all too often at some point in the aging process. Karen came from middle-class, midwestern WASPs who weren't thrilled with her marriage to an out-of-work Jew who had told his fiancée's mother that he'd agree to get married in a church if he could wear a gorilla suit. By the time Ted and Karen got married, Karen had already done her rebelling; now she was ready to return to the fold. So before too long Ted began to annoy her with his behavior. He would do anything for a laugh—embarrass her publicly, torture her in private—and always make her feel uncomfortable and guilty when she didn't see the humor in what he did. And worse: He would point out that she was reacting the way her parents would have reacted. That was one of Ted's strengths; he manipulated you into feeling that you were behaving like your parents.

Once, he threw her a surprise birthday party. I helped organize it. Ted and Karen were supposed to go out to dinner, and just before they left I was supposed to show up at their apartment with Karen's best friend, a gorgeous model named Melissa. (Unfortunately for me, no chance of a repeat older woman–college boy fling; she liked me fine in a pat-on-the-head, cute-younger-brother way, while I pined away for her love and attention.) But when we rang their doorbell, we were accompanied by thirty of their best friends, all carrying different kinds of food and drink. (Ted had cleverly made sure that he wouldn't have to pay for a penny of the party.) What none of us knew was that Ted had bought Karen a beautiful pearl necklace as a present—using their joint checking account—and he'd spent the previous hour trying to convince her to open the door wearing nothing but the pearls. She kept saying, "But Bob will be there," and Ted kept saying, "Oh, don't be such a prude—he'll go wild." Amazingly enough, he almost talked her into it, but then at the last second she changed her mind and threw on a T-shirt and a pair of jeans before opening the door to be greeted by a huge crowd shouting, "Surprise!" She turned to Ted in a fury, started screaming at him, and bolted into the bedroom. He just looked at the crowd and shrugged, as if he had absolutely no idea what she was so upset about.

I saw Ted and Karen often, and over time Karen and I became close friends. We'd talk on the phone at least once a week, and she would confide in me. I'd stay with them when I came to the city. Ted would watch TV or strum his guitar—he could play several instruments well, but he was a superb guitarist—while Karen and I chatted. And despite Ted's obvious flaws, I was still a little in awe of my big brother: his lifestyle, his gorgeous wife, his joie de vivre, his seeming unconcern over his lack of direction and success. His seeming unconcern about anything. As far as I could tell, he had everything he wanted and needed—at least up to this point in his life—and he was embracing it all with a lusty bear hug.

The embrace with Karen lasted three years. Over those years, the marriage got more and more volatile. Karen's work took her out of New York for longer stretches of time; when she came back, she couldn't wait to get away again. Ted spent hours every day writing a screenplay that he insisted he was going to sell only if he was allowed to star in it. "Fuck 'em," he used to say on a regular basis. "If they want this baby, they're gonna have to take *me*." I believed him. *Everyone* believed him, even though none of us ever knew who "they" were.

Unfortunately, we never got a chance to find out what would have happened if "they" wanted his baby but didn't want him. On the day before their third anniversary, Karen came back from a two-week business trip to New Orleans and Chicago, went into the kitchen, and saw new brass faucets on the sink. She came back into the living room, looked at Ted, and said, "What's that?" He shrugged and said, "They were a bargain."

This was almost the final straw. My brother was a compulsive spender. (My father was the opposite. He was a hoarder, so of course Ted was constantly getting rid of things and then buying new things to replace them.) Karen was a saver, planning for the future; Ted refused to admit that anything existed beyond that night's dinner. Months earlier, Karen had forbidden Teddy to spend any more of their money on frivolous things. Particularly appliances—Ted was an appliance freak. He always had to have the latest stove or dishwasher. He had a near fetish for refrigerators; he must have discarded and bought three of them in the time they were married. Of course, neither he nor Karen cooked a lick. He just thought the sleek appliances looked the way a perfect kitchen—and a perfect life, a perfect marriage—should look.

Karen went ballistic over the faucets. She was so angry that she went to a place she'd always been afraid to go: She demanded to see his screenplay. He wouldn't show it to her. She insisted. They argued back and forth until finally she went to his computer, found the screenplay, and opened it, and then saw that it was right out of *The Shining*. It wasn't exactly "All work and no play makes Jack a dull boy," but it was close. In a year and a half, he'd written six pages—including the title page. Two of the pages were verbatim conversations between Ted and Karen. Two more pages were verbatim conversations between Ted and our dad. The final page had a page number at the top and a note in bold type that said, "DEVELOP RELATIONSHIP BETWEEN ED AND CARMEN."

That was the end of the marriage.

It was also the beginning of an intense three weeks for Ted and me. He had a kind of nervous breakdown. I don't know what else to call it; he just kept crying all day and was unable to get out of bed. My dad wouldn't talk to him—by this point, he hadn't talked to him for quite a while—and my mom simply couldn't drop everything and come to the city to help (although since we were both out of the house we were never exactly sure what "everything" actually was), especially if that help put her in between her husband and her son. So I left college behind for a while and stayed with Ted. Took care of him as best I could. Mostly that meant ordering pizza or Chinese food and smoking dope with him and letting him cry and talk. He insisted that I talk, too. He wanted to hear about school and especially about the girl I was pining away for, who would only consider me a close platonic friend even though I was fairly sure she was dating the entire college basketball team, two assistant professors, and a geek from the science lab who doubled as the late-night janitor. Despite my haze of jealous despair, my concern for my brother, and my even greater concern that my efforts at playing emotional nursemaid could lead to disaster—he obviously needed far more caretaking than I was capable of providing—those three weeks were wonderful, if odd and bewildering. It was just like when we were kids and I would go into Ted's room (larger than mine because he was older) and we'd read comics and talk about sports and girlfriends and our favorite flavor of frozen Pepperidge Farm turnovers and all sorts of other crucial things.

By the end of those three weeks, Ted had stopped crying and could order his own pizza. A very attractive neighbor, a dancer wannabe named Melanie, had begun coming over to check up on him. Ted got the great apartment, somehow, and Karen had moved out; Melanie had witnessed the dissolution of the relationship close up. One night I returned home and it was painfully obvious that I had become a third wheel, so I went back to school. Before I left, Teddy hugged me and thanked me. But the hug was another lie: What he really wanted was for me to get the hell out of there and forget that any of this had ever happened. He didn't like being weaker than his younger brother, and I didn't like having to be stronger than him. Even worse was the realization that I *was* stronger than him.

Ted and I skirmished intermittently, but the battle between Ted and my dad went on continuously for years. Periodically, my father would cut my brother off. During those times they wouldn't speak for months, sometimes as long as a year. Eventually, sentiment, blood, and guilt would overwhelm one or both of them and they'd reconcile. Then Ted would set him off again and the war raged anew. During those years—while Ted continued to live off various girlfriends and I went to veterinary school and then became a vet—my father's hair turned white and he grew a bushy mustache. He also assumed a kind of acto-rish, regal manner. And because he smoked four packs of cigarettes a day, his voice became increasingly rough and throaty. At age fifty-nine, my father took a running leap back into his own family's grasp and, just like his father before him, died of lung cancer. Ted was thirty-six and I was thirty.

My mother, my brother, and I were all with our father when he died. Minutes before he closed his eyes for the last time, he nodded at Teddy but didn't speak to him. He tried to blow a kiss toward my mom but couldn't manage it. Then he squeezed my hand and told me to look after her. I don't think my father made this request because he respected me all that much. He certainly didn't respect my chosen profession; he thought that I'd become a vet because I couldn't get into a real medical school. I suspect he told me to take care of my mom because he didn't know what else to say to me. And he couldn't ask my brother because he didn't trust him at all. In my father's defense, he wasn't wrong not to trust Teddy. The last thing I did before my father died was to kiss him on the forehead and say good-bye. The last thing Teddy did before our dad died was to steal his watch from his chest of drawers.

"Why are you so nervous?"

That's what Anna asked me as we were driving to my parents' house for the first time. It was six months after we'd met. Three months after we'd started hanging out together whenever possible, and a month after I'd talked to her about meeting the inmates in the loony bin. My dad still had four years to live, and recently he'd entered a phase where he was somewhat mellower, or at least less judgmental around me— probably because he knew he'd begun the process of dying, although no one other than my mother was privy to that information at the time—which gave me some reason to hope that Anna's first encounter with my family might not be a total disaster. On the other hand, Ted would be there, too.

"I just want them to like you," I replied, glancing over at her as I drove.

She shook her head at her pathetic, misguided boyfriend. "How could they not like me?"

"Yeah, I know. It's just that they're . . . unpredictable."

"Everybody's unpredictable."

"You're not."

"No?" she said.

"No," I said. "You're perfect."

I thought it was a romantic thing to say, but she gave me an odd look, a look that created some distance between us.

"Do you really think that?" she asked.

"Yeah. I really do."

The distance passed and the warmth was back in her eyes, but there was a momentary hint of something else, too. I couldn't tell if it was confusion or exasperation or maybe even sadness.

Anna took my free hand in hers and held it up to her cheek. "I'm not," she said. "I'm really, really not."

"To me you are. I mean . . . whatever you do, I like. And I don't think you could ever do anything wrong. Not really wrong."

"That's a little scary," she said. But she leaned over and kissed me lightly on the lips, which made me think it wasn't all that scary.

Then we pulled into the driveway and went in to meet the Heller family.

My dad took to Anna right away. He was as charming as could be, telling her his favorite soap opera behind-the-scenes moments, which everyone who met him found hard to resist—at least the first time. He regaled Anna with the story about the beloved actress who played the stern matriarch on the show but had to take swigs of gin before every take; he told her about the weird gifts people sent in when characters on the show had babies or got married. And he asked her about all sorts of things: her studies, her parents, her high heels. He even made her take off her shoes so he could hold them in his hands; while he held them, he said to my mom, "Les, how do women wear things like this?" and then to Anna, "Really, how do you wear these things?"

My mom, Leslie Heller, aka Ms. Polite at Any Cost, was extremely reserved, to the point of being unfriendly. It kind of rocked me. I'd seen her upset, I'd seen her crying, I'd seen her angry, although her anger was usually fairly tepid and most often aimed at herself or at people who'd done something to hurt various family members. What I'd never seen directed at any of us, especially me, was blatant disapproval or disappointment. My mom was the stabilizing, calm presence, the generous soul who too often was underappreciated or overlooked. No one realized it then, but she was actually the glue that held us all together. We mistook her quiet strength for being merely quiet. But not that evening. At the first encounter with the woman I was going to marry, my mother acted as if I were a young, innocent chick and Anna were an approaching fox.

Anna tried. She smiled and offered to help with the cooking. (This was little more than a gesture, since Anna knew that my mom was a great cook, whereas the only thing Anna made was microwave popcorn; still, she was hoping it was the thought that counted.) She effusively admired the house and the garden. At one desperate moment, running out of accolades, she even commented on how clean everything was. It didn't matter; nothing worked. All she got in return was a subtle but unmistakable resistance.

As for Anna's meeting with Teddy, it went about as expected.

At first he was charming and funny. Apparently he and my dad had agreed to bury the hatchet for the night, and if my mom seemed indifferent or even a bit hostile toward Anna, Ted appeared to be quite taken with her. At some point, my mom went into the kitchen to wash the dishes and my dad went in to help her, which left just the three of us at the dining table. I was full and had polished off a decent amount of wine. Despite the few snags, I was feeling almost out of the woods. Anna was relaxed, smiling, and had gone from holding my hand surreptitiously under the table to slipping her fingers into mine in plain view.

Then Teddy said something about going to put some money down on the lottery.

Anna said, "Really? You really do that?"

"Sure," he said. "I'm gonna win."

"Come on," she said.

"Okay, but don't come crawling to me when I win my hundred and fifty mil."

She laughed and shook her head in disbelief.

Teddy said, "I'm serious."

By this time, I was poking her under the table, but she missed the cue for silence. And she had no idea that the ice beneath her feet had suddenly become very thin.

"You make it sound like just because you want something, it's going to happen."

"Come on," I interjected. "Let's go to the basement and shoot some pool."

No one took me up on the chance to walk away from the discussion.

"You don't think I can win?" Teddy said to Anna.

"Well . . . sure. I mean you *could* win." She smiled at him, as if to show that she hoped he *would* win.

"Oh, I'm *gonna* win. Sooner or later."

"Just because you want to?"

He shrugged. Teddy would never try to outargue you. Logic wasn't his style. His modus operandi was to charm you into wanting to agree with him. Which definitely was not Anna's style. She believed in stubbornly sticking to logic over all else, even after it became abundantly clear that logic held no sway when people wanted deeply to believe in something.

Anna leaned toward Ted and said, "But if you think that way, then you don't actually have to *do* anything. In fact, it pretty much guarantees that you *won't* do anything. You just wait around for stuff to happen. You don't think that's kinda nuts?"

Teddy smiled and nodded. His charm offensive had clearly failed. So he turned to me, at first looking quizzical, then offering a slow, broad smile, and he said, "I get it. She's a cunt."

That's when my mom and dad came in with dessert.

Anna's mouth was open and her jaw hung slack She looked as if she'd been slapped.

"Apple pie?" my mom said.

From the *New York Daily Examiner:*

Dr. Robert Heller is one of New York's leading veterinarians and is the author of a book about taking care of pets, *They Have Nothing but Their Kindness*. Dr. Bob takes care of cats, dogs, horses, birds, snakes, turtles, frogs, small pigs, and many varieties of rodents. You can e-mail him at AskDrBob@NYDE.com and ask him any question about the animal you love. His column runs every Tuesday in NYC's most popular newspaper.

Dear Medicine Man Bob:

First off: longtime reader, big fan. Loved your comparison of Confused at the Dog Run's pit bull to the whole steroid scandal in sports. Okay, enough sucking up. Sorry about that. On to my problem. It's about a new animal I just brought into the house. I have one cat, Binky, and one dog, Esther, and they get along just swell. But my wife fell in love with a cockatiel and we brought him home and the bird drives the other two animals crazy. I have to say, I've gotten totally attached to the new family member, Baretta, but it has caused real havoc in our household. Any thoughts on how to restore some sanity to our previously copacetic environment?

—Looking for a Return to the Past

Dear Looking:

Let me begin by saying that there can never be too much sucking up to Dr. Bob. So never apologize for that. As to your problem, it's not an easy one to solve. I have two words for you: *time and patience.* Okay, I realize that's actually three words. But I don't think the connective should count as part of the equation. So back to your problem. Having your home space invaded is traumatic. It takes time for things to jell. Not everything can fall into place easily and perfectly. Even in the animal kingdom, there are issues to be negotiated and compromises that have to be made. Cats and dogs get along better than Israelis and Arabs, but now you've gone and thrown a Palestinian into the mix. I admire your courage, but you're going to have to come up with a two- (or even three-) state solution now. The Middle East has managed to hang on for quite a while, despite a lot of volatility, so I suggest you follow a tried and true historical path: Do your best to negotiate, weather the storms, and enjoy the periods of détente. In the meantime, be as attentive to all sides as possible, and show that you have no favorites. I'm sure there will be uprisings on all fronts, so that's where the time and patience come in. It's going to take time. And the only way to survive that is patience.

Note to Dr. Bob's readers: Please don't write nasty comments to your favorite vet because I compared Looking's problem to the Middle East. I think it's a valid comparison. I often wish that the various antagonistic forces over there would take a few lessons on canine and feline togetherness. All abusive e-mails will not only hurt Dr. Bob's feelings, they will be transferred immediately to Trash. If you want to send an abusive e-mail that will be read, feel free to criticize the sudden use of the third person to describe myself.

—Dr. Bob

CHAPTER 3

In retrospect, the first year of our marriage was a little odd.

It didn't seem so to us because getting married was what we desperately wanted to do and it was more important than any potential inconveniences. Also, nothing ever feels odd when you're actually doing it. Only on reflection do you scratch your head and go, "What the hell was that all about?" I know what it was about: We wanted to be together. Even if we couldn't actually be together.

We got married in a civil ceremony at the courthouse near my parents' home. Anna was in graduate school—the second year of a two-year program in interior design—and she came down from Providence, Rhode Island, for the big event and the weekend-long festivities. My parents attended. A few of Anna's friends from college came down, too. Most important (at least to me), my best friend, Phil Colavito, came.

Phil and I had been best friends since we were ten years old. Even though we'd gone in different directions, our friendship was inviolable. I was a year away from becoming a doctor of veterinary medicine. Phil was running the local bowling alley in our hometown, which he'd taken over after his dad had a near-fatal heart attack and couldn't work anymore. At first, I was amazed that Phil had chosen to rescue his father's business. He was a smart and deeply funny guy, with a savagely cynical view of the world. I thought he could be anything, do anything, and go anywhere. But what he wanted—or at least what he decided—was to stay firmly rooted in his hometown, run the family business, and spend a lot of his considerable energy making fun of everything and everyone that surrounded him. His current girlfriend, a local girl named Darlene something-or-other—I'm not a hundred percent sure that Phil actually knew her last name—was a perfectly nice person. Not particularly attractive, not dumb but not smart, and although it was obvious that Phil didn't really care for or about her, they'd been dating for six months. The day before my wedding, I asked him about his relationship with her after working up my nerve while we split a six-pack.

"So what's the story with Darlene?"

"No story. She's just there."

"Well, 'just there' is a story, right?"

"No. It's 'just there' because there's no story. If there was a story, she'd be there 'because' and then there'd be an explanation."

"Jesus Christ."

"Don't Jesus Christ me. You're the one asking the stupid questions."

"You like her?"

"Sure."

"That's not incredibly enthusiastic."

"I'm more subtle than you are."

"Is this, like, a serious thing?"

"Robbo," he said—that's what he'd called me, Robbo, ever since we first met in fifth grade—"is what you're asking me am I gonna marry her? 'Cause if it is, the answer's 'Shit, no.'"

"So—"

"Is the next question gonna be some asshole thing about wasting my time or settling for someone who can't hold a fucking candle to fucking perfect Anna?"

"Do you really think Anna's perfect?"

"Fuck you."

"So, okay, yeah, that was kinda gonna be my next question. More or less."

"Here's the thing," Phil said. "I don't really care that much about any of this shit. Don't really care where I work or what I do. Don't care if I'm with someone or if I'm alone. It all just seems like a lot of shit to me and some of it sticks and some of it doesn't."

"You're not practicing my wedding toast, are you?"

"You think I should leave out the part about the shit?"

"I'd appreciate it."

"I know you think I'm wasting my life."

"Hey," I protested. "I didn't say that."

"You have a very expressive face, though. And I understand why you think that. But you wanna know my whole philosophy of life?"

"I don't think so."

"Tough shit. My philosophy is: There's nothin' wrong with making people happy on any level. And you know what makes people incredibly happy?"

I shook my head.

"Bowling shoes," Phil said. "People love to rent those bowling shoes, put 'em on, and go to their assigned lanes and bowl a couple of games. Really. You should see their faces. They love the feel, the fit, even the smell, I think. So I hand 'em over the shoes and I go home smilin'. And that's the thing about Darlene, too. You know how happy she is havin' me take her out to dinner and sometimes letting her come behind the desk at the bowling alley as if she belongs there? And then on top of that, gettin' a taste of Phil's Magic Ten Pin? The girl's in heaven."

"I have to say, if I knew you were gonna turn out this weird, I'd have asked to move my seat away from yours in Mrs. Bates's class."

"Too late now. And hey, by the way. I don't want to embarrass you by giving you my present in public. So I'll tell you now. Fifty percent off, lifetime, at Colavito's Bowl-More. Except Friday and Saturday. And July Fourth weekend."

"I'm over-fuckin'-whelmed."

That conversation, along with the six-pack, was pretty much my bachelor party. A few of my college buddies had come down, too, to round out the wedding bash. Some were women, so there was none of the usual guy-only stuff. That evening Anna and I took Phil and all our friends out for pizza and more beer. We talked about life and the future and commitment and love, with some sports and fashion thrown in so neither sex felt deprived.

No one from Anna's family was there. She hadn't invited anyone. When I pressed her on it and suggested that she might regret their absence at some point, she just shook her head and said, "I'd only regret it if any of them actually showed up."

During one of our first heart-to-heart-lying-in-each-other's-arms-on-the-couch-at-three-A.M.-after-drugs-and-reading-poetry-aloud-to-each-other conversations, Anna told me that she hadn't spoken to her mother since the day she'd left home for college. Though I was doing a reasonably good job of following the conversation, I was also a little distracted by the thought that maybe we should go out to IHOP for some chocolate chip pancakes. With the image of those delicious, syrupy mounds in my head, I casually tossed off my response. "Well," I said, "what if she dies? Won't you feel bad? Isn't it better just to make peace?"

Anna gave me a look that has haunted me ever since, one that showed she was really disappointed in me, that I'd just exposed myself to her and revealed that I was no different than anyone else. She must have thought I was worth salvaging, though, because she stayed in my arms and said, very softly, "If it was a man who was as abusive to me as my mother was, people would applaud me for leaving and never looking back. But because it's my mother, people think there's some kind of importance to the relationship. There isn't. Abuse is abuse and I had to escape it." I remember feeling incredibly ashamed. I apologized profusely and told her that I completely understood and that I thought it was one of the smartest, bravest things I'd ever heard.

She pulled away from me a bit so she could look me in the eye and make sure I meant what I'd said. Then she stroked my hair and said, "Do you want to go get some chocolate chip pancakes?"

After that, we almost never spoke of her family again. So when we were planning our wedding and in response to my question she said she didn't want any of them to come, I didn't argue. I just asked my question and accepted her answer.

———

Things were not that cut-and-dried with my family, of course. I don't know if that was due to weakness on my part or the fact that the abuse on the Heller side was done in a much sneakier, harder to detect fashion. It wasn't actual abuse. It was just . . . well, it was just family.

Teddy and his new girlfriend flew in Friday afternoon from L.A., arriving in time to join us just as were leaving for the local pizza parlor. The girlfriend's name was Charlie, and when I asked what her real first name was, she said, "Charlie." She was from Oklahoma, and the whole time my brother stared at her with those familiar Teddy goo-goo eyes to show her and everyone else around him how much in love he was. They held hands almost constantly, and from time to time he'd stroke her arm or her cheek, just to add that extra little proof of affection.

Like all the others, Charlie was perfectly nice. She was extremely attractive, with long brownish-red hair and a pale complexion, long legs, and enormous breasts, which she didn't have much compunction about revealing via tight T-shirts or dresses with plunging necklines. And she was interesting, in an offbeat way. Three years younger than Ted, she had spent two years driving on the professional stock car circuit, quitting only after a big pileup in which she'd broken both her legs and her car had caught on fire. She was now working as a receptionist at a small ad agency in L.A., but her goal was to open her own garage. As she told this story, her breasts jutting through her tank top, the awed expressions of the men at the pizza joint resembled what I imagined people must have looked like when Jonas Salk announced his discovery of the polio vaccine. Except along with that awe, there was also a collective hangdog expression of despair that showed an understanding that no one else at the table would ever be able to have sex with a large-breasted ex–stock car driver. On the other end of the spectrum, the women at our table mostly revealed narrow-eyed suspicion or utter indifference.

Charlie was interesting in another way, too: She was pregnant. Which explained why, on Saturday morning, she and Teddy showed up at the courthouse with a guy named Leonard, whom I'd never met or heard of before. When I asked Ted, who was my best man—it seemed the simplest, least hurtful thing to do, and I'd cleared it with Phil, who'd said, "Whatever makes everyone the happiest"—why he'd brought Leonard to my wedding, he told me that Leonard was *his* best man.

"What do you mean?" I said.

"I mean, peckerhead, that we're having a joint ceremony."

He smiled at me triumphantly. It was one of those Ted moments: I was screwed no matter what I did. If I refused to let him go forward with his plan, I was an asshole, ruining this fun-loving, spontaneous, hilarious scheme that Ted had brewed up. He was doing something to bring us closer together; I'd be breaking us apart. He was sharing the love; I'd be spitting on the whole relationship. But if I agreed to the double wedding, I'd be: (1) almost certain to seriously piss off the woman I expected to spend the rest of my life with, (2) diminishing the experience and probably the memory of what should be the best day of my life, and (3) maneuvered by my brother, once again, into doing something I knew was wrong and that would somehow misfire and blow up right in my face.

I went straight to Anna and told her what had happened. It was all of twenty minutes before our ceremony was supposed to begin. This was her exact reaction: She was silent for at least a full minute. Her eyes didn't register anger; they clearly showed someone thinking through this bizarre situation step by step, imagining what implications it might have for many decades of marriage, all the way to old age. The silence lasted long enough to drive me to the brink of desperation and ended at the exact moment I was about to ask her to say something, *anything*. She said, very slowly and carefully, "I know you're really upset. And the fact that you are makes me happy, because I know how much this means to you. But I don't think Ted or anyone else can ruin this day for us. It's our day. A lot of other people are getting married on this day, all over the world, but it's still going to be our day and ours alone. So don't give him the satisfaction of letting this ruin anything. Let's just say okay and we'll have our day and it'll be exactly the way it's supposed to be."

We kissed. I still remember it as one of the nicest kisses I've ever experienced. It's not just that it was long and passionate; it's that our lips seemed to merge together and our tongues tasted sweet, as if we were tasting the future and finding it delicious.

Right before the ceremony, my dad pulled Ted aside and said, "Having a child's not like having a dog, you know. It's not a pet. It's a huge responsibility. It involves a lot of sacrifice."

Ted nodded solemnly, then patted my dad condescendingly on the back and said, "Don't worry about it, okay?"

After Ted walked away to go stroke Charlie's arm some more, I asked my dad if he liked Charlie. He shrugged and said, "She seems nice." Then he said, "She's not exactly what I envisioned as the perfect daughter-in-law."

I said, "How come?"

"Well . . . she's not very classy." He hesitated a moment and then said, "Of course, neither is Ted."

It was a startling moment. A rite of passage. A completely unexpected wedding present from my dad. It was the first time he'd ever spoken to me adult to adult rather than father to son. I didn't ask him what he thought of Anna. Not because I feared the answer—I knew Anna passed all the tests. I didn't want to take a chance that he might say something about *me*. I knew I wasn't his vision of the perfect son, but I had no idea of whether he had such a vision or what it might be. However, having already come close enough to entering the Twilight Zone, I thought it was time to edge away.

Ted and Charlie got married first that Saturday morning. At ten-fifteen they both said, "I do," Charlie crying and Ted smirking. Whoever the hell Leonard was, he handed the ring to Ted, gave Charlie a kiss, and then hugged Ted with one of those "I love you, buddy" man hugs. Teddy hugged him back, a full-body embrace. I guess they both meant it at the time, but I never heard of or saw Leonard again after that day. And I'm not sure Ted did, either.

Anna and I were next. We'd thought about preparing our own vows and then decided it seemed too pretentious. We knew what we meant to each other and didn't feel the need to share any of that with anyone else. The ceremony was our way of letting others into our marriage, but our feelings were private. So we just allowed the judge to do his duty. Teddy, still smirking, handed me the ring. Anna and I said our "I do"s and then the whole group went out to brunch at the best restaurant in town, a steak place that served eggs Benedict on weekend mornings, where we all ate mounds of delicious food, drank lots of champagne, and toasted the bright future.

Afterward, Anna and I went to a small inn about half an hour from my parents' house, on the Massachusetts side of the border. We drank more champagne and made love several times over the next day and a half. There was nothing extraordinary about our lovemaking. It didn't break any boundaries and it certainly didn't break any furniture. It was slow and sensual and extraordinarily emotional. Neither of us was all that experienced, nor were we particularly eager to experiment. We liked kissing and touching and falling into each other's arms when we were done. Even though we'd made love plenty of times before then, that weekend was still special. I think we were both exploring each other's bodies, looking for *something,* though I'm not exactly sure what. Maybe for the promise of whatever would give pleasure in the future, or a sensation we'd remember when we were apart. Mostly, I think, we were simply relishing our time alone and expressing that pleasure in a purely physical way. We said we loved each other, more than once but not so often that we felt as if we were trying to convince ourselves.

That was our honeymoon. On Sunday night, Anna headed to Providence and I went back to Cornell. Anna was interning at an architectural firm and was due to spend the next week designing an ecologically sound bathroom using waterless urinals. On Monday morning, I had to dissect the cancerous liver of a recently deceased poodle.

Over the next year, we talked almost every day on the telephone and got together almost every weekend. I suppose it wasn't everyone's notion of the ideal first year of marriage, but it felt ideal to us. Every weekend was special: We didn't *have* to be with each other, we *wanted* to be with each other. After a couple of months of getting used to a heretofore unknown loneliness coupled with a joyful, if incomplete, sense of togetherness, we fell into a lovely rhythm. And almost every time we saw each other, we agreed that in all our lives we'd never suspected that we could be so happy.

Six months into our marriage—and Ted's—Ted and Charlie had their baby, a boy. They named him Hilts, after the Steve McQueen character in *The Great Escape,* Ted's favorite movie. The weekend after Hilts was born, Anna and I flew out to L.A., as did my parents. At the initial viewing of grandson by grandfather—Ted and Charlie brought the baby over to the hotel, where, courtesy of my parents, we were staying—my dad heard the name for the first time and to give his reaction some perspective, to say that he went ballistic would be akin to calling the Taliban a minor irritation to the women of Afghanistan. He was livid. In his view, Hilts was a pet's name, not a boy's name. He reminded Ted—maybe a dozen times in fifteen minutes—of what he'd said before the wedding: that having a child was not the same thing as having a pet. He lectured Teddy about responsibility and the future and the need to be a grown-up. And every time my dad said the word "pet" he looked at me, as if somehow my choice of profession had been the cause of my new nephew's lifelong humiliation.

Ted ate it up, relishing every moment of my father's fury. Charlie just rolled her eyes with a "Well, that's Ted" expression. My mother tried to calm my father down by saying things like "Greg" (she usually called him "honey" or "dear"; "Greg" was only for emergencies), "a lot of children have eccentric names these days." But my mother's words only caused my dad to breathe even more fire. Meanwhile, Anna and I spent a lot of time that weekend in the hotel's restaurant, drinking coffee and trying to devise worse names for a kid than Hilts. I came up with Zimbabwe, Swami, and Pegasus. Anna went for Mephistopheles, Lanyard, and Papaya Joe.

It was a difficult two days. As often with my brother, I never felt as if he were swinging an axe directly at my head or anyone else's But I did start to feel as if all of us were being pecked to death.

Ted and Charlie were living in a beautiful, too-expensive house in south Beverly Hills. It was below Wilshire, so they were living not among movie stars or studio heads but next to an actor who'd had the third lead on a TV series for four years, and across the street was someone who'd been the assistant director on the last Bruce Willis movie.

As usual, Ted didn't have money of his own; to my knowledge, he'd landed only one acting job since moving to L.A., a small part in an experimental play at a not-for-profit theater. But Ted did have superb taste, and that was very much his own. If he hadn't considered the work so demeaning—no, that's not quite right; it's that he would have found it too ordinary, which I think may have been his biggest fear—Ted would have made a superb antiques dealer or decorator. He knew how to put furnishings together the way some people knew how to combine ingredients in a kitchen. Ted could wander into a shop, spot something, and immediately recognize both its beauty and its value. Almost nothing gave him as much pleasure as having an antiques dealer say to him, "You just picked out the most valuable piece in my store." Or better yet: "I'm not sure I want to sell this; I've grown very attached to it." Say those magic words and whatever was being discussed had about a ninety-nine percent chance of winding up in Ted's collection.

Ted wasn't driven by a craving for money. He simply felt an overwhelming urge to be surrounded by *things*. He didn't actually do anything or produce anything, so he defined himself by his possessions. They became all-important to him, intertwined with his very identity. And his possessions included his wife and his child. It was all about image: What mattered was the surface rather than the core. As long as his life *looked* orderly and successful, then all was okay and the underlying chaos could be ignored. Yet it was always painfully clear to anyone who knew Ted that before long the beautiful picture he'd created would be shattered. The pattern had repeated itself for too long not to be predictable.

But that weekend in L.A., his life looked beautiful. Though she'd just given birth to a baby, Charlie was gorgeous. And Hilts was a lovely baby; he had his mother's angular beauty and his father's dark complexion and handsome features. For his perfect-looking family, Ted had rented an equally ideal 1920s Spanish-style home with all its original detail and heart. He enhanced the house's charm by furnishing it with elegant antiques and, it goes without saying, sleek kitchen appliances. Not only was there an ice machine, the stove had a barbecue grill to go along with the six burners on top, and the dishwasher looked as if it could direct the recovery of astronauts from wayward space stations. God knows where he got the money. As Anna and I were working a combined forty-six hours a day it seemed, trying to steer ourselves toward careers and struggling to pay for three full meals a day, Anna wanted me to have a heart-to-heart with Ted and get some tips so I could find out how the hell he did it. I assumed that Charlie had come from money and made the mistake of opening up a joint checking account, but Anna insisted that this couldn't be the whole story. Though she was not a hater, Anna had not been a big fan of Ted's since the delightful "cunt" incident. Now she was working on the assumption that he had to be a drug dealer, a professional cat burglar, or living so far beyond his means that on our next trip we would be visiting him in debtors' prison.

We went to see the Beverly Hills house the night we arrived. Charlie had ordered delicious take-out Mexican food, and the evening was reasonably friendly and tension-free. My father had quickly put the whole "Hilts" issue behind him; within hours of arriving, he'd fallen completely in love with the idea of having a grandchild, no matter the name. I say "the idea of having a grandchild" rather than that he'd fallen in love with Hilts himself, because there was an odd kind of disconnect in my father's adoration. His skewed perception of Hilts was apparent that initial weekend, and it grew over the next few years. To me, Hilts was a cute, apparently sweet-tempered little kid, but to my dad he was the most amazing, beautiful baby in the history of babies. He was magnificent, a genius, unquestionably a future Nobel Prize winner.

I think a lot of my father's response to Hilts was attributable to the fact that he already knew—although none of us did at the time, except my mom—that he was dying of cancer. The idea of death affects people in many different ways. Sometimes it calms them down; it allows them to accept their own mortality and deal with life as it is while they wait for its natural limitations to come into play. Other people panic or experience deep despair or simply give up. My dad became manic, obsessed with the idea that he had to make every experience crucially important, even if in reality it was banal. So here he was with a fine, normal grandchild. But that didn't fit my dad's new definition of his remaining time. He needed magnificent, not fine. He needed extraordinary, not normal. The only way he could turn ordinary reality into something exceptional was to do what he did best: He acted. He assumed the expansive role of loving grandfather, doting on the world's greatest grandson.

There were other issues involved; there always are. I think my dad felt guilty about Teddy. It's not that he didn't love Ted—he just didn't *like* him very much. Here was a way to make amends for the past. So he didn't simply love Hilts. He devoured him with affection.

Teddy and Charlie had given Greg Heller the greatest possible gift: a small human being he could use to redeem himself with his oldest son.

Amid all this Sturm und Drang, I was simply doing my best to be a good uncle. (Anna was doing her best to just keep quiet and stay out of the way.) Knowing Ted's penchant for antiques, and knowing that our relationship needed some repair, I'd spent a good percentage of my savings account on a late-nineteenth-century baby chair. It was exactly Teddy's taste—beautifully hand-carved maple with simple rustic lines, the chair had been smoothed by years of use—and I thought he'd love the idea of feeding his kid on a 130-year-old seat. I'd found it in a small antiques shop on Bleecker Street, making a special trip into the city a few weeks before Hilts's birth. I couldn't swing the full price all at once, but the owner of the shop saw the urgency in my eyes and agreed to let me pay it off over a few months. Anna thought it was insanely extravagant but I felt good doing it, as if it might help me recapture a bit of the past I'd shared with Ted.

I'd had the chair shipped to our hotel in L.A., and that Friday night I presented it to Ted and Charlie at dinner. My brother smiled when he saw it, but as always by now, his reaction had a double edge. A piece of him, I know, loved and appreciated it. I was sure he understood that I was giving him something special, something tailored exactly to his taste, because I loved him and was willing to love his child. But after I told him that the gift was from both me and Anna, his words were totally lacking in enthusiasm. In a dull monotone, he said, "Thanks, it's very nice."

The distance in his response was startling and painful. I saw immediately that we could no longer connect, not on any level. He wouldn't allow himself to take genuine pleasure in anything I gave him because it would make him too vulnerable. But even more startling was the thought just then taking hold inside my head: Maybe he just couldn't take pleasure in *anything* anymore.

Charlie acted pleased and kissed Anna, then me. But then she brought out the gift her parents had sent her, which happened to be a super-modern, every-possible-bell-and-whistle version of what I'd just given them. My baby chair was a little stand with a seat and a thin fold-down slab of wood to serve as a table for the hungry infant. This other thing was plastic and had wheels and a seat belt. Parts of it lit up, and I'm pretty sure there was a control panel that was compatible with the dishwasher/rocket launcher.

Anna knew how crushed I was and gently took my hand in hers. My mom understood, too. She patted me on the back and must have said at least four times that the antique chair was a lovely gift. And so thoughtful.

My dad was so absorbed in Hilts that I don't think he even saw the chair. Cradling and singing to his grandson, he was busy making up a ditty that managed to work in the words "Hilts," "stilts," "kilts," "wilts," and "quilts." Hilts seemed to like the song quite a lot; he was burbling just like perfect babies are supposed to.

I don't know why I did what I did next, but after Ted had basically said, "Nice try, what else you got?" when it came to my gift, I suddenly declared that I wanted to take everyone—including my parents—out to dinner the next night.

"On me," I said. And then to both Ted and Charlie: "Pick a place you guys like."

Before Anna could even poke me—which she did, hard—Charlie started to say, "Oh, we'd love to but—"

Teddy cut her off, finishing her sentence: "I know you guys flew out here and everything, but Charlie's exhausted. And we really need a night, a whole day, with Hilts. We need to just stay at home with him and let him rest. Some alone time, just the three of us."

"But—" I said, and that was all I got to say before my dad interrupted.

"We'll do Sunday brunch," he announced. "Before we have to head to the airport. Pick a place and it's my treat."

"But—" I said again. "I wanted to—"

"You don't pay when I'm around," my dad said. "Hilts's granddad is treating."

"Great," Teddy said. "That's great."

And that was that. Somehow, I had lost again. I wasn't exactly sure what I'd lost or how. But I felt hollow. My family was not only refusing to accept my gift, they were refusing even to acknowledge my generosity of spirit. I understood my father's response. He had a role to play, one he not only liked but insisted upon playing at all times: the adult. The moral authority. The Father, with a most definite capital F. Once he locked into that part, everyone else had to play his or her own supporting part. Ad-libbing or changing roles was not acceptable. In the family play that was my father's reality, there were no rewrites. The son did not pay. The child did not step in and assume the role of hero. Or even of equal. If that happened, the center would not hold. One wrong move around a check for the cost of eggs Benedict or blueberry pancakes and Greg Heller's universe would explode. I'd seen it all my life and gradually come to understand and even sympathize with my father's need to be the essential player in all our lives.

But Teddy's emptiness was beyond my understanding. We had been growing apart, but I'd thought there was still a link. I was positive that our lifelong bond hadn't broken. But that disinterested look in his eyes when I'd given him the chair, the instant capitulation to our dad's insistence on picking up the tab—he had to know how hurtful all that would be to me. He had to know that he was destroying the foundation of our relationship. And I didn't know why.

Another human trait I was having trouble comprehending: the destruction of something valuable without any rhyme or reason. Maybe that urge was at the center of the history of mankind, but it still made no sense to me.

The next day, Anna and I struck out on our own and wandered around L.A. We did some touristy stuff and talked about my family. Anna was particularly gentle with me, knowing how much the Friday night dinner had stung. After we had tacos and pork buns and hot cinnamon doughnuts at the Farmers Market, she took me back to our hotel and we made love. This was something I could comprehend. It's amazing how much better and more connected I felt stroking her thigh and running my nail along her bare back.

We had dinner with my parents that night at some Italian restaurant by the Pacific Ocean. My dad spent a lot of time talking about how sweet Hilts was and how he hoped having a baby was going to make Teddy more mature. My mother spent a good part of the dinner looking dubious but caring. Anna and I drank ourselves to near oblivion, which wasn't as pleasurable as touching each other when we had no clothes on, but it wasn't too shabby, either. The next morning, we packed up, put our bags in the rental car, and met Ted, Charlie, and Hilts for brunch.

After my second latte, I had to go to the men's room. As I pushed the door open, I practically collided with Randy Kelley. Randy was an actor who worked a little more often than Ted and had been another one of my brother's best-friends-for-life who then disappeared fairly quickly from Teddy's life. We recognized each other because Randy had spent a lot of time with Ted after the divorce from Karen. He'd been gracious and caring during Ted's three-week crying jag, when I'd come down to help put the pieces back together. He had popped in several times with superb grass and good Chinese food. He also played a mean guitar; after we ate, he and Ted would sit and strum their guitars and sing quietly. Ted loved Randy's playing and singing. I did, too, because his enjoyment shone through on everything he played and sang. Ted was equally talented, possibly even more so, but his playing was forced because he had to show his audience how hard he was working, as if effort was what mattered. His singing was a little too sincere, too emotional. He'd get this very serious look on his face, even when singing a lighthearted, frivolous song, similar to the look he got when he was trying to show his girlfriends or wives how much in love with them he was. The real emotion behind the words wasn't important. It only mattered that his audience understood that Ted was feeling something. The result was that no one could ever be sure Ted felt anything.

A few months after that New York trip, I'd asked Ted how Randy was doing and he'd said, "Oh, he turned out to be a real asshole." I hadn't expected that, despite Ted's history of abandoning friends, because Randy didn't remotely fit my definition of "asshole." But Teddy went on: "He turned into a born-again Christian and now he's singing Christian music." I went, "Seriously?" And Teddy had gone, "Who the hell jokes about Christian music?"

So on my bathroom break from brunch that Sunday, I was surprised to run into Randy, who was drying his hands on his jeans on his way out of the men's room. We said hi and I asked him what he was doing. He told me that he was indeed into Christian music now and had just made a recording. He added that he'd be playing at some church in New York and that I should come see him. Before I could say anything back, he said, "Hey, where were you last night?" I kind of shook my head, not understanding his question, and he went, "Why weren't you at Ted's last night?"

"What do you mean?" I said.

"At the coming-out party."

"I'm still not following," I told him.

"Bob," Randy said, as if he were lecturing a small child. "I asked about you last night, and Ted said you were in town. I asked why you weren't at the party, and he said you didn't want to come. Come on, man, you're out here and your brother had a baby—you should have come to the party."

"Was it a big party?" I managed to say.

"Fifty, sixty people. Pretty big. Everybody wanted to see the baby. And see if Ted really and truly was a dad." He laughed. "Good grub, too."

"Where was it?" I asked.

Randy paused before answering that one. Maybe the look on my face gave something away. Finally he said, "At Ted and Charlie's."

"At the house."

"Yeah, at the house. Look . . . if I said something I shouldn't have—I know Ted sometimes—"

"No, no. I mean . . . well, I just wasn't feeling great last night."

We stood there awkwardly for a moment. Then, before he could make his escape, I said, "Does Ted know you're here?"

"At the restaurant?"

I nodded.

"Yeah," he said. "I mentioned it last night. I was gonna come by and say hello, but Ted said it might be awkward. Is it awkward? He told me you had some kind of problem with me. Strange, because I always thought you and I got along pretty well."

I found that I couldn't say anything. My mouth was open half-way—my Nicolas Cage moment—but no words were coming out.

"Seriously," Randy said one more time, now using his best Christian-music tone. "I think you should have gone last night. Even for just a few minutes. I mean, whatever problems the two of you have, you don't have to act like an asshole. Pardon my French."

I shook his hand, took care of my business in the men's room, and went back to the table. I knew that Ted had spotted me talking to Randy; he was smiling, a thin, tight-lipped smile that didn't reflect amusement. It was an oddly startling smile: It didn't convey cynicism or defiance or refusal to conform to normal human behavior, which is what I usually saw in Ted's smirks. What I saw in this smile was fear. He was delighting in my discomfort and anger, but he was also afraid of it. I don't know what he feared. Not retaliation, because what could I do? Not invite him to my next birthday party? Pretend I wasn't home the next time he called? Ring his doorbell and then run and hide behind the bushes? Perhaps he was afraid that I'd tell our parents. But Ted knew me well. Telling our mom and dad that Ted had betrayed us would hurt them tremendously, and if I told them what had happened, *I'd* be the one to hurt them, not Ted. So he could feel safe, knowing I'd keep his nasty secret.

I sat at the table, letting my coffee get cold, trying to put it all together. What could my brother possibly be afraid of? After running through every possibility I could come up with, the only one that made any sense was the simplest: He was afraid that I just plain wouldn't like him anymore. Ted depended on people liking him. Without that, he had no way of manipulating them. And that's what mattered to

Ted: his ability to control friends, lovers, family. That's what he was afraid of now. If I didn't like him anymore, he had no more control over me.

When brunch was over, I kissed Charlie lightly on the cheek and said good-bye. I kissed my little nephew and tweaked his tiny, socked feet. When Ted leaned in to hug me, I let him. When he said, "It was great to see you, thanks for coming. And seriously, thanks for the chair," I let him say it. But when he tried to turn away from me, to avoid looking into my eyes, I kept staring at him. I knew he couldn't let it go. That was the thing about Ted: He couldn't help himself. He always did his best to let himself be caught when he lied. And he had to look back, to see if he'd gotten away with it.

So when he finally met my gaze, I gave him a thin-lipped smile of my own.

I didn't know whose was sadder.

When our year of living separately was finally up, Anna had her graduate degree and I was a vet. We agreed that we'd go where the work was: Whoever got the first great job offer, the other would follow along to that city. I got the first bite, an invitation to join up with several young vets in Miami. At first I was excited—I had visions of tending to sick cocker spaniels while their blond, bikinied owners stood by, and of making emergency house calls to South Beach bars, prescribing miracle cures for scrawny bar cats and then getting free drinks for the rest of my life. On closer inspection, however, I saw that the invitation came from a group of vets in Miami, Ohio, which was just a bit different. The Ohio version of Miami was a solid college town but with many more mittens and down-filled parkas than bikinis or tall drinks with umbrellas stuck in them. The place was also only a couple hours away from Covington, Kentucky, the home of Anna's entire family.

When I told Anna about the offer, the look on her face was one I'd seen only in movies where at least several teenagers are hacked to death with a chain saw. That look was quickly followed by another, an instant attempt to hide the dismay—no, despair is probably closer to the truth—behind her initial reaction. And then came a third and very

different look when I told her I'd already turned the offer down. I
hadn't needed to ask her; I knew that if we lived a short drive away
from her hometown, she would spend her waking hours curled up in
a fetal position on the living room floor, waiting for her family to
come suck the life out of her. I told her I was sure something else would
turn up in a city far enough away from her past that it would give our
future a reasonable chance of working out. I would have turned down
a thousand jobs if I could have kept that third look on her face on a
twenty-four/seven basis.

Anna got the next job offer. A design firm in Tulsa, Oklahoma,
wanted her to start immediately. I did my best to smile and be supportive, but the invisible thought balloons floating above my head filled
with images of cattle and buffaloes requiring urgent veterinary treatment and women in floral stretch pants trying to get me to sign on to
a committee to make automatic weapons mandatory in every American household. I had a difficult time pretending that this was a future
I could get excited about. Fortunately, Anna turned that job down as
quickly as I'd rejected Miami, Ohio.

My father told me what a mistake we were making. "You go where
the work is," he said. My mother sided with him. "What, she can't be
close to her family? What kind of way is that to live? You're acting
young and stupid. Call them back and take the job in Ohio. She'll get
used to it."

The only person who told me we were doing the right thing was
Ted, which made my knees quiver. For some reason, he'd taken to calling me once or twice a week, starting four or five months after we'd
left L.A. I knew something was wrong. At thirty-two, Ted was floun-
dering. Life had begun to move too quickly for him; he didn't seem
able to leap aboard and be a real part of it. It was clear that I was suddenly some kind of lifeline. He was trying to reach back into the past,
but the past was no longer much of a tether between us, so I kept things
as superficial as possible. That was easy, because with Ted any attempt
at digging beneath the surface was dangerous. (Think Laurence Oliv-
ier and Dustin Hoffman in *Marathon Man* with Ted's psyche the fresh,
raw nerve in Hoffman's tooth.) So whenever I asked a question, which
was rarely, I never pushed for real answers because I knew Ted was

never going to *give* me real answers. Keeping things superficial was easier than severing the relationship; it avoided family arguments and rifts and lectures and taking sides and lots of hurt feelings. On the other hand, it meant he was still a part of my life, and that made me uneasy. It was like building a house on a fault line. At any moment, the beams and rafters could start to shake and serious damage could be done.

Anna and I, meanwhile, were certain that the good life was tantalizingly close. The perfect opportunity was just around the corner—we just needed to hold out a little longer. Sometimes, late at night, in bed and wrapped in each other's arms, we would confess our fears that we'd spend the rest of our lives broke, homeless, and with fewer job opportunities than George Bailey in *It's a Wonderful Life*. But mostly we were excited, and in our mid-twenties, excitement—even if it included the possibility that we could fall off a cliff—was what we wanted. We didn't want to settle. We didn't want a routine existence. We didn't want to be real grown-ups yet. But we both knew that when the call came, we'd be ready.

Let's face it: Sometimes it pays to be young and stupid. A month after we rejected the two less-than-perfect jobs in favor of the unknown, I got a call from a vet I'd met at Cornell when she'd guest lectured at the veterinary school. Her name—I swear to god—was Dr. Marjorie Paws. She was sixty-eight years old and had a private practice in New York City, in the West Village. Her specialty was retinal degeneration in dogs, but she was as pure an old-fashioned generalist as I'd ever met. She could talk for hours—and did!—about the skin texture of cats (their skin is one-sixteenth of an inch thick, less than half the thickness of a dog's skin, thus making them far more susceptible to burns and abrasions from collars). She'd made a nearly lifelong study of cat litter and the deadly ingredients in processed pet food and the connection between tooth decay and diseases of the immune system in various species.

I'd been assigned to look after her during her three-day visit to Cornell—drive her around, take her to and from the lecture hall, show her around campus. On the second night, she invited me to dinner and we split a bottle of white wine (this after she'd downed two double scotches on her own) and talked until well after midnight. I told her all about Anna and described exactly what sort of career I imagined for myself; she was so warm and disarming that she made me feel I could be completely open with her. And she was just as open in return. She'd never married, but she told me about several romances (some old, some recent) and regaled me with stories about her patients (the people as well as the animals) and her life in Greenwich Village.

Marjorie had grown up in Hungary and still had a slight Hungarian accent, even though she'd come to Brooklyn when she was ten. She was about five feet tall and rather squat, with wrinkled skin. She wore garish gold jewelry, and her teeth were yellow from years of smoking. What made her my hero, though, was that she spent a big chunk of her income on season tickets to the Knicks. By the end of the night, I'd practically fallen in love with a woman more than forty years my senior and about half my height. She was smart and charming and, except for the nicotine-stained teeth, she had pretty much led the life I was hoping to lead for the next half a century or so.

I hadn't seen Marjorie after that night, nor had I thought much about her. But one afternoon, as Anna and I were eating a late lunch—grilled cheese sandwiches, which was as gourmet as Anna got—I answered the phone and heard Dr. Paws's gravelly voice.

"Heller," she said. During her visit to Cornell, she had only called me by my last name, so I knew exactly who it was.

"Dr. Paws. How great is this, hearing from you?"

Anna snorted and iced tea almost came out of her nose. I'd told her about my evening with this wonderful woman, and though she appreciated my enthusiasm, her own excitement was overwhelmed by how funny she thought the name Paws was.

"Yes, it's nice talking to you too. I got your phone number from the university. Why are you home in the middle of the day?"

"Because I'm having lunch. And 'cause it's better than all the other places I could be, I guess."

"And what are those other places?"

"You know—the racetrack, an opium den, Republican headquarters . . ."

"You're not working?"

"No. Well, I had an offer but . . ." I thought about explaining the problem with Miami, Ohio, and decided against it.

"Would you like to be working or are you happy just staying home? And why are you having lunch at three in the afternoon?"

"I don't know. I mean, I know about working. I don't know about lunch. We just weren't hungry until now. But I'd definitely rather be working than eating a grilled cheese sandwich."

"I thought you loved my grilled cheese sandwiches," Anna said. I waved at her to pipe down.

"Would you like to be working in New York, Heller?"

I froze, afraid to answer. I had the distinct feeling that if I moved or said the word "yes," she'd start laughing and hang up.

"Are you there, Heller?"

I nodded.

"Are you nodding?"

"Yes," I said.

"Well, it's very hard to actually see nodding over the phone, but I imagine you're a little excited at the idea of working with me."

I nodded again.

"Are you nodding again?" she asked.

"Yes."

"Here's the deal. I want you to come to New York and be my junior partner. I don't want to work so hard anymore. I'll still work hard, just not *so* hard. You'll do all the things I don't want to do, especially in all the shitty hours when I don't want to do them. Do you understand?"

"Uh-huh."

"I can teach you everything I know, and you can try to make me laugh on occasion."

"Okay."

"Did I tell you I own the building where my practice is?"

"You did."

"I live above the practice. In this beautiful apartment. Very spacious. Beautiful fireplace. It's a brownstone, and I live on the second and third floors. An outside stairway leads down to a beautiful garden."

"That sounds nice."

"It is. There's also a lovely two-bedroom apartment on the fourth floor. Not fancy but very charming. I rent it out. It pays for almost half the cost of the entire building."

"That sounds nice, too."

"Oh, it is. It's all superb. Except for a shitty little one-bedroom apartment on the top floor. If this were Paris, it'd be a *chambre de service*. Or maybe even a garret. But whatever it is, it's small and shitty. But it's also free. That's where you and Anna will live. Her name is Anna, correct?"

"Yes," I said. "Anna."

Anna looked up at the sound of her name but remained silent. She knew something momentous was happening, but she didn't want to break the spell by speaking or making any sudden movement.

"Are you almost finished with your grilled cheese sandwich, Heller?"

"I'm done."

"So what do you have to say?"

"First . . . well . . . oh my *god*, does this sound good."

"And is there a second?"

"Kind of. I mean, not really."

"I'm already learning that in Heller language that means yes. So go ahead. You can ask me whatever you want."

"Why me? How do you know I'm good enough?"

"Because you drink very well and you're an excellent driver. And I did do my homework. You come highly recommended. You were right to turn down Ohio. This will be much more fun."

"What? How'd you know about Ohio?"

"Heller," she said. "It's a small world, the world of dogs and cats and hamsters. We know what's out there and who's out there. And I also know you're drawn to my holistic, naturopathic approach, and you'd be surprised how many people think I'm . . . how should I put it . . ."

"A kook?"

"No, that's a little too harsh, but thank you very much. I would say 'outside the mainstream.' "

"That's a better way of putting it."

"Thank you."

"Don't you want to, you know, test me out or anything?"

"Oh yes, good thinking. Let's discuss hip dysplasia."

"Right now? On the phone?"

"What better time? Unless you have to make yourself another grilled cheese sandwich."

"No, no. Now is fine."

"How about Anna? Does she need another sandwich?"

"No, she's fine. She's eating some ice cream now."

Anna cocked her head, mouthing the words "What the hell?" Then she whispered, "Tell her it's chocolate chip."

"Anna says to tell you she's eating chocolate chip ice cream."

"Excellent choice. Mint or plain?"

"Mint or plain?" I asked.

"Plain," Anna said, and I relayed the information into the receiver.

"Ah," Marjorie Paws said. "Not quite as good. But still good. So what are the symptoms of hip dysplasia? What would you look for?"

"A reluctance to walk up stairs, difficulty standing up, discomfort while walking or running."

"Are those certain indications of dysplasia?"

"No. It could be other degenerative diseases. Even Lyme disease."

"So what's the first step?"

"A radiographic diagnosis."

"And conventional medicine would treat it how?"

"Conventional medicine says it can't be prevented and its degeneration can't be halted. So they use painkillers to treat the symptoms of inflammation and pain, and surgery to change the angular dynamics of the joint. Maybe even a full hip or socket replacement."

"And if one were to avoid that conventional treatment?"

"Um . . ."

"How about a bio-nutritional analysis?"

"Okay. Sure."

"Explain."

"Well . . . that would allow us to see all of the dog's imbalances, not just his hip condition. In a lot of hip-dysplastic dogs there are imbalances in the pituitary gland in the brain, which controls growth factors in the body. There's usually a need for adrenal support, too."

"What supplements would you prescribe?"

"Potentially AR-Ease for arthritic symptons, Cosequin, chondroi-
tin sulfate . . ."

"That's enough."

"There are other things that can be done."

"I know. I mean, that's all I have to hear. When can you start?"

"When do you *want* me to start?"

"I'll have the shitty little apartment cleaned out in two days. And
I'll repaint, just because I'm so good-hearted."

"What happened to the person who was working for you up till
now?"

"He went to Ohio. Took the job you turned down. I think the poor
guy actually thought he was on his way to South Beach. By the time he
realized what was happening, it was too late."

So Anna and I went to New York, which was where we both wanted
to wind up. We were thrilled that we didn't have to spend years working
our way there. Thanks to my ability to drive slowly and safely, coupled with my talent for drinking with elderly female veterinarians, we
were suddenly heading for our dream destination.

New York had always been my ideal city. I used to love coming to
visit my dad when I was a small boy, and I still get a tingling sensation
at the memory of seeing the skaters in Rockefeller Center and being
overwhelmed by the size of the movie screen at Radio City. Later, visiting Ted, I delighted in all the things most people complain about when
they bash the city: the heat, the congestion, the honking cars, the rude
waiters. I never failed to feel the electricity when I stepped out onto
the streets of Manhattan, and I grew up thinking of it as a kind of para-
disaical haven that would safeguard me from the boredom of normal
life. I don't think Anna had quite the degree of faith I had in the city,
but she, too, aspired to be worthy of it. It is, for a certain kind of person, the ultimate testing ground, and we were both eager to put ourselves to the test.

The fifth-floor garret in Marjorie Paws's brownstone was as small
as Marjorie had said it was, but not nearly as awful. In fact, it was

wonderful—charming and in a perfect location on Greenwich Avenue. Right below us lived Florence and Isaac Schmidt, Marjorie's tenants. In their early sixties, the Schmidts were exceedingly nice and kept to themselves. Our first day in the building they knocked on our door, welcomed us, and Florence said, "Feel free to borrow anything you want or ask if you need anything. Other than that, you'll probably never see us unless we bump into you in the stairway." Isaac added, "We're extremely friendly, but we have plenty of friends and have no desire to make new ones." I immediately fell in love with them.

Marjorie lived below them. Well, she actually lived and slept in the second-floor apartment, which was orderly, comfortable, and inviting, especially the lovely garden, which she tended fanatically, and the outdoor patio. She also had the third-floor apartment, but she didn't exactly live in it. It was part office, part research lab, and part storeroom; it also served as a guest room for the occasional relative, out-of-town friend, and anyone who seemed to need shelter for the night. There were papers everywhere, and odd pieces of furniture positioned in apparently random order. There were framed photos of people I'm not sure even she could identify, odd bric-a-brac she'd bought over the years at flea markets, and New York Knicks paraphernalia on the walls and the fireplace mantel and draped over couches. Marjorie used a Walt Frazier jersey as a throw on her favorite easy chair; I would often find her sitting there in the evenings with her reading glasses on, cloaked by an orange-and-blue number 10, perusing various causes of canine gingivitis or feline renal disorder.

To the left of our building stood a pizza parlor, and the aroma of baking sauce, cheese, and dough wafted up to our windows day and night. To our right was another residential brownstone, this one with a small store on the ground floor providing computer services to the technologically incompetent. One of the two guys who ran the place had more acne than I'd ever seen on a human being over the age of sixteen. The other one had body hair of early caveman proportions. They were both very spacey and even nicer than they were spacey, and it didn't take long for Anna to get them to agree to take in deliveries for us when the clinic was closed (their working hours seemed to be approximately twenty-four hours a day). In exchange for that great convenience, I said I'd treat their pets for free; they didn't have any pets but they assured me they'd take me up on my offer if and when they ever took the plunge. Anna responded by offering to design and decorate their office, which looked like a dumping ground for anything computer-, phone-, or electronic-related. They looked at Anna as if she were a madwoman—and made it clear they thought their tiny, gadget-filled space was as Eden-like as one could get in this life.

Anna and I got settled quickly. Within days we came to understand that Marjorie was not only the perfect landlord, she was also the perfect boss and a completely delightful person. She and Anna became very close; I became her friend and disciple. Some people might have wanted more of a separation between work and home, but I never did. I didn't think there *was* a separation between the two.

My first week at the clinic, someone brought in a kitten that had been put in a shopping bag and left in the street. The bag had been tied with ribbon so the kitten could breathe but not get out. Marjorie was in the process of posting a sign saying, FOUND: INCREDIBLY CUTE KITTEN. WHO WANTS HIM? when I stopped her. At first she didn't say anything; instead, she just watched me as I eyed the cat, who was orange and white and scruffy and meowing his head off.

"We get a lot of these," she said. "We get three-legged dogs and cats people have tried to drown. We once got a Vietnamese pig that some asshole tried to sell to a restaurant in Chinatown, figuring they could stick it on the grill and make it disappear. You can't take them all in."

"How many have *you* taken in?" I asked.

"My apartment is a lot more spacious than yours."

I nodded and waited her out.

"Five cats and two dogs," she admitted. "And briefly a snake. But to be perfectly honest, snakes give me the creeps, although please don't tell anyone. It can't be good for business."

"And how about Lucy?"

Lucy was the office receptionist. She was around thirty-five years old, maybe five foot two, and weighed a good three hundred pounds. She lived with another woman—Alana, who was almost six feet tall and weighed at most one-twenty. They'd been a couple since Lucy had moved to New York and owned at least four animals, all of which I was pretty sure had come from the abandoned list at Marjorie's practice.

"Okay," Marjorie said. "Lucy has taken her fair share, too—including the pig, by the way. But it's a slippery slope. Should you be doing this without discussing it with Anna?"

"Anna? Anna's gonna love this little guy."

"Let me ask you something, Heller. How long have you been married?"

"Over a year now. Sixteen months."

"How come you don't have any animals?"

"What do you mean?"

"I mean, you're a vet. You studied to be a vet for three years, and you probably wanted to be a vet for ten years before that. So why don't you have any cute little pets running all over the place?"

"'Cause we wanted to wait until we got settled somewhere."

"Uh-huh."

"What?" I demanded. "That's a totally legit reason. I'm telling you, Anna will want this little guy as much as I do."

She looked at me, unconvinced, but I didn't say anything more. I just kept waiting until finally she handed the tiny creature over. Marjorie seemed both grumpy and satisfied that I'd won the argument. I didn't rub it in; instead I simply nodded a thank-you and then gave my full attention to the kitten.

"It's not a hard commute," I told him. "And it'll be a lot easier when you learn how to go up and down the stairs."

He meowed at me with complete understanding.

"See," I said to Marjorie. "He and Anna are going to have a lot of interesting conversations."

When our last patient left, I took the kitten upstairs and presented him to Anna. She cooed appropriately and then said, "Um . . . there's something I should probably tell you."

"Feel free," I said. "Although I think the last time you said that to me, I found out you were a totally different nationality than I thought you were."

"This is almost as big." She hesitated and literally took a gulp. "I'm allergic to cats."

A long silence. Then I managed to go, "Uh-huh." Another silence, not quite as long. Then: "You do know I'm a vet, right?"

"I just never had the heart to tell you. I'm okay as long as I don't touch them or anything."

"Okay. You realize you're holding him, which qualifies as total touching."

"I know. And I'm about to start sneezing my head off."

She called it perfectly: The sneezing began on cue. For such an otherwise delicate person, Anna delivered a string of rapid-fire sneezes that were startlingly loud. She sounded the way I imagined Curly of the Three Stooges would sound if he went on a major sneezing jag. I'd never seen this particular quirk of hers, and I could tell by the flash of her eyes that it would not be wise to comment on it. She sneezed seven humongous sneezes. (Later, when we were able to have a rational conversation about this physical anomaly, she told me that she always sneezed seven times; never six, never eight. Once it stopped, she was free to live life the way it should be lived until it was time to sneeze again.) Then she produced a second and third set of seven sneezes—twenty-one sneezes in all.

When the terrifying noise abated, I waited a few moments just to make sure there wasn't going to be a fourth round. Then I said, hesitantly: "What about dogs?"

"Not quite so bad. But not good."

"Is that why you make me wash my hands so often?"

She nodded.

"And do the laundry three times a day?"

"That's an exaggeration, and you know it. But yes."

"So all that talk about waiting to get a dog until we were settled . . ."

"Avoidance."

"How long did you think you could avoid this?" I asked.

"I don't know. Until a safe fell out of a window and landed on my head. I just *couldn't* tell you." She looked miserable, and not just because the skin around her eyes was turning red and puffy.

"So . . . you didn't think this was worth mentioning? I mean, this is kind of like me being allergic to furniture. That would not be good for your job."

"I know. I know. "

"I always thought we'd have a whole bunch of cats and dogs. That was my idea of what our family would be like. You, me, a few cats, a puppy or two, a Vietnamese pig."

"A Vietnamese pig?"

"That probably won't happen. I'm just saying."

Anna was silent for quite a while. Finally, she said, "I can take shots."

"Shots?"

"I checked it out. I talked to Marjorie. I can go to a doctor and get allergy shots once or twice a week."

"That seems kind of crazy."

"No, it doesn't. I can see it on your face. You already love this little guy. I'm not gonna deprive you of that just because my sneezing can practically wake the dead if he gets too close to me."

She was right. I'd already fallen for the little orange-and-white fur ball. It's difficult for me to explain the reaction I have to animals—my heart just goes out to them. I've played basketball with a team of guys, sweated and struggled and fought to win with them, but afterward, once the thrill of victory or the agony of defeat has faded, I have no idea what any of them were thinking. Before I met Anna, I'd made love to women and, afterward, holding them in my arms, I didn't have a clue about what they were feeling or what they wanted.

In truth, most humans were complete ciphers to me. I knew they had emotions, knew there was an awful lot of complexity under the benign layer of skin, but I didn't have any idea what those emotions were or how to tap into their complexity. But I could pet the head of a horse, look into its eyes, and absolutely understand what he wanted, what was pulsing through that insanely strong body. I could tell what different meows meant; I was able to distinguish between "I'm hungry" and "I want to go out" and "I want to be petted" and "I just want to meow and pretend I want to jump on the bed but really I'm staying put." I knew when a dog wanted to wrestle or run or bite or lick. And

I loved that connection to animals. They touched me deeply; I appreciated their independence and willingly accepted their needs. They brought me comfort, something very few people did until I met Anna. And now here was Anna, dropping an atomic bomb on my world. I'd already been grinning at the thought of the little orange cat sleeping on me, of feeling his small body heave up and down to the rhythm of his breathing. In my imagination, I could already feel his weight on my chest, and the idea that I wouldn't ever be able to feel that for real was beyond my comprehension.

"Do you *like* 'em?" I asked Anna.

"What?"

"Animals. Cats, dogs, chickens, you know. All of 'em. We never even discussed it. I just assumed. I mean—"

"I love them. And I always wanted to have them. Well, maybe not chickens or a Vietnamese pig. But cats and dogs, yeah." She laughed. "I want a whole nursery full."

"So," I said, "Marjorie knows about this?"

"I figured she'd know what to do. I knew you'd show up with one of these guys"—she nodded toward the kitten, who was doing his best to get under the refrigerator in our Pullman kitchen—"sooner or later."

"You'd really take shots?"

She nodded, simultaneously making a "what choice do I have?" face. Then she said, "Do you think I don't know?"

"Know what?" I said.

"Know all the things you were thinking while you were standing there panicking about not keeping our new cat."

I stepped forward and kissed her. "No," I said. "I think you know everything about me."

She went quiet for a moment and then asked, "How'd I get to be the lucky one?"

"Lucky how?"

"You're so much better with animals than you are with people. How come I made the grade?"

When I didn't answer, she said, "Seriously."

I nodded. "I don't know if I'd call it lucky. But . . . I trust you."

"I know you do. So tell me."

"I just did. That's my real answer. I don't trust people. Not all that much. I trust animals. And you."

"And Phil. And now Marjorie."

"Yes," I said. "Phil and now Marjorie. I also kind of trust the guy who runs the laundromat on West Fourth. He told me I gave him an extra five bucks by mistake, and he gave it back to me."

"Wow," Anna said. "You're making progress." Then she said, "Oh, and just so you know, I'm not allergic to kids. I mean, in case you're wondering."

I stepped back—a giant step. I couldn't help myself.

"Don't worry," she said. "I just wanted to see your reaction. It was a good one, by the way. A little subtle but effective."

"I thought you didn't want kids."

"I said, 'Don't worry.' Why do you think we're such a good pair? I don't trust people any more than you do. I'm just more civil about it than you are."

I nodded. Anna looked down at the kitten.

"What are we gonna name him?" she asked.

"Rocky," I said.

"I thought you hated those movies."

"Not Stallone Rocky. Jimmy Cagney Rocky."

She looked me blankly.

"Oh my god," I said. "I can't believe you don't know this. *Angels with Dirty Faces*. Cagney plays Rocky Sullivan. He's a total gangster—doesn't give a shit about anything, has zero fear. The Bowery Boys completely idolize him. But he goes to prison and is gonna get the electric chair. Pat O'Brien convinces him to pretend to be terrified so kids everywhere will spit on his memory. So even though we know he's not afraid of dying, he acts like a coward to make sure kids don't idolize a guy like him. The ultimate act of heroism. And the big headline in the paper is 'Rocky Dies Yellow.' That's my fantasy for my obit. I want the *Times* to say, 'Bob Dies Yellow.' "

She peered at me as if I'd lost my marbles. But she didn't seem to mind. I could also see her registering this new bit of information about me, tucking it away for future use. Then she turned her gaze on Rocky.

The look in her eyes was affectionate but not as affectionate as when she looked at me.

"He does have that tough-guy, trench-coat kind of look," she said.

"So you're really okay with this?"

"Look at him," she said.

Rocky was now up on our one kitchen counter, trying his best to stick his nose into a package of Pepperidge Farm double chocolate cookies. I picked him up with one hand, held him against my neck and collarbone. When he meowed, a tiny squeak of a meow, and then started purring, Anna reached over and put her hand on his head.

"How could I resist?" she said.

Then she sneezed fourteen times.

It turned out she *couldn't* resist. Not Rocky, and not Scully (an abandoned black cockapoo; Anna was an *X-Files* fanatic). Not Margo (a lovely little alley cat who'd been cruelly burned by her previous owner and left in a bike basket a block from the clinic; we named her for the lead singer in the Cowboy Junkies), and not Larry (named for Larry Bird because even though I was a Knicks fanatic I loved Larry Bird), an insanely talkative green-and-pink parrot who'd been picked up on a street near the Meatpacking District and liked to greet visitors by saying, "Hello, cocksucker." And definitely not Waverly (a truly dumb but extraordinarily enthusiastic Irish setter who lived, I believe, solely for the pleasure of licking Anna's face; it was Anna who insisted on taking Waverly in and naming her after her favorite Village street). That was our family, and it was a very happy one.

One evening, Anna and I were lying in bed, comfortably leaning against each other. We had just finished making love; we weren't newlyweds any longer, but it was still impossible to imagine taking each other for granted physically. We'd been living in our small apartment for about three years, and life was good: I loved my work, the clinic was thriving, and Anna, in between allergy shots, was beginning to develop a reputation as a gifted designer. Our animals were in various stages of repose on or near the bed except for Margo, who was chasing after something, hopefully not a roach, in the other room. Anna picked up a book; I'm pretty sure it was a Jane Smiley novel. I turned on a *Law & Order* rerun.

At some point before the conclusion of that episode's trial, Anna put her book down and said—no big deal, not whispering, not overly dramatic—"I'm starting to think about kids. I mean real ones. The two-legged kind."

I was a little surprised at how unshaken I was at this pronouncement.

"And what are you thinking?" I asked.

"I'm thinking about whether or not I'd be as terrible a parent as my parents were."

"No," I said. "You'd be a perfect mother."

"You're not a good judge."

"Why not?"

"You think I'd be a perfect anything."

"Well, you pretty much would be."

"That's what I mean. You're a little biased."

"So, what do we do? Go to Judge Judy and see what she thinks? My bias is valid here, unless you're thinking of doing this without me."

Anna ignored me. That was one of her many skills, ignoring things I said that deserved to be ignored. "Are you scared by the idea of having a kid?" she said.

"No."

"Why not?"

"Because I'd be having it with you."

The radiant look on her face: I can still see it, still feel its warmth. "I think that's the nicest thing anyone ever said to me," she said.

I shrugged and did my best to look blasé, but secretly I was thrilled to have made her so happy. "I didn't say it to be nice. It's just the truth."

"Do you want a kid?" she asked.

"I don't know," I said. I looked around the room, at Rocky, who was sprawled, sound asleep, on my chest, and at Margo, who was now at the foot of the bed, playing with a paper clip as if it were the most fascinating invention in the history of the world. And at Waverly, who was, of course, gently licking Anna's cheek, and at Scully, who was on the floor, aggressively spinning in circles, trying to catch his own tail.

Larry was perched on top of the TV and mercifully silent. "It might be a problem," I finally answered. "I think we've run out of names."

"And I think we have to do something," Anna said.

I raised my eyebrows, half happy, half leering. "Try making a baby?" I asked.

"We can do that," she said. "But actually I have something a little less fun in mind."

From the *New York Daily Examiner:*

ASK DR. BOB

Dr. Robert Heller is one of New York's leading veterinarians. He is the author of a book about taking care of pets, *They Have Nothing but Their Kindness,* and appears occasionally on the *Today* show, dispensing advice about animals. Dr. Bob takes care of cats, dogs, horses, birds, snakes, turtles, frogs, small pigs, snails, the occasional fish, and many varieties of rodents. You can e-mail him at AskDrBob@NYDE.com and ask him any question about the animal you love. His column runs every Tuesday in NYC's most popular newspaper.

Dear Bob:

I'm at my wit's end. I've lived alone for a few years, with my three dogs. I thought it would be fun to breed my little Havanese. She might be the sweetest dog that ever lived. I did all my research, found the right breeding partner for her—a top-notch pedigree—and two weeks ago she gave birth. Well, something has definitely snapped in my sweet thing. She isn't nurturing her puppies. At one point I found her growling at the runt—so cute, you could just eat him up!—and I was seriously concerned that she was going to kill him or do him some real damage. As for the others, she doesn't seem to care about them at all or take any interest in them. She just wants to be left alone. I don't know what to do. I've never heard of anything like this. All I know is that I'm so worried for the safety of her children that I haven't slept since they were born. I hope you can help.

—Worried for Her New Kids

Dear Worried:

   A mother who doesn't like her kids and isn't concerned about their welfare? And who doesn't seem to care about what happens to them? Welcome to the real world. My only question is, Where have you been the last several thousand years? Can I help with this problem? Well . . . yes, but not totally. There's nothing you can do about Mom's indifference. I doubt she'll actually do any physical damage—that would be extreme. But you might get the kids away from her as soon as they're physically able to separate. Not because of the physical danger but the potential psychological damage. And make sure the puppies are around as many caring, loving people as possible within the next several weeks—that will help socialize them and minimize the damage done by the mother. Remember, too, that Mom will in all likelihood be just as sweet around you as she ever was. You're not one of her children. And be particularly nice to the kids, especially the runt. They're going to need it.

—Dr. Bob

CHAPTER 4

Anna had decided it was time for me to meet her family. Not only had she relaxed enough to use me as a prop while she read a novel, she had determined that we had passed whatever deadline needed to be passed and were now clearly moving forward into an unknown but permanent future together, a future that required us to wade into particularly murky waters. So something in the relationship part of her brain clicked into the "he needs to see my past for his very own self" mode.

Her family was just a tad different than mine. To begin with, they were from the South. Well, they lived on the border of Kentucky and Ohio, so officially that's not really the southern United States. It's more like southern hell. The Johnsons exhibited none of the repressed neuroses, disappointment, and sense of unfulfilled expectations that dominated the Heller household. They had slightly lower expectations for their lives. Medical school was not an option, for instance; their hopes for the future were more along the lines of not marrying an actual first cousin. Okay, I'm exaggerating a bit. To be fair, those were *my* expectations, partly due to my own prejudice, having read the book and seen the movie *To Kill a Mockingbird* a total of at least thirty times, as well as having obsessed about the woman who washes the car in *Cool Hand Luke* since I was able to operate a videotape player and make the direct connection between her and my erection. But it was undeniably true that Anna's family's personal interactions were played out on a stage that had very little in common with mine. Or with Anna. Anna wasn't just the only member of her family to leave the fold, she was the first one to move farther than a mile away from her parents' house. One of her sisters—she had three as well as three brothers—had briefly fled to a college nearly three hours away but had been whisked back home very quickly after it was discovered that her female born-again roommate was actually a black male coke dealer.

Anna was the oldest of the seven children. Next in line—I was forced to memorize everyone's name and age before we made the trip—was Horace, who hadn't gone to college or done anything else, as near as I could tell. At age twenty-six, he still lived at home, and his life seemed to revolve around beer, guns (or deadly weapons of any kind—if it were possible to keep hydrogen bombs under his bed, there's no question that he would have stashed them away for the Armageddon he knew was coming), cars, and God, in that exact order.

"How is this possible?" I asked Anna soon after we arrived. I'd just been exposed to Horace for the first time; he'd asked me if I wanted to go to the dump with him to shoot refrigerators. I checked with Anna to make sure that "refrigerator" wasn't a code word for "Jew," and she assured me it wasn't. Horace simply liked to spend his afternoons at the dump, firing away at old freezers to watch what happened when the Freon exploded. And believe me on this, what happened was the same exact thing every time: It exploded. Despite Anna's insistence that I'd be safe, I took a pass.

Next in line was Emily, twenty-four. She was married to a CPA who worshipped Ronald Reagan, even though he'd been born after Reagan had seen his last day in the Oval Office. The CPA's name was Roger, and as near as I could tell, the only thing Emily worshipped was Roger's money, of which there was quite a bit. She also clearly had a fondness for turtles—or, rather, turtle replicas—because her entire split-level house was filled with porcelain turtles, oil paintings of turtles, and fluffy turtle pillows.

Rhonda, twenty-two, was the sister who had escaped briefly before being reeled back in. She lived at home, in a small room over the garage.

She didn't have a job yet, and her defining characteristic was that she was bored: with her family, with any form of current event, with any type of discussion, and, I suppose, with life. Her only form of exercise seemed to be rolling her eyes to indicate how bored she was, as if no one could have picked up on that fact without her help.

We were visiting because Anna had decided it was time. But the catalyst for the trip was her brother Dean, the next sibling in line. Ostensibly, we were there for his wedding. Dean was nineteen, and Leonica, his bride, was a thirty-four-year-old dentist's receptionist from Ohio. They had met three months earlier when Dean went on a bender and one evening broke into the dentist's office to try to steal the nitrous oxide dispenser. Leonica was working late, called the police, and had him arrested. He couldn't afford bail and was so broke when he got out of jail, ten days later, that he went back to the dentist's office to see if Leonica could loan him some money. She refused, but since he couldn't afford to stay anyplace that had an actual roof, she took him in. One thing led to another—although I made a point of never asking what any of those things actually were—and now we were at the wedding, along with Leonica's twin fourteen-year-old children and her just-released-from-rehab mother.

Lawrence was sixteen and in high school. His main claim to fame, according to family chatter, was that he was a fantastic football player who, if life were fair, would be getting a college scholarship and a shot at a pro career. Except for one small detail: The life-not-being-fair part was that Lawrence stood five feet four inches tall. He was tough as nails but had a much better shot at riding a Kentucky Derby winner than running for a touchdown in the Sugar Bowl. As a result, he had a perpetual hangdog look. I would have expected him to be angry or bitter or on the road to early alcoholism. Instead, he just seemed resigned to a deep understanding that before his life had begun, his dream was already over.

Deirdre, the last-born sibling, was fourteen years of age, pretty as a picture, and full of life. She had Anna's genes. She was smart and ambitious and liked to talk about books and movies and whatever anyone else wanted to discuss. She was desperate to come see New York, and she was already talking about going to a college where she could spend her junior year in France so she could learn French and experience Paris. But she was also already being smothered by her parents. If she offered an opinion, her mother would almost immediately point out that she didn't have any idea what she was talking about; how could she, since she was so young and not that smart? If she asked her father a question, he would answer in one or two words and then return to whatever world he inhabited inside his own head. The big question was whether Deirdre could escape her parents' clutches and become a full-fledged human being. It would unquestionably be a fight to the death, and after that weekend I gave her a fifty-fifty chance.

How can I put this delicately? Well, if you put every member of Anna's family together, they were like a super-fucked-up, real-life version of the family in *Everybody Loves Raymond*. Except without the sense of humor. That's about as delicate as I can be.

Anna and I had been married for four years by then, so I'd known her for five, and this was my first exposure of any kind to her clan. It was also the first time Anna had seen them since the day she'd gone away to Brown, in Rhode Island.

She'd left home at eighteen, so it had now been a decade since she'd run. In those ten years, she'd lost any trace of a regional accent, become about as well educated as a person could be (ask her anything, on any subject, from astronomy to Zaire, and she could spout explanations, analysis, and history without blinking an eye), launched a career as a successful interior designer, developed an almost eerie natural sophistication (even in her early twenties she'd had a great palate for food and wine and a natural fashion sense that often turned strangers' heads on the street), and come to exude an even eerier sense of calm and self-confidence. On the surface, she was the perfect example of how to escape one's family's tentacles without being scarred for life. Seeing those tentacles up close and feeling them wrap around me for a mere forty-eight hours, I was awed by her accomplishment. And staggered by her apparent lack of anxiety about stepping back into their clutches.

If Anna felt anything about her family, it was guilt over deserting her youngest siblings; she knew she had left them to her father's disinterest and her mother's voraciousness and thus, she felt, to their doom. So after keeping Dean's wedding invitation to herself for over a week, she'd mentioned it right after our impromptu chat about potential Heller-Johnson offspring. In the days leading up to our trip, I didn't see one twitch or hear one stutter. But by then she'd begun peeling away some of the layers of her past, and I knew she could not be as untouched by the experience as she seemed. I decided to make it my job to find the tender spots.

Within days, she became seriously annoyed by my frequent expressions of admiration for her nonneurotic behavior and my simultaneous insistence on poking and probing to get to the bottom of it. In keeping with my chosen profession, I was indeed a poker and prober. I believed in preventive medicine. My need to find out what caused cats to develop progressive retinal atrophy and make them less inclined to go outdoors at night was no different than my insistence on discovering how in hell my lovely wife could stand to be in the same room as Ruby, her terrifying mother.

I asked Anna this question after her mother—five foot five; late forties (she'd had Anna when she was almost a baby herself); thick, black hair that was vaguely Medusa-like; large, surprisingly firm breasts; a scary, gummy smile that revealed protruding teeth and a nasty heart—asked me to get some cooking oil off a high shelf in her pantry the morning of the wedding. As I stretched up to grab the bottle, Ruby crushed her body against mine, grabbed my testicles with one hand and my ass with the other, and asked if I found her attractive. I suppose I didn't handle this as well as I might have. I yelped in terror and waved my hands as if I'd been stung by a five-foot-five-inch bee, managing to knock at least half the cans and bottles off the pantry shelves. The clamor was about a 6.4 on the Richter scale.

I did my best to stroll casually back to the living room and then tell Anna what had happened, although I don't think I needed to. The look on her face showed me I hadn't reported anything surprising.

"What the fuck was that all about?" I asked.

"My mother is a deeply disturbed woman."

"Her nails left indentations in my balls!"

"She's mentally ill. I mean really, seriously, mentally ill."

"More details, please."

"I don't like to talk about it."

"I know. But tell me anyway. This is one of those key marital compromises. Your refusal to talk running smack up against my insatiable desire to hear. It's like one of those immovable objects meeting an irresistible force—"

"I get it," she said. "I get it."

I stayed silent, refusing to back down. She let out an exasperated sigh—although I also sensed some vague relief under the annoyance—and we went outside to sit in her parents' backyard. The wedding party was being held at their house, which resembled an early 1960s bomb shelter. I half-expected Bay of Pigs headlines to be plastered all over the bathroom walls. And yes, I know I sound like one, but I'm really not a snob. Well, okay, I *am* a snob—but only in the good sense, meaning I couldn't care less about class or money or race or religion. I do care about taste and quality and thoughtfulness and compassion. The house where Anna grew up and the family from which she'd escaped had none of those things. The home in which she was raised made Graceland look like the Morgan Library, and the most thoughtful thing I heard all weekend was that "Jews are funny" (although it wasn't *too* thoughtful because I'm pretty sure the speaker, Dean's lovely new bride, was referring to Whoopi Goldberg). As we sat in the untended yard, I wondered how a simple, small patch of land could look shabby and lifeless, but this one did; the evening's shadows provided a welcome dab of contour and life. And after just a brief glimpse of the forces that had done their best to shape her, I also wondered how Anna could so definitively be the embodiment of all the things I admired and cherished in life.

We sat in silence for a while, a silence that I thought was comfortable. It was broken when Anna began to quietly cry. Chalk up another point to my lack of sensitivity when it came to human connections.

"Hey," I said. "This isn't a crying conversation. There's nothing bad. I just want to know more about you, now that I see the monsters in real life flesh and blood."

"I know," she said. "This is embarrassing."

"No." I shook my head. "It's normal. Well, okay, it's not totally normal. But I think it's probably not as weird as you think it is."

"It's just so depressing," Anna said. "The way they live. The way they think. The things they care about. The things they *don't* care about. Their friends. Oh my god, their friends. Did you meet my dad's friend who owns the diaper delivery service? We talked about *stains* for half an hour."

"Was Horace always this into weaponry?"

"What? Yeah, I guess so."

"He told me he didn't know how I could live in New York."

"How come?"

"Because we're not allowed to have automatic weapons. We're not even allowed to have *semi*automatics."

"What did you say?"

"I told him it was hard, but that we muddled through."

"And what did he say to that?"

"Nothing. I think he thought 'muddled' was Yiddish or something, so he didn't feel he had to respond."

"You're not exactly helping the situation, you know. This isn't making me feel a lot better."

"It shouldn't depress you, Anna. You got out."

"I know. But you never get completely out."

"Yes, you do."

She shook her head. "No. Some of it stays with you. *In* you."

"No, it doesn't. At least it doesn't have to. They're not you. They're not even a real part of you. They're part of your past, that's all."

"I wish I could believe that."

"You just think that somehow there's a chance you'll have to come back. That's what's depressing you. But you won't."

"How do you know?"

"Because that would be bad. And I'd never let anything bad happen to you." I knew she'd openly ridicule this grandiose statement, so I immediately followed it up with: "And the only way you'd ever wind up back here is if you came *with* me, because we're together forever, so you couldn't come without me, and there's no fucking way I'd ever come here again, except for a quick stop at that breakfast place that had fried pancakes."

She reached for my hand, and I let her take it.

"Although now that I think about it," I said, "your mom is actually pretty attractive."

She smiled for a fleeting second, then took an affectionate swing at my arm. "You know what my first memory is?"

I shook my head.

"My mother, telling me how sick she was and that it was my fault."

"How old were you?"

Anna shrugged. "I don't know. Three. Four. Five. She used to pull me into a room so no one else could hear and she'd talk to me, her tone nice and kind of sweet, and she'd say stuff like 'I've been sick ever since I gave birth to you' and 'Your father cheats on me. I'd leave him but I could never get another man because of you. Who'd marry me knowing that you'd have to come along with me?' That's what she did to me. To my brothers, she used to say things like 'You have to choose who you love more, me or your father.' They'd start crying and she'd say, 'Well, you better choose me 'cause when he leaves us, he's not gonna want you.'"

"What'd she do to your sisters?"

"Nothing. Well . . . not much. Emily was like a doll. She used to dress her up in these beautiful clothes, and comb her hair all day long, and tell her how lovely she was. She used to say things like 'You're more beautiful than Marilyn Monroe. You're going to marry a prince, maybe even a king.' I swear to god. I don't know about Deirdre. She was so little when I left, four or five. My guess is she's spent the last ten years telling Dee that she's not smart enough to leave home, and that if she ever does, strangers will do horrible things to her."

"Jesus. What the hell was your father doing the whole time?"

"Tuning out. Disappearing. He basically didn't want anything to do with us. He'd *shtup* her every so often and she'd get pregnant, and I guess somehow that got him off the hook. Once the next kid arrived, he'd just kind of disappear again. Not *disappear* disappear. He'd be here. But he was off somewhere in his head. He didn't want to know about any problems. He just wanted to be left alone."

"I don't know if this is the time to bring this up, but it gets me really hot when you say things like *shtup*."

"You're an idiot."

"Thank you so much."

"*Oy gevalt*."

"What?"

"Does that get you hot, too?"

I half-nodded, half-shrugged. "So-so. Not as much as *shtup*."

"How about 'gefilte fish'?"

"No. Whatever the opposite of hot is, that's what 'gefilte fish' does for me. You want flaccid, start talking 'gefilte fish' and 'knish.'"

"*Mishpocheh?*"

"Oh my god, yes. I don't even know what it means, but hearing you say it definitely gets me hot. How do you know *Mishpocheh*?"

"I know many things, my child." She smiled. "*Mishpocheh. Vey iz mir. Tsuris*. Are you totally turned on?"

"Major boner," I assured her. "But I feel really guilty about it."

I leaned over and kissed her, and the kiss turned into a long one. Anna slowly guided me down to the grass, and somehow I ended up on top of her. It was sexy, but actually it was more comforting than sexy. It was almost like we were teenagers, making out on her parents' lawn. For a moment I thought we were going to make love right there in some strange defiance of all the craziness inside the house. It was tempting, but we were married people. If we wanted to, we could just get up, go to our motel room half a mile away, and screw our brains out. We didn't have to define ourselves by our defiance of her family, but for those twenty minutes or so, it was more erotic to act as if we did.

And it was also sexier to talk than to make love right then. It was perhaps the most intimate moment we'd ever spent.

"By the time I was ten, my mom was always sick," Anna said quietly. "Every single day, I'd have to fix the other kids' lunches and diaper the baby 'cause she was too sick to move."

"What was wrong with her?"

"Nothing. She was an incredible hypochondriac. Still is. She went to a million doctors. Every one of them said she was a hundred percent healthy. But she didn't believe 'em. Told them they were all quacks.

She used to say that she just felt things too strongly. I remember her always going, '*Life* makes me sick.' And it did. She hurt all the time. Or she was exhausted, even though she didn't do a fucking thing. My dad would come home from work and I'd make dinner after I did my homework. Horace would bring her the food on a tray and she'd eat in bed. I'd clean up."

Anna adjusted her weight so I wasn't quite so heavy on top of her. She didn't shift enough to topple me off. She wanted me on top of her, which made me happy. "All we did was argue," she went on. "About everything. My clothes. My lipstick—she didn't want me wearing any, and all I wanted to do was wear the brightest, reddest, most garish stuff I could smear on. Does 'smear' get you hot?"

"No. *Schmear* gets me hot. Big difference. 'Smear' is an actual English word."

"Oh. Right. Anyway . . . the biggest fight we had was over a school dance. One day, when I was, I don't know, eleven or twelve, she came into my room on a Saturday, around five o'clock, and said, 'Why aren't you dressed?' And I said, 'For what?' She went, 'Young lady, there is a dance at your school and it starts at six sharp!' I went, 'What are you talking about?' She just kept saying, 'Get dressed! You get dressed now! There are boys goin' to this dance and you are goin' if I have to drag you there myself!' I didn't even know about any dance. And if I did, there was no chance in hell I was gonna go. Boys? Dancing? Getting dressed up? Oh my god, that was a nightmare for me. So I just shook my head. She screamed at me for what seemed like half an hour, but I didn't move or say a word. I just kept shaking my head."

"What'd she do?"

"She went into my closet, took out my favorite skirt, and went downstairs. She came back up with the skirt and a pair of scissors. She said, 'You get dressed right this minute or I'm gonna cut up your favorite skirt.' I didn't move. So she cut it to ribbons. I wanted to cry—I loved that skirt. It was dark green and had these little pleats. But I wouldn't give her the satisfaction. So she took my favorite shirt and she cut that up, too. Then another skirt, and a dress. When she saw that she could cut up every single piece of clothing I had and I still wasn't going to speak to her or go to the damn dance, she left."

"Where'd she go?"

Anna laughed. It was a little harsh but it still was Anna laughing. "To the dance. By herself. I heard from one of my friends that she pretended I was there. She was going up to other mothers and saying things like 'Have you seen my Anna? I don't know *where* she got off to!'"

I started to say something, but she was on a roll now.

"You know what happened to you in the pantry? That wasn't the first time. When I was sixteen, some boy was taking me to the prom. He picked me up at home, here, and when I came downstairs in my prom dress, she was kissing him on the couch. And I mean practically sucking his brains out of his head."

"What did you do?"

"The boy was pretty embarrassed. Thinking back on it . . . can you imagine? He didn't know what the hell to do. But he just kind of hopped off her and acted like nothing had happened, and then he took me to the prom. When we were almost out the door, my mother said, 'Bye, honey, have a wonderful time. I'll be here when you come home.' She wasn't even talking to me. She was talking to Jimmy—Jimmy Williams, that was the boy's name. He didn't come in the house afterward. Actually, he didn't even take me to the prom. He just dropped me off at the gym and ran like hell. I didn't go in. I hung out by myself for a couple of hours, then got a ride home. My mother was waiting in the living room when I got there. All dressed up, tons of makeup. 'Did you have a nice time?' That's what she asked. 'That Jimmy's an awful nice boy. You should bring him around more often.'"

"What'd you say?"

"Nothing. I thought about saying a million things, but I knew it would get really bad if I even opened my mouth. I just went upstairs."

"So why aren't you angry? Or at least angrier."

She thought about this one for a while. Then she said, "'Cause I won. I left home the second I could, I went where I wanted to go, got a scholarship so I didn't have to take anything from them—for two or three years, nobody in my family even knew where I lived. I learned what I wanted to learn, started becoming who I wanted to be." She smiled that smile, the one that could only be meant for me. "I met who

I wanted to meet. Once I learned I didn't have to *be* them, I wasn't angry. I was just relieved."

"So why the tears?"

Now she shifted my weight off her, rolled to her right, and settled on her back. She smiled, happy to breathe freely again. "Because . . . I know I'll never actually have to come back here and live this life. But sometimes you see your past and, I don't know, I can't help thinking that it's still risky. Something could happen that'll turn me from the princess back into Cinderella, no matter where I am." She waved her arm around so that it took in the yard, the town, the whole world. "It's just all so awful. The emptiness. The people. The sadness. Sometimes it feels so overwhelming to me, so inescapable."

"I won't turn into your father," I said. "And you definitely won't become your mother. I'll never be distant from you. I'm always going to be so interested in you and everything you do, you won't be able to stand it. You can wear the most garish lipstick in the world, I will never ask you to go to any place of worship as long as you live, and when we have a guaranteed-to-be-perfect child, I swear I'm going to be so loving and caring that you'll be nauseous just thinking about it. I can't do anything about the emptiness in the real world. All I can do is make sure that our life together is never empty. Or sad. Or anything you don't want it to be."

"I know," she said. "I know you think that. And I love you very much."

"I *am* getting this really weird, overpowering desire to go shoot some form of refrigeration device, however. Is that a problem?"

She said it wasn't.

So we went back inside. Anna's mother didn't grab my testicles again, although she did rub her breasts up against my shoulder twice. Her father spoke to me once, asking me if I wanted a drink. Her brothers were friendly and one of them even patted me on the back and told me to take good care of his sister.

The next day we all met at Emily's house for brunch, which was chipped beef on toast. *Frozen* chipped beef on toast. I was mostly thrilled that the toast wasn't molded into the shape of a turtle.

I found out many things about the Johnsons during that trip, but one of the oddest was that none of them seemed to have any real friends. Even Anna, as I thought about it. She hadn't stayed in close contact with her college pals. She didn't have any childhood chums who called or e-mailed her. The Johnsons' friends were one another, even though none of them seemed to like the others much. They didn't talk about anything of import or share any real intimacy. It was a bit like *Invaders from Mars*—they took the form of humans, but with the exception of Anna they all seemed vaguely alien and soulless.

I was the guy who was supposed to be bad with people, good with things that barked and meowed. But I had relationships. I felt connections. I had people I loved and cared about or, at the very least, was interested in, whether they ran a bowling alley in my hometown or were Norwegian women who cried all the time and annoyed the hell out of me. In some way, I cared about everyone I'd ever gotten close to. My parents were difficult—they'd made mistakes and I didn't always like them, but I loved them. Even Teddy. Maybe especially Teddy. I didn't like the Teddy who lived in the present, but I loved the Teddy from the past probably more than anyone I'd ever known until I met Anna.

Anna and I couldn't pretend that the past didn't exist. But we didn't have to allow it to live with us every minute of every day. Our lives apart, before we met, were entirely different from our life together. We were creating something new. Something we refused to bundle up and throw in with the detritus of our pasts. Still, I was beginning to understand Anna's worries about parenthood. If the Johnson clan had taught me everything I knew about family, I'd have a few hesitations, too. I couldn't help but wonder whether I was really strong enough to beat my way through the Johnson past to make our family work. Worse, I knew that Anna was wondering the same thing.

Despite so many things simmering under the surface, despite the entanglements and the complicated relationships, the weekend went off without a hitch. The wedding was perfectly pleasant as long as one overlooked the total underlying despair that permeated everything from the Swiss cheese chunks served as appetizers to the groom's tuxedo, which was approximately seven sizes too big. The after-party was perfectly palatable. Anna's dad, Todd, downed six or seven scotches and spoke to me a second time. (Okay, he asked me where I'd served in the armed forces, and when I stared at him, bewildered, he said, "I thought you were a vet." The conversation didn't progress much beyond that, but I considered it a solid start.)

The brunch at Emily and Roger's (the Reagan-worshipping CPA) was tolerable. Emily's neighbor, a nasal woman named Gretchen, insisted on telling me about every single piece of artwork in her house and how much each piece cost, but even that didn't really bother me. (I kept myself occupied by imagining how ugly each too-expensive-for-me-to-buy painting or sculpture probably was.) I kept my eye out for Anna and made my way over to her if any interaction looked remotely traumatic or potentially difficult. And I even saw her smile three or four times during the course of the bash.

The brunch started at eleven. The chipped beef was gone by twelve-thirty. The alcohol had pretty much disappeared by one-thirty. At two, we kissed appropriate cheeks, made the necessary thank-yous, wished the best of luck to everyone who needed or expected it, and got a taxi to the airport, telling the driver to step on it. In the back seat of the comfortably rickety cab, smelling of old leather and a decade of fast food sandwiches, all we cared about was that we were together.

Promises had been made and allegiances had been sworn. Now it was time to see if we were capable of making life conform to our desires.

By dinnertime, we were back on Greenwich Avenue with our cats and dogs and our foul-mouthed parrot and the pizza smells and honking car horns and urinating drunk guys on the street. We were where we both wanted to be, and where we both belonged.

From the *New York Daily Examiner:*

ASK DR. BOB

Dr. Robert Heller is one of New York's leading veterinarians. He is the author of a book about taking care of pets, *They Have Nothing but Their Kindness,* and is a regular on the *Today* show, with his monthly segment, "The Vetting Zoo." Dr. Bob takes care of cats, dogs, horses, birds, snakes, turtles, frogs, small pigs, snails, various kinds of fish, and many varieties of rodents. You can e-mail him at AskDrBob@NYDE.com and ask him any question about the animal you love. His column runs Tuesdays and Thursdays in NYC's most popular newspaper.

Dear Dr. Bob:

My husband, Ken, and I have two dogs, Bjorn (a wirehaired fox terrier) and Ivan (a German shepherd). Bjorn, the sweetest little thing imaginable, is not doing well. I know we're going to have to put him down soon, and this has created a problem for Ken and I. Ken wants to get another dog now. He doesn't want Ivan, who has lived with Bjorn since he was a puppy, to mourn and be sad when Bjorn crosses over. He believes that Ivan needs companionship and shouldn't have to experience being an "only dog" (that's the way Ken refers to life after Bjorn). I just can't replace my baby so easily. Bjorn is much more my dog, and Ivan is much more Ken's. Bjorn sleeps next to me, and while Ivan isn't allowed to sleep on the bed because he's so big, he sleeps on the floor on Ken's side and follows Ken wherever he goes. I'm not ready to simply discard Bjorn and pretend to love a newcomer. Ken feels we have to do what is right for Ivan. But I don't think he'll feel a loss like this the same way I will. I feel like I'm about to lose my right arm, and I'm not ready to get a new one. What advice can you give me?

Sincerely,
—Getting Ready to Mourn for Bjorn

Dear Ready:

First of all, I do feel your pain. That's one of the reasons I hate to be so picky, but I'm afraid I can't help myself: It's "a problem for Ken and me" not "Ken and I." I know that people write in for pet advice, not grammar advice, but I'm starting to think that our whole culture is falling apart because no one knows how to communicate properly anymore. Actually, our whole culture is falling apart for many reasons, one of them an amazing (at least to me) lack of compassion for people less fortunate than ourselves. But poor communication skills and bad grammar don't help the cause, okay? I know that, for some weird reason, people think that "I" sounds more intelligent than "me" in sentences like the one you wrote. But it doesn't. It just makes people sound like Judy Holliday in *Born Yesterday*. I will be glad to explain and pontificate further on this subject so that you never make such an error in the future. If you have any desire to get the lecture, e-mail me separately and I promise to keep it private. And now on to your question.

You and Ken do have a problem, and it's a tough one to solve. People express their love in different ways. When love is lost, some people need to replace it right away. That doesn't make their love less valid; it just means that they need a physical representation of their love. They can't love a memory. Or if they can, a memory isn't *enough* for them to love. Other people need time to get over their grief and can't immediately transfer their love to another creature. Grief is cured by one thing and one thing only: time. So these people need to wait a bit before replacing a beloved pet. In the end, there is no perfect solution to your problem because it's rooted in human nature.

I may have a practical solution, however: Make sure you spend as much quality time with Bjorn as you can before he . . . um . . . "passes." (Okay, this is another peeve of mine: I hate euphemisms. It'll actually make it a lot easier to deal with Bjorn's death if you use the real word. Bjorn isn't passing; he's dying.

It's not a bad word. Dying happens to everyone. It's the ultimate common denominator, so I don't understand why it's such an uncommon word. Sorry. I won't digress like this again.) Here's my other important tip: Try loving Ivan as much as possible, too. I know he's Ken's dog, but make a point of petting him. Talk to him. Play with him. See if some of the emotion you feel for Bjorn can be transferred. It might not only help your problem, it might help his. If you feel able to love the dog you already have, it could allow you to feel that kind of love for a brand-new dog sooner rather than later. Here's another thing to consider: A lot of people feel they can't possibly love another pet after a favorite one dies. But when they're confronted with a wonderful new animal, love just naturally follows. So don't feel as if you're being disloyal to Bjorn. And don't worry that your heart won't open again. It will. And it will happen a lot faster than you think, if you realize that not only will you be helping Ivan deal with his loss, you'll also be helping Ken deal with his.

—Dr. Bob

CHAPTER 5

As I became more integrated into the daily life of Marjorie's clinic, I became more connected to and more in tune with the community around me. Gradually, something began to occur that I found astounding: I slowly became as interested in the pet owners as I was in the pets. As they began to learn from me about how best to live with and treat their animals, I began to ascertain some truths—small and large—about life from listening to their stories and seeing how they dealt with their triumphs, their losses, and their day-to-day lives. I observed and learned and then started to keep notes on the people who were becoming an extension of my newly developing family. I'm not a hundred percent certain why I began writing about them, but I suspect it was so I'd have a constant reminder that they were real and that I valued them. I think it was also because I knew that this family would likely prove to be temporary, that it might last only as long as there was a necessary connection: their pets and my ability to ease their pain. And as I got a little older and more attached to their world, I felt an urge to make these people—some remarkable, some remarkably ordinary—a permanent part of my life.

LUCY NELL ROEBUCK

Lucy Nell Roebuck was not technically a client, although we did take care of her many pets. She was our receptionist, and she became a crucial part of my daily existence. I probably spent more time listening to her talk and coo and explain—to me, to patients, to patients' owners, to Marjorie—than I did to Anna.

Greenwich Village has a substantial gay community, and Marjorie had a high percentage of gay pet owners as regulars. Particularly lesbians—I have no idea why, but I would guess that a third of our clientele was composed of lesbian cat owners. Long before I arrived, Lucy had started out as a lesbian cat-owning customer of the clinic. Over time, because she spent so many hours in the clinic and exhibited such curiosity about everything going on while she was there, she became a lesbian cat, dog, and pig owner who doubled as the office receptionist. It wasn't difficult to figure out why she spent so much time hanging out at Marjorie's refuge for injured pets and discombobulated humans: Lucy needed as much care and attention as her two lovely cats, Franklin and Eleanor.

Lucy had come to New York from South Carolina. She thought she wanted to be a schoolteacher, but her parents repeatedly told her that she wasn't intelligent enough. Their reasoning—remarkably faulty, because Lucy was not just bright, she was obsessed with learning—seemed to be based on nothing other than their daughter's size. Lucy was enormously fat; she'd been fat since birth and had gotten ever fatter as she grew older. Her parents berated Lucy for her supposed lack of intelligence when she was quite young, and the fatter she got, the stupider her parents decided she was. When she hit three hundred pounds, her parents decided she wasn't capable of grown-up decisions or grown-up anything else, so they refused to pay for her to go to college. To replace campus life, Lucy got a minimum-wage job at the local Walmart and prepared to spend the rest of her days and nights subsisting on fast food and low-level cable shows, living in the room in which she'd grown up.

After a lifetime spent in the care of her parents, Lucy met Devon, who was shopping at Walmart, looking to buy a tent for a weekend camping trip. One thing led to another, and Lucy went along for the weekend. That led to yet another thing, which was that Lucy had her first sexual experience and fell in love. Lucy's parents were less than thrilled with her sexual awakening and the ensuing loss of control over their daughter, so before long Lucy moved out of the house, moved in with Devon, and became a grown-up.

She understood the true price of being a grown-up when, one evening after nine months of domestic bliss, Lucy came home early from Walmart and found Devon in bed with Erica, whom he'd met that afternoon at a Piggly Wiggly. At first she was completely at a loss about what to do, but having gained confidence from her romance and Devon's constant assurance that Lucy's parents were living in a different era as well as on the planet Mars, Lucy worked up the nerve to move to New York City, specifically to Long Island City, in Queens, which at the time was perhaps the least glamorous neighborhood in all five boroughs. That mattered not a whit to Lucy, because she had fantasized about living in New York for as long as she could remember. She got a cat, got another cat, lost fifty pounds, gained it back again, got a third cat when her second cat jumped off the building's fire escape, never to be heard from again, lost seventy-five pounds, gained it back, and eventually fell in love with a woman named Alana, who was ten years older than Lucy and weighed about two hundred pounds less than she did. When Alana suggested that Lucy move into her studio apartment in the West Village, Lucy happily agreed. And that's where she was living when I met her at Marjorie's.

By the time I arrived, Lucy probably knew at least as much as I did about pet care, and she definitely knew much more about dealing with impatient, depressed, terrified, insecure, and possibly insane people who had complicated relationships with their animals. Her talent for dealing with that very specific group of humans undoubtedly had a lot to do with the fact that Lucy was, on an hourly basis, impatient, depressed, terrified, insecure, and possibly insane. She was like a dog that had been abused in puppyhood. She had made great strides and overcome much of her fear, but although she had become a charming and fascinating adult, I got the feeling that underneath it all she was still expecting to be hit. And hit hard.

I was a bit awed by Lucy's ability to deal with the people who paraded through the waiting room and into the vets' offices. She never got angry, never raised her voice, never even seemed annoyed. She responded with empathy to everyone's problems and saw through everyone's neuroses to find their sadness. And not just to find it but understand it. One of the first things

I told her, after she'd revealed to me a portion of her past, was that she would have made a wonderful teacher. She kissed me. On the lips.

Working many hours a day with Lucy was a joy. I loved her loud, very southern, husky voice, as well as her assured demeanor, which got more assured with each passing day. She calmed me down and made me smile. And yet there was something sad about her, too, though it was a deeper sadness than what I saw in most of the people she empathized with and soothed. After being in such close quarters with Lucy for two and a half years, one day I worked up the nerve to ask her why she didn't lose weight. Her eyes turned sad—not for long, just for a flash—and her voice got uncharacteristically quiet. "Because then I wouldn't have any excuses," she said. "I'd just be the real me. And who knows how that would turn out?"

The thing about dealing with humans and pets is that we're never sure how anything will turn out.

The median life expectancy of dogs is 12.8 years. As always, of course, there are mitigating factors. A rare Mexican breed, the Xoloitzcuintle, has a life span of fifteen to twenty years. The Irish wolfhound has an estimated six-to-eight-year life expectancy. Almost forty percent of small-breed dogs will make it to their tenth birthday, but only thirteen percent of large-breed dogs will. The average fifty-pound dog will live ten to twelve years. But hundred-plus-pounders—Great Danes and deerhounds—are elderly at six to eight years.

The average age of a cat is twelve to fifteen years. With proper care, nutrition, and regular veterinary visits (that's not really a plug, it's just good common sense), a cat kept indoors can reach twenty-one years, barring any serious medical conditions or untimely accidents. Indoor-outdoor cats usually don't last to the average age because of traffic accidents, fights with other cats, poisoning (accidental or intentional), diseases caught from other cats, death caused by predators, and capture and subsequent euthanization by various animal-control organizations. Stray cats, often called "feral cats," usually don't live more than two or three years because of starvation or all of the nasty realities of street life detailed above. Manx and Siamese cats are commonly said to be among the longest-lived pedigreed breeds. And the jaguar is the longest-lived species of cat, sometimes reaching thirty years. According to some sources—and aren't you glad you have me so you don't have to actually know who these sources are?—the longest-lived cat was in Devon, England, a tabby named Puss who passed on to the Great Food Bowl in the Sky after his thirty-sixth birthday, in 1939.

Statistics, of course, do not carry any moral weight, but they do help us understand our parameters and keep things in perspective. Unfortunately, emotion is continually seeping into and clouding our perspective. I once heard Marjorie Paws say to an overwrought man who'd brought his fourteen-year-old dachshund in to be euthanized, "The only thing wrong with our pets is that they don't live as long as we do."

I've since used that line on almost everyone who brings in an animal to be put down. I'm not sure why it provides so much comfort, but the fact that it does proves two points about people. One is that we often love our pets without reservation; we not only *want* them to be perfect, we believe they *are* perfect. Even so, people are incredibly resilient: They love their animals wholeheartedly, and yet when a pet dies, they get another one and usually love that one just as deeply. And that's the second point illuminated by Marjorie's wisdom. People don't just need love; they need to feel that, despite the statistics, love will last as long as they do. Of course, a lot of people believe that love will survive a lot longer than that, which is why pet cemeteries and online pet funerals and all things related to pet heaven are now a billion-dollar business.

I'm not a believer in the idea that love lasts forever. It's my view that if love lasts a lifetime, someone's either doing something awfully damn right or is awfully damn lucky. (When I told that to my buddy Phil, he said he sometimes feels that way about love that lasts for only a weekend.) It's hard enough keeping some sort of perspective about our pets. It gets *really* complicated when we need to take a good, hard look at our own selves. For example: According to the actuarial tables, the odds are that I will live to be 75.6 years old. I try to be objective about that. I tell myself that odds are not real. That they're simply a guide, a way to understand our limits. I tell myself that I don't really need stats; life does an excellent job all by itself of letting us know what our limits are. And there are a hell of a lot of them.

Besides, as all sports fans know, statistics and odds don't always matter when it comes to winning or losing. It's why we have to play the game. Bill James, the venerable baseball analyst and philosopher, has sabermetrically proven that major league ball players peak and have their best year, on average, at age twenty-seven. With luck, they stay close to that level of productivity for five more years, until the age of thirty-two. No one has done a similar study for veterinarians. Or any other group of normal human beings, for that matter; I don't think we non-home-run hitters have captured the American rooting interest quite the same way the Red Sox and the Cardinals have. Nonetheless, anecdotally—a method of deduction we vets tend to believe in—it's not a dissimilar pattern. We might not sign ten-year, two-hundred-million-dollar contracts and have ticker-tape parades to celebrate our success, but we do thrive nonetheless. And we also know that long-term contracts don't guarantee success. Or actual longevity. Often, they just soften the blow when failure comes. In any case, here is what happened to me between my twenty-seventh and my thirty-second birthdays, my so-called peak years:

I was offered a job as a pet columnist for my favorite New York tabloid, the *Daily Examiner*. I'd never written anything for publication before, but Anna urged me to give it a try. Almost instantly, I felt comfortable with this new role. Giving advice came naturally to me. And giving advice to strangers seemed a pretty safe way to start. The surprise was that the people with whom I corresponded quickly stopped feeling like strangers. They soon became a part of my extended human family. Before long Anna and I had a wall full of Christmas cards from "Living with Six Cats" and "A Beagle-Loving Widow."

As a result of my column, I began to be invited to speak to various organizations around the country, ranging from animal rights and rescue groups to women's lunch organizations and businesses looking for speakers at their corporate retreats. (My corporate speech was titled "How You Treat Your Pet: Is That How You Treat Your Job and Your Life?")

Sometimes when traveling, I'd take Rocky with me. He'd become a remarkable companion and although he liked Anna perfectly well, he and I had bonded deeply. He slept on my chest every night, and we had a solid fifteen minutes of quality time every morning while Anna slept (he would cuddle up close to my chin and I'd stroke him—his favorite spot was on his cheeks and under his chin, and sometimes he liked to butt his whole head into my palm—and whisper to him and he'd lick my fingers). He was very protective of his relationship with me around the various other animals in our lives, and he just plain didn't like being away from me. Every morning he insisted on following me downstairs as I went from the apartment to the clinic, and he didn't like it one bit if a closed door ever shut him out of a room I was in. He was especially unhappy when I left the city for more than a day. Anna told me that he moped and cried pitiful little meowing cries and didn't move around very much; if I was gone longer than two days, on the third day he'd state his displeasure at his abandonment very clearly: He'd shit in the bed as a protest. Anna spent a lot of time petting him and assuring him that I'd be back soon, but none of that stopped him from unloading himself on our sheets, so I started to take him with me if I was going to be away for more than forty-eight hours. He was good company and so happy to be with me that he fit in anywhere. He was better behaved at most corporate retreats than the employees I was lecturing to. And at the restaurants that allowed him in, he showed off impeccable table manners.

A segment producer at the *Today* show attended one of my lectures, liked what he saw and heard, and couldn't believe that Rocky sat calmly by my side during the entire talk. As a result I was asked to come on *Today*. It was meant to be a one-time appearance, but I was called back and then called back again. I became their pet advice expert whenever they needed one—I got the call when a chimp violently turned on its owner, a dog saved a family from a fire, a cat found its way home to Maine after being lost in California. I'd bring animals on, sometimes mine and Anna's, sometimes other people's. I would show people how to physically and mentally deal with their pets. Rocky appeared quite a few times with me. He was a TV natural; relaxed and photogenic, he rarely meowed over his allotted time limit. He became something of a minor celebrity (well, in cat circles).

A publisher asked me to write a book, which I did, elaborating upon the advice and observations I offered in my column and on the air. Called *They Have Nothing but Their Kindness*, it wasn't exactly a best seller, but it sold nicely and I still quite like it.

Marjorie Paws retired. Well, semiretired. She didn't walk completely away from the practice, but she did put it at arm's length. After buying a condo in Florida, she began spending more and more time down there. And since she was only in the city two to three months a year, she insisted that Anna and I move into the spacious three-bedroom apartment on the second floor (with the stairway to the garden) and keep the cluttered third floor apartment for our future needs (the latest gambit in Marjorie's continuing campaign to persuade us to have a child as soon as possible). We kept the third-floor apartment pretty much as it was—although doing our best to straighten out what could be straightened out—and used it when Phil or my mom came to visit. When Marjorie came to town, she stayed in the much smaller one-bedroom garret on the top floor. The fourth floor was still rented out to the Schmidts, whom, oddly enough, we still almost never saw or spoke to except when something in their apartment stopped working. We kept the rent well below the market rate, and in return they signed a long-term lease, were friendlier than ever on the rare occasions when we bumped into them, and were never a day late paying their rent.

In time, Marjorie insisted that we work out a formal arrangement to transfer ownership of her brownstone. She had no heirs and claimed that she didn't know anyone else she'd rather see happy and comfortable than the two of us, so she proposed a ridiculously generous deal. An agreed-upon percentage of my share of the clinic's profits went to Marjorie. At a certain point, that money would be credited toward an outright purchase of the entire building. The deal was as simple and straightforward as Marjorie. I even got ten Knicks games from her season-ticket package.

I fell more in love with my wife the longer our marriage went on. Anna's career soared, even faster and higher than mine. She was promoted to vice president of her design firm, Eagle & Schlossberg, and she expanded the business into garden design and landscape architecture. At a community board meeting, she met the city parks commissioner. (Anna often attended those meetings, which would have caused me to beat my head against the wall until I lost consciousness, because she was obsessed with two things: trying to get a stoplight put in at a particularly busy and dangerous corner near the clinic and trying to stop NYU from turning everything below Fourteenth Street into a huge, hideously ugly dorm.) That meeting led to their having coffee; coffee led to lunch and then a dinner that included me and the commissioner's wife. Several dinners *à quatre* later, Eagle & Schlossberg was designing Manhattan's triangle parks.

For much of this period of my life, I felt like Derek Jeter during the Joe Torre years. I wasn't world champion every year, but I was certainly in the conversation.

But other things happened, too, during those five years.

My father died.

It wasn't sudden; cancer had been killing him for several years, although he had hidden that fact from almost everyone (including me) for all but the last six months or so of his life. His death followed the pattern of his life: It was reasonably dramatic, he controlled the circumstances up until the last possible moment, and ultimately it left everyone feeling vaguely dissatisfied.

The death of a parent is a strange and crucial event in anyone's life. There is, of course, the inevitable flow of sadness, guilt, fear, and regret. But the one thing no one ever wants to admit, not out loud anyway, is that when a bond—sometimes tiny and loose, sometimes suffocating and tremendously restricting—is suddenly released, it can be liberating. For some it means the loss of a moral compass; for others it causes the disappearance of a nagging conscience. Mostly, though, I think it's an evolutionary next step in any animal's growth, a neon sign flashing the warning: YOU ARE NOW ON YOUR OWN. YOUR LIFE IS NOW YOURS TO LIVE AS YOU PLEASE. For some people that's a good thing, or at least it's something natural. For others it's like being released from jail: There's no telling if you're ready to go the straight-and-narrow route or if all hell is going to break loose.

My mother had spent most of her adult life trying to please her husband and holding their world together. Once she got over the shock of his death and her very real grief, she began to flourish. She traveled to all sorts of adventurous places and revealed both a stubborn streak and an incredible backbone that no one, probably not even my father, had ever suspected existed. My relationship with her got stronger and more interesting. So did Anna's. We had fun with her when she visited us in the city, and we were both astonished when she began to confide in us about her past: her thoughts, her reasons for making many of the choices she'd made throughout her life, her plans for the future. She knew a lot more about all sorts of things—including me and definitely including Ted—than I ever would have thought.

Among other things, my mother told us that Ted had come to her soon after our dad died, to ask her for some of his inheritance. A payment up front, so to speak. He said he knew our dad had left him some money and he'd like to have it now. When I asked if she gave it to him, she shook her head. "I told him, 'I'm not dead yet and I don't want to rush it. You'll have to wait.'" She said that Ted got furious and stopped talking to her for a few weeks. "Is he talking to you now?" I asked. "Oh, yes," she said. "I have the money, and he doesn't have the balls to stay angry as long as I have something he wants."

Ted reacted to our dad's death as might a little kid left alone in a candy store: The moral straitjacket had been removed; he was now free to grab for whatever he wanted. He got divorced for a second time. By the time I turned thirty-two, he'd spent two years living in Portugal (doing what was anyone's guess), gotten arrested for passing bad checks, gotten arrested for not paying child support, gotten married and divorced for a third time, and bought a brand-new BMW convertible after leaving Portugal and moving back to L.A. (doing what was still anyone's guess). He'd also told me he hated me.

That conversation took place in a quiet little French bistro near the clinic. He'd been visiting our mother (and, we found out sometime later, siphoning money out of her bank account) and came into the city for one night—at least that's what he said—and called me up to invite me and Anna to dinner. No advance warning. It was just "Hey, it's me. I'm in the city. Just got in. Wanna have dinner tonight?" When I said, "Sure," he said, "Great. I already made a reservation for three at the Whistlestop," a restaurant in Chelsea that Ted had frequented and loved when he'd lived in the city and been married to Karen. Anna didn't want to go—she had decided there was no longer any need for her to pretend that Ted was important to her—so I went by myself. Ted had Hilts with him, a detail he hadn't mentioned over the phone, and since he hadn't made a reservation for four, it meant he knew Anna wasn't going to come.

At dinner, Hilts was fine. He behaved just like any other six-year-old. But I found something off about the boy. He wasn't genuine or relaxed; even when he was having fun his smiles and his giggles seemed forced, as if he had to let everyone know he was happy so they'd be pleased. He also seemed distant, as if there was a protective cocoon enveloping him, preventing him from ever hearing or seeing things exactly as they were. I know it's not fair to say—he was only six, after all—but I didn't like him. He wasn't a kid with whom I wanted to be friends.

Even so, I felt sorry for the boy There were reasons for his behavior, and I saw them quite clearly during our dinner.

Teddy was disturbingly abusive to Hilts. Not physically abusive, but somehow menacing. Ted expected him to act like an adult; when he didn't, it was some kind of violation of whatever game Ted was playing. When Hilts filled his straw with Coke and then deliberately released some of it on the table, Ted yelled at him. It was a strange kind of yelling; his voice didn't get all that much louder, but he spoke through clenched teeth—his entire body was clenched—as if he were going to explode. The yelling was sudden and violent and it frightened Hilts. It frightened *me*. I halfheartedly defended the kid—I didn't really think of him as my nephew; there wasn't that kind of connection between us—and said, "Teddy, relax, it's not a big deal." Ted turned to stare at me, as if he were surprised that I had noticed what was happening on the other side of the table.

Then Ted turned back to Hilts and changed the tone of his voice, cooing at him, using much the same tone and facial expressions he did when playing his guitar or showing his girlfriends that he cared about nothing but them. He'd seen Hilts shrink away from him, and he instantly switched from stern father to seductively loving protector. This happened three or four times during dinner: The kid would do something slightly wrong—he'd complain or squirm or whine or knock some string beans onto the floor—and Teddy would scare him half to death with his sudden temper. Within seconds, Ted would follow that up by stroking his son and speaking to him as if he were a little kitten, telling him how much he loved him. In front of Hilts, Teddy told me, "You know, I love him more than anything else in life. He's the most important thing in the world to me." Staring at me as earnestly as a person could stare. Then Hilts would take too big a gulp of soda and make some loud slurping sound and Ted would swat the boy's hand, furious, and tell him to act like a fucking grown-up.

Toward the end of dinner, Ted asked me to loan him some money. I was doing well, no question, but Anna and I were trying to save as much as possible, hoping to have a baby soon, hoping to take ownership of the brownstone as quickly as we could, dreaming of buying a small weekend house in the country. And I knew that money and Ted was a combustible combination. Over the years, he'd conned me plenty of times: ten bucks here, twenty dollars there, even a few hundred dollars when I was in graduate school. I'd never seen a penny of it once it left my hands, and I'd always felt too guilty to ask him to pay it back. Ted had a remarkable knack for making people feel that since they'd worked hard and earned something for themselves, they were some-how obligated to share their success with him—the guy who tried so hard but couldn't ever earn something of his own. Only recently had I come to realize that he didn't *really* try hard to earn his own reward. He worked hard at making people want to give him things so he would never have to compete in the real world.

All that is by way of saying that instead of just telling him, "Sure," I asked how much he wanted.

"How much will you give me?"

It was awkward. I didn't ask what the money was for. It didn't really matter: It was for Ted. It was for Ted to live like Ted. All sorts of things flashed through my mind. I remembered going to the movies with him when I was ten years old; I could feel his sixteen-year-old hand holding mine. Now I looked for some sign of that sixteen-year-old. I couldn't tell if it was there or not.

I knew Anna would kill me, but after a moment I said, "I can let you have five thousand dollars. But it's a loan, right? I mean, it's not a gift. We should probably work out some kind of timetable for paying me back." I thought my response sounded fairly adult and reasonable.

Ted didn't say anything.

"I mean, let's face it, Ted. I've given you money before but I never got anything back. I can't afford to just give you five thousand dollars. I want some kind of assurance that I'll get paid back."

This time the silence continued so long that it was unnerving. When Hilts broke the standoff by starting to say something innocuous, Ted practically spit the words "Shut the fuck up" at him. Hilts sniffled a little bit—it wasn't a real cry, just the beginning of one—and Ted said, venomously, "I told you to shut the fuck up."

Hilts bounced up from his chair as if he were sitting on a spring and sprinted away from the table, toward the front door of the restaurant. Ted went after him in a flash, almost knocking over our table, and caught his son before he got too far. Hilts let out a wail, a loud one, and I was certain that Ted was going to hit him. I was ready to jump up and stop him, though I didn't know exactly how. What I did know was that I couldn't just sit there and let him wallop the kid, not with the fury that was roiling inside him. But instead of hitting the boy, Ted grabbed him and hugged him and told him how much he loved him. He said all this in a soft, gentle voice, rocking his son slowly back and forth.

When he was calm, Hilts said, sniffling, "You shouldn't talk to me like that." And Ted went, "Like what?" Hilts said, "You said bad words to me," and Ted said, "No, I didn't. I'd never say anything bad to you." Hilts said, "But I heard you." Whispering, incredulous, as if he had no idea where Hilts could get such an idea, Ted said, "No, you didn't. I never said anything bad. I'd never say bad things to you. I love you. I love you more than I love anything on the planet Earth."

I wanted to say to Hilts, "Yes, he did! He said bad things to you! You're going to go crazy if you believe what your father says instead of what he does." But I didn't. He was six years old. If I'd said those things, he would have thought it worse than his father telling him to shut the fuck up.

Within several minutes, Ted had the boy back at the table, giggling and happy—genuine giggling this time, no worries about what anyone was thinking. Ted was telling him silly jokes and laughing along with him. At one point he looked up and saw me watching. I was half-smiling at the fact that they were liking each other so much—and half-looking as if the world was melting right in front of me.

Ted announced that it was time to go. Hilts stood up, took a step away from the table. Ted leaned over to me and in a calm, rational voice said, "Good night. And fuck you. I don't want your money. I fucking hate you. You're a selfish prick, and I hope someday you have to go crawling for something you need so someone can tell you to go fuck yourself."

I was so stunned at the contempt dripping from his words that I could barely speak. "I didn't tell you to go fuck yourself," I said. My voice was high and whiny. I'd become ten years old again. "I said I'd give you money."

"I hate you," he said a second time. This time it came out as a hiss. The pain radiated through his voice so powerfully that I couldn't focus on the fact that I was the target of his hatred. "I hope you understand that. I hate your fucking guts."

"What?"

He repeated himself, this time very slowly and deliberately: "I . . . hate . . . your . . . fucking . . . guts."

"Those are bad words," I said. "Or are you going to lie to me, too, and pretend you didn't say them?"

The demons that lived inside Ted came very close to erupting. For a second or two—it seemed like an hour or two—I thought he was going to pick up a knife and stab me in the neck. His face turned red and a blue vein in his forehead throbbed. I did nothing. Just stared at him. I don't even know whether I would have protected myself if he had really come at me violently. But he didn't. He was a tormented soul, and one of his torments was that although he lacked the self-awareness to understand his distorted desires, he had just enough restraint (and lack of courage) to be unable to act on them.

That was the end of it. After some serious chest heaving and facial contortions, he and Hilts simply left. I sat there for a few moments, not knowing whether I was angry or guilty or horrified or depressed or overwhelmingly sad. I sat there until the waiter came over and handed me the check.

When I got home, I crawled into bed next to Anna. I told her what had happened.

"I'm so sorry," she said. "You don't deserve that." Then she looked into my eyes, saw what she saw, saw what was inside me, and said, "Don't let him make you think you deserve it. That's what he does. Don't let him do that."

"I don't know. I think I do deserve some of it. You didn't see him. He was in so much pain. I'm so good at taking pain away from cocker spaniels and Maine coons. I just don't know what the hell I can do for *him*."

"There's nothing you can do."

"Or what I could have done. *Should* have done. I don't mean tonight—I don't know, even tonight. But mostly in the past. Over the last few years. I had so many opportunities to be kind, and I wasn't. Tonight, I could have just given him the money."

"No. You're not rich. And you work all the time. You work hard for your money. You don't owe him."

"It's not a question of owing. I give money to strangers on the street, to homeless people. Teddy needed help, and I just let him slip away."

She shook her head, almost angry. And she just kept saying, "You don't deserve that. You're not responsible."

I kept saying, "Maybe, but I *feel* responsible. You didn't see how unhappy he was."

"That's the thing about people," Anna said. "Sometimes they're just unhappy. And sometimes they hate other people just for *not* being unhappy."

She was right, of course. Intellectually, I understood. But sometimes the brain just can't impose itself on the heart. I've watched people talk to their pets when those animals were in physical agony—bones shattered after being hit by a car, limbs swollen by cancerous tumors, flesh torn and hanging loose after being bitten and clawed. They tell their pets that everything will be all right, that the doctor is going to help, that they will soon feel better. They talk soothingly, as if the animals will understand. But animals only understand that there is pain or no pain. If they feel no pain, they don't fear that it might surface or reappear. If they do feel pain, it overwhelms them because they don't know that someone is capable of easing their misery. That's what Ted was like that night. He saw nothing but his own pain. All he wanted was for it to stop, but I don't think he saw any way of stopping it. All he saw was a chance to spread the pain to someone else—to me. Maybe he thought that spreading it around would diminish it, would banish whatever was chewing him up inside. Or maybe he just wanted someone else to feel what he felt. That deliberate spreading of one's pain: That's purely a human trait.

Anna and I talked about Ted and Hilts and families and happiness until two in the morning. When I finally felt calmer, she touched my arm and told me that she hoped we would have a baby more than she'd ever hoped for anything. She said she knew that what I'd seen tonight between parent and child could never happen to us. When I asked how she could be sure, she said, "Because of you."

It was the only thing in the whole world she could have said that could have made me feel better. And I said, "No. Because of us."

When we made love under the blankets, I felt whole again.

Over the next few years, we didn't have a child, although we sure tried.

Toward the end of those peak years of mine, Anna did finally get pregnant. But we lost the baby.

And there was more.

Between the ages of twenty-seven and thirty-two, I found out that love, no matter how strong and how sincere, is never easy. Sometimes it makes sense; other times it makes no sense at all. Sometimes people do good things for people they don't know and to whom they have no personal connection. Sometimes people do bad things to people they love. Sometimes it takes years to create an experience that lasts only a glorious few seconds. Sometimes it takes seconds to destroy something that was created over many years.

Let's see. Am I leaving anything out?

Oh yeah.

During those five years, my life got turned upside down, ripped wide open, and torn apart.

Signing that long-term contract doesn't guarantee success. It just means that sometimes someone's paying you to fail until the contract ends.

From the *New York Daily Examiner:*

Dr. Robert Heller is one of New York's leading veterinarians. He is the author of two books about taking care of pets, *They Have Nothing but Their Kindness* and *More Than Human,* and is a regular on the *Today* show with his weekly segment, "The Vetting Zoo." Dr. Bob takes care of cats, dogs, horses, birds, snakes, turtles, frogs, small pigs, snails, fish, and many varieties of rodents. You can e-mail him at AskDrBob@NYDE .com and ask him any question about the animal you love. His column runs Tuesdays and Thursdays in NYC's most popular newspaper.

Dear Bob:

Recently, my cat, Ralph, died. (Yes, I read your columns; I'm not afraid of using "died" or "death" or "dead.") I'm not ready to get a new cat. I understand all the arguments for getting one, but damn it all, I'm not ready. Though I am not enjoying my grief, I do need to carry it around with me for a while before I release it. But I'm not writing to you for advice on a replacement cat. I'm writing to you because I'm going through a very weird psychological adjustment and I'm not sure how to deal with it. Or even if I *can* deal with it. I mostly want to see if I'm alone in feeling this way or if it's a common experience. Ralph used to sleep on top of me, either on my chest or on my knees. Sometimes, especially in the summer, he'd decide to sleep right next to me instead of on top of me. But he was always touching me. I could feel his weight on me when I went to sleep, and I could feel his weight on me when I woke up. If it wasn't direct weight, he'd be leaning against me and I could feel this very definable pressure on my side. I grew to love that feeling—and now that Ralph is no longer around, I miss it beyond description. It's almost painful, like an ache, although I suppose it's the exact opposite of that—it's a void. I haven't slept through the night in weeks; I feel too light. I feel something missing that's preventing me from having peace. Do you have any idea what I'm talking about? Any comments? Thoughts? Recommendations for a good psychiatrist?

—Weightless in Seattle

Dear Weightless:

I do indeed know what you're talking about and feeling. Pet weight—the simple name I've given to what you're describing—is one of the most delicious feelings in the whole world. The weight of your animal on top of you or against you is like an extraordinary security blanket. When Ralph slept on top of you, it was as if he was protecting you, and yet, at the same time, you felt as if you were there to shield Ralph from any harm. You could touch him and feel his heart pumping, feel the breath going in and out of him. You could stroke him and pet him and feel his warmth. And you knew how good your touch felt to him. It conveyed your love. And your touch received *his* love, carrying it back to you. Yes, pet weight is an extraordinary feeling, and its absence can be overwhelming. It can feel as if you haven't just lost your pet but your sense of safety. In some ways you feel as if you've lost your entire world.

I guess I don't write the typical advice column. I don't feel that I'm capable of giving advice about this kind of loss. What you're describing is not just losing a pet or a loved one. It's losing a crucial piece of yourself. Is that normal? I don't know. I also don't know how many people share the kind of love you and Ralph had. For those who do, yes, I suppose that feeling of tremendous loss is normal. Is it better not to feel it? Only you can answer that. At times you will almost certainly feel that the answer is yes. You'll wish you'd never experienced pet weight because then you wouldn't be aware of its absence. On the other hand, you've lived through something very special. The real question you're asking, if you're asking a question at all, is, Will I experience that again?

I like to think so, Weightless. I hope so. I don't know if pet weight is really replaceable. You will just have to see when you get your next pet. Good luck in the night.

—Dr. Bob

CHAPTER 6

ANTOINE LEFEBVRE

Antoine has two poodles, two white mice, and a snail. I swear. Sometimes he brings the snail, named Speedo, in for a checkup. He makes an appointment, tells Lucy on the phone that he thinks Speedo seems a bit lackluster—again, I swear this is true—and Lucy will book him, making sure we fit him in almost instantly because she knows that my examination of Speedo will take, tops, three minutes. My exam is almost always exactly the same: I pick Speedo up, put him in my palm, observe him closely for a moment, and then tell Antoine that everything is fine. One time Antoine said to me, a bit peevishly in his thick French accent, "Doctaire 'eller, you do zees every time. You look at Speedo for perhaps two seconds and tell me he eez okay. Don't you think you should really examine heem? Poke or probe or geev heem a shot or somezing?"

I thought about this for a few seconds and then said, "Antoine, here's my thinking. As far as I can tell, snails have two basic states of being: fine and dead. Speedo's alive, so he's got to be fine. I should also point out that I'm not charging you when I examine Speedo." Before Antoine could protest, as I knew he would, I hurried to add, "Not because I think this is a charity case, but because Speedo's such a great snail. I just love to see him." That quieted Antoine down instantly, and I was able to complete my little spiel: "If I really poked and probed, I'd have to charge you. And if you started paying, you might not bring Speedo in so often and then I wouldn't get to see him, not to mention you, nearly as much as I'd like. If I thought there was anything wrong, I'd poke and probe. But believe me, your snail's fine. He's going to live a long and productive life as long as no one smothers him in butter and garlic and eats him."

Antoine spoke often about his love of Paris. Although he'd been coming to the clinic for years, he had a thick-as-tarte-tatin accent. I assumed, quite naturally, that this was because Antoine was from France. But one time, after my quick look-see at Speedo, Antoine got a bit expansive and started talking about his first pet, a spider monkey named "Peep."

"Peep?" I asked.

"Peep," Antoine said. "P-i-p. Peep."

"You had a spider monkey?"

"Ah, oui," Antoine said. " 'E was a lovely monkey. Smart as a wheep."

"Was this in Paris?"

"What do you mean?"

"I mean, was this before you left France?"

"I never left Frahnce."

"I don't mean emotionally. I mean, was it before you moved to New York?"

"But I was born in New York, Doctaire. In ze Bronx."

Sure enough, Antoine had never been out of the tristate area in his life. And he didn't speak one word of French. When he was eleven years old, he saw an Inspector Clouseau movie and began imitating Peter Sellers. It started as a joke, but he grew so comfortable in the role that he has maintained the accent for over thirty years. Antoine's been coming to the clinic at least twice a month since I started working here, and I've never heard him— not even for one word, not even when caught off guard—speak in anything but his thick French accent. I don't think he knows any other way to speak at this point. I don't think he knows any other way to be.

For some reason, my thirty-first birthday made me feel old. Thirty hadn't done it for me, but the following year Anna and I celebrated at home with champagne, grilled cheese sandwiches—with bacon! A special birthday treat!—and pecan pie from Anna's favorite bakery, on West

Fourth Street, with six animals in various positions on or near the dining table (we'd added a small, three-legged black-and-white Havanese we'd cleverly named Che). Biting into my second sandwich, I began to feel the stirrings of a midlife crisis. There was no rhyme or reason for it. I did not feel as if I had reached midlife; nor was there a crisis of any kind. All I knew was that I suddenly felt as though I would wake up the next morning and be celebrating my fortieth birthday, and then a week after that my fiftieth. I sat there, sipping champagne, looking adoringly at my wife, thinking that I didn't want to change anything at all in my life. Simultaneously, I found myself thinking that I wanted to change absolutely everything.

We made love that night—we were trying to have a baby and we were on a strict schedule, all geared around the fertility calendar—and for the very first time since I'd met Anna, as soon as the lovemaking was over I wanted to jump out of bed. She knew it. She knew everything I was thinking; it was a little unnerving. I felt guilty that I wanted to do anything but stay wrapped around her, so we lay in bed until she smiled and said, "Okay, I'm a big girl. I can take it. Go."

I heaved a sigh of relief, rolled over, and hopped out of bed. Joined by Che and Rocky, I sat at the kitchen table, ate some ice cream, and read until Anna was asleep. When I got back under the covers, she stirred and muttered, "Happy birthday." I kissed her lightly on the shoulder. She fell back asleep instantly and I stared at her back, admiring her, wishing I could be like her, loving her, deciding I had to be insane to want to be away from her for even a few seconds, until I, too, fell fast asleep.

About two months later, Rocky and I went away on a weekend corporate retreat in Miami—the real Miami this time, in Florida—for the Starling Insurance Company. I got there late Friday night and had room service in my mini-suite (all courtesy of Starling; I ordered a sirloin steak with French fries, and Rocky had a lovely roast chicken, which I cut up and let him eat off the hotel plate instead of his portable food dish). Late Saturday morning I gave my speech, with Rocky at my side, and got a very enthusiastic response. Saturday night—part of the deal—I had dinner with two hundred and thirty insurance agents from around the country. I was as charming and entertaining as I could be, although not as charming and entertaining as Rocky. I received special attention from the myriad women agents. It was the first time it occurred to me that a boy and his traveling, well-behaved, very handsome cat made for an irresistible combination to certain members of the opposite sex. It was fun and a little exhilarating, as I'd never mastered or even had the chance to master the art of flirting.

On Sunday morning, I spent a couple of hours by the resort's pool, soaking up the rays and recuperating from having to be so charming for such a long stretch. While I was lolling on my chaise longue, Anna called my room, but I'd already checked out, so I didn't get her message. She called my cell phone, but I must have had it on mute or maybe the reception was bad, because I didn't hear it ring. On my way to the airport, I picked up the cell to call her and saw that she'd beaten me to it. Her voice mail message to me said only this: "I tried the hotel and your cell. Call me when you get a chance." Her voice sounded terse and tight, as if it were painful for her to even manage that short sentence. I quickly called the apartment and Anna answered, her voice as tightly controlled as it was on the message.

"What's the matter?" I said. I didn't even say "hello."

She didn't answer at first. She seemed to be gathering herself to speak. "I wasn't sure when you were landing," she said. "That's why I called. To find out."

"My plane leaves in about an hour. So I'll be home around five. What's going on?"

"It's probably nothing," Anna said.

"You sound horrible."

"Thank you so much."

"You know what I meant. You sound like something's wrong."

"I have this pain."

I felt my throat tighten and my stomach clutch. Years ago, after I'd known Anna for several months, I'd told her my definition of love. It was that whenever I knew something bad was happening to her, I always wished it were happening to me instead. The idea of her being in pain made me dizzy.

"What kind of pain?" I asked.

"Stomach. All around there."

"How bad?"

"Bad."

"Have you ever had it before?"

She didn't answer.

"Anna?"

"Yes."

"Often?"

"Not all the time."

"Not *all* the time? That means a lot of the time."

"Some of the time."

"When did it start?"

"About six weeks ago."

"Six weeks! Jesus Christ, why didn't you say something?"

"You've been so busy. And because it's just pain."

"'*Just pain*?' Anna, for god's sake."

"Okay, because you would have made me go to the doctor."

"You're fucking right I would!"

There was a silence. My silence said: *You're not your mother. You're too old to have to prove over and over that you're not your mother.*

Her silence said: *I know everything you're thinking is right, but I don't want to hear it. I don't even want you to keep thinking it. I just want you to concentrate on me and make me feel better.*

It's strange how people who know each other so well can communicate without words or facial expressions. Love is its own kind of telepathy. It is both a wonderful and a scary thing.

Anna broke the silence, letting me hear the resigned tone in her voice, her way of acknowledging that I had a point. "Okay, okay. I'm saying something now."

"Look," I said, slowly. "I'm not angry. I'm sorry if I sounded angry. I just can't stand it when you sound like this. And I know you hate doctors and I understand all the weird reasons you hate them. But you have to go to a doctor. Go to Alfredson. I'll call him right now and—"

"It can wait until you come home."

"Anna—"

"I'm sorry I called you. I know you worry about me more than I worry about me."

"I do."

There was another silence. I couldn't interpret this one. She wasn't just tamping down her own pain or fear. She was holding something back, something she wanted to ask or reveal. This was typical Anna; she thought sharing anything complicated—anything she hadn't yet defined or understood on her own—was somehow unseemly. I once had a friend who was too embarrassed to speak Italian until he could speak it fluently, which of course meant that he never spoke a word since you can't become good at anything without practice. He understood the language better than any non-Italian person I knew, but he wouldn't use it to communicate, so his knowledge was basically useless. Anna was similar in her approach to people. She wouldn't let you inside unless she'd already decided it was safe to let you in. I could often guess what was there, or intuit it. But not always; love has its limits. This time I was pretty sure what she wanted to say, but I absolutely didn't want to face it. Denial can also play a big part in love.

"Look," I said. "I'll call Alfredson now and make an appointment, okay?"

"Okay."

"Really?"

"Uh-huh."

"Jesus."

Almost in a whisper, she said, "What?"

"You agreed without any argument. You must really feel like shit."

Silence.

"Can you go to sleep?" I asked.

"I'll try."

"Try. I'll call you as soon as I get in, okay?"

More silence. All I could hear was light breathing on the other end of the phone.

"Okay, Anna?"

"Okay."

We hung up. As soon as I was disconnected, all I wanted was to hear her breathe again. I put my hand inside Rocky's bag, let my fingers gently stroke him, and felt his tiny breaths pulse into my palm, and that calmed me down. He started making these sweet little whistles and snorts that he made when he slept, and I felt some of the tension go out of my body. Not all, but some. For the first time since I'd heard that Anna had called the hotel, my own breathing returned to normal.

The plane landed at four o'clock and I called home as soon as the wheels touched down. Anna sounded a little better, or at least better enough to fight me for a few seconds about going to the doctor. But I didn't back down. When my cab pulled up to our brownstone, I had the driver wait while I went upstairs to get her. There was a lot of barking and meowing and a few "Hello, cocksucker"s while I let Rocky loose and made my way to our bedroom. Anna wasn't sleeping. She was lying in bed, not propped up but flat on the mattress, with no pillow under head, curled into a kind of S shape.

I kissed her lightly, kissed her again a little less lightly, and then helped her up. She was wearing her favorite pajamas; they were goofy as hell, with flowers all over them, and made her look as if she were eleven years old. She wanted to get dressed but I told her no, I just wanted to get her to Dr. Alfredson as soon as possible. She didn't resist. So all we did was add some slippers to her outfit and throw on a robe and get outside as quickly as we could manage.

The cab was still waiting when we got downstairs, and we made it to the doctor's office, in SoHo, by six o'clock.

Dr. Stephen Alfredson had been our doctor since we'd arrived in New York. Recommended by a friend, he was just a few years older than we were. His office was relatively close by, but since Anna never went to the doctor and I went rarely, we didn't know him particularly well. Still, he seemed competent and nice, and he was very polite to me the one time I went to him for a physical and he had to do the bad thing, so I liked him.

Dr. Alfredson—I just can't bring myself to call a doctor by his first name when we're in a professional situation—knew me well enough to keep me out of his examining room while he took a look at Anna. She was in there for half an hour or so while I sat in the waiting room, biting my fingernails to the nub and reading a three-week-old *Sports Illustrated*.

When she came out, she looked better and said she felt a lot better. Dr. Alfredson said it was because he'd given her a strong pain reliever. He had a perfect bedside manner; he was quiet and calm and his voice had a deep timbre. In fact, he was so calm that when he told me we needed to go straight to the emergency room, I didn't panic; instead I just nodded as if going to the ER were the most natural thing in the world.

Anna protested but it was pretty weak as far as protests go. We found another cab; Anna half-dozed against my shoulder while we drove to a hospital on the Upper East Side. It was a large, impersonal place, but they were exceedingly nice to us because Dr. Alfredson had told them to be. After Anna was rushed in, we wound up waiting there until morning before we got any information. During the night, the nurses helped her onto a gurney that was parked in the hallway. Three different orderlies came at three different times and asked the exact same questions. A doctor came by around two in the morning and took Anna away for an MRI. When she was brought back, we both fell asleep—Anna in her bed, me in a chair—periodically disturbed by the occasional scream and angry outburst and urine test. A few feet away from us, partially hidden behind a curtain, was a guy handcuffed to his bed. An armed guard sat nearby.

Inevitably, I kept comparing everything in the hospital to my own clinic. My patients waited in a room decorated with photographs of animals, and the floor was strewn with pet toys. I encountered plenty of human beings who were nervous and sad; often their animals were in pain. Yet where I worked there was a sense of hope. Most people and their pets came to me for mundane ailments, and they walked out into a world of sunlight and cappuccinos and brownstones. But there was nothing mundane about this emergency room. The people in here would walk out into a world of gunshot wounds and drug addiction and wheelchairs.

Around six in the morning, Anna was taken into a small room with an actual door. Dr. Alfredson was there, along with another doctor, Dr. Barry Liebowitz. Taking turns, they gave us the following news:

Dr. Liebowitz told us that Anna was pregnant.

She lit up with joy, and I asked if that's what had been causing her such extreme pain.

Liebowitz said, "Partly," then turned to Dr. Alfredson as if they were a well-rehearsed vaudeville team.

But they needed to work on their act: Alfredson looked directly at me and said, "Anna, you also have stomach cancer."

I said, "That's impossible."

Alfredson turned to look at Anna now. His voice kept the same calm tone he'd used the previous evening. And while I wanted to believe he was lying or making a terrible joke, his eyes belied the lack of emotion in his voice. Their deep blue color had faded, as if hope itself had passed from them.

"It's spread very quickly. We'd like to operate as soon as possible. Dr. Liebowitz has arranged for you to be taken in this morning. He's one of the best oncologists in the country. You'll be in very good hands."

I moved to stand next to Anna. I grabbed her hand; she squeezed mine as hard as she could but didn't say anything.

"What's going to happen?" I asked. "I mean . . . I don't really know what I mean. But what are you going to do?"

"We're going to do our best to remove as much of the tumor as possible. It looks like it has spread beyond the stomach, but I won't know how far until we get inside." This was Liebowitz.

I shuddered at the word "inside." Anna felt my tremor. I tried to cover it up with an encouraging look, but I was a lot closer to tears and despair than encouragement.

Alfredson said, "Anna, you're going to lose the baby. It won't survive the operation."

I didn't flinch at this news. I didn't care about the baby. I only cared about my wife, the thirty-year-old woman in the hospital bed who still hadn't said a word since learning she had cancer. I didn't know if the news about the baby had registered with her. Her expression hadn't changed since Dr. Alfredson had first spoken.

I asked a few more questions, none of which I really remember. And I don't have any idea what the answers were. I had dealt with cancer, had performed operations on a variety of animals to remove tumors. So the two doctors gave me dispassionate, clinical appraisals, as they would with any other doctor. I understood the technical aspects of what they were about to do, but I couldn't begin to express the emotional turmoil churning beneath my attempt at rational conversation. I do recall that at some point Liebowitz said, "If you'd come to us when you first started feeling the pain . . ." But then he stopped. There was no point in finishing the statement.

Soon after that, they left us alone. I sat with Anna, holding her, telling her how much I loved her, assuring her that everything would be all right. She told me that she loved me, too, and that she was very frightened. She said, "Do you wish you had cancer instead of me?" and when I said yes, I really and truly did, she smiled, a real smile, and then she burst into tears. I held her tightly after that; our flesh had always been a comfort to us both when pressed against each other's. I held her until an aide came and wheeled her bed away, toward the operating room.

It was a four-and-a-half-hour operation. While she was still in recovery, Alfredson came to Anna's little room, where I was sitting alone just staring into space. He told me that her body was riddled with cancer and that she would be lucky to live for another few months.

She stayed in the hospital for several days because they thought it would be too risky to move her, and too painful. After that, she came home, along with a hospice worker, an enormously empathetic and comforting elderly black woman named Liza.

My mother came down from upstate New York. She helped feed and bathe Anna, and she let me cry when we were alone.

Teddy and Hilts flew in from California. I didn't ask Teddy to come; he just showed up. He made sure to tell me that a friend in L.A. had paid his airfare. I didn't have the strength to dislike him or shoo him away. He hugged me a lot and told me he loved me. "Whatever our problems," he said, "this is more important. This trumps everything."

He insisted on taking me out for a drink and I burst into tears at the bar. He was remarkably comforting. It was a strange reversal of roles: I was the one collapsing and he was the one holding me up. He asked me questions, just like the old days, and I answered. I was relieved to have someone I could confess to, someone who would allow me to share my doubts and fears and weaknesses. I told him things I had barely been able to face up to myself, and it was remarkable how the simple fact that Ted was family made it all right.

My brother let me talk and sob myself to near exhaustion. And when the exhaustion came, it brought a deep relief, until I looked up at him to say thank you. What I saw chilled me to the bone. He was staring at me with a kind of contempt. No, not contempt—that's too simplistic; his expression was more triumphant than that. It was as if we were engaged in some kind of mammoth struggle and he'd just won this round. He now knew things about me, secrets he could use, and that's what was most chilling: What I saw in his eyes was that he knew that he'd just been given privileged information and was already formulating ways to use it.

I ran into the men's room and threw up the alcohol I'd just poured down my throat. It came up in a coarse-tasting, thin, brown stream. I went back to the bar, wiping my mouth with my hands. Ted came over and hugged me again and assured me that everything would be all right. This time, instead of giving me comfort, his touch gave me the creeps and his words rang disturbingly hollow. I broke into a cold sweat and was still sweating when we got back to the apartment, where Hilts was waiting with my mother. The boy was terrified by everything surrounding him, from Anna's sickly appearance—he was afraid to look at her, much less talk to her or touch her—to my tears and my mother's sadness. He didn't really understand what was happening, and his struggle to comprehend was not easy to watch. Ted quietly explained the concept of death to his son. Listening to him talk about peace and heaven and the human soul made me want to puke a second time. Knowing that he had used my vulnerability to pierce my protective armor made my pain even more palpable. And the memory of what I'd told him was like a throbbing headache that I knew wouldn't disappear anytime soon.

I called Anna's father, which only added to the surreal fog enveloping me. When I told him the news, he didn't know what to say to me, didn't have any way to cope with the emotion he must have been feeling. He said I should tell Anna that he loved her. I said that I would. He did not offer to come to see her, and I didn't ask.

Anna's mother called me an hour later. She said she was flying to New York. I asked her not to. I wanted to tell her that she had killed her own daughter, that she and her fucked-up family had destroyed her daughter's life. But in the end all I said was that she would be a lot more help to her family in Kentucky than she could be to Anna. She called again the next day, and the next, each time sobbing louder than the day before. After the third day, I stopped taking her calls.

Eight days after Anna came back to our apartment, Liza called me into the bedroom. Anna was surrounded by our animals, all of them standing guard, all of them bewildered and wondering why the woman they loved and had depended on for so long now barely acknowledged their existence. Waverly, Anna's special Irish setter, was on the bed, licking Anna's cheek and making noises that sounded like whimpers.

Liza told me that I shouldn't be afraid to touch Anna, and I said that I wasn't. I could never be afraid of touching my wife.

I put my hand against her cheek, and she stirred. A tiny smile appeared on her lips.

"I called you," she said. Her voice was tiny and cracked.

"When?" I asked.

"At the hotel."

"What hotel?"

"Florida. I called you. When I was sick. You weren't there."

"I know."

"She said you'd checked out."

"Who, sweetie?"

"The woman at the hotel."

"Yes," I said. "I'd already checked out."

"I forgive you," she said. "I forgive you."

When I didn't answer, she repeated it: "I really forgive you."

"Oh, Jesus," I said. "I love you so much. Please don't leave me."

"I love you, too," Anna said. "I told you, didn't I?"

"You've told me everything there is to tell."

She smiled again. And very gently shook her head.

She did her best to move her hand. It grazed Waverly's coat, and her fingers splayed, just a tiny bit, so I knew she was somehow including Rocky and Margo, Scully and Larry and Che, who was snuggled up under Anna's armpit.

"Not everything," she said. She rolled her eyes to take in the animals. "Them."

"The guys?" That's what we called our menagerie.

She nodded. "You love them."

I nodded. "I do."

"Do you think they're more than human?"

"What?" I said.

She didn't answer. I don't think she could. The faint movement, the quiet whispering had exhausted her.

A minute or two went by. Then, in a stronger voice, almost clear, she said, "They're not. Don't let them be. It's too easy."

I didn't know exactly what she meant, but I nodded and said, "Okay."

"But they really are," she whispered. "More than human. They really are." And still whispering, but urgently now, the most important message in the world: "I'm not," she said. "I'm *not*."

She gave me one more smile. A very, very faint one before saying: "I knew I shouldn't've gone to the doctor."

Then she stopped speaking.

Liza explained to me that soon a glow would come over Anna; it was why people thought there was often something mystical about death. She said it wasn't mystical at all; it would be the last rush of energy leaving her body. She said I would understand what death was when I looked in Anna's eyes after she took her last breath.

I told her I knew what death was and wasn't scared by it. I'd seen it up close many times. It was not anything terrifying; it was just the end, the absence of life. But this wasn't just an end. It was the end of Anna. It was the end of love. What I really thought was that it was also the end of me.

Liza left the room, and I stayed. I stayed until that rush of energy came and then Anna's eyes turned cold and still. I leaned in close to her. I kissed her cheek and told her I loved her. It seemed inadequate, but I didn't have anything else to say.

I stayed by her side for quite a while. I'm not sure exactly how long. It was light when she died and it was dark when I went through the living room and into the kitchen. Waverly stayed on the bed next to her, one paw over her arm. The other animals only left because I did. And I only left because Rocky was rubbing up against my leg, quietly meowing. He was hungry.

It was time to eat.

PART TWO

———

CAMILLA

From the *New York Daily Examiner:*

ASK DR. BOB

Dr. Robert Heller is one of New York's leading veterinarians. He is the author of two books about taking care of pets, *They Have Nothing but Their Kindness* and *More Than Human,* and is a regular on the Today show with his weekly segment, "The Vetting Zoo." Dr. Bob takes care of cats, dogs, horses, birds, snakes, turtles, frogs, snails, small pigs, a surprising number of fish, and many varieties of rodents. You can e-mail him at AskDrBob@NYDE.com and ask him any question about the animal you love. His column runs Tuesdays and Thursdays in NYC's most popular newspaper.

Dear Dr. Bob:

I will try to make this as simple as possible. I was moving into a new apartment several months ago, and in the moving process a lamp fell off a table and hit my gorgeous little Pekingese, Leyla. She suffered a broken leg, and I do mean suffered. The operation was a success, and the only trace of what happened is that Leyla walks with a slight limp. Even that should disappear in time, according to the vet who performed the surgery. The problem is that Leyla isn't the same dog. She seems sadder. She's less active. She used to talk to me all the time, but now she barely barks at all. She also seems a bit skittish, as if frightened that some new calamity might strike her at any minute. I just don't know what to do. Can you help?

—Leyla's Mom

Dear Mom:

Here's the thing: Wounds heal on the surface. Broken bones mend, physical scars fade, cuts and bruises ultimately become invisible. But that doesn't mean that they didn't happen. And it doesn't mean that the effects of those wounds disappear when they can no longer be seen. This is when Leyla needs the most attention. It's easy to pamper someone when their physical problems demand that they be pampered. It's much harder on us when we have to remember to pamper someone whose pain is under the surface. Just because people look normal, it doesn't mean that they have recovered from their pain and returned to their normal lives. The same applies to our pets. Things may look all right, but we need to peer below the surface and intuit the possible turmoil that lingers on. Please remember: Wounds do heal, but that doesn't mean they don't have a permanent impact. Leyla's leg may look fine and may even *be* fine, but she is not the same dog she was before the accident. She is a different animal, a different Leyla. Treat her as such. She is still the dog you love. She is just changed, even if she looks the same.

—Dr. Bob

CHAPTER 7

NATALIE SPITZLE

Natalie had been coming to Marjorie's clinic longer than any other person. By the time I arrived on the scene, she was in her mid-seventies, had been bringing her pets in for twenty-seven years, and was on her ninth cat (no, she was not a feline serial killer; she usually had three or four at a time). Natalie was also on her fifth husband. Actually, she was on her sixth, but she'd married the third one twice.

She drank the cheapest possible scotch and smoked three packs a day. She hadn't been to a doctor or a dentist in several decades; she didn't care about her teeth (partly because she had very few left), and she didn't believe that doctors knew anything (although she thought that vets knew everything; she tried many times to convince me to treat her as well as her cats). Natalie had, at various times, been a professional backgammon player, a book editor, and a saxophone player with a touring jazz band. When I began treating three of her cats, all rescued from shelters, she was a cashier at a delicatessen on the Upper West Side. She told me that she should have retired several years ago but two things held her back: She dreaded the idea of being isolated, and she didn't have any money. Her fear of isolation was understandable; despite her many husbands, she had no children. Her lack of money was even easier to explain: Natalie was a compulsive gambler.

Every Tuesday and Thursday at six a.m., she took the bus to Atlantic City.
She would spend more than ten hours gambling and then take the nine p.m.
bus back to the city. She loved nothing better than playing craps and black-
jack, she told me, and that included eating, sex, living in a nice apartment,
and visiting friends.

She tried repeatedly to describe the thrill of a hot craps table to me, and
it frustrated her that I was unable to comprehend the appeal. One day, after
I'd completed an acupuncture treatment on her oldest cat to ease the pain
from his arthritis—a technique I'd taken six months of classes to learn—she
grabbed hold of my wrist and said she wanted to talk to me.

"Everything's a gamble," she said. "Everything."

I told her that I understood the concept.

"You can't win if you don't play," she continued.

I told her that I understood that as well.

"Yeah, well, maybe you do. But there's something nobody understands
who don't gamble," Natalie said.

"Okay," I said. "I'll bite. What's that?"

"People think that if you don't gamble, you can't lose."

"And that's wrong?"

"You bet your ass it's wrong," she said. "I want you to listen to me."

"I'm listening."

"I mean really listen."

"I'm really listening."

She looked at me intently, trying to determine whether I was telling her
the truth. I could see that she wasn't totally convinced, but she gripped my
wrist even tighter, grinned her semi-toothless smile—a crazily angelic smile—
and said, "The only way you can ever lose is if you don't play."

I met Elizabeth Gold under what I would call imperfect conditions.

It was four o'clock in the afternoon, nearly three years to the day
after Anna died, and I was standing in Anna's closet, smelling her clothes,
reminding myself of her odor, which was fading from my memory as
well as from her blouses and skirts and jackets, which I still couldn't
bear to give away. Trying hard to conjure the lovely combination of
powder and shampoo, sweat and skin, I was holding a light gray sun-

dress to my face, smothering myself in it. As I inhaled deeply, I began
to cry quiet tears. That's what time does. It not only slowly removes all
physical traces of a presence both real and ethereal, it also dissipates
your grief, no matter how much you want to keep hold of it. I don't
know if it's a kindness or not, but time eventually reduces sobs to
quiet tears.

I was not, thank god, talking to either myself or my dead wife—I
was never reduced to either of those practices. I was not crazy or
newly spiritual; I was just deeply, deeply sad, and had been since the
day Anna died.

But I was, let's face it, wrapped in a dress and crying. And standing
in a closet filled with my dead wife's clothes.

That's when Elizabeth walked in to introduce herself. It was not
my most dignified moment.

She handled it well, looking appropriately embarrassed but also
concerned. She was able to almost completely hide her suspicion that
there was a reasonable chance that she was staring at an unstable
transvestite having a nervous breakdown. She wasn't at all sure
whether she should stick around or quietly make her way back down
the stairs—at which point she could pretend that none of this had ever
happened, at least until she was in the safe confines of some cocktail
party and found a good opportunity to say, "You think *you* had a weird
day . . ."

I, on the other hand, wasn't just mortified. I was shocked and
bewildered, because I couldn't figure out what this woman, whom I
didn't know, was doing in my apartment, much less my closet. She was
attractive in a slightly severe way: tall, maybe five foot ten, and thin,
with close-cropped, dark red hair (it was a distinctive color, one I can
only compare to a shade described in my favorite childhood books of
all time, *The Black Stallion* series by Walter Farley, in which a second
stallion, Flame, competed with the Black and in fact eventually wound
up with his own series of books, *The Island Stallion,* and Flame was said
to be dark, dark red, and that's the color I always thought of when I
looked at Elizabeth), and she was wearing a very professional-looking
woman's suit, a tweedy kind of jacket with a matching mid-thigh-
length skirt and a white shirt under the jacket, and she had good legs

and remarkably clear skin—and yes, I did notice all of that in my initial glance over at her, even as I was crying and smelling Anna's dress. Whatever else I am, I'm a guy, and we guys will notice every detail about an attractive woman even if we're being stomped on by a herd of wild elephants.

It turned out that I had an appointment with Elizabeth Gold, although I'd forgotten all about it in my outburst of grief. She was a professor-turned-administrator at Cornell, where I'd gone to veterinarian school, and where I'd met Marjorie Paws. Over the past month or two, Elizabeth and I had been e-mailing; she'd been trying to work out some kind of arrangement for me to be a guest lecturer at the vet school for a semester or two, and when she mentioned that she would be in the city on school business we'd made a date to meet and talk. Initially she'd gone to the clinic on the main floor, and because Lucy, at the reception desk, knew about the appointment, she'd just sent Elizabeth upstairs. Elizabeth had knocked on the door, but I was crying in the closet, which made it difficult to hear a delicate rap several rooms away. So she'd turned the knob, found the door open, and stepped inside. As she walked through the apartment she met most of the menagerie except for Rocky, who was sitting at my feet in the closet, half-wondering why I was making odd noises and half-wondering why I wasn't petting him every moment.

Elizabeth and I stared at each other for what I'm sure seemed to both of us like several days but was, in fact, three or four seconds. I lowered the sundress from my face, decided I could escape this whole awkward situation by saying something witty and clever, so opened my mouth to do just that. Instead, as I said the words "This may look bad, but . . ." I totally lost control and began sobbing. Deep, lung-choking, horrible-sounding noises that came out like some combination of wild despair, an asthmatic attack, and a hundred-and-seventy-five-pound goose trying to warn his mate that danger was imminent.

Elizabeth hurriedly stepped into the closet and took my arm. She gently guided me to the corner of the bed and not so gently pushed me down into a sitting position. I didn't resist or say a word. I just kept sobbing, now sitting, holding the sundress to my chest as if it were a dishrag.

"I don't know who you are, but I think it's safe to say this is the most humiliating moment of my life," I said.

And here's the thing about having a relationship like the one I had with Anna: I knew that if this tall, sharp-featured woman had been Anna, she would have said, "I hate to say this, but it's going to be even more humiliating when you find out who I am." That would have made me laugh, and also would have made me curious. The combination of the two would have made me stop crying and would have relaxed me into being at least fifty percent over my discomfort and embarrassment.

But this woman wasn't Anna. So at first Elizabeth didn't say anything. And when I didn't say anything back, she took my hands in hers—her hands were not soft and warm but rather rough and scratchy, as if she spent much of her day nervously picking at them—and said, "There's no reason to be humiliated. Sadness should never be humiliating."

"How about pitied?" I said.

She didn't smile or even bother to answer that one. Instead, she put a hand on my back and began patting me as if I were a small child. It was strangely intimate. I instantly felt as if I'd known her for years, although of course I'd only met her minutes before and didn't even know her name.

After several dozen gentle pats on the back and a gradual reduction of cries and gasps and wheezes, it seemed appropriate to have a formal introduction.

"I'm Bob Heller," I said.

"I know. I'm Elizabeth Gold."

"Oh, Jesus!" I said. "Tell me you're a total stranger who just happened to wander in and has the same name as the Elizabeth Gold who works at Cornell."

This stumped her for a second. I came to know that Elizabeth did have a sense of humor, but it was a slow and subtle one. She had to absorb things before finding them funny. So she just peered at me for a moment, then released a slight upturn of her lips.

"I'm afraid I'm the Cornell one," she said.

I nodded and murmured something along the lines of "Just my luck." Then said, "So is this the strangest job interview of your life?"

She pondered a bit. Then said, "I was interviewing a woman once who told me that she was a transsexual. I thought that was pretty strange. Especially because I hadn't asked and, in fact, it was illegal for me to ask in the context of the interview, even though I suspected that was the case."

"What made you suspect she was a transsexual?"

"She looked like a man who'd put on a dress and stuck a mop on his head."

"So are you saying that was a stranger interview than this one?"

She shook her head. "No, I don't think so. But this one is way more interesting, if that makes you feel any better."

I said that it did, if just a little. Elizabeth explained that she found the whole situation interesting, partly because she knew about Anna's death and had heard all sorts of wonderful things about her from, among others, Marjorie. She also told me about her job at Cornell, and a bit about her past, and I talked a lot about Anna and our marriage and her death and my life in the three years since she'd died. I talked about our animals—after three years I still spoke in the plural when it came to everyday life—and how they had coped with Life After Anna.

We spoke about all sorts of things into the early evening and then late into the night. We did the same thing the next night: dinner and long, involved conversation, talking about nothing in particular this second time, just about movies and television and animals and work. She came down to New York the following weekend, and we had dinner twice. Being with her was remarkably comfortable and easy. Neither of us felt any awkwardness during the inevitable silences, neither of us felt any disorienting electric spark. (At least I didn't, and I got the distinct feeling that Elizabeth was not about electric sparks; she was about quiet affection and being interested in people.) She didn't come down the weekend after that, and I missed her. I had dinner with the guys—Rocky sat on the table, a couple of the dogs sat on chairs; Waverly sat by my feet, as he used to do with Anna; Larry hopped about the apartment swearing—and I felt a chilling sort of loneliness.

The next weekend Elizabeth did come down. Friday was dinner at a restaurant. Saturday, I cooked. Nothing fancy—pasta and salad and a nice bottle of wine—and after dinner we went into the bedroom and made love. It was not urgent lovemaking; it was languid and tender and tentative on both our parts, and it felt natural and unforced. This was not the first time I'd made love since Anna died, but it was the first time I felt better instead of worse when it was over.

Elizabeth Gold and I began seeing each other after that. I went up to Cornell when I could, and she spent every other weekend, sometimes more, in the city, staying with me. I think it's fair to say that she genuinely saved my life, nursing me back to mental health and bringing me to a point where I was able to not just live in the present but appreciate it again. Even hunger for it. She worried about me and nagged at me in the most pleasant way when she thought I was working too hard or not eating well or not exercising enough. She granted me the kind of emotional privacy I needed, understanding that I could not and did not want to let go of the past completely. I know she fell in love with me, but even so she understood that she could not be a replacement for Anna and was simply the next step in my recovery. It does not sound particularly romantic, I realize, but in its own way it was. It was romantic in its solidness and its strength and in the way Elizabeth remade her life to prepare for a future with me.

In exchange, I cared for her deeply and did my best to be as kind and good to her as I could be. I tried to love her. Instead, after three and a half years, I broke her heart.

Life is a constant surprise, a constant throw of the dice. And any time there's gambling involved, there are regrets and unpredictability and surges of excitement bouncing off flatlines of despair. And, of course, whenever there's gambling, there's also a lot of losing going on.

I didn't have hordes of people descend on me after Anna died. What I did do, for the most part, was stay close to the people in my life who really mattered.

Even before it hit me where I live, I'd always believed that grief is something intimate, much like love. I would never go on national TV to bounce around like a spinning top, declaiming my passion for another person and exulting in the beginning of something stirring and delightful. Nor would I go on CNN to talk about my personal tragedy if a loved one was killed in a surprise terrorist attack or crushed by a wayward meteor. If love is a gradual acceptance of the opening of a special relationship—and I would define love as a constant opening—then grief is a gradual acceptance of the closing of that relationship. They are equally personal to me. I don't need mass understanding of either. I just need to share a bit of both with people who know me well enough to appreciate and understand the joy as well as the pain.

Phil came down to the city immediately. He didn't call or e-mail, he was just there, the morning after Anna's death. He showed up at my apartment around six A.M., knowing I'd be awake, even knowing that I was planning on going downstairs to work at the clinic, which opened at eight. He walked in my door and said, "Don't be an asshole. You're not going to work."

I started to protest, said something along the lines of "It'll help me; it'll take my mind off it."

Phil said, "Anna died yesterday, pal. Your mind's not gonna be off it for a long, long time. I already called Lucy, and she's already got a vet lined up to replace you for a couple of weeks. So sit down and let's dive into this." By "this" he meant a huge bottle of Gran Patron Platinum tequila.

"It's six o'clock in the morning."

"The whole fuckin' world turned upside down last night. Day is night. God is the devil. The Knicks are division winners. This is new territory for everybody. All good things are gonna be for shit for a while. So what the fuck difference does it make what time it is? We should get drunk. I sure as hell am going to."

And that's what we did. We sipped from the bottle and talked. The alcohol relaxed me and clouded my brain, which needed some serious clouding; it also sent a warm glow of melancholy throughout my entire body. Phil talked about himself for a while, partly as a way of distracting and entertaining me, partly because Anna's death was causing great pain for him, too, and he needed to let some of it escape.

Ever since I'd gone off to college, Phil and I had spoken on the phone nearly every day; more recently, we'd also exchanged e-mails several times a week. But staying in touch wasn't the same as sitting across the room from each other, face to face, with a tequila high and Anna's ghost hovering between us. As he often did, Phil talked about how life sucked, and the thing about Phil was that he absolutely meant it. Yet the suckiness didn't really matter to him: He was a guy who saw the glass as three-quarters empty, but he got an extraordinary amount of pleasure from gulping down the remaining quarter of whatever liquid the glass held. That day he told me new stories about his life and the bowling alley and his latest girlfriend, whose name was Darlene, though she wasn't the same Darlene he'd brought to our wedding. He made me laugh and provided a relaxed solace with both his cynical view of life and his subtle insistence that everything, and I mean every-thing, had to be kept at a distance, because otherwise you'd lose the essential awareness that life, at its core, was one grand, miserable, painful, ecstatic joke.

Eventually he got around to Anna. "Not all jokes are funny," he said. "And anything truly funny comes from something tragic. Just keep that in mind, will ya? Everything that seems tragic at the time ultimately becomes part of the cosmic joke that's being played on all of us." Then, with no attempt to make sense of the transition, he said, "Hey, when was the Old Testament written?"

"I don't know," I said. "Before my time." I almost said, "That's the kind of thing Anna knows, ask her," but I caught myself.

"Two thousand years ago?" he asked.

"Sure. Let's call it that."

"Okay, a fuck of a long time. You want to know what I learned? And this is no bullshit—just in case you thought I was brilliant and that I always know the right thing to say. I do my research."

"What are you talking about?"

"I learned something about your hallowed religion. Isaac—he was one of the patriarchs of the Jews."

"If you say so."

"Jesus, you're a bad Jew. Don't you even know who Isaac is?"

"I thought he was one of the Chipmunks."

"Not a bad guess, actually. But no. Isaac, or Yitzak, as you people say—you want to know what the name means?"

"Sure."

"It means 'jester.' " He said this as if it were some sort of momentous announcement. I didn't quite see the momentousness.

"So?"

"*So?*" he said. "The patriarch of the entire Jewish people is named Jester! It means that right from the beginning, God was planning on fucking you over!"

"You don't even believe in God."

"You're missing the point. I mean, it's like if we found out that 'Jesus' means 'Bozo' in whatever the hell language 'Jesus' is. Or if it meant 'lying scumbag.' Come on! *Jester?* You're fucked. And everything makes sense once you put it in context!"

"You're an asshole," I said.

"Right! So imagine if I was the fucking patriarch of the Jews! Exactly my point."

While we talked, the guys came and gathered around us. Rocky sat on my lap, as always. Margo sat by my feet, occasionally reaching out her paw to touch my ankle, as if to let me know that she was there if I needed her. Scully, the little sweet cockapoo, sat by my side, too, occasionally trying to displace Rocky, to no avail (he was obviously frustrated by his inability to be of more comfort). Che, the three-legged Havanese, cuddled up to Phil. Larry, for the first time in memory, stayed reasonably quiet. Every half hour or so he'd mumble "cocksucker" or "fuckin' a-hole," but it was almost a whisper compared to his normal boom.

Only Waverly, who worshipped Anna—she was Anna's dog and merely tolerated the rest of us—stayed separate from the group. She paced and whined, as if waiting for Anna's return. It was heartbreaking; I couldn't seem to offer her any real solace. Of course, I was not in great shape myself and so probably not the best person to provide solace. Once, I got up and petted her and tried to tell her that Anna wasn't coming back but I'd take good care of her. But I started to cry, so I returned to my chair and let Phil go back to talking about life back home. At some point, I knew, I'd be able to stop crying and could help sweet, sweet Wave cope. Phil knew it, too, which is why he didn't feel the need to either encourage me to let the tears flow or help me stop.

Phil stayed with me until two days after Anna's funeral. He checked into a hotel a few blocks from my apartment—I'm sure he wanted to give me some space but I'm even more certain he needed to periodically escape the suffocating grief that was emanating from the brownstone—but each day he was at my place when I woke up, and he was there when I passed out from exhaustion at night. The day after the funeral, we sat together in silence for a while, the late afternoon shadows creeping around the living room. He looked into my eyes, told me he knew I'd be okay, and said he'd decided he could go home. When I asked him how the hell he knew I'd be okay, he said, "Because I know you. I can already see that you're beginning to understand that you're going to be deeply sad for a long time. In some ways, maybe forever."

"And that makes you think I'm going to be all right? That I know I'm going to be sad the rest of my life?"

"Sadness is normal, pal. If you weren't sad, you'd be insane. And a few days ago, that's what I thought you were—insane. You weren't sad, you didn't know what the fuck was going on. Now you do. So whatever happens from here on in, you'll deal with it."

"I'm not just sad, Phil. I'm *overwhelmingly* sad."

"Yeah," he said. "I know. Me, too. Not like you, but everybody else is, too. But you can survive that. Deep down, you know you're *going* to survive that."

"Oh god. I sense a bowling metaphor coming on."

Phil nodded. "Life is like a seven-ten split. It looks ugly and fucks up your game, but every so often, you luck out and make the spare."

"I don't think that even makes sense."

"You want the gutter ball one instead?"

I shook my head. We gave each other a half handshake, half hug, and sat around for the rest of the night talking about our childhoods, our families, and Anna. The next morning he headed back upstate to Darlene and life among the rented bowling shoes.

My mom came down the same day as Phil, but later in the afternoon. She didn't make much of a fuss; she just appeared, straightened up the apartment, made enough food to last several lifetimes, and paid attention to the animals, all of whom seemed happy to be petted by someone who wasn't trembling or tearing up. Even Waverly perked up; she began following my mother wherever she went and insisted that my mom and only my mom take her for her thrice-daily walks. My mother moved into the guest room, and the nicest thing about having her there was that she never asked me how I was; she acted as if she knew. She became my mom for the first time in a long, long time and just took care of me.

Marjorie Paws came up from Florida. She stayed for two weeks, living in the small top-floor apartment where Anna and I had started, which she still maintained. She roared back into action at the clinic, working full-time and continuously shuttling back and forth to my apartment, complaining about the climb every time she came up and sighing about the steps every time she went down, insisting that it was the damn steps that drove her to Florida. She was like a backup mother: She touched me constantly—the back of my neck, my arm, my cheek— and her rough, callused hands were remarkably soothing. Her touch conveyed warmth and life, and I understood, yet again, why she was so wonderful with animals. I saw why a cocker spaniel who'd been hit by a car or a German shepherd with bone cancer would immediately calm down when she put a hand on their back. Her touch helped lift the pain and promised eventual relief. It was an extraordinary skill, although it probably shouldn't be called a skill. Better simply to call it being Marjorie.

Part of being Marjorie was to fuss over me and ask me questions no one else would ask (except Phil, who rather than asking usually just told me what I was feeling and thinking). Another part of being Marjorie, possibly the best part, was that she treated me as if nothing all that unusual had happened. She asked me about animals she was treating at the clinic, testing to see if I'd kept up on the latest research and theories. She nattered on about the weather and the traffic. And she asked me about Anna, which no one else did: why she had done certain things; why the spice cabinet was arranged the way it was; how she had handled the pain of her cancer. To Marjorie it was all of a piece. Just because my wife had died, that didn't mean I could get away with drinking milk out of the container when other people would be sharing it.

The clinic contributed its share of mourners and sympathetic hand-holders, too. Lucy was magnificent. She set herself up as a one-woman barrier: If you wanted to get to me for any reason, you had to go through her. If she decided you weren't supportive enough, you didn't have a chance. She was like a tiger ferociously protecting her wounded cub. But she knew when to let through the various eccentrics who populated the clinic, all of whom had had some connection with Anna: Antoine the fake Frenchman; Paige, a seventy-year-old actress who hadn't actually acted in forty years; Leslie, a line chef at a nearby restaurant who looked alarmingly like her Afghan, whom she even more alarmingly had decided to also name Leslie; Victor, who owned a pair of beautiful Siamese cats and who'd been in love with Anna from afar (he'd send her charming notes, admiring her beauty and style, attached to strange presents he'd bought for her—inexpensive salt and pepper shakers, a necklace made out of old presidential campaign buttons, a DVD of an old movie he thought she'd like, usually starring Donald O'Connor). There were others: Francis, Elaine, Rosy, Mike, and Bernie, cat and dog and snake owners all. I came to understand that they thought of me as part of their family circle, their *inner* family circle, and part of their daily lives. From time to time I had helped ease their pain over the past several years, and now they were eager to reciprocate. It was amazing to me that these people—who I too often took for granted, who interested me, yes, even touched me on occasion, but who had all seemed so replaceable—were all insisting on being key participants in my restructured world. They all wanted to help with my care and feeding and regeneration. They all wanted to make me part of *their* family.

Teddy, too, was there—but, as always, not there. He was too uncomfortable to stay in my apartment for more than a few minutes at a time. He mostly showed up, paced around, ate what was in the fridge, said he had some business appointments, and dropped Hilts off so our mother could look after him. We were convenient babysitters for the boy; mourning was keeping us close to home, which made it easy for Ted to do whatever it was he did out in the world.

For a week, I spent as much time with Hilts as with anyone else. He was a month or so shy of his eighth birthday so still too young to be allowed to wander off on his own down the mean streets of Manhattan (though I did tell my mother that the meanest thing that could possibly happen to him in my neighborhood was that he'd get run over by a speeding bike messenger). He did his best to entertain himself with video games and DVDs and TV, but the specter of death in the apartment had its own irresistible allure. It was his first exposure to it, and I could see that although it frightened him, it also attracted him, like a somewhat scary magnet. He knew death was something he had to understand and, to his credit, he did try.

Hilts had enough of his father in him to make me uncomfortable; in particular, he, too, had a certain hollowness at his core. When he told me how sorry he was that Aunt Anna had died, he didn't seem especially sorry. He behaved as if he knew he *should* be sorry, but he seemed more curious than sad. After a while, I realized that he was also strangely pleased. Not that Anna had died—the boy was not a monster, not even close; he was just a fucked-up kid stuck with a more fucked-up father—but pleased that something out of the ordinary was happening. He got to be in this strange apartment with a sarcastic uncle who periodically burst into tears; his uncle's friend who drank tequila or beer all day long and talked about despair, bowling, and his favorite porn titles, in no particular order; animals who alternated between a desperate urge to be petted and a languid sadness; a loving grandmother who only wanted to make sure he was happy and well-fed; and eccentric characters who slipped in and out of the apartment at all times of the day, sometimes bringing birds, dogs, or a snail. For Hilts, this was a whole lot better than enduring the endless routine of school, or feeding his father's neediness, or coping with his mother's overprotective and almost psychotic sternness, which most likely stemmed from a deep-rooted fear that her son was going to turn out like his father.

I talked a lot with Hilts, which was sometimes awkward because I still didn't like him much. I felt a little bad about that, but not *that* bad. For one thing, I had a few other things to feel truly bad about. For another, there was nothing likable or interesting about him. He was remarkably mundane. He could talk about sports and his church (his mother was a churchgoer now, so Hilts was, too) and several other features of his narrow world. But he had no grasp of any aspect of life that fell outside those boundaries, and he had little capacity for original thought.

Hilts was also becoming something of a fantasist. He told me he had ridden a Jet Ski (he hadn't) and had gone 120 miles per hour (he definitely hadn't) and that his mother saw him do it (no way in hell). He said he was taking martial arts lessons (possibly true) and could now beat the eleven- and twelve-year-old kids in his dojo (untrue). His Little League coach, he reported, had already told him that he could get him a baseball scholarship when he was ready to go to college. (I could only shake my head and do my best not to scream at this one.) The tree in his backyard, he assured me, was the largest tree in Los Angeles.

No matter how outlandish the claim, Hilts seemed to believe everything he was saying. He simply couldn't help himself: He leapt at any vague suggestion of something positive and turned it into an absolute truth. My guess, for instance, is that his Little League coach had at some point asked him what he wanted to do when he grew up and Hilts probably said, "play baseball." The coach then went, "That's great. It's a good goal to have, and when the time comes, I'm sure everyone will help you do that." The coach probably told him how hard it was to make it to the majors and that he should think of high school and college ball. And that became: "I guarantee I'll get you a scholarship." It was a slight variation on his father's fantasies; Hilts wasn't manipulative, and there was no real gain other than trying to impress. But his reflexive lying pushed my buttons, and for some reason, it was the one about the tree that really got to me. Instead of keeping quiet, I felt an irresistible urge to challenge him, probably because I know that's exactly what Anna would have done. So I asked him about the tree and how he knew it was the biggest—what were his sources? I wouldn't let it go and pushed far past the point of reasonableness. Before long I began to challenge him on almost everything he said. He never could verify any of his wild claims. And I could never make him understand the damage that could pile up over the years from believing so strongly in a fantasy.

My mother saw none of this. When it came to Hilts, she had crossed over to the berserk grandmother side—I think it was her loyalty to my father and his obsession with their grandson that did it. She delighted in his every movement and utterance. She thought he was brilliant, funny, charming. If he glanced outside, saw clouds, and said it looked like it was going to rain, she practically burst into applause at his ability to predict the future. One night when Ted came by and picked Hilts up to take him to a friend's house for dinner, I made the mistake of telling my mother that the kid seemed a bit distant and troubled. She practically whacked me over the head with a frying pan. Under other circumstances I'm sure she would have really torn into me, but in this case she probably chalked up my heresy to the fact that I was in deep mourning.

But there *was* something off about the kid. Not serial-killer off— he was just too disconnected and too self-protective and too . . . sad. He was in a sad house, so his demeanor wasn't inappropriate. But I didn't think he was sad for Anna or for me. I think he was sad for himself. And for his dad. I couldn't blame him, either; he was slowly becoming aware that this was the family he would have to deal with for the next sixty or seventy years. He could go to church all he wanted, but his dad was still going to steal dollar bills from the collection plate.

One evening Hilts wandered into my bedroom. I had most of the menagerie in there with me and was focusing on Waverly, doing my best to scratch her ears exactly as Anna used to. I thought I was doing a pretty good job, though she seemed less than impressed.

"Is she sad?" Hilts asked.

"Waverly?" I said. "Yes, she's very unhappy."

"How do you know when a dog's unhappy?"

"Pretty much the same way you know when a person's unhappy. She's not eating much, she's kind of moping around, she's not very playful."

"But she can't *say* anything. So you don't really *know*."

"No, that's right. But words aren't the only way to communicate. Don't you sometimes feel things that you don't talk about?"

Hilts didn't respond. For a moment I thought he was being incredibly clever—not talking about the idea of not talking—but I was giving him too much credit. He was merely thinking over what I'd said, and it was a slow process.

"I don't know," he said. "My dad usually knows what I'm feeling and he just tells me."

"And is he always right?"

"Well, yeah. He's my dad. He knows a lot more than me."

I hesitated. This was dangerous territory, especially in my weakened condition.

"Give me an example," I said, "of something where you're feeling one thing and your dad tells you you're wrong."

"I don't know," he said.

"Try."

"Well," he said. "There was one time when he took me out of school."

"What do you mean, took you out of school?"

"I was supposed to give a book report on this book I really liked. It was really cool—it made me think of you because it was about this guy and his relationship with a cat. But my dad called the school and said there was a family 'mergency and he picked me up."

"What was the emergency?"

"There wasn't one. He made it up."

"Why?"

"There was this really cool movie I wanted to see. It was about this killer—he killed people just by thinking about them. It was R-rated and everything."

"So he just took you to see the movie?"

"Yeah."

"And what, you didn't want to go? You wanted to stay in school?"

"No. It was so cool that he took me out. We went to the movie and then we got a hamburger and a milkshake. It was way better than school."

I tried not to shake my head in exasperation. "So how does this mean he knows what you're really thinking?"

" 'Cause my mom was really mad when she found out. The school called her to make sure everything was all right. She got super pissed off. She had this long talk with me and told me that it was wrong to do what we did and she kinda made me think she was right."

"Yeah?"

"So then the next weekend I was with my dad and I told him what Mom said. I told him she was probably right and that I needed to do stuff like my book report or I'd get in trouble and not get good grades."

"What'd he say?"

"He said my mom was wrong. I mean, he said she was right in that I needed to get good grades. But he said that a lot of stuff was more important than school and good grades. He said that family was way more important and that it was good the two of us could spend some time together like that. He said I'd remember that day at the movies way longer than I'd remember giving a book report. And then . . ." Hilts hesitated.

I said, "Don't worry. You can tell me whatever you want. I won't tell anyone if you don't want me to."

"Grandpa was your dad, too, right?"

I nodded.

"So don't get mad. He just said something not so nice about Grandpa."

"I won't get mad. What'd he say?"

"He said that Grandpa never took him to the movies. He said that people like Grandpa don't really care about other people and what happens to them. He said . . ."

"It's okay. I told you. You can say anything you want."

"He said you were like Grandpa. You didn't care what happened to him or to me. He also said Mom didn't understand what really mattered, so we had to stick together. We were the only two who could understand."

"And did you think he was right?"

"Not at first. I mean, I don't know about Grandpa or you. I know my mom would never take me out of school to go see a movie. So I guess he was right. 'Cause I liked it a lot more than school. And a lot more than just doing work, you know?"

"Yeah, I know," I said.

"You're not angry?"

"About what?"

"That my dad said something not so nice about you?"

I shook my head. "Nah. I've got bigger things on my mind."

"I know," he said. "I'm sorry for your loss."

I couldn't help myself. I laughed. "Where did you pull that phrase from?"

"TV. All the cop shows. That's what they say when someone dies."

"Thanks," I said. "I appreciate it."

"Do you think my dad was right?"

"You want to know what I really think?"

"Yeah."

"I think it's extremely complicated. I think that sometimes family's more important than school. But I think everything has to be thought out on its own. And I think what your dad did was wrong."

"Why?"

"Because I don't think he did it for you. I think he really did it for himself."

"Because he was lonesome?"

"Yup. And needy. He needs you to like him and love him."

"I do. I mean, he's my dad, right?"

"Right. I'm glad to hear you say that. Try to remember that as you get older. 'Cause sometimes he makes it kind of hard."

It's difficult to know what registers with an eight-year-old. But I think he took note of what I said because I saw something flicker in the back of his eyes. He was a kid who expressed almost no emotion, and at that moment I thought I understood why. If he'd allowed himself to deal with all the emotions that were whirling inside him and all the responsibilities and all the psychological burdens that were being piled on top of him, he probably would have exploded like the human piñata he was becoming.

Dealing with Ted and Hilts wasn't easy, but it wasn't my biggest challenge. The person who worried me the most—who had the most potential to rip open the wound I was trying so hard to keep stitched together—was Anna's mother, Ruby. One of Anna's brothers, Lawrence—the short one who couldn't get a football scholarship—wrote me a lovely note, saying that I was lucky to have had Anna as long as I did because she was such a special and wonderful person. He said I should be at peace with the knowledge that I had made her so happy, something her own family had never been able to do. It was touching and perceptive, particularly because that was the only communication I had from her family, the only acknowledgment that Anna had been a part of their lives but was no longer—except for the barrage of calls from Ruby.

"My life is now unbearable," she told me over the phone in her first call. "No one has any idea how much I loved my oldest daughter."

"I can't go on living without Anna," she said in her second. "You have it easy. She was with you these last few years. She ignored me. I don't have anything to fall back on."

During the third call, the last one I took, she said, "You can't keep me from coming to the funeral. She was my child. I was there when she was born. I have to see her buried."

"I'm not going to keep you from coming, I'm just asking you not to come. Anna wouldn't want you there."

"You're a hateful, hateful man," Ruby said to me, two days after my wife had died. "I know she wanted to be with me, only you wouldn't let her." Before I could say anything, not that I really had any kind of comeback for that, she reversed field completely. "And Anna was a hateful daughter, if truth be known. She treated me like shit, and I never deserved that. She's gonna rot in hell for what she did to me." Then she burst into tears, saying how much she loved Anna, how much she loved me, even though she'd only been allowed to meet me once. She insisted that she was totally misunderstood and then told me that she might kill herself, since she had no reason to live without Anna.

After that, I had my mom deal with her. The two mothers-in-law spoke several times—Ruby called every two hours or so—then my mom told me that although Anna's mother was obviously mean and deranged, she was coming to the funeral and I was just going to have to deal with it. My mom said she'd shield me as much as possible but that the woman had a right to grieve for her own daughter, no matter what we thought of her. I was in no condition to argue or disagree, but I did feel a little more at ease when Marjorie answered the phone the last time Ruby called, the day before the funeral, and told Anna's mom that if she bothered me in any way or made me feel worse than I already felt, she would cut her heart out with a scalpel and let the rats eat the rest of her on the streets of New York. She ended the conversation by saying that if Ruby didn't believe what she had just said and came to the funeral anyway, she should keep an eye out for the woman with the scalpel.

I had a lot of trouble deciding where we should hold the service. A church or a temple was out of the question. God had not been a part of either of our lives. Nor were rabbis, priests, or religious groups of any kind. I basically thought the whole idea of religion was absurd. Just because Judaism and Christianity were old, burning bushes and turning water into wine and miraculous births without sex were no less absurd than the angel Moroni delivering his message on tablets with the handy provision that men could have sex with as many women as they wanted, or that spaceships were supposed to meet mass suicides up in the sky to take them to whatever heaven existed for insane idiots.

I tried to imagine what Anna would have wanted and soon began to panic, overcome by a strange kind of helplessness when I couldn't come up with anything that would have pleased her. I felt a sudden disconnect from her, as if she were already fading from my life, something I was not remotely prepared for. The panic turned into a full-fledged attack around four A.M., the second night after she died. I woke up sweating, my forehead and neck soaked, the pillow wet through. What flashed through my mind was that I was unable to do the very last thing I needed to do for the woman I loved. I told myself that I hadn't really known her. And that I had never deserved her. I lay in bed shaking, clammy, trying to stay silent so as not to disturb the humans and pets who were trying their best to see me through these impossible hours. All I could do was lie there, breathing heavily, eyes wide open, paralyzed, feeling as if I were having a heart attack.

I don't know how long I stayed like that. I do know that I woke up sometime around six A.M., so I must have fallen asleep for some period of time. When I awoke, my sheets felt as if they'd been washed, then placed on the bed without having gone through the dryer. They were cold and I was colder. But I was no longer in a panic because I knew exactly what I was going to do.

Phil was already up and sitting in my living room, drinking a tomato-juice-and-tequila concoction. (It was healthy, he said, because of the celery stalk he'd rammed into it.) He took one look at me and made me a drink of my own, which I gulped rather than sipped. When I told him my idea, he just nodded, as if I'd made the easiest, most natural decision in the world. I asked him if he thought it would be allowed. He said he had no idea, but within seconds we were on my computer—weirdly like little kids again, as if hunting for treasure or, when we were slightly older, looking through magazine racks for porn—and soon we found what I needed to find.

Suddenly my idea seemed wildly crazy and impossible to fulfill. I wanted Phil to make the call, but for the first time since Anna died, he shook his head and said that I should do it. He stared at me in such a way that I knew I wasn't going to win this argument, so I checked the number on my computer screen, picked up the phone, and called a temple up in Morningside Heights. A woman answered, and I suddenly realized I didn't even know whom to ask for. I stumbled a bit over my explanation and finally she said, "You need to talk to the rabbi." I said okay and as I waited, I wondered if I'd ever spoken to a rabbi before. I decided the answer was no just seconds before I heard a fairly high-pitched man's voice say, "Hello, may I help you?"

I was calling the rabbi because Anna had come to love Greenwich Village as much and possibly even more than I did. She loved strolling around, finding little nooks and crannies and unexpected pleasures. She loved the few remaining wooden stand-alone houses, and she spotted things almost no one else saw or paid attention to: historical plaques on brownstones and tenement buildings, unique moldings and the stray gargoyle, rooftop gardens that could barely been seen from the street, antique glass left in townhouse windows. She was fascinated by the history behind the century-old cast iron figures attached to the fronts of several buildings in the West Village. (They were indications that you had fire insurance; if you were wealthy enough to have a cast iron emblem on your house and your house caught on fire, the fire department would rush to save it. If you didn't have one, you were fresh out of luck and your house would, in all likelihood, burn to the ground without anyone offering to help. I'd bought her two of them for her twenty-eighth birthday and she was as delighted as I'd ever seen her; she told me she knew they'd protect her as well as our home.)

Most of all, Anna loved the little cemetery on West Eleventh Street. It was a tiny plot of land, and the gravestones dated back to the early 1800s. She used to walk by and rest her hands on the metal gate, which was always locked; we never saw it open. She considered it the most peaceful spot in Manhattan. It was a Sephardic Jewish cemetery, but that had no meaning for her; she was thrilled only by the link to the past and the fact that it could survive in the midst of hundreds of years of building and reconstruction and rezoning. She had done some research on the cemetery a few years before and discovered that it was owned by the oldest Jewish congregation in North America. She also learned that in fact there were three Sephardic cemeteries in Manhattan.

One Sunday we had a cemetery date: We started downtown at the oldest one, near Chatham Square in Chinatown. It operated as a cemetery from 1683 until 1828; buried there, among others, are twenty-two veterans of the Revolutionary War and the first American-born rabbi. We then strolled up to the third cemetery (third going chronologically), which is on Twenty-first Street just west of Sixth Avenue. This cemetery opened in 1829; it's jarring to see it today, since it's stuck in between unattractive buildings, looking anonymous and lost. We stopped off and had lunch at Eisenberg's on Fifth Avenue, a classic diner that has not just the best egg creams in the city but also perfect grilled cheese sandwiches, which of course pleased Anna to no end. Anna didn't just like to make grilled cheese sandwiches, she liked to sample the gourmet outside-the-home versions.

After lunch we walked down to her favorite place in the city, the graveyard on Eleventh Street. We stood there for twenty minutes or so and didn't speak much. We thought about the past and the present and let our arms touch as we occasionally swayed back and forth. We held hands. When we did talk, we wondered about the people buried there and if they had any descendants still in New York. This one, the second of the Sephardic cemeteries, opened—if cemeteries open; I guess it's not like movies or plays, although it's the same basic concept—in 1805, and although it was eventually cut back in size, twenty original headstones are still there. The best thing Anna learned about this strange little enclave was that it was originally next to a red brick building that became a Civil War tavern known as the Grapevine. While Union officers drank, Southern spies listened surreptitiously, and thus was born the phrase "I heard it through the grapevine." Anna loved that story. I know that if there were such a thing as a time machine, the first place she would have traveled to would have been the Grapevine, to have a drink and then to linger in front of the West Eleventh Street cemetery.

So when the rabbi at the temple answered the phone and asked what he could do for me, all I could say was "My wife died two days ago and I'd like to have the memorial service in your cemetery."

He was silent for so long that I began babbling. "The thing is, Rabbi, my wife was this really amazing person. And she loved the cemetery on Eleventh Street. The old Sephardic one. I mean, really loved it. She'd walk by it three or four times a week. Not just walk by it, go there specifically to see it. It brought her a certain kind of peace. And . . . and . . . I'm cremating her because that's what I think she would have wanted. I mean, we're too young to have even talked about something like this. And when she got sick she wanted to talk to me about it, but I couldn't bear it. A few days before she died she said, 'You do whatever you want. After I die, whatever happens is for you, not me.' Except I don't want it to be for me. I want this to be for her. And I can't think of anything else to do that would really be for her."

Actually, I think I went on a lot longer than that. But when I eventually did stop, the rabbi said, "So what are you asking, exactly?"

"I . . . I'm asking if you could open the gate. She never saw it open and I don't know if you ever even open it, although I guess you must because somebody has to mow the grass and take care of the flowers and stuff. But—"

"Please," the rabbi said. "Slow down. Take a breath and tell me what you want."

I followed instructions. Took a deep breath. Phil was watching me. He nodded encouragingly. "I want to have the memorial service there. I want to have her friends and family go inside and talk about her in her favorite place. What I'd really like to do is scatter her ashes there, but I understand if you don't want that or if it's forbidden or . . . if it's sacrilegious or something. But I want her to be inside there. Just once if not forever."

"Was your wife Jewish?" he asked.

"Jewish? Um . . . no," I said.

"Are you Jewish?"

"Yes."

"Are you observant?"

"No," I told him. "No, neither of us is religious. Was. I'm sorry, I don't even know what tense to use when I'm talking about her. But we just kind of ignored religion."

I saw Phil roll his eyes. He gave me the thumbs-up sign. Clearly sarcastic.

"You have to understand," I said before the rabbi could respond, "my wife was a really, really good person. I think she was the best person I ever met. And anyone who knew her would tell you the same thing. She was kind and unbelievably smart and I don't think she ever did a mean thing to anybody in her whole life. And she hardly ever asked for anything or inflicted herself on anybody. She was just kind of perfect and . . . and . . . I want to do something really special for her. I just want her to get inside that fucking cemetery, just once, because it's the only thing I can think of that she ever really wanted. Oh shit, I'm sorry. I didn't mean to say 'fucking.' Oh god, I didn't mean to say 'shit,' either, and I'm sorry I said it again and I'm sorry I said 'god.' I'm kind of not myself because Anna, that's my wife, she's only been dead two days, I think I told you that already. I'm sorry. I guess I'm not making a very good case for this. But please. Please. It would be so important to her."

Now Phil had his head in his hands, and he was shaking it back and forth as he held it.

"Are you still there, Rabbi?" I said very quietly into the phone.

"What's your name, son?" he said.

"My name? Heller. Bob Heller."

"Your wife's name was Anna?"

"Yes. Anna Johnson. She didn't change her name to Heller. She didn't believe in changing her name. Maybe that's too much information. Probably it is. I should stop talking so much."

"When would you like for Anna to be inside the cemetery?"

"Really?" I said. "Um . . . I don't know exactly. I think her ashes . . ." At the word "ashes," I started to cry. "I'm sorry," I said. "It's very hard for me to think of her as just ashes."

"Compose yourself," he said. His voice was soothing and rhythmic. "Take your time."

It took longer than I wanted before I could finish my sentence. I tried twice but each time got too choked up to speak. On the third try I finally succeeded: "I think her ashes will be back tomorrow. So maybe the day after that. Just to be, you know, sure."

"What time would you like the gate to be open?" he said.

"Lunchtime," I said. "Around twelve-thirty. That's when she usually went there. I don't know how to thank you. If there's anything I can do—"

"I can't allow you to bury her there, Mr. Heller. Leaving aside the temple's restrictions, it's illegal to bury someone in that ground. The city won't allow it."

"I understand. I wasn't going to bury her. I was thinking of scattering her ashes. I think that's what she would like. To just be present there forever."

"I can't give you permission. Even putting her above the ground, her ashes, is not permissible. But what I will tell you is that during your visit, no one from our congregation will be present. I'll have the gardener open the gate at twelve-thirty. And I'll tell him to leave your group alone for an hour. Is that enough time?"

"Yes. Yes. That's plenty. That's incredibly nice."

"Do you understand what I'm saying to you? Your group will be totally alone, with no supervision."

"Yes. I think so. I don't know what to say."

"That land is extremely important to members of my congregation. We're the oldest Jewish congregation in North American, descendants of Spanish Jews, exiled during the Inquisition."

"I know. I mean, Anna knew. She knew all about you."

"I'm honored that she valued the history and the meaning of this cemetery."

"She did," I said. "She really did. It made her happy that it was there."

"Then we should all be happy that she will be there. Even if it's just once and not forever."

"Well . . . it's very hard for me to think about being happy, Rabbi. Because she was only thirty fucking years old, and from my perspective anything or anybody who decided it was time for her to die is pretty fucking evil. But yes . . . I agree. Theoretically, anyway."

"I suppose this is not the time to have a theological discussion with you."

"No, sir. Not really."

"Well, if you ever have the urge to join a temple, Mr. Heller, you should pay us a visit."

I took another deep breath, this time without being told to do so. I think it was only the second real breath I'd taken since the conversation began. "Okay," I said. "I probably won't have that urge but if I do, sure, I'll pay you a visit."

"I'll look forward to it," he said. "And thank you for calling."

I hung up the phone. Phil looked at me and said, "You are the most unbelievable fucking guy in the whole fucking world."

Two days later, we had the funeral. I carried Anna's ashes, walking from the clinic to the Sephardic cemetery. I went by myself, having convinced Phil and my mother and Marjorie that I wanted to make the stroll alone. It was no easy task—the convincing as well as making my way along the streets carrying the remains of my wife. But it felt right.

I got to Eleventh Street about twelve-fifteen and waited, trying not to focus on anything. It didn't work: Seeing the cemetery, knowing what was about to ensue, my breaths started coming in short, asthmatic gasps. My brain kept telling me to stay calm, but my body wasn't paying any attention. The gardener showed up two or three minutes later. He was Hispanic and didn't say anything to me. He just unlocked the metal gate and walked away. I stepped inside, breathing heavily. I had expected some sort of relief once I put my feet on the hallowed ground, but there wasn't any relief. There was just more pressure on my chest and more sweat dripping down my face and neck. I wanted to do something corny, say something aloud to Anna, but I couldn't. It felt too much like a Steven Spielberg movie as it was. I didn't believe Anna could hear me. I didn't believe her soul was hovering nearby. I didn't believe there was anything left of her except bone fragments and ashes. So I just held those remnants and waited silently.

Five minutes later, Phil and my mother and Marjorie arrived. Moments after that, Ruby Johnson pulled up in a taxi. She was wearing a tight black skirt and a red blouse that revealed too much bosom. Her high heels were too high; she wobbled rather than walked. Her makeup was a bit garish, too red and powdery. Teetering, she stepped through the gate. To nobody in particular, she muttered into the thick air, "Oh my god, this is a place for Jews." Then she came up to me, smiled forlornly, and kissed me gently on the cheek. I could feel that her lipstick had left a smudge and I moved to wipe it off with my hand the moment her sticky lips left my skin.

"I'm sorry," she said.

I nodded.

"I'm sorry for so many things," she said. She didn't say anything else because she glanced to her left and saw Marjorie, who was gripping the handle of a scalpel that she was pulling out of her purse. After that Ruby moved away from me and attached herself to my mother, who assumed the role of saint for the rest of the hour.

By twelve-forty, everyone who'd been invited had shown up: our New York City friends, the patients from the clinic, my brother and nephew. About twenty-five people stood quietly in the little cemetery.

I hadn't actually thought this through. I guess I figured that people would spontaneously step up and begin talking about Anna. But they were all looking at me, waiting for me to lead. I suddenly realized that although I'd kind of rehearsed the service in my head, I hadn't actually linked my thoughts together and had no coherent plan for proceeding. Every time I tried to speak about Anna I burst into tears, another minor obstacle to my preparation and not something I was eager to do at that particular moment.

Phil nodded at me. So did Marjorie. I saw Ruby step forward as if she was going to launch into a tirade, and that provided strong motivation. I immediately cut her off and, still holding the urn, said, "Um . . . I know this will sound strange, but I didn't really prepare anything to say. The thing about my relationship with Anna was that neither of us ever had to prepare anything to say. There was never an awkward moment or an uncomfortable silence. There was never anything fake or pretend between us. And I don't think either of us ever got bored listening to the other person. At least I know *I* didn't. I . . ."

I had to catch my breath, had to blink back tears. I was determined to do this and say what I now realized I needed to say. "I picked this spot because Anna loved it. She didn't actually care what the history was—who's buried here, what the religious significance is, who's allowed in or who's kept out. What she cared about was that it existed. That it survived. Anna was all about protecting things she thought were lovely. Protecting people she cared about. Protecting the world as she saw it and wanted it to be. She was bewildered by meanness and hatred. She didn't understand them. And that's why she loved it here. I didn't think of this until just a few minutes ago, but I think she understood that here there was an end to meanness. An end to hatred. It's a place untouched by time. It's a sad place because it's a place of death. But it's also a hopeful place because it has survived while everything around it has been knocked down, renovated, destroyed. Anna understood that life is all about a combination of hope and sadness. Love and kindness. And endings and forever."

I opened the lid of the urn. "Anna liked to do things she knew she shouldn't do, as long as they were the right things. She never minded pissing people off if she was right. So I'm pretty sure I'm doing the right thing now, for Anna and for me and for everybody here because now she'll be here forever, in this place she loved. How could that be wrong?"

With that, I began to pour her ashes around the cemetery. I scattered them over several gravestones and in the bushes. My wife trickled out of a can like some kind of plant food, which is what, in fact, she was going to be.

Nobody said anything. Ruby was sobbing, loudly and dramatically. Oddly, no one else was crying.

When I was done dispersing the ashes, I said, "I think my wife was perfect. I know I've told some of you that the only thing wrong with our pets is that they don't live as long as we do. It's not fair that she didn't live as long as I will. It's just . . . well . . . it's just plain wrong. And I don't know if I'll ever get over it. But at least now I know I've done something perfect for her. I wish I could have done something perfect for her when she was alive."

With that I sort of smoothed my foot over one small mound of ash. Marjorie stepped forward and said, "You did do something perfect for her when she was alive. You made her happy."

That was when I started to cry again, and Ruby began screaming: "My baby girl, my baby girl!" She keened and bent over as if she were in great pain. My mother stepped forward and kissed me. One by one, everyone else came up to hug or kiss me. We all scanned the cemetery, looking down at the ashes, which were spread as evenly as I could manage.

Several passersby peered in at us from the sidewalk. I think Ruby's wailing kept them on the other side of the fence.

Gradually people filtered out of the cemetery. By the time our allotted hour was over, I was alone again, standing inside the gate, holding an empty urn.

The Hispanic gardener came by exactly at one-thirty. He still didn't say anything, but he didn't have to. I nodded and stepped outside the cemetery. He locked the gate behind me, shook my hand, and left.

I threw the urn into a wire garbage pail on Sixth Avenue and Twelfth Street.

And walked, by myself, back to the clinic and the place where I now lived without Anna.

Most of the people who attended the funeral had come back to the apartment. My mother had thought to order sandwiches and coffee and various desserts, as well as wine and beer. At first everyone ate and drank a little and talked quietly. As time passed, their voices got louder and less solemn. People started telling stories and even laughing. Phil told a story about the first time he met Anna, about giving her two left bowling shoes to wear, and suddenly I was laughing so hard that tears were streaming down my face.

Ruby came over to me. Tentatively, as if I might lash out at her. She stood several inches away, her perfume overpoweringly strong, and for quite a while she said nothing. Finally she spoke: "You think I'm crazy. A lot of people think I'm crazy. Maybe I am. I do a lot of crazy things that hurt a lot of people. I lie about a lot of things and make people very uncomfortable. But I'm going to tell you something. I don't know if you'll believe me, and I guess I don't really care. I'm past the stage of caring about anything very much. But I loved my daughter. I also hated her."

"Please," I said. "I don't want to have this conversation. I really and truly don't."

"I hated her because right from the time she was a little girl, a baby really, she was every single thing I wanted to be but knew I wasn't. She was smart and beautiful and adventurous. And she had a great amount of courage. Oh my Lord, she wasn't afraid of anything or anybody, especially me or her daddy. You were right, what you said in that Jewish cemetery place. If she thought what she was doing was right, nothin' could stop her from doin' it. She was stubborn as a god-damn mule, and mostly what she wanted was to get the hell away from us. Startin' when she was five or six, all she used to talk about was moving moving moving. Goin' someplace we weren't. She was maybe seven when she told us she was gonna fall in love and move to New York and be a big success. Did you know that? Did she ever tell you that?"

I shook my head. "No."

"It's true. I used to tell her when she was a baby that I wanted to live in New York and go to Broadway shows and eat at fancy restaurants. And she used to ask me why I didn't just do it."

"Why didn't you?"

"What I told her was that I was too scared. Me in New York? What the hell would I have been here? I was pretty enough and smart enough for where I was. But here? Uh-uh. I'da been stomped on pretty quick, and I knew it. I didn't have the nerve to do what she did. Ever. She lived the life I wanted to live, so I hated her. But I also loved her for it. And was jealous of her. Envious. Competitive. I wouldn'ta minded if she'd failed, which is a pretty terrible thing to say. But deep down I didn't want her to. I really didn't want her to. I wanted her to get what she finally got. You know—you, all her success. I guess a mom's not supposed to feel any of those things. But I sure did. And I'll tell you something—it was a lot easier than hating myself for not bein' her."

The whole time she spoke, it was in a quiet southern drawl. I had to lean in toward her to hear what she was saying; it was the first time I'd ever heard her speak in anything but a bellow.

After she finished, I looked at her for a long time without saying a word. For once I wasn't seeing her through Anna's eyes, and suddenly she didn't look like a monster. She looked like what she was: a sad, lonely, destructive woman who had no real place left in the world.

So when I finally gathered myself to speak, I said, just as quietly as she had spoken, "I think in a lot of ways you killed your daughter. She tried so hard not to be you that it did her in. But I heard what you said, and I'm pretty sure I know why you said it. So I want you to know: I don't hate you."

She stared at me. Her black eyes flared, then turned cold again.

"That's why you told me all that, isn't it?" I said. "Because I'm your only link to your daughter and you don't want me to hate you. So you can go home and find some small bit of peace and tell yourself whatever it is you're gonna have to tell yourself to keep on going. Well, it worked. I don't like you, but I don't hate you, either. Not anymore."

She dropped her stare and looked away. Then she raised her head again.

"Can I call you from time to time? Or maybe drop you an e-mail? So I can just see how you're doing?"

I nodded. I couldn't believe I did, but I definitely nodded.

And then she went back from whence she came.

Everybody else did, too. People got back to their lives fairly quickly. Phil went back upstate, after telling me that he knew I was going to be fine because I was sad. The clinic regulars brought me food—pastas and cakes, mostly; Goldie, a tiny woman, several inches under five feet tall, and perhaps the jolliest woman who ever lived, and who had the largest and most languid Great Dane imaginable, brought over a week's supply of beef stew and approximately two tons of mashed potatoes. But the visits and the food and the forced companionship only lasted a week or so. For the most part, acquaintances and clients soon stopped asking me how I was doing and went back to being more concerned about their Peanut Butters and Carmelos and their Loveys. Which was all as it should have been. Life goes on. I understood that, and I found it vaguely reassuring.

When Teddy and Hilts left to go back to L.A., Hilts gave me a quick hug. He didn't linger, probably because Teddy was watching. Teddy also gave me a quick hug. He didn't linger either, but of course there was no reason for him to. Then he gave our mom a kiss good-bye, though he didn't say anything to go along with the kiss. Hilts kissed her, too, and to my surprise, he hugged her quite fiercely. She loved it, of course, and smiled in a way I'd rarely seen her smile. For whatever reason, she loved this little boy. And he knew it. And he responded to it. I don't think anyone else had ever loved him without wanting something in return.

That hug Hilts gave my mother was the first genuine thing I'd seen him do since he'd come to New York, and it made me think there might be hope for us all.

From the *New York Daily Examiner:*

ASK DR. BOB

Dr. Robert Heller is one of New York's leading veterinarians. He is the author of two books about taking care of pets, *They Have Nothing but Their Kindness* and the fleeting *New York Times* best seller *More Than Human*. He is also a regular on the *Today* show with his weekly segment, "The Vetting Zoo." Dr. Bob takes care of cats, dogs, horses, birds, snakes, turtles, frogs, fish, snails, small pigs, and many varieties of rodents. You can e-mail him at AskDrBob@NYDE.com and ask him any question about the animal you love. His column runs Tuesdays and Thursdays in NYC's most popular newspaper.

Dear Dr. Bob:

People write to you about such a wide variety of pet topics, I felt it was all right for me to ask you about something that might seem silly: pet plastic surgery.

My five-year-old boxer, Smokin' Joe, had mouth cancer and, as a result, lost a piece of his jaw. He's a wonderful guy, as friendly as a dog can be, but because of this deformity, I've noticed, some people shy away from him on the street, especially children. It makes him look mean or dangerous, I guess, and of course he's neither. But, as with people, looks can be deceiving. His vet mentioned to me that there is such a thing these days as dog plastic surgery. Is this something I should consider? My sister had a nose job when she was sixteen years old, so I suppose it's okay for a dog to have cosmetic surgery on his jaw, no?

—Smokin' Joe's Dad

Dear Dad:

This is indeed a tough one. Ultimately, you will have to make the decision based on your level of comfort with Smokin' Joe's appearance and Joe's own level of ease with the way people respond to him. But this is my thinking: Everyone has some kind of scar—it's simply a question of how many we get and how we bounce back from them. Some scars are on the surface. Some disappear quickly. Some linger before fading. But every time we're nicked and scarred, we're altered. It doesn't mean we're a lesser or better version of ourselves, but we are different. As for Smokin' Joe . . . I don't think having a reconstructed jaw will make a difference to him. He probably knows what he is and can live with it. If it makes a difference to you, then go for the plastic surgery. The truth will remain the same—as will Joe—whichever way you go.

—Dr. Bob

CHAPTER 8

PAIGE MACKENZIE

Paige was sixty-eight years old when she first brought her long-haired dachshund to me. She had just come from an audition for a Broadway revival of Where's Charley? She explained that she'd gone on an equity "cattle call," as it's known—every stage show in New York is required to have an open call for anyone with an Actors' Equity card so that, ostensibly, any actor in the city has a fair shot to get a role. Paige said the role she'd tried out for was an ingénue in her young twenties and claimed that she was perfect for it. When I hesitantly asked her if perhaps she was just a tad too old for that particular part, she was not at all offended. Instead, she looked at me as if I were a naïve and innocent rube and said, "When they say twenty, they really mean forty. Experience is the greatest requirement for any role in the theater." I said, "Okay," and refrained from pointing out that she was quite a few years past forty.

I saw Paige again several months later; her dachshund was suffering from arthritis. I asked her if she'd gotten the part. She looked at me, bewildered. I said, "Where's Charley? The ingénue." And she said, "Dear boy, that was dozens of auditions ago. Try to keep up."

I learned that Paige went to at least three auditions per week—Broadway, off-Broadway, touring companies, summer stock. Mostly for parts for which she had absolutely no shot. She went to open calls for the parts of Anita in West Side Story, the oldest daughter in The Sound of Music, and for one of the backup singers in Dreamgirls. (I couldn't help myself when I heard about that one and pointed out to Paige that she was most definitely a Caucasian. She acknowledged the accuracy of my comment but said she still felt the part was within her range.) Over time, I came to understand that she had not landed a part in over forty years but still considered herself a working actress. Clearly Paige didn't know—or refused to accept—the difference between auditioning and actually working. She spoke happily about showing up at a theater, presenting herself to a director or casting person, and being rejected out of hand. She described these experiences in such glowing terms that I began to think of them as successful ventures for her. Periodically I had to catch myself and recall that I was talking to a woman who existed in a world far removed from reality.

I went to Paige's apartment once when she had pneumonia and couldn't bring Molloy, her dachshund, in for his shots. She lived in the smallest studio apartment I've ever seen. In the main room there was space for a single bed, a chair, a rug that was maybe two feet by four, the dog, and five-foot-high stacks of Playbills. The kitchen was built into the wall of her one room and consisted of a tiny stove, a small sink, and two shelves above that, which were eighty percent filled with cans of dog food.

I asked how she—Paige—was feeling, but she wouldn't acknowledge being under the weather. She said she was trying to get as much rest as possible because she was going to an audition the next day for a revival of 42nd Street. She told me that she'd bought a tap dance lesson DVD and had been watching it over and over again so she could be certain to get her moves right.

I asked her if she'd ever tap-danced before and she said, "Dear boy, all movement comes naturally to me."

I made her a cup of tea before I left. When I handed it to her she clutched at my sleeve and said, "I know you think I'm a silly old woman."

I shook my head and assured her that I didn't find her silly at all.

"It's all right," she said. "I don't mind. Offstage, it doesn't matter how silly I seem. It's onstage that matters. That's when I can be anything I want to be."

"What do you most want to be?" I asked her.

Her eyes flew around the room and she said, "Anything else, dear boy.
Anything else."

A few weeks after the funeral, life returned to something like normal,
minus one crucial ingredient: Anna.

I carried on, as people do. I went back to work, I grieved, I fell into
a regular, if different, routine. The grief eventually turned from a stabbing pain into a dull ache and then into a small, private throb, like a
separate heartbeat, that was mostly quiet and benign except when it
suddenly exploded. The explosions became less and less common over
time.

After I met Elizabeth Gold, Anna began to recede even more. She
was always present, always a part of me, and I never wanted to let
go of her. But she became more a part of my memory and less a part
of my present. Except for one day: the day I was at the hotel in Miami
and Anna called me and a woman answered the phone and said I'd
checked out. The day Anna called me to say her stomach hurt. The day
we found out she was going to die. That day lived inside me always,
the images and the conversations playing over and over and over
again, not just inside my brain but inside my gut. Even during the time
I spent with Elizabeth, that day was never far away from my very core.

And then Camilla Hayden walked into the clinic with a three-year-
old alley cat named Rags. Camilla Hayden didn't like cats, especially
this one. It wasn't hers; she was cat-sitting in exchange for an apartment in the city. She wasn't happy to be spending money to help a cat
she didn't like and that wasn't even hers. She particularly didn't like
seeing a vet in the late afternoon on a day when she was supposed to
be drinking with a friend from Holland who was in for one day. And
she even more particularly didn't like seeing the vet who wrote the
Ask Dr. Bob column, because she had a friend whose ex-boyfriend had
written a letter to me two years before and I'd told him, in print, that
either his girlfriend needed a change of attitude or he needed a new
girlfriend, and he'd apparently agreed with me because he dumped the
girlfriend soon after that. That's why her first words to me were "Oh

my god, you're *that* Dr. Bob! I've been wanting to tell you for two years what an asshole you are."

She was angry and aggressive and agitated. Her foot tapped impatiently, and she checked her BlackBerry for messages almost every minute she was in the clinic. When she wasn't checking for messages, she was swearing at the fact that she couldn't get a signal to get her messages. She had cuts on her hands, although her fingers were noticeably delicate and her fingernails were perfectly manicured. Her hair was dirty blond, shaped to be practical rather than stylish. She wore a blouse that was oddly frilly—it didn't match her agitated personality at all—along with boots and a short skirt. Her skin was remarkably white, her nose was a bit flat, her ears were small, and her eyes were large, and deep blue and irresistible. She didn't smile with her mouth, she smiled with her eyes. Taken individually, her features shouldn't have worked. But they did. Her beauty took my breath away. It turned out she was English; she spoke with a well-educated, upper-crusty accent. I thought she was captivating if vaguely terrifying.

She complained so much about missing her one opportunity to have drinks with her Dutch friend that when I finished examining her cat—who had gastritis, which was why he'd been vomiting and not eating; I explained that she needed to put him on a fast for several days, giving him only small amounts of liquid, even just an ice cube to lick periodically, and ease him onto a diet of chicken or turkey with rice and chicken broth, all of which she should cook for him; I also told her that she should bring Rags back to see me in five days, which produced another outburst of foul and abusive language—I asked her if she'd like to have a drink with me.

It wasn't exactly a James Bond moment. Even considering the natural difficulty of transitioning from talking about feline gastritis to asking her out, the pivot was not super cool. It wasn't "So I know a great little bar where we can get martinis and talk." It was more like "Um . . . Don't get offended by this or anything, but . . . I mean, since you're new here and maybe don't know that many people . . . and since you had to miss your Dutch friend . . . could I maybe take you out for a drink? I'll understand if you can't, don't worry, I just thought

I'd offer." Actually, I think I'm downplaying how ridiculously stiff and pathetic this was as far as drink invitations go.

She laughed, rather harshly. "Do I look like someone who doesn't know people? I know *too* many people here."

I backtracked immediately. "Sorry. I didn't mean to offend you."

That seemed to offend her even more. "You didn't offend me."

"Oh. Good. You just seem kind of angry or hostile or something."

"I'm not angry or hostile. I just don't want to have a drink."

I didn't mean to look quite as crushed as I suppose I did. But maybe my obvious disappointment was a good thing, because when she saw the look in my eyes, she took a leisurely step back, swaying on her right leg, and said, "But I could meet you around eight o'clock if you want to take me to dinner instead. And you're really going to have to take me because your fee for looking at this fucking cat is pretty much my meal money for the rest of the week."

I said that seemed reasonable.

She tugged at the sleeve of her frilly blouse, something I came to learn was a nervous habit of hers. She tugged and fiddled with anything she could. Her hair. Her fingers. Her clothing. I can't tell you why, but watching her restless, very elegant fingers made me smile. Their perpetual movement, so incongruous with her tough veneer, hinted at some very difficult-to-reach vulnerability.

I realized that she was looking me over and studying me as carefully as I was her. Her gaze made me uncomfortable; her eyes had a natural taunt to them. I hadn't done anything to make her taunt me, at least not that I was aware of. But then I got the overwhelming feeling that this was not about anything specific; this stranger seemed to be challenging my whole way of life. I had a brief flash of Anna: In our entire life together, she had never looked at me in such a way. Nor had Elizabeth. Even when she was in full academic mode, I never got the sense that Elizabeth was judging me, only that she wanted to help and support and understand me.

I opened my mouth to say to Camilla Hayden, "I just remembered, I can't do dinner tonight." I knew that was the right thing to say and do. I should go home, call Elizabeth, who was up in Cornell, and listen to her tell me about her day. Then I should feed the menagerie, take whoever needed walking out for a walk, and read or do the crossword puzzle or watch a DVD. I didn't need a complication in my life, especially not a complication I found both extremely off-putting and overwhelmingly attractive. So I was a little startled when what actually came out of my mouth was "Do you like Italian?"

I was even more surprised when she said, "No," and then waited for me to say something in response. When I didn't, she laughed again, this time less harshly, and flipped her hair and said, "I'll meet you here at eight-thirty. Try to come up with something better by then."

Then she picked up the cat she didn't like and was gone.

Within a minute, Lucy came back to my examining room. She didn't say anything. She just looked me over and nodded.

"What?" I asked.

"Nothing," she said. "I just wanted to make sure you were all right."

She went back to the reception desk. I was well aware that I hadn't answered her nonquestion.

How could I? I wasn't at all sure of the answer.

I was outside my clinic at eight twenty-five and waited for Camilla Hayden for twenty minutes. At eight forty-five she came careening around the corner, talking on her cell phone, walking fast, kind of barreling down Greenwich Avenue. She walked as if she were playing football (or, considering her nationality, rugby): ready, it seemed, to shove anyone who got in her way onto the sidelines. She looked agitated; she seemed to always look agitated. But when she was about half a block away, she glanced up, saw me, smiled, and waved. Her teeth were brilliantly white, and her smile lit up the whole block. Her wave was not a rugby player's wave; it was a little girl's wave. It indicated delight, and her delight filled me with a strange joy. From that moment on, after that one early glimpse of the person beneath the protective veneer, my one overriding desire when I was around Camilla was to bring that person back to the surface and to make it possible for that to be her natural state.

Thinking back, what I most wanted with Anna was always to be worthy of her. I loved her almost religiously, and I always strove to match her kind of perfection. She, of course, would never have thought of herself as worthy of such devotion, and if she had, she would never have used it to her advantage in our relationship. With Elizabeth, it was more as if I never wanted to disappoint her. She saw things in terms of rules and the need to adhere to those rules. An academician to her very core, she saw life in terms of grades; a slip in standards or a lazy moment or an inability to live up to a promise could damage one's final report card.

To my way of thinking, I failed in my attempts to be worthy of both women. Maybe that is the key to human relationships: We pick impossible goals, try to fulfill them, and when we fail we wait to see if the center will still hold.

Camilla's flash of delight had dissipated by the time she reached me on the street. Whoever she was talking to on the phone had aggravated it away.

Standing a foot or two from me, she chattered on for another minute, kept saying into her cell, "I have to go . . . I have to go . . . I really must hang up . . ." When she finally did hang up, she smiled brightly again and said, "I'm starving."

"I've narrowed it down to Indian or Japanese," I told her.

"Japanese," she said. "Sushi. I'm trying to be healthy. Been drinking way too much, so I'm off alcohol for a few weeks. I love all those *dosas* and things but too much starch. Let's do sushi."

So we walked to a great sushi place on Sixth Avenue that I'd read about. I could eat sushi every day, but since Anna didn't like it, we never went to Japanese restaurants. Once Elizabeth came into the picture, I never suggested sushi because . . . well, it somehow seemed as if I were cheating on Anna. I wasn't ready for the freedom of going someplace I wanted to go; more accurately, I wasn't ready for the pleasure it would bring me. (It doesn't really make much sense, I know, but this is the way it works when your wife dies at age thirty-one.) As a result, it had been nearly thirteen years since I'd gone to a Japanese restaurant, and it was kind of thrilling to be walking casually down the street with a beautiful woman to go eat raw fish. At the same time, I felt sad. And guilty. It was a complicated five-block walk.

That entire dinner was fairly complicated. There was a fascinating inconsistency to Camilla. As soon as we sat down, she asked if we could order a bottle of sake.

"Of course," I said. "But I thought you weren't drinking."

"Oh, fuck it," she said. "You can't eat sushi at a place like this without a good bottle of sake."

I shrugged agreeably and ordered a good bottle. (I knew nothing about good or bad sake but the waitress seemed to, so I let her pick. Judging from the satisfied look on Camilla's face after her first sip, the waitress knew what she was doing.)

I'd never seen anyone eat the way Camilla did. Anna had a superb palate and she understood the science of food—what made something sweet, which ingredients dominated a dish, what seasoning needed to be added to put the food world in perfect harmony. She appreciated food on a high level, but it was not a love of hers—other than her precious grilled cheese sandwiches, which brought her to a nearly rapturous state. Elizabeth was no kind of foodie: She saw meals as a break from daily life rather than a part of life, and she cared less about what she ate than maintaining some kind of order and striking the right kind of balance with where and how she ate. As with most things, Elizabeth saw food in terms of purity and structure. But that first night, Camilla ate with such glee and satisfaction that it was a little bit like stumbling upon an elegant soft-core porn movie on late-night cable. As she bit into her toro and yellowtail and giant clam, she would roll her eyes and moan quietly and lick her fingers and take a sip of cold sake and look at me with a kind of wonder and say, "This is *so* good!" I think she spoke to me chiefly to remind herself that she was not the only person in the restaurant. That's the way she ate: as if no one else was anywhere near her and she was in her own little chamber of sensual delight. But then, in between tastes, she would switch gears completely and go back to having a normal conversation. At least until she'd take another bite of something that really struck her fancy, at which point she'd get distracted and drift off into a few more moments of food ecstasy.

I watched, a bit awestruck, as she made her way through several courses and, between moans, told me pieces of her life story. That night I heard only the bare bones of the story, as it turned out. That was another contradiction hardwired into her being: She wasn't just a genuine intellectual who happened to be the most sensual person I'd ever met, she was also reticent to the point of catatonia about revealing anything personal. But she also had a healthy enough ego that once she got going, she held nothing back. And when she did, she demanded full attention and comprehension.

If Cammy—yes, I did eventually call her that; I got a lot of resistance, but she succumbed with a certain amount of embarrassed enjoyment—told you something about herself that she considered important or personal, run for cover if you either forgot the details or didn't take the revelation seriously or used it against her to make a point at some later date. The rage that would emerge was both scathing and a bit terrifying. Not terrifying because of the damage she could do to others (although she could certainly do that), but because of the damage you could see she was doing to herself. That was another compelling and bewildering divide in her character: I had met few people who cared as deeply as Camilla did about humanity on both a grand and an individual scale. Yet I had never encountered anyone who could be so hurtful and deadly cold to people she cared about. Her insistence on seeking the truth about others could cut to the bone. Her fear of dealing with certain truths about herself could engender a fierce and often devastating response.

But that finger-licking, sake-drinking night, I didn't see rage or contradictions or anything else that might have given me pause. I saw a spectacular woman who enthralled me with her manner and her stories.

Cam was English, London-born. Her parents were well-to-do but not upper class. They could afford a spacious flat in the city, as well as a small cottage in Sussex, where they spent happy weekends together. That was all I heard about her family that first night. I poked a little, as is my wont, but got no deeper than that. I also listened carefully as she spilled all the details of her academic and professional life. She'd left England—again, no details on the circumstances—to come to New York when she was eighteen. She went to Columbia University and then to Columbia's med school.

When Camilla told me she was a doctor, she gave me a funny look. That hint of a challenge came into her eyes, though I wasn't exactly sure what she was challenging. For an instant her expression made me shrink back; then the look was gone. Reflecting on the moment later, I thought I'd imagined it, because she plowed ahead with her story without hesitation. But I hadn't. I definitely hadn't.

By the time she graduated from med school she loved New York and wanted to stay. She was able to because she got accepted for her residency at Lenox Hill Hospital, on East Seventy-seventh Street. She lived in a tiny studio apartment way the hell out in Brooklyn and spent the next three years learning how to be a doctor. She specialized in family medicine; she wanted to be an old-fashioned GP, helping people who might not have health insurance, healing poor people who might not otherwise heal. Having a purpose in life was important to Camilla (as long as the purpose was outside of England, a place to which she most definitely did not want to return). The passion behind her words as she described her sense of purpose was a wonderful thing to behold.

When she finished her residency, she felt strongly that she had to get out of New York. She was afraid—although she would never have used that word—of falling into the various traps New York can set: success, status, money, and all the other seductions that didn't sit well with her desire to have a purposeful life. She wanted to escape New York for personal reasons as well, she said, although when I pressed her about what those were she just waved me away, as if I were interrupting her story for unimportant, meaningless details. That, too, became a familiar trait: Anytime Camilla didn't want to deal with something, she would simply dismiss it as unimportant.

She spent a year in the ER at Lenox Hill, a necessary prerequisite to getting a job with Doctors Without Borders, or, as she said in perfect French, Médecins sans Frontières. It was simple, she said: She wanted to help people and figured that MSF would be the best way to do that. So they sent her to North Kivu, in the Congo, where a war had—and has—been raging for several years (that night, I didn't tell Cammy that I had never actually heard of North Kivu; I certainly had heard of the Congo, although I couldn't have told you exactly where it was).

She took a deep breath before continuing with this part of the story, and then she rushed through it.

"With MSF, they ask what you want to specialize in. You can go to areas with infectious diseases or places where starvation and malnutrition are the most important issues or go to natural disasters. I asked for armed conflict."

"Jesus. Why?"

She waved me off again. It wasn't important. At least it wasn't important that she tell me that first night. With Cam, you had to earn the right to hear the important stuff. It was a question of trust: She had to trust you to understand. And she had to trust herself enough to tell the truth.

"I was sent to the Rutshuru region. They had a hospital there. My first day, seventy-eight people were carried in, and all of them required emergency surgery. The second week, one of the doctors I was working with was killed. Blown up by a grenade."

I said her name—"Cam"—and reached for her hand. The move was instinctive; I wanted to offer her a comforting touch, and that was all. It didn't provide much comfort, apparently, because she quickly jerked her hand away—it was as if I'd burned her instead of gently patted her. She looked down, embarrassed for a moment, then said, "Can we get some more sake?"

I ordered a half bottle this time, and we drank it fairly quickly while she told me more about her life in the Congo: how she got to love her translators, the people she cared for, and the doctors; how she was caught in several battles and watched people get shot while standing next to her. She told the whole story very evenly but at the same time with obvious anger and a deep, lurking emotion. And just as suddenly as she'd begun, she decided the time for personal revelation was over. The challenge I'd seen in her eyes earlier returned.

"Why do you do what you do?" she asked.

"I'm not sure I understand the question."

Her anger was under control but still evident, hidden but ever so present. "Why do you waste your talent?"

"You want to think about phrasing that a little differently?"

"No. You have all this medical skill, all this knowledge. And all your effort is spent on . . . creatures. There are all these people in pain and you take care of cats." The contempt practically dripped out of her when she said the word "cats."

I didn't answer. I was trying to control my own anger. But I was also trying to formulate an answer.

Before I came up with anything, though, she said, "I can't be the first person who ever asked you this."

"You are, actually," I told her.

"Amazing." For the first time, I heard a vague slur in her speech. The sake had caught up with her.

"Not really," I said. "Most people I talk to aren't as positive as you are that they're the only ones who know exactly what's right."

"I am right," she said.

"You go into the jungle and stitch people up who've been blown to pieces. And what happens?"

"They go on living."

"They go back outside and get blown to pieces again. You fix people so they can go right back out and get killed in a different way. You don't think that's a waste of talent and knowledge? I have respect for what you've done. I respect anyone who spends his or her life being unselfish. But everyone has a different reason for doing what they do. I don't know what your reason is. Maybe you think you're really making a difference. Maybe you just like to see people blown up. Maybe it's a lot easier when you don't have to see people again after you've done your job, when you don't have to see what happens to them."

"That's why you stitch up cute little kittens?"

"I like cute little kittens. They don't bullshit themselves, like most of the people I know. But mostly, when I fix them, they stick around and bring a lot of pleasure to the people who brought them to me."

She stared at me. Not angry. Mostly just curious now.

"Do you really believe all that?"

"No," I said. "Well, sometimes. I think the reasons people do things are never as simple as what we tell ourselves they are."

"Let's go," she said. "Let's get out of here."

I walked her home. The apartment she was staying in was on Twelfth Street, almost to the Hudson River. I asked her whose place it was and all she said was "Just someone I know."

"The person with the cat."

"Yes. The goddamn cat."

We didn't say much else during the walk. She seemed lost in thought. I assumed her thoughts were about her friend who got blown up by a grenade and the people she knew who were shot. Or maybe they were about the people who brought me cute little puppies to be neutered or rabbits to have their ear infections checked out. I was kind of pre-occupied myself. Mostly I was thinking about how I'd probably never see her again. But when we got to the front of the apartment building she said, "Thank you. That was an amazing dinner. I loved it."

"I'm glad. I did, too."

"Even though I was so rude to you?"

"You weren't rude. You were just . . ."

". . . incredibly insulting?"

"Yeah. Okay. That's a fair assessment. But yes. Even though."

I was about to make a bumbling attempt to see if we could have another dinner sometime soon, but before I could say another word she asked if I wanted to come in for a drink. I hesitated and she shrugged her shoulders; apparently she couldn't care less if I came in or not. She took a step toward the building door and then, much to my surprise, I went, "I'd love to come in."

She turned back toward me and nodded, not at all surprised. If anything, perhaps, just a touch satisfied.

I followed her in. The apartment was a simple but well-appointed one-bedroom. The furniture was neutral, but there were some personal touches and surprisingly feminine decorations that had to be Cam's and gave the place real charm. Considering how beautiful she was, I don't know why I kept being surprised at how much "girl" was still in Cam. It seemed much more normal for her to be talking about rebels being blown up in Kivu than for her to coo over a perfect rose in a vase—she liked the idea of a single perfect flower more than a lush bouquet—or a photo of a sunset that she'd taken from her building's rooftop. And yet she swerved back and forth between the two extremes, equally comfortable with both.

She poured each of us a glass of white wine. We didn't speak at all— she seemed distracted and I couldn't come up with anything to say. My mind was racing for a subject that would engage her. Her cat's flatulence? No. (Although Rags did greet me like a long-lost friend when we walked in the door—I don't think he got a lot of attention from his new sitter.) My various animals? Uh-uh. My dead wife? A definite pass. The relationship I'd been in for the last few years? Nope. Weather, politics, art? No, no, no. Panicking, I was just about to back-track to the whole sushi conversation when she put her glass down, leaned forward, grabbed the back of my head, and kissed me. Not a soft, gentle kiss. This was passionate. Almost desperate. And I matched her desperation—more than matched it—when I returned the kiss.

In an instant she was clawing at me and I was clawing right back and we were both moaning and gasping, although hers were raw and animal-like and coming from an erotic place deep inside her, while I have a feeling mine sounded as if they were coming through the rusty throat of a long-dormant robot. She stood up to lead me to the bed-room and I stood up to follow, then she grabbed me and wrapped her legs around my waist. I carried her like that—something I'd always fantasized about but figured that because I wasn't actually the young Jack Nicholson in *Five Easy Pieces* or Ryan Gosling in what I imag-ined to be his real life, I'd never get to do—into the bedroom, where we ripped our clothes off and fell onto the bed. We were kissing and grabbing as wildly as if we'd just survived a shipwreck, found our-selves on a desert island, and were making love to reassure ourselves that we were indeed alive.

I had never experienced anything remotely like it. On my part, it was a combination of overpowering lust and a sudden letting go after years of holding myself back. In a single great rush, I cast aside the over-whelming horror of Anna's death, my ensuing grief, my slow recovery, and my gentle nurturing back to health by Elizabeth. There was noth-ing gentle about this, nothing sad. There were no thoughts running through my head, no guilt or tenderness; there was nothing but abso-lute desire. It was savage and almost violent in its intensity, and although I understood that the intensity had been initiated by her, I was thrilled to be overwhelmed by it. Before we were done making love I thought my heart might burst, literally and figuratively.

I didn't know what was causing the frenzy within Camilla. She seemed almost in a dreamlike state, part lioness and part kitten. She started out so aggressively, scratching my back, biting me, telling me to pull her hair, which I did and which felt insanely sexy—silken and rough at the same time—in my hands, then making me tell her over and over again how much I wanted to fuck her, which I did until I was screaming the words "I want to fuck you!" at the top of my lungs. Then as we thrashed around naked on her bed she became more and more passive, speaking quietly, almost in the voice of a small child, asking if I wanted to spank her, asking if I wanted to tie her up, demanding answers, insisting I tell her what I would do to her and what my fantasies were, then begging me to go inside her—but the way she said it, her voice was trembling and I didn't know if this was a game or if she was suddenly afraid or if this was just another strange way of controlling the situation she was in. It didn't really matter. Whatever she wanted, I did. She insisted on climbing on top of me, lunging up and down while I was inside her, and she came first, shaking as she did, shuddering, her entire body in spasm. I was desperate to explode but she wouldn't let me; she wouldn't (or couldn't) move and she just stayed on top of me, squeezing me tightly, and whimpered, "No, no, stay still, don't move." She grabbed my face, holding me down, as if she were going to smother me with a pillow, but she just wanted peace after the violence of her orgasm. I lay as still as I could, my chest heaving, trying to control my breathing. I tried to speak but she shook her head crazily back and forth. She wanted silence to go with the peace. So I stayed silent until some form of life came back into her eyes. Then she rolled over to lie next to me, pulled me gently on top of her, put me inside her, and we rocked together very slowly at first, then faster, and faster still and then I was done. I collapsed on top of her, sweating profusely, sopping wet and spent.

She only let me stay there for a few seconds; then she pushed me off, not with any great force but making it clear that I wasn't welcome. Our intimacy began to fracture immediately, but I wanted that closeness more than I'd wanted anything in a long time. So even as I toppled off beside her, still breathing heavily, I reached over to wrap my arm around her and hug her, to bring our bodies together, but she burst into tears and turned away from me. Startled, I asked her what was wrong, but she wouldn't answer or look at me. I sat up, watching her for a long while. Her eyes were closed but she wasn't sleeping. The tears were still coming. I tried stroking her beautiful bare back—her skin was achingly smooth—but she jerked away. Moments later I put my hand on her hair and ran my fingers gently along her dark blond strands. That seemed to please her. Although I got no reaction, when I stopped doing it she reached for my hand, still not looking at me, and placed it on the side of her head.

I combed through and stroked Camilla's hair for what must have been half an hour. Before she fell asleep, I whispered into her ear, "That was amazing. I love making love to you." I could see and feel her stiffen, and in a muffled, icily dismissive tone, the anger seeping out of her once again, she said, "We didn't make love. We fucked." I started to say something, but the harshness of her words left me speechless. I wondered if she was lying next to me, eyes closed, hating me. I wondered what she was going to say to me next. Tell me to get the hell out? Tell me I was an asshole to think this was anything but a one-night stand? And then I realized she wasn't going to tell me anything: She'd fallen sound asleep.

I, on the other hand, was wide awake. Her words had stung and bewildered me. I didn't have a clue what to do. I was fairly certain she would leap up and scream if she woke to find me next to her in bed in the morning, but the thought of leaving was unbearable. More than anything I wanted to touch her again, to feel her lovely smooth skin against mine, to kiss her gently and then passionately and taste her tongue in my mouth again, pressing her as close to me as our sweaty bodies could get.

Instead, I slid off the bed so as not to disturb her. Pulled my clothes on. Found a piece of paper and a pen, and left a note on her kitchen counter that was as far from doing justice to the few hours we'd just spent together as any note in the history of the written word. "I wanted to stay but wasn't sure if you wanted me to," I wrote. "I hope to see you soon. Thanks. P.S. I think Rags is doing better already."

Then I walked the five or six blocks back to my apartment, careening dizzily between elation and despair. I wasn't in bed more than a few minutes when my phone rang. I jumped for it, thinking it might be Cam—but of course she didn't even have my number. It was Elizabeth.

"I've been calling you all night," she said. "You didn't answer your cell."

"I . . . I turned it off, I guess," I told her. "I'm sorry. I was out to dinner."

"I'm glad you're home. I worry about you. You know, the crazy city and all that."

"You shouldn't worry," I said quietly.

"I can't help it. Who'd you have dinner with?"

"A new patient," I said.

"Really? That's so unlike you."

"I know, but . . . he was a really nice guy and didn't know anybody in town."

"What's his name?"

I felt myself getting in deeper and deeper. "Kevin."

"I'm stunned. A new friend for Dr. Bob."

"Maybe," I said. "We'll see."

"But you had a good time?"

"Yeah. You know, nothing special. But yeah, it was fine."

"Well, I'm glad you're home. Sleep well and I'll talk you to in the morning."

Of course she would: We spoke on the phone nearly every morning. Even if we'd talked right before going to bed the night before. There was never any purpose; it was just a routine we'd fallen into. *Did you sleep well? . . . What's your day like? . . . Did you hear about the earthquake in Afghanistan? . . . Okay, we'll talk later.*

"Okay," I said. "And you, too. Sleep well."

"Bob," she said, "are you all right?"

"I'm fine," I told her. "Talk to you in the morning."

We each hung up. I lay in my bed with the light on, staring up the ceiling, feeling Camilla on me. Tasting her.

Wave clambered onto the bed and slung her long, reddish-brown body next to mine. Rocky seemed a little distant, but eventually he hopped up, too, and curled into a ball on my chest, his paws stretched out to rest on the Irish setter's head.

The other animals slept or played somewhere nearby. I heard the shuffling of some paper, probably Margo, finding a new toy-that-wasn't-supposed-to-be-a-toy.

I could smell Camilla—she was in my pores, in my mouth, on my skin—as I closed my eyes. And for the first time in nearly fifteen years, I fell asleep without touching, thinking of, or crying about Anna.

From the *New York Daily Examiner:*

Dr. Robert Heller is one of New York's leading veterinarians. He is the author of two books about taking care of pets, *They Have Nothing but Their Kindness* and *More Than Human,* and is a regular on the *Today* show with his weekly segment, "The Vetting Zoo." Dr. Bob takes care of cats, dogs, horses, birds, snakes, turtles, frogs, fish, snails, small pigs, and many varieties of rodents. You can e-mail him at AskDrBob@NYDE. com and ask him any question about the animal you love. His column runs Tuesdays, Thursdays, and Sundays in the tristate area's most popular newspaper.

Dear Bob:

I'm twenty-two years old and have my first serious boyfriend. I have had cats my entire life, and although I live in a studio apartment in Williamsburg—the first time I've lived on my own—I still have three of them. I love having them, and I think of them as my children. My boyfriend, Fred, thinks that I have way too much of an emotional investment in my cats. He thinks that I don't pay enough attention to him and he thinks it's because I'm too afraid to make a commitment to a human being, as compared to a much less complicated entanglement with my feline babies. Being attached to another person is indeed much more complicated for me. More painful, more time-consuming, more dangerous. My question is: Is it worth it? I get a lot out of my relationships with Tater, Gabby, and Glory. Do we really get so much more love and satisfaction from human beings that it's worth all the problems that come with those relationships? Thank you for your time and consideration.

—Tempted to Stick with Cats

Dear Tempted:

I don't know. I think so. I hope—for your sake, my sake, and everyone's sake—that we do. But I don't know.

—Dr. Bob

CHAPTER 9

ROSY AND MIKE APPESIN

They often came in together with Strudel, their basset hound. Sometimes they even came with their grown children, Micheline and Audrey. For Rosy and Mike, a visit to the clinic was a family affair. They lived in a small Archie Bunker–type house in Queens, but the dog came to work in the Village every day with her doting owners, and that's how they wound up at our clinic on Greenwich Avenue.

    Even before I arrived, Rosy and Mike had been seeing Marjorie Paws for two decades. Prior to Strudel they'd had Glinda, also a basset hound, and Juliet, a cocker spaniel. When I first met Rosy and Mike, she was in her early sixties and he was five or so years older. He was Armenian and spoke with a growling accent; she was a typical Jewish mother and wife from Long Island. When we weren't talking about Strudel's health issues, we were talking about her hairdresser (who drove her crazy but whom she'd gone to for eleven years), or her favorite Chinese restaurant, or his obsession with the local laundromat and their tendency to put too much starch in his shirts. They owned a stationery store a block from the clinic; Anna and I were good customers, buying paper and pens and whatever else we needed, and Lucy bought all our office supplies there, too. Rosy and Mike always insisted on giving us a discount. We always insisted on paying full price. They won eighty percent of the battles because they were both so nice you couldn't argue with them. For three months after Anna died, they refused to take my money for any personal stationery needs. Then they went back to giving me a discount.

A year or so after Anna died, Lucy told me that Strudel was due for his checkup but that Mike and Rosy hadn't responded to her usual notice. She had called them and left a voice mail message that morning, but she still hadn't heard back. On my lunch break, I strolled over to the stationery store and saw that it wasn't open. It didn't seem to be permanently closed, but it was odd that the store would be shut tight on a sunny Tuesday afternoon.

The next morning, as soon as I walked in the door, Lucy, crying, showed me the front page of the New York Post. *The headline read: "Brutal Ending Penned for Store Owner." The photo on the front page showed Rosy and Mike's stationery store, in front of which stood an EMR gurney carrying a body covered by a cloth. The body was Mike's. He'd been murdered the evening before. As he was closing up the store, around seven p.m., someone had come in and bludgeoned him to death with some kind of mallet. I called Rosy immediately; she didn't come to the phone, but I spoke to her younger daughter, Audrey. I didn't press for details, just sent my love. The next morning, Lucy sent over a big food basket.*

Two days later, the Post *ran a second story about the murder. This time Lucy wasn't crying when she unfolded it for me at her desk. Her eyes were wide with shock and disbelief. It turned out that gentle, charming, warmhearted Mike had been laundering money through his stationery store for a Mexican drug cartel. The NYPD suspected that Mike had been skimming money off the top and that the Mexican mob, none too pleased, decided to send him a rather definitive warning by bashing his brains in. The police also seemed to think that neither Rosy nor the two kids had anything to do with Mike's scam or even suspected its existence.*

I didn't see Rosy for two months, but then one day she showed up with Strudel for his overdue appointment. It was a freezing February afternoon, and Rosie, who usually wore an inexpensive cloth winter coat with fake fur lining, strolled through the door wearing a full-length mink. I stared at her in astonishment but did my best to steer clear of any delicate questions. But Rosy was the type who didn't need much prompting, so as I examined her delightfully friendly basset hound, Rosy gave me the lowdown on her life post-Mike.

She told me she'd had no idea what Mike had been up to—and had,
apparently, been up to for fifteen years. At first, she didn't believe a word of
the story the police told her. It seemed crazy and impossible. She said she
didn't even know any Mexicans except for a guy who'd once done some work
on their kitchen in Queens. She only knew his first name, and the police
were now doing their best to find him—to which she said, with a dismissive
wave of her hand, "Good luck to them." Then she fingered her coat. "Nice,
huh?"

I had to agree with her. That's when she lowered her voice and said,
"The craziest thing happened. A few weeks ago, we had a leak in the bath-
room. A plumber came over and had to break through the wall next to the
toilet. And guess what? Inside the wall he found an envelope, a padded
eleven-by-fourteen, manila, with the peel-off seal at the top—we sell a mil-
lion of 'em. Anyway, after the plumber leaves, I open the envelope, and guess
what's in there?"

"I can't imagine."

"Fifty thousand dollars. Cash. Big bills."

Poor Strudel squealed. At the words "fifty thousand dollars" I must have
squeezed him harder than I should have.

"So it got me to thinking. For years, poor Mikey was always up in the
middle of the night, fixing things and plastering things. All kinds of
mishegoss. *He said he couldn't sleep and it relaxed him. I used to say, 'Well,*
it doesn't relax me, all that hammering and pounding.' But you know, you
get used to anything after a while, especially when you're in love. Anyway, I
went to a couple of places I remembered him fixing. I took a hammer and
smashed through the wall and found nothin' but cash. I've found six more
envelopes. Three hundred and seventy-two thousand bucks so far."

I stared at her in amazement. "I don't think you should tell too many
people about this, Rosy."

"Oh, don't worry, I'm not telling anyone except Audrey and Micheline.
And you—I figure I can trust you. Isn't there, like, a doctor-patient confiden-
tiality thing or something?"

"I don't think that works with vets. But I won't tell anybody, don't worry.
I just think you have to be careful."

"Yeah, I know. I don't want no Mexicans barging in in the middle of the
night. The only annoying thing is that I can't sell the goddamn house now.

For all I know, there's a couple of mil stashed away in the goddamn walls. I can't risk it. I figure it'll take me another year or so to bash through the places I think Mike mighta worked on. Then maybe it'll be safe to sell."

When I finished examining Strudel, Rosy gave me a kiss on the cheek.

"You've been a good friend, Doc," she said. "If I find enough cash in the walls, I'll give some to the clinic."

"Thanks," I said.

For the next eighteen months, Rosy brought Strudel in for regular check-ups and to get various ailments taken care of. Then she let me know that they were moving down to Florida. During that year and a half, she never said another word about the money hidden in her house, and I never asked. But she did start wearing expensive jewelry, and one day she tipped Lucy a hundred dollars. Lucy came into my examining room, holding the bill and saying she didn't want to take it but that Rosy had insisted. " 'Take it, darling, you deserve it'—that's what she said. What should I do?"

"Keep it," I said. "You do deserve it."

Rosy died soon after her seventh-fifth birthday—of natural causes, happily. I hadn't seen or heard from her in years, but I know she died because she left five thousand dollars to the clinic in her will. Her lawyer sent me a check, saying that Rosy wanted to cover the expenses of treating animals whose owners couldn't afford our fees.

Lucy let several of our customers know about the endowment and told them to send any of their friends our way if their friends had animals but not much money. We got ten new clients through that grapevine. Lucy's five grand ran out long ago. But we still treat those animals without charging the owners.

Communicating with Camilla made me feel as if I were a geeky fifteen-year-old in high school, instead of the geeky almost-forty-year-old professional I actually was. I called her twice the day after our dinner. The first time, I left a message on her voice mail that said, "Hi, this is Bob. You know, the . . . um . . . the vet. Uhhh . . . I just wanted to say that I had a really nice time and I hope you did, too, and I hope we can do it again soon. Have dinner, I mean. Not . . . well . . . I'd really like to take you out to dinner again. So give me a call." I gave

her the clinic number and my cell phone number. I sta[rted]
the number for the landline in my apartment but stop[ped,] suddenly I had a gut-wrenching picture of Camilla calli[ng]
while Elizabeth was there and I started to get all clam[my on]
the message. I handled my change of heart very coolly[: "—and]
the last number is two-one-two two-five-five . . . oh, nev[er mind, I've]
got enough numbers for me. My cell is probably best. [Bye."]

I thought about my goofy message for several h[ours, then]
couldn't stand it any longer, so I called back. I got her v[oice mail]
and this time said, "I realize I didn't specify a date for d[inner"—as the]
words came out of my mouth I thought, and may have actually muttered aloud to myself, *"Specify a date?" Jesus!*—"so I'm just calling
back to see if maybe you can have dinner tomorrow night. The weekend is bad for me, but if tomorrow doesn't work, maybe next week?
Next week I'm totally free, so name your night. Monday, Tuesday,
Wednesday, Thursday, whatever. Jeez, I can't believe I just listed the
days of the week on your machine. Okay, I'm hanging up now. I think
I'm talking gibberish." But I didn't hang up. I left my clinic and cell
phone numbers a second time, just to make myself seem even more of
a nerd, and then I hung up.

I saw patients practically every minute that day, but all I could
think about was how idiotic my messages had been, and I was sure she
wouldn't call me back. I was like a cross between Charlie Brown with
the Little Red-Haired Girl and a dog in heat. A really big, stupid, panting dog. Our original dinner was on a Tuesday night. I left my messages on Wednesday. Wednesday night I stayed home, tried to read
a Peter Robinson Inspector Banks novel, and couldn't concentrate
enough to get past five pages. I did a lot of pacing, played with the
animals even more than usual, and didn't fall asleep until two A.M.
Most of the sleepless part of the night was spent wondering why I was
such a schmuck.

Camilla finally called me back on Thursday, in the late morning—
okay, she called at exactly eleven-thirteen, according to my iPhone,
not that I was obsessively keeping track or anything—and said we
could have dinner the next night, Friday. Her tone was light and casual;
she gave no indication that she'd either (a) noticed how moronic my

messages were, or (b) remembered that we'd just spent an insanely passionate night together. She spoke to me as if I were already a friend, which made me happy. But she didn't speak to me as if I were a new lover, which sent me into a semi-panic. Worse, I couldn't have dinner with her the next evening, because Elizabeth would be in town.

My stomach clutched and churned when I said that I couldn't see her this coming weekend (and I simultaneously felt even more school-boyish than I had earlier, because now I was worrying about the fact that she obviously hadn't bothered to pay close attention to the details in my idiotic voice messages). When I asked her about next week, she said she could do something Monday and I said that was fine. The conversation stopped there, though we lingered on the phone for a few extra seconds, as if each of us was trying to think of something more to say. But neither of us came up with anything, so it ended with an "Okay, see you Monday" and we hung up. As soon as I was off the phone, I thought of at least ten things I wanted to say to her, but there was no way I was calling her back. I knew that if I did, all ten things would go flying out of my mind. Or they'd sound a lot dumber out loud than they did inside my head.

I spent Thursday night pacing, playing with the menagerie, and rereading the same five Peter Robinson pages. Friday morning I went to work earlier than usual—I was already there by the time Lucy showed up—and did my best to focus on the patients and their own-ers instead of thinking about cupping Camilla's perfect breasts in my hands.

Elizabeth arrived in the midafternoon. As usual, she dropped her stuff in the apartment before popping into the clinic. She sat patiently in the waiting room, as she always did, until I came out of the examin-ing room, a little white Pekingese named Lydia panting and bouncing along behind me. I made the transfer of dog to owner—a rail-thin, bearded man named Carl, who looked as if he were about to burst into tears—and told him I'd call him tomorrow with the results from the blood test. I was reasonably certain that Lydia was experiencing some kind of early and very treatable renal failure, and I was equally certain that Carl was already in despair and planning the dog's funeral service.

Once Carl was out the door, Elizabeth kissed me on the cheek. She had a self-satisfied look in her eyes and held up two tickets. I peered closer, but she just blurted out, "Offenbach's *La Périchole*." Unfortunately, I wasn't able to plaster the appropriate look of delight on my face. Part of me was thinking how nice it would be to go to Lincoln Center on the spur of the moment to see an opera with the woman I'd been with for nearly four years. A much bigger part of me was thinking that I wouldn't see Camilla for three and a half days, and that thought was making my soul ache.

Elizabeth said, "You take these things too hard."

I jerked my head toward her sharply, then realized she was talking about Carl and his Pekingese. I smiled at her—I had to smile; she was worried about me, and as always her concern softened my heart—and told her she was right. I said I'd be finished at the clinic around five P.M. When she asked what I wanted to do for dinner, I said, "Let's just play it by ear. We'll walk around after the opera until we find a place that looks right."

Elizabeth frowned. Spontaneity and improvisation were not her strengths. "It's Friday night. We'll never get in anyplace."

"Okay," I said. "Why don't you just make a reservation."

"Italian?" she said.

"That'd be perfect."

Over the years Elizabeth and I had developed something of a routine for our weekends together. We tried to schedule one interesting event each weekend—this time it was the opera; Elizabeth loved opera and reveled in every aspect of it, while I was happy to sit, absorb, and seem more sophisticated than I was—and have one nice meal at home. That Saturday night, I made a delicious pasta with cauliflower, pine nuts, currants, and anchovies. We each had a glass of Chianti. Elizabeth rarely drank more than that. I was in the mood to finish the bottle, but that seemed a tad excessive, so I just matched her sip for sip.

During our weekend visits we also left some time just to talk face to face; it was our way of making sure that we were fully a part of each other's separate worlds. She knew the names of many of my clients, two- as well as four-legged, and I knew what all her co-workers looked like and thought. We made love Friday night but not Saturday night. The second night we read in bed after dinner, until we fell comfortably asleep. On Sunday we went out to brunch in the West Village. And, as I did every Sunday in the late afternoon, I put her in a taxi to LaGuardia, where she caught a small plane to the Ithaca airport.

That Sunday, we kissed before she got into the cab. A light kiss on the lips.

"That was a particularly nice weekend," she said.

I nodded and smiled.

"You come to me next weekend, right?"

I nodded and smiled again.

"I'm already looking forward to it."

I kept smiling and nodded twice.

Then she was gone.

The entire weekend, I thought I might explode. At the opera, I saw three women with similar hair color to Camilla's, and my heart started racing. When Elizabeth and I had brunch, two women walked by who had Camilla's strong, distinctive gait, and I could barely finish my meal. As I was kissing Elizabeth before putting her in the cab, I was positive I heard Camilla's voice and pulled away as if being tugged by a capricious puppeteer. Basically, I felt as if I were losing my mind.

I didn't relax until I saw the real Camilla on Monday night. We went to a different sushi place, this one in the East Village. We talked about all sorts of things—or, more accurately, she got me talking as I drank my sake. I told her about my childhood in upstate New York, and a lot about Teddy and Phil and my parents, and a little bit about Hilts. I told her about my wedding and the early days of my marriage, and she asked me questions about Anna, leading me gently through the details of her death. She pushed for insights into my relationship with Anna, the different levels it had had and whether I thought it was a completely honest relationship. I answered as best I could but was uncomfortable with some of the scrutiny, and I know I came off as a bit evasive. Camilla could be a cipher when talking about herself, but when she was listening to someone else's story her face became an IMAX 3-D presentation. As I spoke, she registered high degrees of sympathy, disbelief, curiosity, understanding, and disdain, along with an occasional verbal response, most of which sounded either like "hmmm" or "agghh" or "tsk tsk," and all of which was mixed in with various sighs and moans indicating her delight with the raw fish.

When we finished our encore half bottle of sake (polished off after Camilla once again told me she wouldn't be drinking with dinner), I was drained from the grilling. I also realized that, as before, I'd learned almost nothing about her.

It was drizzling when we left the restaurant, so there was no leisurely stroll home. We grabbed a cab, and when she offered to drop me off I'm sure she heard my sharp intake of breath and saw the look of disappointment that turned my face into something Buster Keaton-ish. I insisted on dropping her off first, hoping silently that when we got to her place she'd again invite me in for a drink. The cab stopped and she stared into my eyes before opening the door. Whatever she saw there she must have liked, because she shrugged and said, "Come on." I followed, puppy dog–like.

I greeted Rags, the cat, who ignored her and ran to me. Camilla opened a bottle of Chilean white wine I'd never heard of and, sitting next to each other on the couch, we drank the entire bottle and talked until three in the morning. As we talked, she kicked off her boots and tucked her bare legs and feet under her. I found the position intimate and strangely touching: Her bare feet somehow made her look ten years younger. At one point she saw me looking at her legs and said, "I hate my calves. My mother used to tell me that I got them from her Uncle Sean, who was a rugby player."

She noticed the thin smile on my face and went, "What?"

I shook my head. When I'd seen her walking down the street toward me the other night, I'd thought, *Rugby player* but decided that was best left unsaid.

She didn't mind that I didn't answer. I could tell she understood that it was something that didn't need answering. I liked her even more for not minding and for not pressing me. And something must have clicked—maybe it was my own silence—because she then began to tell me a bit about herself and her family.

Her father was a British character actor and radio and TV

announcer. He had a wonderful voice, she said, and he could talk with an actor's stage whisper. She remembered him whispering to her all the time when she was a little girl, and she could hear his whisper all the way across the room. She would whisper back and he would keep saying, "What?" until she'd wind up screaming at him in a hoarse voice while he laughed. She smiled recounting the story. I knew she was hearing her father's whisper inside her head.

Her mother was a fashion designer. Not high fashion: T-shirts and crazy, colorful socks and fun accessories. She said her father was always whispering to her: *Look how beautiful your mother is. Look how she can turn a little ribbon into something magical.* And she could, Camilla said. That was her memory of her parents: lovely whispers and magical ribbons.

The way she talked about them, I couldn't tell if either or both of her parents were alive or dead. I'd had enough alcohol and was drowsy enough that at some point I asked the question. Cammy looked up at the ceiling and waved my question away.

"Come on," I said. My words were a little slurred. My brain was a lot slurred. "You have to tell me something sometime."

So she looked at me and said, "Dead."

Without another word, she got up and walked toward the bedroom. As she did, she began stripping off her clothes, leaving them casually strewn behind her. It didn't take me long to follow. But when I got to her bed, she wouldn't let me undress. She insisted on holding me while she was naked and I was fully clothed.

"You're seeing someone," she said. It wasn't a question.

"Yes," I said. As quietly as I could.

"Do you love her?"

"No."

"Have you ever loved her?"

"I don't think so. No."

"How long have you been with her?"

"Oh, Jesus. Do we have to—"

"How long?"

"Three years. Almost four, I guess."

"Does she know? That you don't love her?"

"I don't know. But she's very smart."

"Why has she stayed with you for so long?"

"I don't know."

"Why do you think?"

"Because we get along really well. We like each other a lot. It's all very . . ."

"Easy?"

I shook my head. "Nice." Then I shrugged. "And easy."

"That's not enough. And it's depressing as hell. There has to be more."

"There is."

She waited. Then waved her hand, asking me to continue.

"Because she's in love with me," I said. "And because she thinks I'm too afraid to ever leave her."

"Afraid of what?"

I took longer to answer this one. "Of being alone."

She took a moment to consider this. "And you don't mind cheating on her?"

"Yes. I mind."

"But you'll do it."

"Yes."

"Why?"

"Camilla—"

She pulled the hair at the back of my neck. It made me melt.

"Why?"

"Because all I can think about is making love to you."

"We're—"

"Don't tell me we're just fucking! We're not!"

"Oh, now you have a temper, now that we're talking about you cheating on your girlfriend."

I didn't respond.

Camilla went: "Is that all you think about, making love to me?"

"No. I think . . . everything about you. I think about talking to you and eating with you and listening to your voice and . . . Mostly I think about how all I want to do is be with you."

She nodded. And kissed my neck. I shuddered with pleasure.

"Are you?" she asked.

"Am I what?"

"Afraid of being alone?"

"No."

"Then why does she think that?"

"Who, Eliza—"

"No!" She almost jumped up. Waved her hand at me as if she were a deranged traffic cop. "Don't tell me her name!" She calmed down. Her body relaxed, and her voice returned to normal. "I don't want to know anything about her. Just tell me why she thinks that."

"Because *she's* afraid of being alone. It makes it easier if she believes I am, too."

"But you're not."

"I've never been afraid of being alone. What I'm afraid of is not being in love."

"Don't you mean not having someone love you?"

"No." Then I said, "Well, I kind of think they're the same thing."

"Oh my god are you wrong," Cam said. "Are you that much of a romantic?"

"I guess I am."

She took some time to absorb this. I had surprised her.

"I have a boyfriend," she said.

"What?"

"You're so shocked?"

"No. I mean . . . I was wondering, but . . ."

"We have a pretty crazy relationship. And I found out last week that he's been seeing a friend of mine on the side, the prick."

"Not much of a friend."

"No. Not much of a boyfriend, either. Actually, that's not true. He's pretty great. He's just a prick."

"So . . . what am I? Payback?"

"Yes," she said. "At least you were last week."

I didn't say anything. Focused on breathing slowly in and out.

"Do you mind?" she asked.

"No," I said. "I don't give a shit."

We kissed for a long time; then all she said was: "The shoes."

I kicked my shoes off and we kissed some more. Then she said, "Socks." I pulled them off as quickly as I could, and that's the way it went. She would tell me to remove one piece of clothing and after I did, we'd roll on the bed and touch and kiss, and then she'd tell me to get rid of the next item. Luckily, I wasn't wearing layers of clothing, so it didn't take all that long before we were both naked. And as soon as we were, I was inside her and we were making love and then she was shaking and shivering and crying again.

"Are you okay?" I said. "Did I do something wrong?"

She shook her head after both questions. Quick, firm, dismissive shakes. And before I could ask or do anything else she said, "Just hold me and go to sleep."

It felt so natural to be there with her. I was still confused, still wondering who and what she really was, but I didn't truly care. I just wanted to do exactly what she told me to do, which was hold her and go to sleep and be with her all night long.

That is exactly what I did. And I did it until my cell phone rang, around five o'clock in the morning. Camilla stirred as I left the bed and searched for my pants. Once I found them, I tried to dig the ringing phone out of my left front pocket. I was sure it was Elizabeth and I didn't have a clue what I'd do—if I'd answer or click off. But it was too early for Elizabeth to call, and when I looked at the caller ID it was an upstate number. The same area code as my hometown, but not a number I recognized.

So I answered, saying a wary "Hello," and a woman's voice on the other end said, "Is this Bob Heller?"

I said yes and she said, "This is Marta Hendrix."

It took me a moment. "Marta as in my mother's next-door neighbor?"

"Yes," she said. "I don't know how to tell you this. But last night around eleven o'clock, I came home. I was visiting my daughter in Buffalo and the train was delayed and . . . well, I noticed that your mother's newspaper was on the front stoop, which isn't normal—she takes it in as soon as she gets up. But the light was on. And I knew she wasn't away. So I knocked on the door and—"

"Marta," I said. "Is my mother okay?"

"She's had a stroke," she said. "A big one. I don't know how long she'd been there, she was lying on the floor in the kitchen, but it was a while. I think because the paper was there maybe all day. Or even twenty-four hours. The ambulance came and took her to the hospital. I went with her and I just got home. Your apartment number's listed, but you weren't there and I didn't have your cell number. I just got home and I went into your mom's house and I found your cell phone number in her address book."

"Is she okay?"

"Well, she's alive," Marta said. "I don't know if that's the same as okay."

"No," I said. "I don't know either."

There was a car rental place not too far from my apartment, but it didn't open until seven A.M. Driving would be faster than flying; it would also be easier on my peace of mind than waiting for a train. Camilla woke up and slipped out from under her duvet (she just had a bottom sheet and slept under only the quilted duvet). She was naked, and she came to me unself-consciously and hugged me. We sat next to each other, her legs and feet once again tucked under her, and I apologized to her several times—for waking her up, for dragging my personal problems into her apartment—until she told me, very gently, to shut up. She seemed to realize that she was naked at that moment, went to a bedroom closet, and pulled out a blue silk robe that came down to her mid-thigh. She tightened the belt around her waist, came back to sit next to me, held my hand, and asked me questions about my mom for half an hour. I saw why she was a good doctor: I immediately felt under her care. Her touch was comforting and warm, her voice soft and caring, and I could tell that she was, to some extent, absorbing my pain. What I wanted to do was kiss her neck and her shoulders and then get back into bed with her, our bodies wrapped together. Instead I told her I should go home and get ready to head upstate. At the door, she kissed me lightly on the lips and told me that after I spoke to my mother's doctors I should call her with any questions.

Back in my apartment, I showered and changed my clothes, lost in a reverie of sadness and disbelief about my mom and quiet exhilaration about the woman with whom I was quickly falling in love. I hurriedly walked Scully, Wave, and Che, impatiently urging them to do what needed to be done, rushed back inside to feed and briefly pet all the guys, nodded in agreement when Larry called me a cocksucker, and gathered Rocky up and put him in his traveling bag. The others could be alone, and I could be without the others. But Rocky was going to be with me.

At seven o'clock, on the dot, I was at the car rental place, and at seven-fifteen I was on the road, driving north in a silver Toyota. I felt as if I were driving in a *Twilight Zone* episode about a world of conformity, because every other car on the road looked exactly like mine. At seven-thirty I called Elizabeth. She started to ask me where I'd been, said she'd called last night and left a message. I stayed silent for as long as I could manage; then all I said was "My mother had a stroke. I'm driving up to see her."

That ended any possible discussion and erased all suspicions. I told her I was driving to the hospital and would play everything by ear once I got there, but that I'd probably spend at least a few days upstate and would most likely stay at my mother's house. Elizabeth didn't miss a beat: She was instantly caring, supportive, and organized. She would call ahead, get the attending doctor's name, and let him know that I'd be coming. She would use her contacts at Cornell's med school to find and then talk with their stroke expert. She volunteered to meet me at the hospital and help out in whatever way possible, but I told her it would be best to wait and see what happened once I got there. In truth, I wanted to be alone. I wanted to handle whatever the situation turned out to be without having to either lean on or fend off anyone else. I also just wanted to be by myself to try to sort out my thoughts about my past and present. And possibly future.

I called Lucy to tell her what had happened and ask her to take care of my guys and figure out how to get an emergency replacement at the clinic for the next few days. After that I was pretty much of a blank slate for the three-plus hour drive. I plugged in my iPad and blared rock and roll for much of the ride, occasionally switching to opera when I felt my brain cells deadening but mostly sticking with the Stones, Florence and the Machine, Pearl Jam, and, as my way of rebelling against Elizabeth and women in general, about twenty minutes of Meat Loaf. By the time I pulled into the parking lot of the hospital and reached the automatic door leading to the lobby, I was in a weirdly good mood. Mick Jagger and Eddie Vedder had cleared my head of all thoughts of lust, sadness, or longing. I just wanted to find out what the hell was going on with my mom and figure out what the hell I could do about it.

The answers to both questions were, in order, a lot and not much. But like with any visit to a hospital where the situation is critical, by the time I left to get some dinner, I was exhausted, discouraged, enraged, and impressed.

My mother had suffered a massive stroke in the dead center of her brain. The doctors believed that it had happened sometime between six A.M., about the time she usually woke up, and eight A.M., when the newspaper was usually delivered to her house. They told me that to have any sort of reasonable recovery from this kind of stroke, my mom needed to have been discovered and tended to within two hours. Instead, she'd been lying on the floor of her kitchen in a puddle of her own urine, unable to move and going in and out of consciousness for approximately seventeen hours. As a result, the young doctors told me, she would very likely have locked-in syndrome, which meant she would never talk or move again.

Marta, her neighbor, told me that in addition to the hours she'd spent sprawled on the kitchen floor, my mother had lain for several hours on a gurney in the hallway of the hospital, waiting for an MRI of her brain. Marta had stayed with her until she'd finally gotten into a room. It wasn't a private room. She was sharing with an elderly black woman who moaned constantly and never quietly and occasionally let loose with a scream that could bring the house down.

I made my way to my mom's room, walked past the moaning black woman, and saw my mother. She appeared to be sleeping, her mouth partway open, her right arm outside the blanket, bent at the elbow and tight against her side, her right fist curled into a ball that looked as if it would never uncurl. Her eyes moved slightly as I stepped into her line of vision.

She looked as if she'd lost fifty pounds and any sense of normal human life. From what the doctors had told me, I was expecting her to be in a near-vegetative state, and that's certainly what it seemed like at first glance. Her hair was stringy and flat. Her skin had had a dull greenish hue. Sweat dripped down her neck, and snot hung from one nostril. But when I took her left hand—her good hand—and said, "Well . . . I've seen you look worse," my mom let loose with a raspy "haw" that was clearly a laugh. She rolled her eyes as if to say, "Can you believe it?" and I laughed back at her.

At the time, I had no understanding of my mom's extraordinary strength and no idea of what she'd be able to accomplish over the next few months. All I knew was that a woman who happened to be my mother—someone I was close to and loved but ultimately didn't know all that well—had suffered a serious stroke and now stared up at me from a near-fetal position on the bed. She looked like she'd been run over by a truck, sprayed with a fire hose to clean her up, and dropped off at the hospital in a laundry bag.

Rocky and I sat with her for several hours. Cats were forbidden in the hospital, but no one seemed to notice that I had one. Intermittently I spoke to doctors and nurses, all of whom told me something worse than the previous doctor or nurse. I got a rundown of the planned treatment, which was basically to wait two or three days to see how the swelling in her brain went down and then determine the level of therapy she'd be capable of. Until they saw the actual physical damage done by the stroke, the doctors couldn't give me much information (other than their dire predictions). I asked why it had happened, and as near as they could tell from the blood tests they'd taken and the brief conversation they'd had with her family doctor, my mother had been on blood pressure medicine designed to limit the potential for a stroke (for which she'd been at risk—news that came as a complete surprise to me). The medicine worked so well and she was feeling so chipper, she stopped taking it. Result: major stroke. One of the doctors told me that as people got older, this sort of thing happened fairly often. They wanted to believe that they could be healthy and young on their own. So as soon as they felt well, they destroyed themselves by eliminating the thing that made them feel well.

My patients never did this. They did not have self-destructive or self-delusional instincts. They happily and gratefully accepted whatever was good for them. I was also pretty sure that dogs and cats and small rodents and large horses never burst into tears after making love. Or stayed up at night worrying that they had barked, meowed, twitched, or neighed something stupid to a member of the opposite sex. I had the urge to call Camilla and tell her this: There was a lot to be said for the animal side of the pets-versus-people argument. At that moment, the people side was not a case I'd have liked to argue before the Supreme Court.

The nurses asked me to leave at eight o'clock. If I'd resisted they probably would have let me stay, but there was no real purpose to my sticking around. My mother was mostly sleeping, and the black woman's moans were getting louder and more regular. I asked if there was any way for my mom to be moved and one nurse said it probably wouldn't be necessary, that the black woman would most likely be gone by tomorrow. The nurse who told me this finally seemed to notice the cat in the room. She eyed him suspiciously, but before she could say anything, I said, "He's a therapy cat. I have permission to bring him in." She shrugged—people always shrug in relief when told they don't have to be responsible for a decision—and left without saying another word.

I drove with Rocky toward my childhood home, stopping along the way at a Taco Bell in a dismal mall that had gone up fifteen or so years earlier and had been in steady decline ever since. I got the fast food back to my car and just sat there, unable to either restart the engine or unwrap the vaguely burrito-like thing I'd paid nearly four bucks for. Eventually, I managed to muster the energy to drive the remaining few miles home. Good neighbor Marta Hendrix had left a key for me under the mat, and I used it on the front door. I hadn't been inside the house in years, and I'd *never* been in the house when it was this absolutely still and quiet and dark. I reached for the living room light, muscle memory getting my hand to the switch on the first try.

I saw my childhood through the shadows cast by the lamp and sat down heavily on the couch. I'd called Camilla twice from the hospital, stepping away from my mother's room; both times I'd left voice messages. And now I left a third one. I said, "It's Bob," and realized how exhausted my voice sounded. "I . . . I just felt like calling you. Sorry if I'm being a pest. I won't be up too late tonight, so maybe we'll talk tomorrow." I clicked the phone off and sat in silence for several minutes, almost drifting off.

But suddenly I didn't want the silence. Eight hours in a hospital made me want to reach out to living, breathing people. I called Phil, realizing that not only was he close by, he'd want to know what had happened. (Over the years, he'd checked in on my mom periodically, stopping by to chat or to help her with something that needed to be repaired. His visits made her happy, reminded her of a simpler and less fractured life.) I called the bowling alley, but he'd gone home. Called his cell but got his voice mail. I briefly explained what had happened and told him to call me in the morning, because even though I was in the midst of calling him, I was too tired to really talk that night.

I sat, phone in hand, for several minutes before dialing Elizabeth's number. I could hear myself saying to Camilla that I wasn't afraid of being alone. But right now I was, and though Rocky sat curled in my lap, I needed more than a sweet and brilliant cat. I needed comfort, so I went to the only place where I absolutely knew I would get it.

Elizabeth heard the heaviness in my voice and listened quietly while I filled her in. "You sound tired," she said.

"Yeah," I said.

"I can come there on Friday morning," she told me. "If you'd like me to."

"I don't think there's all that much that can be done," I said. "I don't know what you can do if you come."

"I can take care of you," she said.

I looked at my burrito, still wrapped in paper and now nearly cold.

"I'll see you Friday," I said softly.

I ate my burrito, went up to the room I'd slept in as a child—which now was some kind of combination guest room–sewing room; my single bed had been replaced by a couch that converted to a pull-out bed, and my teenage posters of Lawrence Taylor and Michelle Pfeiffer had been replaced by a wall of family photos and a painting that my dad had worked on laboriously during the year he'd spent deciding it was a good thing to be painting bad abstract art—and managed to plug in my cell and kick my shoes off before passing out fully dressed. I slept nearly twelve hours, and when I woke up it took me a few moments to realize where I was and what had happened. Then I got out of bed and tried to conjure a plan. The best I could come up with was to brush my teeth (a miracle: I'd remembered a toothbrush and toothpaste), change my clothes, and go back to the hospital.

Over the next few days, my routine was simple. I spent from ten A.M. to eight P.M. either in my mother's room or in various hospital offices talking to doctors, social workers, therapists, or administrators. They were all nice, seemingly competent, and dispassionate, except for the primary social worker, who was very concerned that I do the right things and explained precisely what I needed to do to make sure my mother got the best care possible. For the first two days, I called Camilla two or three times a day and each time left messages on her voice mail. The third day, I left one message. I didn't get any calls in return.

For three days, there was almost no change in my mother's condition. The physical therapists tried to get her to move but didn't have much luck. The speech therapist tried to get her to talk but, other than a few incoherent syllables, got nowhere. Phil came by to sit with us—me, my mother, and Rocky—for a couple of hours each day. At night he and Rocky and I went to the bowling alley, where Phil and I drank beer and ate burgers and hot dogs while Rocky prowled the lanes before settling in at the shoe desk, where he was petted incessantly by the very attractive high school girl who worked there.

"It's gotta be strange," Phil said to me one night in between bites of an excellent cheeseburger.

"What is?"

"It's like your return to childhood except everything's turned upside down. Your mom's like a two-year-old. Can't feed herself, can barely talk. Your job is to take care of her the way she used to take care of you. It's like one big surreal cycle."

I nodded, had another beer, and debated talking to him about Camilla. I was desperate to, but I held back. For one thing, Phil knew Elizabeth. Not well but we'd had several dinners together and he liked her. It somehow would have been demeaning to Elizabeth to discuss another woman with him. For another thing, I didn't know what I would say. Camilla still hadn't called me back, and her silence was eating me up. I didn't think it would make for much of a conversation if I described a relationship with a woman who wouldn't return my calls.

On Friday two things changed. Elizabeth arrived from Cornell, and the doctor told me that the swelling in my mother's brain had receded a lot more than they'd thought possible. Almost simultaneously with that news, as I was holding my mom's hand she squeezed me back and said, weakly but quite distinctly, "Can you believe this shit?"

The doctors were astonished and the therapists practically fell over each other to show me what they could do now that the patient had exhibited some signs of life. Elizabeth and I sat through my mother's first speech therapy session. The therapist, an earnest young woman in her early twenties, said she was going to start with some very simple exercises. Sitting by my mom's side, she explained that she was going to say a phrase or a sentence and leave one word blank; it was my mom's job to fill in the blank. She asked if my mother understood and practically danced a jig when my mother nodded and said, "Yes."

"I'm going to the blank to get a carton of milk," the therapist said.

"Cow," my mother answered.

I started to laugh. The therapist and Elizabeth both shot me nasty looks.

"That's good," the therapist said, smiling at my mom but managing to send one last frown in my direction. "And it's right. But it's not really correct. You don't really go to a cow to get milk, do you?"

"No," my mom said.

"Where do you go?"

"Cow."

"How about a store?"

My mother nodded and her eyes blinked to show that she was angry at herself. "Yes. That's . . . where . . . I . . . go."

"Excellent! That was a superb sentence. That's really, really good, Mrs. Heller. So let's try it again. Can you just say the word 'store'?"

My mother nodded. "Cow."

"Okay. Let's try another one. You're going to make a sandwich of peanut butter and . . ."

"Salt," my mother said.

"You know, that's a very good answer but not quite right. Peanuts are very salty—is that why you answered that way?"

My mother nodded. This was clearly exhausting her.

"But you wouldn't make a peanut-butter-and-salt sandwich, would you?"

My mother shook her head.

"Mom," I said. "You know the word, don't you? It's just not coming out right."

She nodded. "Didn't . . . mean . . . salt."

"So what word did you mean?" the therapist asked.

"Salt," my mother said.

It went on like that for half an hour, until my mom fell asleep in the middle of a question. She got about fifty percent of the words right; for almost all the others there was a reasonable connection, like cow to milk and salt to peanut. She also produced some oddly esoteric, even arcane terms. The therapist was trying to elicit the word "hallway" and my mom came up with "vestibule." For "television" she said "console." When she missed a word, she scowled; if she could have moved her right hand, I think she would have slapped herself. But every time she got one right, she beamed like a proud third grader.

It was exhausting to listen to her and even more so to watch her work with her physical therapist, who tried to get her to uncurl her right fist and relax her right arm. The left side of her body was working reasonably well, her right arm somewhat, and her right leg not at all. The doctors assured me that she was making amazing progress.

Friday night, Elizabeth and I had dinner by ourselves. She wanted to cook, but I insisted on going out. We went to the local diner, exactly what we were in the mood for. I ate an open-faced roast beef sandwich drenched in thick, brown gravy. She ate a Greek salad. As we discussed my mom's condition and she told me about her work, she patted my arm and touched me in ways that were intended to be comforting but made me want to recoil. By the time we got home, I was repelled by my own behavior, and at my instigation, we made love as tenderly and romantically as I was capable of. She fell asleep quickly after that, her body against mine, her arm wrapped around my chest. I stayed awake for an hour, staring up at the ceiling, trying to wipe away every single thought that swarmed inside my brain.

On Saturday, Phil joined us for dinner. We went to a decent French bistro. Phil showed some restraint and drank no more than his share of a single bottle of wine. We talked about his new girlfriend and I updated him on my mom; over dessert, Phil asked what I was going to do about Ted. I hadn't told my brother what had happened yet, though I had called several of my mother's friends. I'd been checking my mother's phone machine regularly; Ted had called twice, but I hadn't found the strength to return his calls. I knew that no matter how I handled it—called to tell him I was taking care of things; called to ask him to come right away; called to tell him that whatever he wanted to do was fine—it would get ugly. And I couldn't handle that kind of ugly right now. Elizabeth thought I was making a mistake. Phil was in total agreement with keeping Ted away.

At some point during the dinner, Elizabeth said, "It does make you think about how we really have to seize the day, doesn't it?"

Phil snorted and said, "Oh, please. Not that shit."

"Excuse me?" she said.

"Don't get him started," I told her.

Too late.

"You know what drove me crazy," Phil said. "After 9/11, people were going, 'Oh, it really makes you realize how short life is . . . Oh, we really have to live for the moment . . . Oh, it really makes you think about what we're doing with our lives.' Give me a fucking break."

"You don't think 9/11 should have affected people?"

"That's not what he means," I said.

"People need to grieve," Elizabeth said.

Phil said nothing. I, too, stayed quiet.

"It's natural for people to think about their own lives when something like that happens."

"Okay," Phil said.

And then it just poured out of me. I tried to stop it—really I did. But I couldn't.

"What he means," I said, "is that if it takes a fucking plane flying into a fucking building for someone to wake up and realize he's going to die one day, or that he might not die on his own fucking schedule, then he's pretty fucking stupid!"

It came out just a tad harsher and more contemptuous than I intended. Phil didn't seem to notice, however. Or maybe he enjoyed the outburst, because all he did was nod as if that was exactly the point he'd been trying to make.

Elizabeth looked down at her plate. That was my cue to leave it alone, but I didn't. I kept going. Getting angrier and angrier. I was practically snarling now.

"Someone who smokes gets cancer, and suddenly he discovers the evils of smoking, turns into a proselytizer before he dies. Some son of a bitch gets a brain tumor and suddenly finds Jesus and wants to apologize for all the bad shit he did in his life. Somebody's husband gets killed in a terrorist attack and wow, who knew—life's a dangerous, tenuous thing! You're supposed to realize that fires are fucking hot after the age of two when you stick your hand in one. But people spend their whole lives oblivious to other people's pain or tragedy—no, not even tragedy—to just the simple, everyday fucking things that happen to every fucking one of us. We get hit by drunk drivers, we get shot by maniacs with automatic weapons in movie theaters, we get sent off to war by asshole politicians . . . Christ! Until it happens to them! And then people are surprised every single time! Seize the fucking day! Make the most of every moment! What the hell are people thinking? That if a plane doesn't crash with someone's fucking uncle on it then they're all going to live forever? That no one's gonna get a stroke or have a heart attack or die of stomach cancer? And no one's gonna . . . gonna . . ."

Suddenly I realized what I was about to say, and I didn't want to say it. But I absolutely couldn't help myself. I was no longer in control. I did, however, manage to lower my voice, not quite to a whisper but not far above it. Let's call it a nasty hiss. "And no one's gonna look back at their lives and realize the one thing that's sucking the breath out of them, the one thing that sucks it out of all of us, is that we wind up looking back and none of us gives a shit about what we've done, we only regret the things we never had the balls to do."

I looked at Phil. All the emotion had drained out of my voice. As quietly as I could, I said, "It's not fucking 9/11 or cancer that means anything to anybody. It's our own regret that we wasted our own fucking lives doing things we didn't really want to do." I took a deep breath and lowered my voice even more. It was steady and calm when I said to Elizabeth, "That's what he fucking means."

I guess I must have gotten a little overwrought during my diatribe, because when I finished, several people at nearby tables were staring at me as if O. J. Simpson were dining next to them.

Phil said, "Um . . . I think he's a little more stressed out than he's acknowledging."

"You think?" Elizabeth said. But although she tried to keep it light, the hurt in her eyes betrayed her tone.

And that's the moment Camilla chose to finally return my calls. I stared at my cell phone as if I'd never seen it before. Then I took a deep breath and answered.

"Hello," I said.

She didn't identify herself, just started right in. "I'm sorry I didn't call you back. I've been away."

"It's okay," I said.

"Is everything all right? How's your mum?"

"Better." To say I was speaking in a monotone would be giving me way too much credit for showing emotion.

"You sound funny. Don't be mad at me, okay?"

"I'm not. It's fine."

"Tell me what's going on? Is your mother okay? When are you coming back?"

"Can I call you later? Or tomorrow?"

"I picked a bad time to call."

"Kind of."

"Is the girlfriend there?"

I didn't answer.

"Call me when you can," she said. "I'd really like to talk to you."

"Okay. Thanks."

I clicked off the phone and looked up. Phil was watching me, curious and confused. Elizabeth couldn't bring herself to look at me.

"Maybe we should go," I said. Those were my quietest words yet.

"Yes," Elizabeth said. "I think we should."

"Why do I have a feeling a plane just crashed into a building?" Phil said.

Elizabeth and I didn't say a word to each other in the car. We didn't speak at all until we were upstairs in my mother's house, in my childhood bedroom.

"I genuinely wish we were having this conversation anywhere but here."

She didn't laugh. Or even smile. I guess it was too much to hope for.

"That was your 'friend' who called."

I nodded.

"Kevin," she said.

Another nod.

"I assume her name's not Kevin."

"Camilla."

"When were you going to tell me?" she asked. She was livid and in pain but she was holding it in. There was the slightest tremor to her voice but other than that no betrayal of emotion.

"Tonight."

"Even if she hadn't called?"

"Yes. I wanted to all weekend. I tried."

"And what happened?"

"Every time I tried to tell you, I . . . I thought about how much it was going to hurt you, and more than anything in life, Elizabeth, I don't want to hurt you."

"Not more than anything," she said.

"No," I told her. "I guess not."

The silence that ensued made me feel inadequate, incapable of telling her what was really inside me.

"How long has it been going on?"

"Nothing's even been going on. I mean . . . not really. A week. Less. A few days."

"And you're already in love with her?"

"I don't know. Yes. I think I am. I hardly know her."

"Is she in love with you?"

"No. I don't know. Probably not. Jesus. I'm sorry."

She shook her head and a thin, sad smile crossed her thin, sad lips. "This is kind of ridiculous," she said, "but I actually feel sorry for you. I don't like seeing you in this kind of pain."

I breathed out what was supposed to be a laugh. "Thanks."

There was another silence. This one was more comfortable.

"You know," she said, "I understood that you never were in love with me. But I didn't really care. I thought you would come around in time. And we were so nice and comfortable together, I suppose I forgot that it never seemed to happen. I thought perhaps we didn't need it."

I smiled at her. "I think you're the only person I've ever met who uses 'perhaps' when you're actually speaking."

She looked like she was suddenly going to cry, so I hurriedly said, "Elizabeth, I like you so much. And I do love you. Really. I just . . . I need . . . I don't know. I suddenly need more. I didn't know that I did, I swear. I had no idea."

"I was never able to make you forget Anna."

"I can't forget Anna. I don't want to forget Anna. And that's not what this is about."

"Isn't it?"

"It's not about forgetting. It's about . . . I'm sorry, Elizabeth. It's about figuring out how I can rediscover the things that make me want to stay alive."

"The thing is," she said, "none of that mattered to me. You make me happy. I like taking care of you. I like the way you take care of me.

I find you exciting. I don't know why I find a vet who's hung up on his dead wife exciting, but I do."

"Elizabeth . . ."

"Oh god, please don't say you want to stay friends. I couldn't bear that."

"I would like to. At some point, anyway."

"Bob," she said. "What I'm going to say is very humiliating for me, so please don't respond."

"I—"

"Please."

I waited.

She took a deep breath. "If things don't work out with you and . . . Kevin . . . whatever her name is—no, don't tell me again, I don't really care—I'm available. I mean that I'm available for you. I don't have any pride about this. I'm sure I'll be resentful and I might be mean to you for a little while but that wouldn't last long. So . . . well, I guess there's no 'so.' There's just that." She shook her red hair. "God, I'm giving women a bad name."

"Thank you," I said. And then: "I've never ended anything before. Ever. I've only had things"—I paused—"ended. I'm sorry."

"What you said earlier. About looking back and regretting the things you didn't do. Is that the way you're going to think back on our time together? With regret?"

"No," I said. "I treasure what we've had. I don't have one minute of regret about these years."

She waited for the kicker. She knew it was coming. So I finished:

"But if we kept going, I would. If I didn't end it now, I'd regret it the rest of my life."

"Congratulations," Elizabeth said. "I think that's the cruelest thing anyone's ever said to me."

"I didn't mean it to be. I'm just trying to make you understand."

"You think understanding something makes it easier to bear? It doesn't."

We looked at each other for a moment or two, but there was nothing more to say. She packed up her overnight bag, went downstairs, outside to her car, and drove away.

Rocky, who'd stayed away during the entire conversation, came tiptoeing into the room now and hopped up on my lap. I stroked him as he purred loudly. And I waited, trying to be as respectful as I could, although I wasn't really sure what I was being respectful of.

I didn't wait long. I picked up my cell phone and dialed.

"Hello," Camilla said.

"Hello," I said.

Neither of us spoke a word. For some strange, bewildering, exhilarating reason, we didn't have to.

From the *New York Daily Herald-Examiner*:

Dr. Robert Heller is one of New York's leading veterinarians. He is the author of two books about taking care of pets, *They Have Nothing but Their Kindness* and the fleeting *New York Times* best seller *More Than Human*. He is also a regular on the *Today* show with his weekly segment, "The Vetting Zoo." Dr. Bob takes care of cats, dogs, horses, birds, snakes, turtles, frogs, snails, fish, small pigs, and many varieties of rodents. You can e-mail him at AskDrBob@HeraldCo.com and ask him any question about the animal you love. His column runs Tuesdays, Thursdays, and Sundays in the tristate area's most popular newspaper.

Dear Dr. Bob:

I just got a new kitten. When I took him to my local vet, she told me that Goya was a very smart cat but very, very willful. She said that I needed to socialize him as quickly as possible and that if I didn't expose him to lots of different people, I'd never be able to control him. I told her that I didn't really want to control him. I said, "What's the point of having a cat if you can control him?" She said that even cats need some sort of control. She said that if I didn't work on socializing him— "socializing" is her word—he'd be hard to play with because he'd scratch and bite me (not maliciously, just because he'd think that anything and everything was a toy being placed before him for his pleasure). She said he'd insist on being fed when he wanted to be fed rather than on my schedule. And that he'd never learn how to stop clawing the furniture or come when I called him over for a petting. I like my vet. She, too, is very smart.

But somehow I don't think she understands. I don't want to break my cat's will. I want him to be a cat. I will love him even more for being what he is. Do *you* understand, Dr. Bob?

—A True Cat Lover

Dear Lover:

Yes, I do understand. And I hate to sound so wishy-washy, but you both have a point. If I had to choose, however, I'd come down on the side of your (smart and obviously also willful) vet. Look at it like this: Swap the word "control" for the word "convince." We shouldn't want to control our pets any more than we want to control our friends or our mates. It's not simply that having control over someone is just too much responsibility; it's ultimately not very satisfying. But we *do* want to be with someone we can "convince." Wouldn't you like to have your cat *want* to hop up on the bed to get petted? Don't you *want* Goya to let you scratch his belly without biting or clawing you, even if it's in fun? Animals need to learn. Animals need to be socialized. Then, when they are, they can decide to have or not have the kind of relationship with us that they want. And we can decide how hard we want to work to convince them to play with us and listen to us and love us. It's a fine line to walk, but it's a line that has to be respected and a stroll that needs to be taken or no one will ever be satisfied. And one final thing, Lover (I do like saying that, I must admit): Every one of our pets is socialized to some degree; don't pretend otherwise. If they weren't, we wouldn't want to get anywhere near their claws or their teeth. They'd be too unpredictable, too dangerous. I do understand, by the way, that unpredictable plus dangerous can be an appealing combination, in both humans and pets. But only up to a point. Once that point is passed, there are only two possibilities: (1) We get our hearts broken; (2) We wind up as food.

—Dr. Bob

CHAPTER 10

ISADORE BARNES

Isadore was a thirty-five-year-old Trinidadian woman who looked as if she were sixteen. But I knew she couldn't be sixteen because within months of my treating the gray-and-white ragamuffin of a cat she'd rescued from the street, she told me she had an eighteen-year-old daughter. She saw my astonished look—when she'd mentioned a daughter, I was figuring four or five, maybe eight years old, tops—and said in the clearest, most mellifluous island accent imaginable, without a hint of embarrassment, shame, or pain, "Oh, I was raped when I was fifteen."

I muttered the usual things—"Oh my god" and "I'm so sorry"—but she just smiled beatifically and said, "I thought it was a terrible thing at the time. But it gave me my daughter, and I love her more than anything in the world, so I don't think it's so terrible anymore."

Isadore had very little education and not much money, but she was determined that her daughter would have every chance at success. So Isadore worked several jobs and had since the girl was born; now Lena, the daughter, was about to start college. Isadore practically burst with pride when she told me that.

"She has never gotten into any trouble," she said. "She is a wonderful student. And now she's going to college. Can you imagine that? College." She said the word as if it were some kind of magical incantation. "In Boston," she said. "College in Boston. I have never been to Boston, have you?"

"Yes," I told her.

"It sounds like a wonderful place."

I nodded. "I'm sure it will be for Lena."

Isadore worked hard, but she could never land a job that seemed worthy of her smarts and skills. She loved taking care of people, and she had long dreamed of becoming a nurse.

"You should go to school, too," I said. "To become a nurse. You'd be a great nurse."

"I don't have any money, Dr. Bob. To be a nurse, you need money. Maybe when Lena is finished in Boston. Maybe then she can support me and I can help everybody in the world get healthy." She broke into a huge laugh. She had an incredible laugh—it made the whole world seem like one big entertainment.

Everyone worried about Isadore except Isadore. She lived in a dangerous neighborhood in the Bronx and never had a penny. Sometimes she didn't show up for appointments because she didn't want to spend the money on a subway ride. She couldn't ever seem to hold a job for more than a few months. I once asked Lucy, who loved Isadore, why the woman couldn't keep a job.

"Does she drink?" I asked. "Take drugs? What the hell is it? She seems so smart and lovely."

"She's too smart," Lucy said. "People hire her for low-level jobs and she's smarter than they are. It makes them uncomfortable after a while."

Chalk up another one for the nonhumans. Rarely do pets reject one of their own because they're too smart.

We hired Isadore from time to time to substitute for Lucy or to help her out. She was indeed smart. And nice and competent and without any apparent flaws, either personally or professionally.

One day, she was helping Lucy with office paperwork and filing—Isadore was also extremely adept on the computer, which Lucy most definitely was not—when a golden retriever was brought in with a badly mangled leg. She'd been hit by a car and was in extreme pain. The dog was carried in by her owner and two strangers who'd seen the accident, taken off various pieces of clothing to wrap around the poor creature, and helped get her to *the clinic. The dog was howling and whimpering, and when I got near the wound to give her a shot to help deaden the pain, she snapped at me, taking a nice little chunk out of the fleshy part of my hand.*

It was not a happy operation—lots of blood and hysteria. The entire experience was very emotional for everyone involved, from the doctor to the patient to the patient's owner to the Good Samaritans who'd injected themselves into the situation. After it was over—the retriever lived but would have a substantial limp the rest of her life—I found Isadore crying in the short hallway behind Lucy's usual seat.

"It's all right," I told her. "The dog's gonna be okay. She'll be fine."

"You're a good doctor," Isadore said.

"I'm just a doctor," I said.

"No, no, that dog bit you hard and you didn't care. I once saw a little baby bite her own mother and the mother slapped her so hard, she almost took the baby's head off."

"The dog was in pain. She didn't mean to bite me."

"That baby didn't mean to bite his mommy, either."

"I don't know what to tell you, Isadore. Pain makes people do strange things. Animals, too."

"I can't stand seeing people when they hurt," she said. "I just want to make people feel better."

"That's a good thing," I told her.

"No," she said. "Not really. Because no one lets me. No one lets me make them feel better."

"How 'bout your daughter? Lena lets you."

"Yes. And Lena's leaving now."

"But she's only able to leave because you were so good to her. Because you made her feel so good for eighteen years."

"Okay," she said. "But she's still leaving. And I have nobody to help now."

I nodded and gave her a little hug. I felt bad for Isadore, but it made me happy to know someone whose main worry in life was that she needed more people to take care of.

The next few months of my life were, to put it mildly, un-fucking-real.

My mother's recovery was an extraordinary thing to behold. The doctors had told me she wouldn't talk or move again. She was talking and moving within three days. They'd told me she wouldn't walk; a week later she was walking. They'd also told me that she would probably have to spend the rest of her life in a nursing home. My mother, when she got that bit of news, raised her left hand—the one she could lift without too much of a struggle—and crooked her index finger at me to draw me closer, and when I leaned in, she said as clearly as she could muster, "If I have to spend the rest of my life in a place with old, sick people, just smother me with a pillow now." I promised her I'd let her know when that particular decision had to be made.

I stayed upstate for five more days after Elizabeth left. Not long before I was about to head back to the city, the hospital said they were kicking my mom out. She would have to leave in three days.

"You're kidding," I said to the social worker who broke the news to me. "What the hell is she going to do? She can't live in her house. She can barely move."

The woman explained that since my mother had stabilized, she was no longer the hospital's responsibility. She told me that my mom needed to go to a rehab center, where she would either get better or get progressively worse. If she got better, she could so home. If she got worse, she'd stay there until it was pillow time. To be fair, that was my interpretation; the social worker made it clear that any good rehab center would take loving care of any patient until he or she passed on to a better place.

Somehow I managed to hold my tongue. The struggle to ignore the pious assurance that there was a "better place" collided with the thought of trying to deal all by myself with a woman who couldn't feed herself or go to the bathroom without assistance. That put me in something of a tizzy, and I think the social worker noticed my inner turmoil because she hastily gave me a list of local rehab centers as well as several in Manhattan and then explained to me in some detail exactly what I needed to ask when I went to check out each institution. I left her office a bit shell-shocked and called Camilla. She said she'd call me right back and, despite my paranoid concern that I wouldn't hear from her for days, she called back in fifteen minutes with the names of three good nursing homes in Manhattan.

I told my mother what was going on and said I was going back to the city in the morning to try to get her set up. It made more sense to have her in rehab, where I could keep an eye on her. She fought back a bit—she wanted to stay close to her home—but she eased off when I told her that if she did well in rehab it would make it a lot easier for her to get back into her own house sooner rather than later.

Rocky and I spent one final night at the ol' homestead. I made an omelet for myself and cooked him some shrimp and broccoli rabe as a special treat (he loved broccoli rabe). I tried to feel sentimental when I left in the morning, telling myself that in a literal sense I was about to close the door on my past when I turned the key and put it back under the mat, but the sentiment didn't come. That door had been closed a long time ago, either when I realized that the family of my adulthood was not the family of my childhood or when the Lawrence Taylor poster had been taken off my bedroom wall and demolished. Or maybe it was when I realized that I'd spent years rooting my New York Giants heart out for a drug-crazed child molester.

By early afternoon I was back in my apartment. The guys were delighted to have me and Rocky home safe and sound. By late afternoon, I'd visited the three nursing homes Camilla had recommended. The first two places were horrifying. In the first joint, my mother would have been put in a room the size of a steamer trunk with a roommate who was attached to some kind of breathing device. I stayed in the room for about ten minutes, trying to imagine anyone I knew, much less my own mother, stuck in such a place. At one point, the nurse showing me around said, "Mrs. Lapner would be a very quiet roommate for your mother." Since the woman in the tiny bed hadn't moved since I'd been there, I said to the nurse, "That's because I think Mrs. Lapner's dead."

The second place was a little better but not much. For four hundred dollars a night, my mother would get round-the-clock care, three hot meals, and at least two cockroaches under her bed. I'm sure there were more roaches capable of making an appearance, but that was the number I saw before I got the hell out of the place.

The third one was a winner. Quiet, clean, and my mother could get a private room, at least for two or three weeks. I needed to figure out

the insurance issues, but I felt sure I could make this work. She could
live in this place without feeling as if she were dying in this place.

By dinnertime, I was in bed with Camilla. We made love—there
was the same urgency and passion and sexy kinkiness, but this time no
postcoital crying or depression or anger; there was even a sense of
affection and tenderness on her part—and then ordered in Chinese
food and beer. We ate and drank in bed and talked until well past midnight. I still had questions I would have liked answered—why she hadn't
called me back the first several days I was upstate was paramount in
my mind—but there was a delicate balance to whatever was happening with us, and I didn't want to upset that balance. I did tell her about
everything that had happened while I was gone: the first days at the
hospital, my mother's surprising recovery, my blowup and rant at dinner, the breakup with Elizabeth. She absorbed it all and seemed to
relish hearing the details of a life she was just getting to know and
understand. I didn't get much feedback in return, though. I decided
that for the moment I was satisfied to have earned her interest in *my*
life. I'd earn her willingness to share her own life sometime later.

I wasn't sure whether she wanted me to spend the night. So somewhere around one A.M., I said that I should probably go home and
walk the critters. She said, "Okay," without any emotion whatsoever. I
then said, while pulling on my socks, that I could come back after they
were walked so I could spend the night with her if she wanted, and she
said, "Okay," in the same exact tone. But when I looked over at her
she flashed me a smile, and it gave me the same sensation I'd experienced when I saw her for the first time on the street, when she'd waved
at me from half a block away. There was enormous pleasure in her
smile, and it made me light-headed to know that I was the one providing that pleasure.

I strolled home, walked and played with the animals that needed
walking and playing with—they did seem a bit confused; they were
used to a lot more attention, especially Rocky—and then headed back
to Camilla's as quickly as I could. She was under the duvet when
I returned, shivering slightly because she'd gotten up to buzz me in. I
stripped down and hopped into bed beside her. We wrapped our arms
around each other, kissed, and held on as tightly as we could. Her

naked flesh was so firm and smooth and soft, I felt I could disappear into it. We fell asleep clutching each other and woke up the same way.

Her cat slept on the bed with us. When Camilla woke up, seeing the little critter there startled her more than seeing me in the exact same position she'd seen me in six hours earlier. She burrowed under the duvet, sighed contentedly, and smiled. The cat came up and plopped down on my shoulder. Camilla hesitated, then reached out from under the cover and petted him.

"I still don't like him," she said. "I still don't see the point of him."

I shrugged and Rags kept on purring. It might have been the loudest purring I've ever heard.

Two days after that, an ambulance brought my mother down to New York and into rehab. She was pleased with the choice of the facility, although as soon as we were alone she said, "I'm not staying here long." I said that was up to her. And that first night, she was forced to walk, speak, and feed herself. To her, this was the equivalent of full-contact preseason football scrimmages in the NFL: pure torture but necessary if one wants to make the team.

The next morning I paced around my apartment for ten minutes, took a deep breath, and called Ted. It went quickly to voice mail. Rattled—I wasn't prepared to simply leave a message saying that our mom had had a stroke—I heard my voice turn overly serious as I asked him to call me back as soon as he could. When I hung up, I realized that if I picked up a message like that, I'd assume someone had died. So I immediately called back and told him not worry, that no one had died but he should still call me. I hung up, called back again, and said, "Oh shit, this is ridiculous. I'm calling because Mom had a stroke. It's very serious but she's fine. I've taken care of everything. She's in a rehab place in the city; I can give you all the info when you call me back. I know she'd like to talk to you and see you. Sorry to have to tell you this in a message."

I never heard back from him.

I e-mailed him a day later, writing a more cogent version of the scattershot messages I'd left by phone. No e-mail came in return. A few days later, I went up to the rehab clinic to visit my mom—she was having to learn to eat again; they were teaching her how to swallow solid food, so I usually brought her milk shakes and pudding and better versions of hospital food that she could easily ingest—and I told her that I'd been trying to reach Teddy to tell him what had happened but that I hadn't had any luck.

"Called me," she rasped.

"What?"

She nodded.

I couldn't believe it. I thought she had to be confused. "Teddy called you? Are you sure?"

"Sure."

"How'd he know where you were?"

This one was hard. "Friend," she said.

"His friend?"

She shook her head.

"Your friend?"

A nod.

"Who the hell does he know who's your friend?"

She stared at me. She'd given me all the help she could give.

"From back home? A neighbor from home?"

A head shake.

"In the city?"

Another shake.

"In California?"

She nodded.

"Who the hell could it be? Wait a second. Mimi and Fred?"

My mother nodded and breathed a shallow sigh of relief.

Mimi and Fred Stiles were old friends of my parents'. She was an actress and he wrote bad sitcoms. She'd also started her own religion. She owned a building called the Church of the Good, and the slogan over the entryway was "Put God Back in Good." Even her husband thought she was a nut, but they'd been true friends to my mom after my father died. I'd called them after she'd had her stroke, figuring they'd worry if they called and didn't hear back. I'd also e-mailed them when I'd chosen the rehab center and asked them to let her friends know what had happened and where she'd be. Mimi said she'd pray for us. She didn't say anything about Teddy, though. I realized that what must have happened was that they'd called him before I'd left my string of voice mail messages, and he must have gotten furious that I'd excised him from the entire process. For a moment I felt a surge of guilt, but then I shrugged it off. I wasn't trying to exclude him. I was just waiting until I thought my mother was strong enough to survive his inclusion.

"He keeps in touch with them? I didn't know that."

"Yes."

"What did he say when he called you?"

"Wants to come."

"Is he going to?"

She shook her head. Just a tiny shake. "Can't . . . leave . . . Hilts."

"He could bring him. I'm sure Hilts would like to see you, too."

"Would like that."

"Okay," I said. "I'll tell him."

That night, knowing Ted would never pick up the phone, imagining the anger that was gnawing away at him, I e-mailed him. I apologized for not letting him know about the stroke immediately. I explained that my whole focus had simply been on trying to solve a somewhat overwhelming problem. I also told him that I knew he'd spoken to our mom and said that she'd love to see both him and Hilts. Again I got no response.

The next day I e-mailed Hilts. I apologized to him as well for not letting him know about his grandmother's stroke and, as delicately as possible, explained my reasoning. I got a return e-mail within minutes. He said that he'd had no idea about Grandma's stroke and to please send her his love. He asked for a phone number where he could reach her, and I sent it to him, explaining that it was difficult for her to talk but adding that I was sure she'd love to just hear his voice. Thinking I must have misunderstood something, I asked him if Teddy had told him what had happened, and Hilts typed back, "No. I can't understand it. Will find out why the hell not."

Two days later, I went uptown to see my mom. When I walked through the door she said, "Hilts called," and her whole face lit up with pleasure. That night, Hilts called me, too. I was having dinner with Cam, who'd decided to cook a dish she remembered her mother making for her as a little child: shepherd's pie. My cell rang just as I'd taken my first bite.

"Hey, Uncle Bob," Hilts said. "I'm sorry to bother you, but something kind of important's come up."

I tried to remember if I'd ever gotten a call from my nephew before; I didn't think I had. I called him on his birthdays. Or at least I tried to remember to do that. I must have missed one or two, because his voice was deeper than I remembered.

"What's up?" I said.

And Hilts Heller said, "Someone in my school is trying to kill me."

He then proceeded to tell a story that periodically made me squint at the phone in astonishment, look at Cam and mouth the words "You're not going to believe this," and finally, when he was done talking, simply stare at the phone in silence, having no idea how to respond.

The story Hilts told me, and told me with a straight face, was this:

He'd befriended a boy—also fifteen—who Hilts didn't realize was mixed up with a really bad crowd. This kid, whose name was Arky, was selling drugs. According to Hilts, Arky asked him to pass an envelope along to another kid, this one black, named T.J. Hilts didn't know what was in the envelope, and apparently it was a surprise to T.J. as well, because he was expecting to find high-quality cocaine. Instead, he was handed some strange powder that was not worth anything like the large sum of money he'd paid Arky. T.J. didn't just blame Arky, he also blamed Hilts. And T.J. said he was going to kill both of them.

I tried to interrupt at this point, but Hilts wasn't through. He went on to say that T.J. wasn't just some tough, mean kid—he was the son of an African diplomat who was friends with murderous dictators. According to Hilts, T.J. had diplomatic immunity and could kill him and walk away scot-free. There was a lot more, but at some point I tuned out because all I could think was: *Is Ted standing behind you and coaching you on this bullshit?* In the end I simply said, "What do you want me to do?"

I expected him to ask for money so he could get out of town, and I felt pretty sure that the next time I saw him he'd be wearing a thousand-dollar leather jacket. Instead he surprised me.

"I don't know," my nephew said. "I'm just really scared and I didn't know who else to call."

"Okay," I said. "Have you told any of this to your dad?"

"Yeah."

"What did he say?"

"He said he's going to try to get me a gun so I can protect myself."

"*What?*"

"That's what he said."

"Where would Teddy get a gun?"

"I don't know. He said he knows people."

"Listen to me. Whatever happens, don't let him give you a gun. I don't think he's really going to do that, but he's so crazy you never know. If he really does show up with a gun, don't take it. Okay?"

Simultaneously, I heard Hilts say, "Okay," and Camilla say, "What the fuck is going on?"

I waved Camilla off and said into the phone, "Hilts, I mean it. Promise me you won't take a gun from your dad on the slim, insane chance that he comes up with one. Promise me right now."

Behind me, I heard Camilla again going, "Seriously, what the fuck is happening?" with Hilts mumbling at the same time, "Okay, I won't. I promise."

"Where are you now?"

"I'm at my mom's apartment."

"Where's she?"

There was a long pause.

"Hilts?" I said. "Where's your mom?"

"She's in Portland."

"Portland, Oregon?"

"Yeah."

"Who's in Portland, Oregon? Bob, what the fuck is going on?" That was Camilla again. I did my best to fend her off by rolling my eyes and holding up my hand. It was about as effective as using the gesture to stop a speeding train from hitting me head-on.

"How long is she going to be in Oregon?" I asked the boy.

"She moved there."

"Excuse me?"

"She moved there. About three months ago."

"You're living in her place by yourself?"

"No. I'm . . . uh . . . living here with Arky and T.J."

The rest of the story got even crazier. Hilts's mom, Charlie, had left for Portland with a new husband. The hubby had no desire to be burdened by a troubled teenager and Charlie chose hubby over son, so they kept the lease on the apartment and left Hilts there. Charlie decided that was a far preferable solution to having her son live with Ted (I had to admit it was a tough call). Arky didn't have close parental supervision either; his mother had died the year before, at which point, thanks to a combination of grief and alcohol, his father lost interest in most things, including his son. T.J.'s father, meanwhile, was several thousand miles away; the aunt with whom he was staying didn't quite understand the way America and American teenage boys worked, so she thought T.J.'s decision to move into a vacant apartment with two friends was fairly normal. And Ted, of course, was not going to jeopardize his son's friendship and love by imposing any form of parental discipline, so voilà: a two-bedroom, three-screwed-up-teenagers disaster was created from the rubble.

I calmed Hilts down as best I could. By the next morning, I'd done the following: spoken to Arky's father and roused him from his widower's haze; after that conversation, I felt pretty sure that Arky would be grounded until well past his fiftieth birthday. I'd also spoken to Hilts's high school principal, who explained to me that Hilts was a bit of a fantasist. The principal said that Hilts had been caught smoking marijuana recently, as had Arky. They'd been suspended from school for a week and ordered to take several counseling sessions. Without saying so outright, the principal made it clear that Arky was a dangerous influence; she also said that although Hilts was not a bad kid, he was both insecure and too easily influenced. Finally, she told me that the mysterious and dangerous T.J. was not quite what Hilts had made him out to be. His father wasn't a diplomat, he was a banker. And it was possible he knew a dictator or two but only if they'd taken out car loans.

I spoke to T.J. Senior, too, who said that his son was a bit out of control and that T.J.'s aunt wasn't capable of reining him in. Mr. T.J. regretted the fact that he traveled so much and said that he would now be more proactive in the rearing of his son. He would also, he said, insist that the boy immediately swear off any more talk about diplomatic immunity and murder. He ended the conversation by repeatedly assuring me that his son had not put out a hit on anyone, particularly my nephew. T.J., his father told me, might have a tendency to mouth off, but he promised me that anything his son said was nothing more than empty boasts.

I then arranged for Hilts to move in temporarily with none other than the self-appointed head of the Church of the Good. Mimi and Fred knew how much Hilts meant to my mother, so they were glad to take him in for a few weeks until things got straightened out.

With all that done, I blew off steam by writing an e-mail to Teddy to find out what the fuck was going on and what the fuck he was thinking. I didn't hear back.

Finally, figuring I should tell Hilts's principal what I'd learned, I put in a second call to her. As we were finishing up our conversation, she said to me, "You have to understand. Hilts is a very frightened boy."

"Frightened?" I said. "What's he frightened of?"

"You name it," she told me. "He just seems to be afraid of life."

"I'm surprised," I said.

"That he's so afraid?"

"No," I told the principal. "That he's smarter than I thought."

The day after his first call to me, Hilts and I talked again. I said, "Now you have to make me one more promise."

"What?" he asked. He spoke in a monotone; this shitstorm had knocked all the bravado out of him.

"You don't get to ask what. You fucked up in a major way, and I'm helping you straighten all this out. Your job is just to say yes and then do whatever the hell I tell you to do."

"Okay," he said. "Yes."

"Good. The promise you just made is this: You have to tell me the truth about everything from now on. You lied about all sorts of stuff when you told me what was going on with Arky and T.J. I will always be here, and I'll always have your back. Unless you lie to me. If you do, I won't help you again. Do you understand that?"

"Yes," he said.

"Good," I told him. "That's definitely a good thing."

At some point during the madness, when I was back at her apartment, Camilla touched me on the arm and said, "This isn't your responsibility, you know."

I said, "I know. But who the hell else is gonna do it?"

"How did we wind up this way?" she asked.

"What way?"

"Feeling as if we have to take care of all the wounded people." She looked at Margo, the alley cat who still had scars on her neck and back from her burns, and at Che, my three-legged Havanese. "And all the wounded animals, too."

While my mom learned to walk, think, and even breathe again, I was doing something similar with Camilla. As our relationship kicked into high gear, I discovered that she had certain, shall we say, eccentricities—she didn't think we should see each other two nights in a row, that was too claustrophobic for her; she couldn't stand watching television, because it made her angry to do anything she perceived as mindless entertainment; and she didn't enjoy lingering over breakfast in the morning, because she could not bear to allow herself to be unproductive—but we fit together remarkably well. We went to the movies and saw a lot of jazz and classical music; she was extraordinarily opinionated, capable of walking out of a film in a fit of pique or boredom within minutes if she decided it was worthless. There were a lot of museum and gallery visits; Camilla loved contemporary art and possessed what seemed to me an unfathomable amount of information and knowledge at her fingertips. She reacted very emotionally to art and dismissed artists who couldn't elicit a strong response from her. At a Boetti exhibit at MoMA, she walked me around as if I were a child on a class trip, explaining the meaning behind each piece of art, making me see the obsession with order and disorder that dictated the artist's quest to find patterns to art and, more importantly, life. By the end of the tour, I perceived for the first time the deep feeling behind seem-ingly dispassionate works of color and texture and geometry.

We spent a lot of time eating and talking and exploring each other. She loved food; when it was prepared in a way she approved of, it inspired a sensuous and sensual response. But a restaurant had to be perfect for Camilla to bother with it. If she didn't like the chairs or the plates or the color of the walls, that place was immediately crossed off her list. Sometimes we didn't even make it through a whole meal. She'd look at me in the middle of our appetizer and say, "Those candle-sticks are driving me crazy. Can we go somewhere else?" We'd both apologize to the waiter—she would happily accept the blame—and we'd move on to a restaurant that either had nicer candlesticks or nothing at all to distract her from the reason she was there: to satisfy her extraordinary palate. One near-perfect place—friendly waitstaff, delicious food, lovely setting—served American comfort food in bowls that had an unusual rim around the interior, rendering them ridicu-lously shallow in Cam's view. That was the end of the evening—the bowls were too off-putting. And the bowls didn't just spoil the food, they made her angry: *How could a chef with such good taste in food put his food in such horrible bowls?* Even as my eyes rolled in exas-peration, I delighted in the specifics and strength of her opinions and passions. Even when they struck me as truly weird, I still thrilled to them.

She also talked a lot about her career. Would she go back to Doc-tors Without Borders? Would she go back to a danger zone? Her instinct was that she would, that she had to, because it was what made her feel worthwhile. It gave her purpose. But at the moment she wasn't ready to go back, wasn't a hundred percent sure that she'd ever be ready to go back. She often seemed on the verge of telling me more about that danger zone and what drew her to it. But I was never able to push too far or too deep. When I tried, she'd shut down. Revert to simple scenarios and platitudes. What would she do if she stayed here? Open up a practice. Go on staff at a hospital. Partner with another doctor. It all seemed so tame to her. But she had to do something; she couldn't afford to be unemployed for too much longer.

The thought of her going away terrified me. When she talked about leaving the country, I felt as if I were choking. When she conjured a life without me, I was afraid that I'd start weeping. But I listened and said little because I knew that's what she wanted me to do. Sometimes I'd go home and write copious letters and e-mails, telling her what I felt, what I wished she would do, and what I wanted us to do together. But I never sent them; I never even saved them. Every single one was deleted. Over and over I watched my desires and my passion disappear in a blink on my computer screen.

We had our squabbles and had real differences of opinion and comfort levels. I also had to shed some longtime habits. She didn't like talking on the phone, so I had to cure myself quickly of morning and evening check-in calls. On occasion, I'd get bored or have an over-whelming desire to hear her voice and would call her. She would often be cold and distant or sound annoyed, as if I were intruding on her life, and get me off the phone quickly. But sometimes she would call me and we'd talk for two hours. She would sip wine on the other end of the phone and rant about politics or art or someone she'd met at dinner the night before or something she'd read in the paper that either angered her or moved her. I would hang up the phone feeling ever more like a teenager—smitten and frustrated at the same time; closer to her than anyone else in my life yet unable to reach over and touch her.

And she slowly began to become more and more enthusiastic about my appreciation of her quirks. Although she was still hesitant to tell me very much about her past life, she began to trust the fact that she could reveal her true self to me. It started with her disdain of shallow bowls; I was hoping it would soon lead to revelations of greater substance.

She was constant and unwavering when it came to her ideals and convictions about the world but contradictory and inconsistent about anything that had to do with her daily life. She would tell me that she didn't want children—she'd shudder as if a cold chill had come over her—but then she'd giggle like a little girl when we'd see an adorable baby on the street. She'd coo over the kid and talk to the mother about everything from baby clothes to baby food. After one cooing and giggling encounter, she asked me if I thought she'd be a good mother. I told her I thought she would be a good anything she wanted to be.

As soon as I said that, I saw something change in her. I saw her soften and I felt a level of resistance disappear. She kissed me on the cheek, and I don't know exactly how to describe what that kiss felt like. It was a kind of surrender. Though Camilla was powerfully intellectual, her life was guided by her emotions. Up to that moment in our relationship, passion and anger had been the two emotions I'd seen and experienced most often. But now there was a warmth that hadn't been there before, affection that had never surfaced so nakedly. I sensed that she needed me and wanted me. As her lips lingered on my cheek that day, I realized for the first time that Camilla cared about me on a deep, emotional level, maybe even loved me.

That sense of caring and love and, yes, that sense of surrender were what I'd wanted almost from the moment she'd walked into the clinic. Its absence had nearly driven me mad. But now, here it was, on the verge of becoming reality rather than a sleepless fantasy.

Her face was still close to mine when she said, "Why don't we go away this weekend? To a little inn or something. Someplace romantic."

"I thought you didn't believe in romance," I said.

"I never said that."

"Oh, you just don't believe in love." I heard the coolness in my voice. I thought: *What the hell are you doing?* But I couldn't stop doing it.

"I never said that, either."

"You did. You got angry when I told you I loved you."

"What I don't believe in," she said, "is easy love. Or convenient love. Or words that don't really prove anything."

"Oh," I mumbled.

There was an awkward silence. Then Camilla said, "Would you like to go away this weekend?"

"What about your two-days-in-a-row rule?"

"I'll waive it."

I didn't answer right away. I felt my throat constricting. And finally I said, "I can't this weekend. I have to work."

Camilla looked down, as if she was embarrassed. I said, "Maybe next weekend. Or the weekend after."

She didn't say anything. Just nodded. And then we didn't speak to or see each other for five days.

On the sixth day, I called her and asked if she wanted to have dinner. I took a deep breath and said that I missed her and didn't like not talking to her. She didn't respond to that. She just asked me when I wanted to get together, and I said, "Tonight." All she said to that was "Okay."

It's funny. I knew her well enough to know that I was supposed to go to her apartment, and I knew that I was supposed to get there at seven-thirty. I was even pretty sure I knew where she'd want to go for dinner—back to that original sushi restaurant. But I didn't know how she was feeling about me. Or how the evening would go. I didn't know if this would be the last time I'd ever see her. I just knew that I wouldn't be able to stand it if it was. And yet . . . and yet . . . Why did there always seem to be an "and yet" for almost every big event in my life? But here it was: And yet there would also be a sense of relief if our relationship ended. I didn't understand it. It almost made me physically ill to even think about it. But it was true. I knew I'd done something to damage our relationship. I just didn't know exactly what I'd done or why I'd done it.

The evening went very well, it turned out. It was a little awkward for a bit, but there was too much between us—too much knowledge, too much genuine affection, too much interest, too much involvement and emotional attachment—for the awkwardness to last long. I apologized for my behavior. I told her I wanted to go away with her for a weekend. Any weekend she picked. I told her it was just an asshole moment that had occurred and that it wouldn't happen again. And then I blurted out that I was very sure that I was in love with her and I didn't know why it frightened me so much but that she had to give me another chance. Awkward had turned into passion and then panic before I even knew what hit me.

Camilla listened. She didn't say much other than her usual oohs and aahs and moans over the sashimi and sake. After I'd given the waitress my credit card, Camilla touched my hand—she didn't hold it, she just touched it, let two fingers rest on the end of my fingers—and said, "It shouldn't take the idea of losing me to make you tell me that you love me."

That was pretty much that. She didn't invite me in when I walked her home, even after my ineloquent hints. We didn't talk for a couple of days afterward; then we did, and it seemed as if our relationship picked up exactly as it was before my panic attack, before I'd been given exactly what I'd been praying for and had basically stomped all over it. We saw each other often—but not two days in a row—and we made love sometimes, always at her unspoken instigation, but more often not. Nothing gave me more pleasure than talking to her and listening to her, with the possible exception of touching her. And I was fairly sure she felt the same way. Although there was definitely a new wariness on her part. She had made a huge step forward, I'd fucked up big-time, and so she'd taken two giant steps backward. Along with the wariness, I also felt a certain edginess to her behavior. I'd hurt her, even though I hadn't meant to. And I knew that meant there had to be some kind of payback.

Over a glass of wine one day, after we'd had lunch in her apartment, we went for a stroll and she took the recurring conversation about having a baby further than she ever had before. It was the first time the subject had come up since the going-away-for-the-weekend fiasco. "Seriously," she said, "no playing around and no sweet talk: Would I be a good mom?"

When I said yes, yes, of course, she asked me why I thought so. I told her, "Because you wouldn't become a mom if you didn't think you'd be good at it. You wouldn't do *anything* unless you thought you'd be good at it. You'd be a great mother because you'd be in love with the father and want to have his baby. And the first time you ever saw your kid, the amount of love that would be surging through you would be unbelievable. So yes, I think you'd be a wonderful mom."

Camilla looked thoughtful—she was usually thoughtful, except when she was angry—and she wanted to know if Anna had ever asked me about being a mother. I nodded. Camilla asked how I'd answered and I said I'd told Anna that she would be a great mother because she and I would be the parents, and together we could make things right. I said to Camilla, "I always thought of Anna as a part of me, so

I couldn't imagine her having a child unless I was a part of it. I couldn't separate the two things or think of her doing it on her own. I don't think she could, either."

"Thinking about it now, would she have been a good mother on her own? Without you?"

"I still can't think of it that way," I said. "It's not something that would ever have happened."

"She didn't exist unless it was as part of you?" Camilla asked, and now there was an edge to her voice.

"In some ways, that's right. At least that's the way I saw it."

"But for me, you see me as something separate."

"Don't you?" I asked.

She nodded.

"I don't think Anna could have had a child without me. I was too entwined with her, too much a part of her present and her past. We were completely dependent on each other, so it's not something that would ever have happened unless I was part of it. Not then, anyway. And probably not ever."

"But you'll never know that, will you?"

Her words weren't spoken harshly, but they were pointed and they caused me to take a step backward.

"That's right," I said slowly and carefully.

"She died before you could find out a lot of things about each other."

I didn't answer.

"Is it hard for you to talk about that?"

"I think we knew everything about each other," I said.

I could feel the hurt seeping out of my words. Glancing up at Camilla, I suddenly realized that I could barely stand to look at her. Anna had appeared before me like an apparition, dragging me back into the past.

"Everything about each other," Camilla said, "except what you would have become."

I said nothing. But I could feel my heart beating faster and my chest heaving and falling underneath my shirt.

"I have to get going," I told her.

"I've upset you," she said. I could see a bit of panic in her eyes. Fear that she'd crossed some line. Regret that she'd crossed it. And yet . . . it was a line she was going to cross again and again. We both knew that. She couldn't help herself. She reached for my hand, this time trying to hold it.

"I didn't mean to," she said. "Please don't go."

It wasn't the first time I'd ever said no to her, but it was the first time I'd ever *wanted* to say no to her. I had to get away, so I muttered something unsatisfying and evasive about having things to do and left her standing on the street. I walked back to my apartment, trying not to run, and when I got there I fell against the living room wall, using it to keep me upright. I didn't turn on a light, didn't make any motion to pet a dog or cat or bird. I did nothing but wait until I caught my breath.

I didn't know what the hell had upset me so much. Didn't know what the hell was going on. I wanted this woman. Loved her. And yet . . . there it was again. The dread "and yet." I didn't know all of what was scaring me. But I sure knew that what Camilla had said about Anna scared the shit out of me.

I spent the rest of the afternoon going over some records. Around seven P.M. I went down to the clinic and stayed there until after ten. I made myself focus on the charts and numbers and notations in front of me, and then read some fairly complex new research on vaccinations. The whole time I was hoping Camilla would call and hoping she wouldn't.

Around ten-fifteen, my cell phone rang. Caller ID showed a Los Angeles number. I suspected that it was Ted and could feel the tension rise up in my throat. I hadn't spoken to him in months, not since our mother's stroke. I let the call go and later noticed that the caller hadn't left a message.

I got into bed around eleven-thirty. Tried to watch a *Law & Order* but found that I couldn't. I flicked off the TV and reached over to pick up a paperback copy of *The Shock of the New,* a great critic's overview of modern art. The book was probably twenty-five years old, but Camilla had given it to me and said I would learn a lot from it and like it. She said I would agree with it—and she said she knew I only liked to know about things I inherently agreed with. She smiled when she said it. I smiled back at her, silently acknowledging that she had a pretty good understanding of the way my brain worked.

Before I could even open the book, my phone rang. It was my landline. Camilla never used the landline; she always called my cell. Maybe because I hadn't given her that number when we first met. She held grudges—even against phone numbers. But when I picked up the receiver and said hello, it was indeed Camilla.

"I don't like making you unhappy," she said. "I'm sorry that I did."

I had been feeling miserable for many hours: knots tightening my stomach, anger clenching my fists. And then I heard her voice. One sentence. One nice thing. And the misery and anger and fear washed away instantly.

"I'm sorry, too," I said. "I acted like a child. I don't know why. But I apologize."

"Hey," she said. "This is my apology call. You had the last one. Don't steal my thunder."

"I'm sorry."

"You've got to cut that out."

She laughed. I laughed back. Jesus, life was good. Jesus, life was crazy.

We lingered on the phone then, in silence. It wasn't awkward; instead it was remarkably intimate. Somehow we both realized that words would only get in the way, would push us further apart rather than keep us close. So neither of us spoke. We listened to each other breathe; I swear she was listening to me think. After three or four minutes, she said, in a whisper that was so seductive in its simplicity that it sent shivers down my spine, "Do you want to come over?"

I couldn't begin to whisper like that, so I did my best to speak in my normal tone, although I failed miserably and sounded like one of those idiots in a movie who drinks homemade whiskey in a prison-of-war camp and can barely get the word "good" out of his mouth.

"I can't," I croaked. "I'm just so exhausted from what happened today."

"Having an argument exhausts you?"

"Yes. I feel a little ridiculous when you put it that way, but yes."

There was another silence. Not like the first one. I could feel her thinking, feel her concern, but I couldn't tell if it was me she was concerned about or herself.

"I think you should come over," she said.

"I want to, but I think I just need to go to sleep."

"Would you like me to come to you?" she asked.

She had never set foot in my apartment. I'd asked, she'd avoided. Spending the night at my place had never seemed to be an option. It was another line waiting to be crossed.

"Yes," I said finally. "Yes, I would."

So she came to me. She was there in fifteen minutes. Looked around the apartment, nodded her quiet approval. Didn't quite know how to react to the menagerie that greeted her individually, one by one making their way over to sniff, rub up against, or demand to be petted by the newcomer. She dealt with the inspection passably well, but it clearly wasn't her favorite moment in life.

When we walked into my bedroom, she wasn't quite sure how to handle Rocky, who was curled up in bed exactly where Camilla wanted to plant herself. I smiled to show her that she was on her own. She got undressed, folded her clothes neatly and put them on top of my dresser, came back, peered down at Rocky, and frowned. After a moment she gently picked him up and placed him at the foot of the bed. Grumbling a bit, he tried to settle in but soon hopped off, landing on the floor with a graceless thud. I propped myself on an elbow and looked down at him: Since the day I'd gotten Rocky, he had never slept anywhere but on my chest or curled up against my side. Then Camilla pulled back the covers and got into my bed and I had no more thoughts about annoyed felines or bewildered dogs.

We kissed.

"The blue walls in the living room," she said. "That has to go."

"But—"

"Haven't you ever heard of white? Walls are supposed to be white."

"I—"

She kissed me again.

"I'm glad that's settled," she said.

She pulled me over to her and turned her back to me so my chest was against her back, my mouth in her hair. I fell asleep smelling her shampoo.

We woke up at the same time in the morning. I'd rolled back over, and now her arms were wrapped around me. I felt her fingers move and I turned to face her. Larry, Margo, Waverly, and Che were all on the bed. Larry was perched on Waverly's head. When we stirred, I heard Rocky scamper around on the floor. But he didn't come up to join the rest of us. Camilla kissed my neck and let her lips linger there. Her face nestled up against mine.

"Are they always like this?"

"Who?"

"All these weird animals."

"Yes. Well . . . when they feel like it. They must like you."

"Of course they do. But they make me a little uncomfortable."

"Of course they do. Because they like you."

"Don't be such a smart-ass."

"If it'll make you feel better, Rocky is clearly pissed off."

"Which one is he?"

"The orange cat. He's my special bud. He doesn't want anything to do with you."

"His loss."

"He'll come around."

"I'm sorry I'm disrupting your household."

"I'm not."

"No?"

"I'm happy," I said.

She accepted that with a quick nod. "You know what I noticed last night?"

"No."

"I mean, other than your weird animals. You have really good yoga feet."

"What?"

"Do you do yoga?"

"No."

"You should. You have really good feet for it."

"I'll take that as a compliment."

"You should."

We lay there for a few minutes longer, neither of us fully awake, reveling in the closeness of our bodies, reveling in the many pounds of animals hunkered together around us. At least I was reveling, and I'm almost certain she was, too, although reveling in the face of drooling dogs and needy cats was not really in Camilla's DNA.

"I'm glad," Camilla said after a long, comfortable silence. "I'm really glad you're happy."

Her words surprised me and touched me. Hearing her say them was a bit like seeing her naked. Every time she took her clothes off, she smiled. It was a self-conscious smile that made her seem so young and innocent, but it was also a joyously sexy and knowing smile that made her seem so in control. Sometimes she would slink into bed like a seductress or a secret mistress; sometimes she would bounce into bed without a stitch on, giggling and cackling and waving me to join her and it was as if she were a teenager leaping onto a trampoline, ready to celebrate anything and everything without a care in the world. And sometimes her nakedness was so quiet and subdued it was as if she was revealing more than her breasts and her legs and her ass. It was as if she was making her soul vulnerable to my gaze.

I heard all of that in her words that morning. They were innocent and sexy, seductive and joyous, revealing and vulnerable. I believed they were the first words she'd ever spoken to me that were totally unprotected and unafraid.

The next thing she said, she put her lips to my ear and spoke very quietly: "You make me feel safe."

"Don't jump out of bed or hit me or go crazy," I said. "But I think you feel that way because I'm in love with you."

She ignored that and said, "The problem is, I don't really like feeling safe."

"That's because you don't trust me."

"How do you know I don't trust you?"

"Do you?"

"No," she said. "Not yet."

"But you're getting there?"

"Maybe. I'm not sure. There are a lot of hurdles to overcome."

"I'm going to get better, I swear. I know I screwed up, but—"

"No," she said. "Not on your side. On mine."

"Really?"

She nodded. "Really."

"Such as?"

She breathed out a nervous little laugh. "Oh my god, you have no idea."

"Try me."

"You don't know what you're asking for."

"Maybe not. But that's my new goal," I said. "To make you trust me."

"It's a good goal," she said. "But it's not as easy as you think."

"Nothing's ever as easy as I think. But I never learn. It's part of my charm."

"You really are a romantic, aren't you? You think that love can make the whole world go 'round."

"I don't," I said, in all seriousness. "I just think it's a good place to start."

She laughed, a real laugh this time. "Okay, we'll see. After we get rid of the blue walls, we can deal with the curtains. Then we'll figure out the whole trust thing."

I froze and then pulled away from her a bit. "What's wrong with the curtains?"

Camilla waited a moment. Then, not exactly a statement, not exactly a question, more of a realization: "Your wife picked those."

I nodded. "She had superb taste."

"But very different than mine."

I nodded and slowly allowed my body to relax. But I could feel hers stiffen now.

"Camilla," I said. "I'm sorry. It's a reflex. I just have to learn how to . . ."

"How to what?"

"Nothing major. How to forget about my whole life so I can just love you the way you deserve."

I could feel the tension ease out of her, as well. But not entirely. Her eyes didn't soften. They stared at me. It felt as if they were staring through me.

"Do you want to know why I didn't call you back, those days when you were with your mother after her stroke?"

"I don't know," I said. "Do I?"

"No, you probably don't. But I'm going to tell you."

"Camilla . . ."

"I was with Alex. The boyfriend I told you about. He came to New York to see me, and we stayed together. Do you want to know more about it?"

"Christ," I said, "I don't know."

"He's a doctor, too. I met him through Médecins sans Frontières. In North Kivu. He's amazing. I saw him operate on people while bombs were exploding around him. When there were blackouts. And he had to work in the dark with no electricity and no machines. I was terrified. Sick to my stomach. He never stopped."

"Where is he now?"

"Back in Rutshuru. He came to the city to try to talk me into going back there with him."

"Are you going to go?"

"I don't know. Do you understand why I'm telling you all this?"

"To make me want to kill myself?"

She smiled. "No," she said. "I swear. To make you understand that you can trust me."

"You have a very strange way of doing that."

"I'm not with him now, am I?"

"No," I said. "You're not."

"What aren't you telling me?" Camilla said.

"Nothing."

"Uh-uh. There's so *much* you're not telling me."

I put my hand on her shoulder and drew her closer to me. I could feel her heart beating in rhythm with my own.

"I *am* strange," Camilla said. "I'm strange and I'm complicated and I'm not easy. And you know why? You know what else I am?"

"What?" I asked.

"I'm not dead."

With animals, you feed them, house them, pet them, and, when needed, you take away their pain—and for that they trust and love you. It should be that simple with humans, but of course it isn't. We try to make it that simple, but it never is.

That, I've come to understand, is what makes us human. We are not simple. We run from things we're attracted to. We destroy the things we love. We want the things we can't have. We take the things we don't want. We're hurt by truths and soothed by lies. We live for such a short time and all we yearn for is something that will last forever.

That morning, holding Camilla, feeling her beating heart, knowing all the things I was afraid to do or say, all the things I was afraid she would do or say, I began to think that, in spite of it all, the hurdles in front of us were surmountable.

Maybe that's why Camilla chose that day to tell me all about herself and her past.

From the *New York Daily Herald-Examiner:*

ASK DR. BOB

Dr. Robert Heller is one of New York's leading veterinarians. He is the author of two books about taking care of pets, *They Have Nothing but Their Kindness* and *More Than Human,* and is a regular on the *Today* show with his weekly segment, "The Vetting Zoo." Dr. Bob takes care of cats, dogs, horses, birds, snakes, turtles, frogs, snails, fish, small pigs, and many varieties of rodents. You can e-mail him at AskDr.Bob@Herald Co.com and ask him any question about the animal you love. His column runs Tuesdays, Thursdays, and Sundays in the tristate area's most popular newspaper. His columns can also be read on the *Herald-Examiner* website: www.HeraldCo.com/AskDrBob.

Dear Dr. Bob:

I don't know if you'll remember me or my dilemma, but I wrote to you a couple of years ago about the death of my cat, Ralph. Your response to me was a bit evasive and vague—you didn't really make a firm commitment in your answer—but despite your waffling you were extraordinarily helpful. Sometimes an answer that is based in reality is a lot more valuable than one that tries to be encouraging or supportive.

I'm writing to you again—and I swear that I am not a nut who writes letters to the editor or fan letters to celebrities; you are the first and only stranger to whom I've ever written— because I have had a resolution of sorts to my problem. In your response you wrote that you hoped I'd rediscover the pleasures of what you dubbed "pet weight." I have, in fact, rediscovered that pleasure, but in a way I did not ever expect. I was a cat person my whole life. Well, about fifteen months after Ralph died, I heard a screech outside my apartment. It sounded as if something bad had happened, which it certainly had. A small cocker spaniel had been struck by a hit-and-run driver. The poor dog was in tremendous pain; I could see the bone in his leg sticking through the skin. I took off my sweater, wrapped him in it, hailed a taxi, and brought the poor thing to my vet (who, of course, I hadn't seen since Ralph had died). I was nervous touching an animal in such pain, particularly a dog, since I was not at all familiar with dogs. But this little guy was so gentle and seemingly grateful that in the cab I found myself stroking his head and talking to him in as reassuring a manner as I could manage. I realize this letter is going on and on, so let me get to the point. The point is that the owner of the cocker spaniel could not be found. The vet fixed his leg—he didn't lose it, but he does still limp noticeably—and put him up for adoption. I couldn't stop thinking about him, and I wound up doing the adopting. I have renamed him Derek, and he sleeps next to me. Not *on* me, the way Ralph used to, but by my side, usually down around my legs. So the real point of this letter is to say I have indeed rediscovered "pet weight." It's different in every conceivable way. But it's lovely.

—No Longer Weightless in Seattle

Dear No Longer Weightless:

You don't need my advice, you need my congratulations. Rediscovering "pet weight"—and let's call a spade a spade: We are really talking around the idea of love, just using cute euphemisms so as not to appear too treacly—is a rare and, I believe, wonderful thing. You are someone who must have a great capacity for love, and you are therefore able to embrace it on a deep emotional level. Many mere mortals are not capable of such resilience and rediscovery, and I suppose there are many reasons for being so closed off. Those reasons run the gamut from fear to bitterness to a simple lack of opportunity. Speaking for all of us on that end of the human spectrum, I salute, embrace, and revere you.

—Dr. Bob

CHAPTER 11

CAMILLA HAYDEN

Here's what I learned about Camilla that day:

She was eight years, nine months, two weeks, and four days younger than I. But her mother's best friend, an Englishwoman who owned a seed catalog and was always giving exotic seeds to Camilla to plant in their small garden, once said to her, "My child, you were born old." I think the friend was right. Or more to the point, "old" was forced upon Camilla.

She was born in London; her father, Lewis, was British and her mother, Constance, was American. She grew up thinking about her family, as I did about mine, that they were strong and stable and that any problems that might exist in the world would be solved simply because everybody loved each other so much.

Her mother made beautiful things—gloves and jangly bracelets and socks that glowed in the dark—designing them for her own pleasure as well as for her business and selling them to small, upscale boutiques in Chelsea. One women's clothing store in Paris, in the fourth arrondissement, also carried her distinctive line. The Paris store, which was owned by a woman named Maude, sold more of Connie's socks than anyone else's.

Lew was an actor (we were both startled to hear that our fathers shared a profession and that we'd run as far away, conceptually, from that profession as we could, opting for precision and caring for others rather than inventiveness and vanity). He acted in plays occasionally, usually taking small to medium parts in companies that toured the British countryside. He did some television, often playing the bewildered bureaucrat or the friendly neighbor. But his real living came from voice-overs. He was the voice behind ubiquitous dancing tea bags and the narrator of BBC nature documentaries; he also extolled the virtue of the BMW's ability to take curves and hold the road on the iciest of nights.

Camilla's mother doted on her, dressing her up in frilly dresses and decorating her with her own inventions and designs as if Camilla were a living, breathing doll. Her father loved to watch his daughter prance around in elegant ribbons and jangly costume jewelry and iridescent socks. But he also warned her to be careful. When she was eight years old, he told her, "Men love all the shiny things—it's what attracts them. But you have to have more than shine. You have to have substance underneath." She understood what he was trying to tell her, especially when he pointed to her perfect mother and said, "She understands. Look how she shines. Look how she glitters. But underneath your mother there's a lot more than glitter."

Camilla was Lew and Connie's only child. She got lonely sometimes and used to ask her parents why she couldn't have a sister or a brother. They would tell her that they had gotten so lucky with a perfect child the first time around that they didn't want to tempt fate.

Young Cammy went to a top school as a child, an essential step up the ladder in class-conscious England. She rode horses in Hyde Park and in the Sussex countryside, where Lew and Connie had a small nineteenth-century cottage. The cottage had a lovely little garden, and it was here that Camilla planted all the seeds her mother's best friend gave her. On weekends she couldn't wait to see if her own special flowers had come to life or sprung up several more inches or wilted away while she was separated from them. Until the age of twelve, that was the worst thing that had ever happened to her: flowers in the garden wilting and dying while Camilla was in London in her flat on Gloucester Road.

Then her mother made a major career change. Connie had long been satisfied with a business that was small and exclusive, but now she decided to go big-time, or at least bigger. She took a job with an up-and-coming British designer who wanted to branch out into accessories. Suddenly Camilla's mom was a vice president and so busy that she often had to work late and, more often than not, spend weekends in the city. Lew, who was several years older than his wife, was not thrilled with the new arrangement. He loved it when his wife sparkled and shone at home, when she showed her inner substance only to him. He was not so crazy about Connie shimmering elsewhere and getting a big salary in exchange for showing the world how smart and talented she was. Lew loved routine even above substance, and his routine was now very much in disarray.

Things only got worse when Connie had a sudden realization: It wasn't routine her husband craved, it was control. It also hit her that he'd been subtly controlling her all these years, and the awareness staggered her. One Friday, Cammy overheard an argument between her parents. It stunned her because she'd never before heard a cross word pass between them. Since Lew was English, it was a quiet argument. He never raised his voice or allowed his tone to turn angry. He let Connie handle that end. Lew simply said that he couldn't go on this way and that if Connie insisted on continuing along this path, he'd have to do something about it. She pleaded with him; she loved the new job, told him how happy it made her. He didn't care. He said he was taping a voice-over for a new frozen pudding that afternoon for BBC Radio and that he expected her to be ready to leave for Sussex by five p.m. sharp. Connie began to swear and yell while Lewis sat quietly, his arms folded, until she was done. She didn't finish until young Cammy broke into the room, ran to her mother, and pleaded with her to come to Sussex for the weekend. Connie stroked her daughter's hair, stared at her husband, and said she would be ready to leave at five p.m.

The drive out to the cottage was subdued and tense. That night, Camilla overheard another argument before she fell asleep. Her mother couldn't understand why Lew didn't see how important her work was to her. Lew couldn't understand how anything could be more important than the perfect life they'd had for fifteen years. Camilla remembered her mother saying, "Sweetheart, things change. People change. It doesn't mean everything has to fall apart. Change can make things better. You just have to trust me." And she remembered her father responding very quietly, in that actor's stage whisper that up until that moment she'd found so alluring and romantic, "You've betrayed me."

The next morning, Lew told Camilla that he'd arranged for her to go horseback riding.

"I don't want to," she said. "I'd rather stay with you and Mum."

"You can be with me and Mum this afternoon," he said. He seemed particularly jovial, so Cam thought that maybe they'd worked everything out last night after she'd fallen asleep. A neighbor came by to take her, with the neighbor's daughter, to the nearby stable. Cam suddenly felt a powerful need to say good-bye to her mother, but Lew said she was still sleeping.

"We'll have a lovely lunch when you come home, ducks." Cam couldn't remember where the nickname came from, but he sometimes called her "ducks," and it always made her giggle. She giggled this time, too; she couldn't help herself. Then she ran to the car and went horseback riding.

When she came home at lunchtime, there was a local police car parked outside the cottage. She knew immediately what had happened—she just knew—and ran toward the house. A policeman tried to grab her, but she eluded his grasp.

Camilla raced inside and saw her father dangling from a rope strung up to the bedroom rafter. He was wearing a suit; in his jacket pocket, in place of a dress handkerchief, was a pair of shiny, sparkly socks, Connie's latest design. Before he'd hung himself, he had stabbed his wife to death, plunging a kitchen knife into her eleven times. The police later determined that he had killed her before Cam had gone riding that morning. Connie's body was sprawled on the bedroom floor, and Lew's was hanging above it. The image of his dead wife had to have been the last thing he'd seen before the rope snapped his neck.

Camilla's father had not told her he loved her when he sent her off to the stable that morning. He did not express any form of regret or agitation. He just said good-bye and told her he'd see her when she got home.

But he did leave a note for her. The police found it and at some point handed it to the hysterical little girl. Lew Hayden wrote the following words as his suicide note: "Ducks, I'm sorry we betrayed you. It doesn't mean we don't love you. Love, Da."

Camilla was taken in by her father's sister and brother-in-law, who lived in a London suburb. They were very sympathetic and kind—for a while. But they were unable to understand the depths of the girl's confusion about how and why her life had been shattered so abruptly and so insanely, and they couldn't comprehend why, at some point, she didn't just pull herself up by her British bootstraps and get over it. They treated Camilla as if she had some kind of disease. Camilla told me that she did: terminal sadness.

Sadness often shifts toward anger, but when Camilla was fifteen, her anger turned into full-blown rage. Her aunt and uncle knew even less about how to deal with that. She started drinking and doing drugs. And she discovered sex, which became an excellent way for her to express her fury at the living as well as the dead and, of course, at herself. At sixteen, she left home. She also left behind a fair amount of money, because her aunt and uncle had somehow used the British court system to assume control of Lewis and Connie's estate. It wasn't all that sizable but it was bigger than nothing, which is what Camilla now had. For the next two years, the teenager lived with friends, mostly boys. She was rootless and restless, unable to feel comfortable anywhere. Everywhere she turned she saw betrayal.

The one thing that didn't suffer during this period, miraculously enough, was her schoolwork. School became a valued escape from all her frustrations and self-destructive behavior; when she turned eighteen, she was able to get a scholarship to Columbia University, in New York. But her rage continued unabated, as did the powerful desire to run as far away from home as possible. Not just the home that had been shattered or the home that had been forced upon her—she ran away from any home, all homes, anywhere. She lived with several men, but as soon as they got serious, she dumped them. She shared several apartments with roommates, but the moment a roommate started buying furniture or making the place comfortable and lived-in, Camilla either threw the roommate out or moved out herself. She left people and possessions behind without a second glance.

She loved medical school because it left her no time to think about her life. She loved her residency even more because it was her life. She lived at the hospital five nights a week, ate all her meals there. Her entire existence was devoted to eliminating other people's pain, which gave her no time to experience her own.

When she finished with school, she felt lost for a bit. She hung out in bars, met men, sometimes went home with them, usually didn't. She liked to make them listen to her tale, liked to watch their faces when she told them about her parents. She began to embellish the story, honing the details of what she'd seen when she'd raced past the policemen and into the cottage.

She delighted in seeing how the tragedy scared many men away, excited others, and made some vulnerable to her manipulation. She liked the pity and the shock. Sometimes when she told the story she was casual and hard; sometimes she would go for the sentiment and the tears. It was all an act, because she never felt anything when she told her story except the deep sense of betrayal that her father had apologized for in his suicide note. He had taken away her belief that anything would be all right ever again. He had stolen her faith that the center could ever hold.

In med school, she realized that she was drawn to the patients who were seriously wounded or dying. Stabbings, car crashes, suicide attempts—that's what she wanted to be around and surrounded by. And one night, drinking in a bar on the Upper East Side, telling her story to some advertising guy who was dreaming of getting into her pants, she realized that she wasn't drawn to dying patients. She was drawn to death.

She went home to her barely furnished studio apartment, got into a warm bath, and took a kitchen knife with her. She imagined that it was identical to the knife her father had used to kill her mother. She drank most of a bottle of gin and prepared to slit her wrists, sink into the water, and join her parents. But something held her back; she didn't know if it was cowardice or if she just wasn't ready, but the final urge to end her life never came. She stayed in the tub for six hours, until the water was cold and her teeth were chattering. Then she got out, padded naked into the kitchen, put the knife back in its proper drawer, and fell asleep on the unmade mattress in the middle of the floor.

The next day she got in touch with Médecins sans Frontières. When she learned that she needed to spend a year in a big-city emergency room if she wanted to work for them, she didn't hesitate. She slogged through twelve grueling months at a New York hospital's ER and gained the experience that would enable her to put herself directly into the hands of death.

As soon as she had the necessary qualifications, Camilla headed to the Congo and the center of the fighting in North Kivu. She worked amid gunfire and explosions and saw friends and patients murdered in front of her eyes. She treated soldiers who'd been shot and babies who hadn't eaten in days and small children whose limbs had been blown off. She had a torrid affair with a Spanish doctor named Alex García and thought she was in love with him. Then she discovered that, in the midst of their romance, he'd also started sleeping with a friend of hers, a nurse who'd been working with them in the Rutshuru hospital. It was another betrayal, but she'd already come to understand that she didn't love him. He only came to life when surrounded by death. It was what excited him and motivated him and sustained him. She had begun to thirst for something else. She had seen enough; something invincibly alive had sprouted within her. Now Camilla wanted to run from death. She wanted to run from betrayal. So she came back to New York, a place where she felt she might belong, and sublet a friend's small apartment for a modest amount of money and a promise to take care of a cat named Rags.

She met me. I fell in love with her. She wanted to fall in love with me. But although she was on the run from her dark side, she hadn't escaped it altogether. She couldn't bring herself to believe that love and family didn't go hand in hand with betrayal. She was caught in the middle, pulled apart by two magnets of equal strength. One magnet was everything she had experienced and knew to be true. The other was me.

My family fell apart because of neuroses and competition and fears that played out and festered over decades. But, thanks in large part to Anna, my family didn't destroy me or even come close. My brother lied and cut a wide swath of destruction, and my parents were sometimes hurtful and caused some inadvertent harm, but in the end, all it added up to was the kind of normal, everyday, distasteful human behavior that makes the world go round. Camilla's family blew itself apart and shattered a lovely little girl.

What happened to my family was a war game. What happened to Camilla's was a real war.

We were two people incapable of escaping our ghosts. My ghost was so perfect that she made the past so much better—incomparably better—than the present. Camilla's ghost was so murderous that he tried to kill his child's future.

And there we were.

While Camilla and I were trying to convince ourselves that we could overcome the entanglements of the past, my mother was trying to come to terms with the enormous burden of what her future might be. It was an extraordinary thing to watch, especially because, at least to me, it was so unexpected. Perhaps the biggest surprise one can have is when you've known someone for your entire life, then discover that you don't actually know her at all.

My mother's doctor told me that he'd never seen willpower remotely comparable to hers. She refused to succumb to her fate. She didn't get depressed. She didn't get angry. She didn't yield to the physical or mental obstacles thrown directly in her path. She just went about her business—which, I began to realize, was what she'd been doing her (and my) entire life.

I was told that my mother would likely be in the rehab center for at least six months to a year, if she ever got out at all. Exactly three months later, I installed a motorized seat that attached to the stairway railing in my building; the next day, my mother moved into the third-floor apartment. I had cleaned up the apartment as much as possible and shipped a lot of Marjorie's more esoteric items—a totem pole from a South Seas island; teacups with pictures of all the key Disney characters (as well as a teapot shaped like Goofy; the lid had ears as floppy as ceramic ears could be); a nutcracker shaped like a naked woman (the nuts were cracked between her legs)—down to her in Florida. Marjorie's New York trips had become less and less frequent, and when she came she rarely stayed in the garret anymore. It was too hard a climb, so she stayed in a hotel instead.

Having an extra apartment as a spare storeroom was a ridiculous luxury in Manhattan, so in came my mom. And to live with her and be her aide, I hired Isadore, the very special Trinidadian who only wanted to care for and help people. My mother needed plenty of help and care: She couldn't walk by herself or go to the bathroom by herself or cook or clean. Isadore happily moved out of her Bronx apartment and into the brownstone on Greenwich Avenue. She couldn't believe her luck. She was now living in a beautiful apartment and had someone new to love and look after.

I remembered Phil's words when my mom was in the hospital. He was right: This *was* like a surreal version of my childhood. Life had begun to come full circle. I had in no way escaped my family; I had only reconfigured it. I was now living with one dead wife, one dead father, one stroke-ridden mother, and one semi-missing brother. And I was in the midst of a serious relationship with a living, breathing, fully functioning woman with whom I'd fallen in love and who wouldn't see me two days in a row.

It all seemed fairly normal to me.

Camilla's first encounter with my mother was quite different from Anna's. My mom was fairly aphasic now. Her memory was perfect; she simply couldn't come up with a lot of pesky nouns or proper names. Conversation was difficult at times, although with enough patience we could get where we needed to go. Sometimes her words flowed easily; sometimes she struggled to come up with the simplest of questions or statements. But she never stopped pushing herself. I'd go downstairs to my apartment, and two hours later the phone would ring.

"Do you have a new dog?" she'd ask. Her voice had become weaker since the stroke. It quivered a bit, as if the effort of stringing words together was strangling her vocal cords.

"Is that what you wanted to ask me earlier?"

"Yes."

"No, I don't. Why do you think so?"

"There was a dog in the . . . you know . . . where I come in."

"The stairway."

"Yes. I'd never seen him before."

"What kind was it?" I knew she'd have trouble with that one. But the doctor had told me to keep peppering her with specific questions so her brain would keep working hard.

"It was a . . . a . . . oh, god, I hate this."

"Describe it."

"It was blue."

"Really? Blue?"

"No. Not blue. Didn't mean blue. Light-colored. Like at the beach."

"Tan?"

"Yes. It was tan."

"Like light brown?"

"Yes. And long hair."

"Was it big?"

"No. The size of Hilts."

"Hilts? That'd be a pony."

"Not Hilts now! Young."

"How old? Five?"

"Younger."

"A baby?"

"Yes."

"Okay. A small, light brown dog with long hair."

"Yes."

"That was pretty impressive—you nailed it. It was a cocker spaniel. I was treating it, but the owner let it run out the door and into the hallway. It's not mine."

"Oh. Good. You have enough dogs. Time to have a real one."

"A real dog?"

"Don't be a smart-ass. You know what I mean."

"A baby."

"Yes."

"I'm hanging up on you now, Mom."

"I knew you would."

Over breakfast one morning I asked her if she'd always been this stubborn. She nodded.

"Living with your father," she said. "Had to be stubborn."

"Why?"

"He was part-time husband. Part-time father. Not easy holding things together."

"You did a good job," I said.

She shook her head. "No. Didn't do good with Ted."

"Why not?"

"Made mistakes. Was too afraid."

"Too afraid of what?"

"Of making mistakes."

She laughed at herself after that. It was a rueful laugh, but it was genuine. I think my mother got funnier after her stroke.

So when I finally introduced her to Camilla, my mother was in some respects a different woman than the one who'd met Anna. In some ways she was diminished; in most ways she was much more secure and understanding and generous.

She and Camilla hit it off. For one thing, Camilla had a superb bedside manner. She didn't speak to my mother as if she were some kind of victim; she dealt with her as an equal. When my mom couldn't come up with a word, Camilla immediately fell into the rhythm of helping her tease it out. It was all fairly easy because my mother liked Camilla and Camilla was comfortable around my mom.

From that point on, the four of us (Isadore was always at my mother's side) had dinner together at least once a week and on occasion went to the movies. Several times Camilla took my mother out—in her wheelchair—to museums and galleries when I was too busy to go. My mother also took to hanging out in the clinic's waiting room for a good chunk of the day. At any given moment it was a safe bet that you'd find the room filled with lesbian cat owners, a hypochondriacal snail (or snail owner), barking dogs, homeless pet owners receiving free treatment thanks to the scholarship money that came from a Mexican drug cartel, a Trinidadian caretaker, an obese receptionist who would occasionally burst into tears (now more frequently than ever, because Alana, Lucy's longtime partner, had just dumped Lucy in favor of an even more obese woman, and the three of them were living in Alana's studio apartment, which would have made me cry a lot more often than Lucy did), and an elderly stroke victim, who somehow managed to comfort them all.

A couple of months after my mom moved in, I went upstairs to check on her during a short break between patients. Camilla had gone with her to the Morgan Library that morning to see an exhibition of rare manuscripts.

"You like her," I said. It wasn't a question.

My mom nodded.

"We liked her right from day one," Isadore chipped in from across the room, nodding more energetically than my mother.

I waved my hand, acknowledging her approval, then turned back to my mother. "You didn't like Anna when you first met her, did you?"

I wasn't sure she'd even remember that first meeting. But, as usual, I'd underestimated her.

"You're right," my mother said. "I didn't like her that day."

"Yeah, but why?"

"You liked her too much."

"What?"

"You asked. That's the reason."

"I know, but . . . what do you mean? Teddy used to bring all these women home, and he could barely speak in front of 'em he was so smitten and lovesick."

She waved her one good hand in the air, dismissing the comparison. "Teddy fell in love every day of the week," she said.

"And me?"

"You were gonna fall in love once. That was it."

I looked at her in amazement.

"What?" she said. "Don't look so surprised. I was always smarter than you thought."

"Mom," I said. "You still haven't answered the question."

"Get me a . . ." She drifted away for a moment; her brow furrowed as she tried to remember something. "Goddamnit," she said. "I hate not being able to remember words."

"What do you want?" I asked. "You can do it."

"The second drawer on the left in that thing in the dining room. The second drawer on top. I need the thing to wipe my mouth."

"A napkin?"

She nodded in relief, then sighed in frustration.

I got her the napkin, watched her wipe her mouth, and waited.

Finally, she said, "I thought she'd break your heart."

"From the moment you met her?"

She nodded.

"When did you start to like her?"

"Oh, soon after. Very soon after."

I smiled, teasing her. "So you admit you were wrong, huh?"

"About what?"

"About her breaking my heart."

She didn't say anything.

I laughed now, and shook my head. "Come on. After all this time, you can't admit you were wrong?"

She wiped her mouth again and gave a little cough into the napkin. "Was I?" she said. "There's still time."

I thought perhaps she'd gotten confused. "Mom," I said, "we're talking about Anna. She died. Almost ten years ago."

"I know," she said. "I'm not an idiot."

"Then how can she still break my heart?"

"Does this one want to get married?"

"Camilla?"

"Yes."

"It's complicated."

"That's what I mean."

"It's not just me."

"Have you asked her? Shit, what's her name again?"

"Camilla."

My mother nodded as if trying to make sure she stored the name in her brain so it would keep. "Have you asked her? Shoot. I can't believe it. I already forgot her name."

"Camilla. And no. It's too early."

"No, it's not. You have that look in your eye. Not like Ted. The real look."

"Maybe."

"She has it, too."

"Really? You think so?"

"Know so," my mother said. She was starting to get tired; that's when her sentences turned into fragments.

"It's still complicated," I said.

"I had . . . a stroke," my mother said.

"I know."

"I had stroke, not you."

"I know, Mom."

"But I know . . . Anna's dead."

"So do I. Believe me, so do I."

"No," she said. "She's still . . . breaking . . . your heart."

Camilla and I were having dinner one night—sushi and sake back at our usual haunt—when she told me she had a job offer. My breath didn't seem to want to leave my body, and then I managed to say, "Where?"

"A doctor I knew from med school. He's kind of my Marjorie Paws."

"In New York?"

She looked at me, surprised. "Yes. In Tribeca. Is that all right?"

"Yes. I mean . . . it's not all right, it's great."

"Would it make you happy if I stayed in New York?"

I closed my eyes and breathed a long sigh of relief. "Very happy," I told her.

"Happy enough to tell me all the things you still haven't told me?"

"Cammy, there's almost nothing I haven't told you."

"Almost nothing isn't the same thing as everything, is it?"

"When do you start the new job?"

"In a few weeks."

"I'm very, very glad," I said. "You have no idea."

"Shall we go back to your place and celebrate?"

I leaned over and kissed her. Normally, any public display of affection mortified her. Holding hands was barely acceptable, tolerated only on rare occasions. Kissing in restaurants was verboten. But this time she didn't pull away or swat at me. She kissed me back. Then we got up to leave.

Ten minutes later, we were in front of my apartment. An ambulance and two EMT workers were standing by. I rushed over to them and asked what had happened. Before they could respond, two other EMT guys carried a stretcher out the front door. On it was a body covered by a sheet.

"Oh shit," I said. "After all that."

Cam put her hand on my neck, but even her healing touch didn't ease the frustration and sadness that flooded through me. But what she said right after that did.

"Bob. Your mother's fine."

"What?"

"Your mother just came out of the building."

Sure enough, right behind the stretcher was Isadore, wheeling my mom.

"Then who's this?" I said to the EMT standing next to me.

"Florence Schmidt. Fourth floor. Heart attack."

And then I saw, behind Isadore, Florence's husband, Isaac, my neighbor for the last fifteen years. He was crying, staggering a bit, not sure who or what to hold on to.

Before I could get to him, my mother reached out with her good hand to hold one of his hands. He bowed his head as if he were in church.

"It's never dull around here," Camilla whispered.

Truer words were never spoken. A few minutes after that, we stepped inside my apartment, where, the moment I closed the door behind us, I was shocked to hear a familiar voice—deep but not quite a man's voice—say, "Hello, Uncle Bob."

"What are you doing here?" I said. "Camilla, this is Hilts, who shouldn't be here."

"Hi," Hilts said to Camilla. "Nice to meet you."

"Ditto."

"Enough with the pleasantries," I interrupted. "What the hell are you doing here?"

"I don't know. I sort of ran away."

"From who?"

"Everybody, I guess."

"How'd you get in here?"

"The fat woman let me in."

"We call her Lucy."

"Right. Lucy. She let me in."

"And how the hell did you get to New York?"

"I flew. JetBlue. It's really cheap."

"Yeah, I know. But how'd you pay for it?"

"I put it on one of Mimi's credit cards."

"Oh, Jesus."

"I figured I'd pay her back when I got here. I mean, you would. And then I'd pay you back. As soon as I can."

"What about school?"

He shrugged.

"What about your mom? And Ted?"

He shrugged again.

"Hilts, your father's gonna hit the roof."

"Let him."

It was hard to counter that one.

"What happened?" Camilla asked him quietly.

Hilts didn't say anything.

She looked at him intently. "Something must have happened to make you do this."

He nodded.

"What?" she said.

Hilts didn't move for a few moments. The kindness from Camilla's voice seemed to envelop him. Then he undid two buttons of his shirt and pulled the shirt open. On his chest was an ugly-looking red mark.

"Who hit you?" Cam asked. "The people you're staying with?"

"No," I told her. "They wouldn't do that."

My eyes met Hilts's. A tear came out of one of his.

"That's Ted," I told Camilla. "That's definitely his father who did that."

I got Hilts something to eat—leftovers, but he was so ravenous I could have given him cat food—and the three of us stayed up talking for an hour or so, then Hilts fell asleep on the couch. Cam covered him with a blanket, and we went to bed.

"He's such a skinny little kid," she said, lying next to me. "How could your brother hit him like that?"

"Hilts did something pretty dangerous," I told her. "If he's for real."

"It sure sounded real."

"Yeah," I said. "But Ted used to sound like he was for real, too."

"You're suspicious."

"I've just learned not to rush into believing everything my family says."

"I don't think he was making that up."

"No," I said. "I agree."

"Then why?"

"It's hard to know. But it sounds like Hilts did something he shouldn't have done. He made Ted face the truth. It's like dropping a lit match into a tank of gasoline."

According to Hilts, my brother had insisted on taking him to a movie and then to dinner. He let the sixteen-year-old kid drink half a bottle of wine at the restaurant. Afterward, in the parking lot, Ted told his son what he wanted him to do: call his grandmother—our mother—and say that he needed money. Ted had the story all ready. Hilts was to say that he'd been practicing driving and taken his friend's father's car and crashed it. He needed five thousand dollars or he was going to be in real trouble.

Hilts refused to make the call. His grandma was probably the only person in his young life who had loved him unconditionally, who hadn't wanted anything in exchange for that love, and he couldn't do this to her. Ted got angry. Then angrier. But rather than back down, Hilts told his father than just because Ted was a liar and a loser, he wasn't going to turn him into the same thing. Ted reacted instinctively: He lashed out with a clenched fist and hit Hilts in the chest, right above his heart. Hilts told us he doubled over and threw up. It took him twenty minutes to get his breath back. Ted tried to help him, as if Hilts had just gotten sick all on his own. As if the punch had nothing to do with it. As if the punch had never happened.

For the first time in his life, Hilts saw his father in the harsh light of reality. He saw the truth of his father's actions rather than just hearing Ted's words. (My guess is that Hilts's clarity of vision had as much to do with the fact that he had vomited all the wine he'd drunk as it did with his father's violent and indefensible punch.)

Ted started yelling at him, trying to convince his son—and himself—that Hilts had *made* Ted hit him, that it was really the boy's fault because Ted would never do anything to hurt him. But Hilts had the raw welt and the stabbing pain in his chest to prove that Ted had indeed hit him. And hurt him badly and viciously.

Ted used all his powers of persuasion to get Hilts in his car and then tried to take the boy back to his house. As he drove, Ted was soothing, cajoling. Hilts could barely focus on the words and was almost overwhelmed by the rhythm of Ted's insistent chant: *I didn't really hit you. I didn't really hurt you. Nothing happened. Everything is okay.*

Everything is going to be fine. But at a red light, Hilts jumped out of the car and ran. He had no idea where he was or where he was going—he just ran. Eventually he made it back to his room at Fred and Mimi's. For the next couple of weeks, Ted called him ten times a day, maybe more often than that, but Hilts wouldn't answer or call him back. Ted came by Fred and Mimi's house, but Hilts ducked out the back door. That's when he had the bright idea of running away. Running to me.

"What are you going to do?" Cam asked. Her bare left arm snaked over my chest.

"I don't know," I said. "I don't even like the kid very much."

She smiled. "I know what you're going to do."

"What?"

She just looked at me.

"Yeah, I know." I sighed. "Take care of the wounded."

"Poor Bob," she said. "You try so hard, but you just can't get away from all the damaged people."

It took a little time to work out the details, but before long Mr. Schmidt decided to leave for his long-planned Florida retreat earlier—and sadder—than planned. And I had two new tenants in the clinic townhouse: Hilts Heller and Lucy Nell Roebuck. Hilts couldn't live alone, and Lucy needed a new place to stay. Since Lucy's life revolved around the clinic, she welcomed the idea of actually living upstairs, even with a befuddled teenage boy as a roommate. Although I was willing to take unofficial responsibility for my confused nephew, having him live two flights up from me was a much more appealing option than having him in the bedroom next to mine. We had a win-win situation all around.

My mother was deeply disturbed by the mess Teddy had made of her grandson's life, and she immediately began trying to repair the relationship between father and son. But she was also thrilled that Hilts was now in her life full-time. Hilts responded in kind: He spent much of his free time with his grandma, taking her out for walks (or rolls), movies, and visits to any and all New York sights that struck their fancy. He took my mother to the sex museum on lower Fifth Avenue (yes, that one actually stopped me in my tracks), and she introduced him to the Frick and the Met. He worked endlessly with her on speech exercises and goaded her into getting back on the computer (not only was its keyboard good for her dexterity, it offered all sorts of speech and cognitive learning programs for stroke victims). Under Hilts's guidance, she improved mentally and physically every day. I saw, in him, the same stubborn resolve that kept my mom going.

I put Hilts in school. Camilla helped me do the research, and after a group discussion—Cam, me, Hilts, Lucy, my mom, Isadore, and Rocky (okay, he didn't contribute much to the conversation, but he alternated between sitting on my lap and strolling over to Hilts to rub against his leg, which was comforting to both humans)—we settled on a small school in the Village that catered to Europeans and transient students. It had a long history of being both progressive and scholastically stringent. I went with Hilts to meet the head of the school, who was sympathetic to our circumstances and our need for a quick solution. Within a week, Hilts was back in the classroom and had three friends, who all seemed like a big step up from T.J. and Arky.

I can't say I felt any new respect for Teddy and the challenges he'd faced as a parent, but I did begin to appreciate the difficulties and the responsibilities that come with raising a child. And I began to hear my dad's words ringing in my ears several times a day: *Having a child's not like having a dog.*

Hilts was not a genius. But he was mature enough to understand that he had to grapple with legitimate problems—loneliness, girls, his parents, the fear of rapidly approaching adulthood, new and different forms of worry and ennui on a seemingly hourly basis—and my job became to help him grapple. In some ways, my initial lack of emotional involvement with the boy was an advantage. I could be objective and dispassionate when dispensing advice. On the other hand, I felt his pain—and his insecurities and his discomfort and his neuroses—and before long I began to understand how and why he'd become what he was. Slowly but surely I began to get sucked into the boy's life, despite my best efforts to resist emotional involvement. I had missed Hilts's formative years, when instead of being formed he had nearly been dismantled. I was now left with the reconstruction. I hoped I could handle it.

Teddy was not entirely absent. He surfaced just often enough to cause disturbances, setbacks, and anger. Teddy could no longer command his son's love. But if he was responsible for a bit of fear, that was almost as satisfying. He could not be forgotten or ignored, and at this point that was enough to keep my brother present in Hilts's life. I spoke to the kid about how to deal with his father, and he said that he was ignoring Ted as much as possible—he didn't return Ted's numerous phone calls, and when they did happen to speak, he revealed nothing personal about himself, his life, or me. I told him that for the moment that was the best and safest route. I did make an attempt to explain to him that Teddy was sick and very unhappy. I told Hilts that he'd be unhappy, too, if he let himself hate his father for what he'd done. They did not have to be friends, I told him, but he shouldn't think of his father as his enemy. Just engaging in battle meant that, in some sense, Ted had won.

In saying this, maybe I was talking as much to myself as to Hilts, because Ted often seemed like a relentless adversary. Teddy was furious at me for taking Hilts in, and as a consequence he did his best to wreak havoc in my life. He sent me a steady stream of e-mails, which alternated between expressing his rage at my role in stealing his son and offering up sentimental gibberish about our past together and our separate existences in the present. When he wasn't trashing me, he rhapsodized about childhood events that never happened. He sent a meandering and affectionate reflection on what he said was one of his happiest childhood experiences—except that it hadn't happened to him, it had happened to me. His own life had become so indistinct, he had resorted to stealing other people's memories.

Whatever the tenor of Ted's stories and rants and comments, I did my best to respond as vaguely and noncommittally as possible. But his words always left me feeling uneasy and anxious. In one sense Hilts and I felt much the same about Ted: My brother could no longer claim my love and affection, but he could insinuate himself into my dreams. Sometimes, in the middle of the night, I could feel his presence smothering me. A black snake would uncoil in my guts, slither up my throat, and I would wake up trembling and sweating.

Fending Ted off on a day-to-day basis was not particularly difficult, but it was draining. And of all the elements in the life of my new and ever-shifting family unit, it was the thing that engendered the most fear inside me.

I was right to fear Ted.

One night I was in bed with Camilla. I thought she was asleep and so did Waverly, who never ventured onto the bed until Camilla dozed off. But when Wave put her forepaws on the edge of the mattress, Camilla stirred. With no hesitation, she pushed the sweet Irish setter firmly away. Waverly slunk off to another corner of the room.

"Can I ask you something?" Camilla said.

"Anything."

"Actually, let me tell you something first."

"Okay."

"I admire what you're doing. Taking care of your mother. Taking care of Hilts. Assuming responsibility for all these new people. I mean, seriously. Forget those two, I don't know where Lucy or Isadore would be without you."

"I don't think it's all that admirable," I said. "It's not like I searched them out. They all kind of fell into my lap. I didn't have much of a choice."

"Maybe that's what I think is admirable. You think you didn't have a choice."

"Well, I accept that I had a choice. But the choice was pretty much: be a decent human being or be an asshole."

"I still admire it. And I know it's not easy on you. Even though you make it look reasonably easy."

"So what's the question?" I asked.

"Why are you doing it?"

"I told you. Human being versus asshole. It's pretty simple."

"No. That's not all."

"What are you asking, exactly?"

She gave me a long look. "I think I need a drink."

"What's going on, Cam?"

She got out of bed, flashing that thin, uncomfortable smile when she realized I was very much aware of her nakedness. She went into the kitchen and came back with a bottle of cognac and two glasses. She filled them both and handed one to me. Then she sat in a chair, a couple of feet away in the corner of the bedroom, while I propped myself up in bed.

"Your brother called today," she said.

"He called *you*?"

"No. He called here. I answered."

"What did he say?"

"He knew who I was."

"How do you know?"

"I could tell. He asked me a couple of questions. He knew about me."

"How—"

"Hilts."

"I thought Hilts wasn't talking to him. At least wasn't saying anything to him."

"Bobby . . . Hilts is a very insecure boy. I don't think he even realizes what he's saying when he talks to Ted. He's very easy to manipulate. He doesn't mean any harm, he just doesn't understand what his father's doing to him."

"What did Ted know about you?"

"It doesn't matter. Nothing important."

"Then what—"

"He told me to ask you something."

I almost doubled over. My stomach cramped, and I clenched my fist. I nodded at her to tell me. A nod was way easier than speaking. And she didn't have to tell me what Ted had said to her.

"He told me to ask you about the day you heard that Anna had cancer."

It took me a very long time to say anything. When I did, all I could manage was "Did he tell you what I was going to say?"

"No. He just said that he would tell me the truth if you wouldn't. He scared me. He was so . . . I don't quite know how to put it . . ."

"Friendly."

"Yes. He was talking to me as if I were a close friend. But I knew he was saying something that was going to hurt you a great deal."

"And you," I said.

"Do you want to tell me?" Camilla asked.

I nodded. Took a deep breath. Gathered myself. When I answered, I could hear myself talking in a monotone. I wasn't trying to keep emotion out of my voice. I couldn't help it. I felt dead inside.

"The day Anna got sick . . . the day we found out she was sick . . . I was away, speaking at some convention. To make a little money and, I guess, to get some attention. It was fun to, you know, be a star for a day. Among real people. Or any kind of people."

I hesitated. She nodded for me to go on. I took another deep breath, exhaled it quickly, and then spewed out everything as quickly as I could. I barely breathed at all as I told her what had happened.

"I cheated on her that day. There was some insurance person, a woman who sat next to me at dinner and she was flirting and, I know this sounds crazy, but I was feeling kind of old, I don't know why—I can't even explain it. I felt hemmed in. Smothered. Like I could see my whole life laid out in front of me and everything was all so neat and planned and unchangeable. I didn't want to change it, not for real, just for . . . just for a moment. And it was just easy and sexy and I'd never even thought of sleeping with anyone else, it never even occurred to me, but there it was. And the next morning I checked out of the room and left the woman still in there—she didn't want to come out into the hallway with me. But while I was checking out, Anna called, and they put her through to the room. The woman answered. Told Anna I'd checked out. I don't know what Anna really thought but . . . she knew. She knew why that woman answered the phone. She called my cell but it wasn't on, and then when I finally saw that she'd called, I heard the pain, she was in so much pain, and I knew she knew what I'd done, which made it so much worse. I thought *I* caused her pain—I mean, I thought I was the reason she felt so sick. And then I rushed her to the doctor and we found out . . . it wasn't me. It was much, much worse than just me. Christ, I never told anybody about this, not one fucking person, not Phil, not anybody. Except my fucking brother, who caught me at the one fucking moment when I had to talk, when I just couldn't keep it inside, and somehow I trusted him one more time, the way I used to as a kid. And I *knew,* as soon as I did it, I knew I'd done something bad. I can still see his face. Like he'd tricked me. Like he'd won some horrible competition."

A sudden sense of relief flooded over me. I felt unburdened in front of Camilla: At last there were no more barriers between us. I didn't excuse what I'd done, but somehow it didn't feel so terrible deep down in my soul. And I knew how Camilla was going to respond. She was going to tell me it was okay, that what I'd done was in the past, that it wasn't a reason to keep torturing myself. That she was thrilled I'd finally come clean and that we could now finally move forward with no secrets between us. I reached over to touch her.

My fingers hit only air. Pulling away from me, she said: "You felt like he was going to betray you."

"Yes."

"You knew that he would. You were certain that he would."

My sense of relief was fading, replaced by a feeling that things were about to spin out of control.

"Yes," I said.

"The way you betrayed Anna."

Those were, by far, the five worst words I had ever heard. Her tone was cold, distant. The barriers hadn't dropped away at all; now they'd become an insurmountable cement wall keeping us from each other.

I nodded, felt my shoulders sag, and barely managed the strength to say, once again, "Yes."

She put her drink down, got back into bed, pulled the covers over her.

"I wanted to tell you. I really wanted to tell you."

"Why did you wait? Why did you let him do this?"

I no longer had the strength to give a coherent answer, but I knew exactly why I had waited. I hadn't told her about that day because I was afraid of admitting to myself what I'd done, and I was equally fearful of how she'd respond. I was ashamed of my weakness, of my dishonesty. I was afraid of telling the one person for whom I wanted to be strong and honest. So I'd said nothing. And I said nothing now. I just shook my head and shrugged. Even the simple shrug felt as if I had several thousand pounds clamping down on my shoulders.

She didn't speak after that. I waited until I began to feel silly not touching her, so I gingerly slid over so my chest was against her back, my knees inside the backs of her knees, my arm around her, holding her close. Her skin was cold, and I wondered if this was how we were to sleep, with that wall between us. But at some point she shifted her position, turned so her breasts were against my chest and her lips were so close to mine I could feel the warmth of her breath. She kissed me, slowly and deliberately, and we made love. She didn't speak or moan or sigh. It wasn't soft and gentle lovemaking, but it wasn't violent or harsh. It was determined, purposeful. And silent. Afterward, I hugged her and put my head into the crook of her neck. We fell asleep.

In the morning, she was gone. That wasn't surprising; she often left early to go to her Tribeca practice. I didn't hear from her that night, but that wasn't so strange, either. Although not as fanatical as she had been, she still tried to hold to her no-two-nights-in-a-row rule. But the next morning she didn't return my call, and I didn't hear from her the rest of that day.

After three nights of silence, and many voice mail messages left on her cell phone, I walked over to her apartment. I knocked on the door; when there was no answer, I inserted the key she'd given me into the lock. Then I heard a rustling from inside; I removed the key and waited.

The door opened. I was facing a man in his early to mid-thirties. Sandy-colored hair, cut short. He was too thin. His collarbone seemed about to jut through his skin.

"You must be Bob," he said. When I just stared at him, he said, "Cam told me you had a key."

"Is she here?"

"No. That's why I'm here."

"I don't understand," I said. That's when Rags came to the door and slid between the skinny guy's legs, purring. And then I understood.

"Thank you for taking care of him," the guy said to me.

"Rags is your cat."

He nodded.

"And this is your apartment."

He nodded again.

"Where's Camilla?"

"She went back to the Congo. She left yesterday."

"That's impossible," I said. He started to say something else, but I pushed past him. Stormed into the apartment and started looking around, although there was really nowhere to look and nothing to look for.

"Hey," he said angrily. "I don't know what's going on, but get the hell out of my apartment."

"She's really gone?" I said.

Something in my voice caused his annoyance to quickly fade. "She's gone," he said quietly. "I'm sorry."

Rags appeared at my feet. I reached down and rubbed my fingers from his scrawny neck to the end of his tail.

I handed the skinny guy my key to his apartment and left.

Before I went back to Greenwich Avenue, I walked slowly over to the Sephardic cemetery on Eleventh Street. I put my hands on the locked gate, wrapped my fingers around the bars. I felt as if I were a prisoner locked inside the real world, instead of outside the small patch of land where I really wanted to be—the quiet remnant from the past that held several dozen dead bodies and an unknown number of beckoning ghosts.

Dear Dr. Bob:

I am assuming this won't make the final cut for your column. Jesus—at least I sure hope not. I don't know if you'll even read this. I imagine you're so angry at me. It's almost unbearable to me how much I must have hurt you by leaving the way I did. I'm hoping that by sending this as an "official" e-mail to your column address, you'll read it and perhaps even be a little more objective about us and me. More than anything, I hope that after these several months, you're not still hurting. Or at least not quite so much. I know how resilient you are. Anyone so capable of helping us wounded has to know a fair amount about how to heal himself.

As difficult as this might be for you to believe, I have wanted to get in touch with you often since I disappeared on you. But I couldn't. I was too angry. Too afraid. Too confused and too me. I know you'll actually understand the "too me" part. That's one of the reasons it's been so hard to be away from you—your understanding. So let me try to explain myself and hope that one more time you can understand.

You probably know me better than anyone I've ever known. Don't think I'm unaware of it. You not only know what I'm going to order in a restaurant before I even look at the menu, you know when I'm going to get angry and when I'm going to retreat and what I'll think is funny. You know where to touch me to excite me and where to lay your hands to calm me down. You know when I need space—god, I hate that phrase; sorry to actually put it in print—and when I need to be close to someone. I have never had a relationship like that, and I'm not sure I ever will again. This was probably a wasted paragraph because you already know all of this. It's kind of annoying, now that I think about it. You know so much. Maybe too much.

But there are a few things you probably don't know. I wish I'd been able to tell you about them in person, but I think I'm incapable of saying something like this face to face. Perhaps it's because I wouldn't be able to rationalize to myself the hurt I caused; seeing it close up would be more than I could bear. Or perhaps it's because if I did have this conversation with you, I might not have fled. I think I'm a lot weaker than I appear. And if I weakened and stayed with you, I probably would have wound up hating you. I'd hate you for all the things I'd believe you'd do to me. This way I can be far away and love you. And regret the fact that I wasn't strong enough to stay and find out if you really would have done those things.

Is that complicated enough for you? Jesus. I'm a bloody mess.

Here's the thing: It has taken me most of my adult life to trust someone, and unfortunately for you, you were that someone. I finally let myself believe that with you I'd be safe from the kind of destruction I've seen all around me for my entire life. But when you told me about your being unfaithful to Anna, it truly was like waking from a bad dream and finding myself in a real-life nightmare. I had envisioned such a perfect relationship between you two, one that was nearly impossible to compete with. I admired that relationship so much while at the same time hating and resenting it. And then, suddenly, you blew it up. It was as if I'd discovered that what I thought was a glimpse of heaven was actually nothing more than an illusion—that what I was really seeing was a well-disguised hell. I can't quite explain what I felt, except to say that all I saw in my future was more betrayal and more destruction. If you could betray Anna, I was sure I had no chance. What I thought I had finally escaped suddenly seemed inescapable. And that realization overwhelmed and terrified me.

So I went back into the heart of the nightmare. I am back in North Kivu. I am helping people who desperately need my help. There is genuine destruction all around me. I am, once again, seeing limbs blown off and people dying. The crazy thing is that up until recently, I found all this less terrifying than what I feared might happen with us. How insane and unwieldy is the human heart?

The good news, at least for me, is that I can't stay here anymore. I have to get away to someplace safer. I am ready to come back to a world where death may certainly be present but is not life's constant companion. The problem is, I don't know what I'm coming back to. Or what I want to come back to.

I need help, Dr. Bob. I need real help. Not platitudes. Not promises. I'm not sure exactly what I need to know . . . and I have no idea If you'll even be willing to reengage with me or even if you've read this far without pressing the delete button. But I need to know something that will bring me back, and I'm turning to the person who seems always to know what I need.

—Frightened of Ordinary, Corrupt Human Love

Dear Frightened:

I can make this fairly short, if not all that sweet.

No platitudes, I hope. And definitely no promises. Here's what I've learned. For me this knowledge is comforting, in a strange kind of way. I don't know whether you'll feel the same, but it's all I can offer.

All guarantees are worthless. I suppose you realized that long before I did. But you see it as something terrible and destructive. I now see it as what it really is: normal life. I could tell you that I'd never be unfaithful to you or that I'd never hurt you. Or that nothing bad will ever happen to you or . . . or . . . or . . . you can fill in your own blank. It's all bullshit. (At last: I can finally use the word "bullshit" since you're right—I'm reasonably sure I won't be selecting this to be printed in New York's most popular newspaper.)

Here's what *isn't* bullshit: the idea of someone trying as hard as humanly possible never to be unfaithful. And trying never to hurt you. And to never let anything bad happen to you. At some point, yes, one is finally judged by one's successes. But it's the process that defines us as we move through life. I can't go back and prevent the wound from ever happening. I can only do my best to stitch it up and take away the pain and hope the scar is as invisible as possible.

Here's a borderline platitude (see? it's very hard not to be treacherous on some level): Good people sometimes do bad things. People make mistakes. I have made several. Okay, plenty. But I think sometimes moments are just moments; sometimes a mistake defines a life, but sometimes it doesn't have to. I believe we can rise above moments of failure. Maybe what goodness is about is *trying* to be perfect. (And, of course, not failing all that often.) And maybe what love is about is dealing with the failure to be perfect. Knowing when to stay in the face of failure. And then knowing when it's time to leave.

Here's what this knowledge has left me with: a family. A weird family, but a family.

Hilts is doing really well. He's healing. My mother's healing. Lucy is healing. Isadore is healing. I think that's what family does, when one chooses one's family correctly: They help the healing.

Teddy called me recently. It was a strange call. I realized that he thought being family was an unbreakable bond, that he thought everything he did would ultimately be forgiven because he was a member of my family. But I realized that he's not. Blood does not a family make. (Uh-oh—does that count as a platitude? If so, I apologize.) And so I cut him loose. I didn't tell him that's what I was doing, but he knew. I could tell he understood. Toward the end of our inconsequential conversation, he said, "You're a bigger prick than I ever realized." When I didn't answer, he just said, "Congratulations. I guess my job is done here." And then he hung up. I don't think I'll ever hear from him again. And if I do, it will no longer matter.

The bottom line, Frightened? Life ends badly. There are no happy endings. A safe could fall on your head tomorrow. Whoever I marry next might die of stomach cancer, and whoever you decide to love might do all of the bad things you dread. But what happens if you skip that whole part between life and death? What will you have?

I'm not big on opening myself up to too many wounds. But I'll open myself up to this one: I don't want to live in the graveyard any longer. I want you to be part of my family. I need you to be part of my family. I don't care what you've done in various moments we've spent—or not spent—together. I care about what and who you are, not every mistake you've ever made. So if that's what you want to come back to, the offer's on the table. I will try to be faithful. I will try to do an excellent job of choosing your food when you don't know what to order. I will touch you whenever and wherever you need touching. In return, you just have to be you. Not a perfect version of yourself. Not Anna. Not anyone or anything else. Just you.

Here's the simplest way I can say what I believe (and it's only taken me my entire life to learn it):

Pet weight is a wonderful, comforting thing.

But it's nothing compared to ordinary, corrupt human love.

—Dr. Bob

CHAPTER 12

HILTS HELLER

For weeks after Camilla disappeared, I lived in a kind of daze. I took care of my patients and their pets, I took care of my mother, I took care of all the wounded people and creatures in my life. But I had no clear idea about how to take care of myself.

To my great surprise, having Hilts around helped a lot. My nephew fit into his new world much more easily than I'd expected. Perhaps that's because a sixteen-year-old's most exhilarating skill is the ability to look forward rather than backward.

For the first couple of months he was with me, I spoke to his teachers and his principal on a regular basis, hoping to hear that he was making friends, hoping to hear that he was making the right kind of friends—trying to make sure that he wasn't heading toward a repeat of the Arky and T.J. fiasco—and doing whatever I could to help him, in fact, move forward. Hilts was not particularly verbal, nor was he easy to read emotionally. Getting him to talk was an effort; getting him to reveal his feelings was almost impossible. Understandably, he had wrapped himself in a protective cocoon; he was unwilling to trust other people and make himself vulnerable. His father had done a lot more than sucker punch him in the chest; he had stuck a dagger in his heart. I guess there was a lot of that going around.

Hilts was an easy mark for anyone who was nice to him, and I came to understand that this was the source of his fantasizing. Eager to live in a kinder world than the one in which he'd grown up, he responded to kindness much like a small puppy—with no discernment and no awareness of motive. If he were younger, he'd be prey for a child molester. At his age, he was open mostly to either manipulation or misinterpretation. Over and over, he would take a simple human gesture and exaggerate it into whatever he so desperately wanted it to be.

One day he came home and told me that Mrs. Elander, his English teacher, had said she was definitely going to get him into Harvard. I tried not to sound too skeptical, but I explained that it was hard to get into Harvard with a B-minus average and a deficit of about eighty percent of the tuition. He countered by insisting that she had guaranteed it—and that she would get him a scholarship, too. I said, probably not as gently as I should have, that I doubted an English teacher at a small school in the West Village had that kind of pull with any Ivy League college, but he was adamant.

He was so adamant that ten percent of me believed him (he was, after all, Teddy's son), so I called Mrs. Elander, a lovely, caring woman, to find out what she'd really said to him. It turned out, of course, that all she'd done was be nice to the boy. She asked him what his goals were, and he replied that he wanted to go to a great school like Oxford or Harvard. (He didn't realize that Oxford was in England or that Harvard was anywhere real; they were just concepts to him, magical places where people went to get educated so they could ultimately wind up with great jobs.) Mrs. Elander told him that to get into a top-flight university, he'd have to study hard, improve his grades, and start getting involved in a lot of extracurricular activities. He asked if she could help and she, of course, said yes. Somehow, in his hunger to please and to find someone to whom he could attach himself, he had morphed this conversation into a guarantee that she'd get him into Harvard. It was Little League coach redux.

Keeping Hilts positive but disabusing him of his fantasies was a delicate line to walk. I was pretty good at it, mostly because I could understand his instincts. I'd come to realize that I wasn't so far from being a fantasist myself. After all, I'd done a pretty good job of creating a past and a present that weren't really what I thought they were.

Hilts was still not an easy boy to like. I saw too much of Ted in him; I worried that he, too, might be empty at the core. But as we became closer *and began to trust each other, I realized that at heart he was a decent boy. He didn't always know the decent thing to do, but he did understand that decency was the ultimate goal. What motivated him more than anything else was this: He was terrified that he'd grow up to be like his father.*

I spent a lot of time trying to help Hilts understand both of his parents, hoping that understanding might replace hatred or resentment. I didn't know Charlie well enough to really comprehend what made her tick, but I could say with confidence that she was not deliberately destructive. I spoke about her in terms of choices made and not made, and I told Hilts that it was difficult to condemn someone for her choices—at least on this kind of personal level—without knowing what caused her to make them. Ted was harder to explain away. When Hilts asked me if I liked Ted, I said no, I didn't, but that being his brother was not the same as being his son. And I said that Hilts didn't have to like his father; he just had to avoid hating him.

It took Hilts a while to ask me about Anna. He remembered her but not clearly. Her death had assumed a kind of glamorous patina to him; coming to New York after she died had been an exotic vacation for the small boy, a glimpse into a scary but somehow exciting future. I told him as much as was appropriate and appreciated the fact that he didn't just absorb the information; he used it to round out his understanding of me. Hilts was beginning to learn that with knowledge came a certain amount of power and that he had to use it carefully and delicately, unlike his father, who used it only to slice, dice, and butcher.

He also asked about Camilla, and I was honest with him there, too. I said I didn't really know why she had left. I said that I had hurt her but in a way that didn't really have anything to do with her. I'm sure he didn't understand—how could he?—but he didn't press me when I wouldn't go any further. When I said I didn't think she'd be coming back, I saw the sorrow in his eyes and liked him all the more for it. He was not just expressing his own sadness, he was appreciating mine.

As time went on, he accepted discipline from me. In fact, he seemed to crave it—he wanted to better understand the difference between right and wrong. He was grateful that I talked to him like a man while acknowledging that he was still a boy. One evening, after a particularly good talk, I realized a surprising truth: He liked me and I liked him. Love was not there, not yet. But liking was a big step for both of us.

Hilts did love his grandmother, and it was a wonderful thing to watch them grow closer every day. She wanted nothing from him, demanded nothing from him; she took him for who he was and loved him for it. Whatever fears she'd had about making mistakes with Ted or me seemed long gone; she was confident and decisive when dealing with her grandson. She encouraged him and doted on him, but she was not uncritical. When he boasted or hinted at something unethical, she called him on it immediately. She could produce in him instant shame or regret or embarrassment. He wanted to live up to her standards. And though she kept her standards high, they were not unrealistic.

Their relationship was not a one-way street. He worked with her, helping her in small and large ways to get better. He wheeled her to museums and to the grocery store. He confided in her and treated her with gentle respect. As tough and stubborn as my mother was, I believe it was Hilts who gave her the will to push herself to get healthier. Now more than ever, she had a great incentive to live: She wanted to see her grandson grow up.

Hilts also began to love Lucy. He spent more time with her than with anyone else. She was the unlikeliest of roommates, but he delighted in bringing friends home from school and introducing her to them. He could joke with her and make fun of her—but if one of his school friends ever went too far, ever made the wrong kind of comment, there was hell to pay. She fell hard for him, too; she treated him like a puppy left in her permanent care. She made sure the apartment was clean and that he got off to school okay. He often made dinner for her, insisting she eat healthy and watch her weight. One holiday weekend they watched the entire boxed set of The Wire together, and it may have been the happiest seventy-two hours either of them had ever spent.

The clinic, meanwhile, seemed to have become the social mecca of the West Village. Most afternoons I would come out of my examining room to find my mother in her wheelchair, along with Isadore, Hilts, and one or two of Hilts's friends. Someone was always chatting with Lucy, who sat behind the receptionist's desk, and everyone else was talking with the patients who'd managed to squeeze into the room with their animals.

When I'd closed the door on my childhood home, I'd left behind the idols of my youth and all the memories. I had never quite understood where home had gone and how I had lost it. I had loved the feeling of having one place in the world that was my place, a place where I believed I belonged *and where the center did indeed hold. For years, I'd been positive that this place had been real, even if I could no longer define it or even prove its existence. I'd found that feeling with Anna, and then it had been yanked away from me. And then I'd begun to doubt the veracity of its existence. Now I felt something very similar about my new home, and I believe Hilts shared that feeling. Neither of us was exactly sure how it had happened. Or exactly what it was.*

But it most definitely was.

I didn't hear from Camilla after our e-mail exchange.

I had almost deleted my response to her without sending it. But I just couldn't do it. That may be the craziest thing about life: The door might slam in our face ten times in a row, but we always have hope that it'll stay open the eleventh time. Where that hope comes from is an exquisite mystery. All of which is to say I pressed the send button and spent the next month checking my e-mail approximately seven hundred times a day. But no. Nothing.

Six weeks after Camilla had briefly interjected herself into my life again and then once more disappeared, I got a call from Elizabeth. She said she was in town and asked if we could have a drink. I said yes, and we met at a wine bar we used to go to. The waitress remembered us and said she hadn't seen us in a while. I shrugged, and Elizabeth looked uncomfortable. I don't think the waitress noticed.

"So," Elizabeth said. "How's . . . Kevin?"

It took me a moment; then I nodded, acknowledging her subtle bitterness. "Over," I said.

She looked surprised. "For how long?"

"A while."

"Does it hurt?"

"Yes."

"I'm sorry."

I must have looked surprised because she said, "What? You think I'd enjoy it?"

"I guess I did think that."

"I don't want you to be unhappy."

"Thank you." Then: "I don't think I'm unhappy, actually. I just hurt really a lot."

"Well, I don't want you hurting, either."

I clinked her glass with mine in appreciation.

"How's your mother?" she asked.

"Toughing it out," I said. "She's kind of amazing. I think she's at the ballet with Hilts."

"Hilts?"

It seemed natural to be talking to her and I'd momentarily forgotten that she'd been out of the loop, so told her a bit about what had been going on: with my mom, with Hilts, with Ted, even a little about Camilla.

When I finished, Elizabeth said, "Would you like me to spend the night tonight?"

I actually thought that would be pretty swell, but what I said was "No."

"Why not? No strings attached."

"There are always strings, Elizabeth."

"I suppose. But really—why not?"

"I don't know. I'm being faithful."

"To whom?"

I laughed. "Nobody really. Maybe just to myself."

She kept her eyes on my face. I remembered that scrutinizing gaze: It meant she was trying to figure something out and wasn't having any luck.

We finished our wine. I walked her to a taxi and kissed her on the cheek before she got in.

"I don't think I'll call you again," Elizabeth said.

"I understand," I told her.

"I still don't," she said. Then she got in the cab and headed uptown.

Three weeks later, I was home alone. Well, I was never home alone. I was home feeding, petting, and brushing various three-legged, four-legged, and feathered friends before cooking dinner when my phone rang. It was Lucy.

"Could you come down to the clinic?" she said. "We have an emergency patient."

"Can't you send him to Fifteenth Street?" I asked. There was a twenty-four-hour pet emergency room on Fifteenth and Fifth.

"I think you'd better come down," Lucy said.

I sighed. Gave Larry a final pat on his tiny green head and climbed down the one flight of stairs. The door to the clinic was open.

Camilla stood in the waiting room. Lucy was nowhere to be found.

I tried to speak, but my goddamn heart was beating so fast I couldn't manage it.

"Don't be mad at Lucy," Camilla said. "I didn't think you'd see me unless she called."

"Nice trick," I managed, a little surprised to get even that much out.

"I did think it was kind of clever. Are you glad to see me?"

"How can you ask me something like that?"

"Are you?" she said.

"No," I said. Then: "Fuck. Yes. I'm unbelievably happy to see you."

"Me, too," she said. "The good news is, a safe didn't fall on my head while I was walking over here."

I didn't say anything.

"Well," she said, "at least I thought it was good news."

"I guess you got my e-mail."

"I got it. Thank you."

"For what?"

She smiled. "Not sure. It just seemed appropriate to say, 'Thank you.' How is everyone?"

"Everyone's fine."

"And how are you?"

"How can you be so goddamn casual about this?"

"I'm not casual. I think I'm being pretty determined. And I'd like to know how you are. It's important to me."

"I'm fine, too. I'm glad we're both fine. You want to talk about the weather now? Why are you here?"

"Because you invited me."

"Cam—"

"You invited me. You asked me to be part of your family."

"I invited you months ago. And you never bothered to answer me."

"Yes, I did."

"When?"

"Now," she said. "This is my answer. You said to be me. This is me. This is what I am. And this is my answer. Now it's up to you where you really want to live."

"Do you mind if I sit down?"

She swept her hand in the direction of one of the patient chairs. I sat slowly.

"Your leaving almost destroyed me," I said.

She nodded. "I know. But you left me, too," she said. "I might have been gone physically, but you left emotionally. That didn't do wonders for me, either."

"It's the history of the world, I guess. People do their best to destroy each other, and then they want someone to help put everything back into place."

"We're doctors. That's our job. To put things back into place. To repair things after the destruction."

"I don't know how to repair people," I said. "I only know how to fix dogs and cats. And Vietnamese pigs."

"I don't believe that. But that's why I came back. To see if you want us to learn how to put each other back together."

She looked beautiful and vulnerable and perfect. She looked dangerous as hell.

I wanted to hold her. I wanted my lips against hers. I wanted to run for my life.

"Do you want to come in?" I asked. "Upstairs, I mean."

"Do you want me to?"

"I want you to," I said.

I turned and stepped out of the clinic and climbed back up the one flight of stairs. Camilla followed.

I opened the door to my apartment. She hesitated.

"Are there any changes?" she asked. "Anything I should be prepared for?"

"New curtains," I said.

"Seriously?"

I nodded.

"Are they nice?"

"You'll have to see for yourself."

She nodded, then took a deep breath, as if bracing herself.

She put one foot across the doorway, hesitated yet again. Then Camilla stepped forward, into my apartment. She looked back into the hallway, a lingering look, as if memorizing what she was leaving in the outside world.

Various pets came forward. There were meows and barks. Larry screeched, as loud as a bird can screech. "Fuckin' A," he said. "Fuckin' fuckin' A."

Camilla closed the door behind her.

BOB HELLER

*One of the things that happens as you get older—and while Camilla was
away, I celebrated my forty-second birthday—is that you begin to realize that
your life isn't really about you. It's about all the other people around you.
That's both an unnerving and a strangely reassuring realization. It's unnerving because you begin to suspect that you're not so crucial in the overall
scheme of things. It's reassuring because if the people around you are good
and truly care about you, then you might not be so insignificant after all.*

*Soon after his seventeenth birthday, Hilts was accepted at Syracuse Uni-
versity. I was happy he would be staying reasonably close to home—it was an
easy weekend trip back and forth. He was even happier because his girlfriend, Tracy, also got into Syracuse. She was a lovely girl, smart and polite,
with just the right amount of wild streak to her. Hilts spent much of his time
staring at her with a loving gaze—a very familiar loving gaze—and I often
heard them making plans for their future. I thought about telling him that
the odds were approximately a million to one that they'd even recognize each
other by the time they got out of school. But my job was not to save him from
the roller coaster he was about to ride through the rest of his life. My job was
to tell him how proud I was of what he'd accomplished. When he told me
that he intended to pay me back every penny I was spending on his college*

education, I was extremely happy to tell him that it was my gift to him. He hugged me when I gave him the news, the first time he'd ever reached for me like that. We held each other for quite a long time. Then he called Tracy, told her what I'd done, and went back to talking like a lovesick idiot.

I'd never seen my mom as thrilled as the day she went to Hilts's high school graduation. For her, it seemed to be some kind of validation of the past, when my father had seen his baby grandson and decided he was the Second Coming. He certainly wasn't that, but Hilts had turned out all right, in no small way because of my mother's support. He didn't remember his grandfather, but he knew all about him. On his graduation day, my mom gave him a gift: a month-long trip to Europe, ticket and cash included. On the same day, Hilts gave my mother a gift he said he'd found at the bottom of a suitcase: a CD recording of my dad singing that goofy little song he'd made up just days after Hilts had been born. I suspected that Ted had sent it to his son, but I could never prove it. Ted didn't come to Hilts's graduation. The last any of us had heard, he was living somewhere in Central America. Nobody knew exactly what he was doing.

My mother died while Hilts was in Europe. She had another stroke, and this one killed her instantly. Hilts wanted to fly back from wherever he was when he found out, but I told him that my mother wouldn't have wanted him to. She would want him to continue his adventure and to enjoy life, not mourn her death. I told him to have a glass of wine and toast her memory, toast her strength and her life. He burst into tears on the phone. I let him cry and then told him I loved him.

When he stopped crying, I also told him that Camilla and I had had dinner with his grandma the night before she died. Her speech was as good as it had been in years. She'd talked about my dad and a little bit about Ted—she was still guilty and full of regret—and a lot about her grandson. She talked about Anna and to Camilla, and while I was eating a slice of pecan pie, for dessert, she reached across the table and patted my hand. Her skin was loose, what there was of it, but her touch warmed me through and through. I told Hilts that she was happy; she was grateful to be alive and glad to have seen all the things she'd seen along the way. The next morning, when Isadore came to tell me that my mom was dead, she said that the stroke had occurred while my mother was listening to the CD of my dad singing his song to Hilts.

I e-mailed Ted with the news of our mother's death, and though I gave him the details of the service I didn't expect him to come. When he walked up to me just before the funeral started, it was jarring. I didn't recognize him at first—he had aged tremendously. He was not yet fifty, but his skin was slack and his hair was bone-white. He was subdued and nervous. Furtive. He brought a young Spanish woman, whose name, he said, was Angel. That was all he told us about her. When he met Camilla, he leaned over, kissed her on the cheek, and mumbled something indistinct to her. After the funeral, he handed me a piece of paper with his address on it and told me that's where I could reach him after the will was settled. He also went to hug me, but I drew away. Then I shook my head, as if clearing it, and embraced him slightly. Refusing to touch him at all seemed as ridiculous as giving him a warm and loving hug. I did not feel good or bad when he left. It was like saying good-bye to a stranger.

Not long after that, I took a new partner into the clinic, a young woman who had just graduated from Cornell's veterinary school. At Elizabeth's instigation, I'd recently gone up to Cornell to give a lecture, and Kendra Boudreaux had driven me around during my time on campus. Kendra was a pretty good drinker and a very good driver, and she was a superb listener when I told her all about Rocky and Waverly and Larry and Scully and Margo and Che. She moved into the apartment I'd first lived in with Anna. Lucy stayed on the fourth floor and kept Hilts's bedroom ready for whenever he returned. Izzy didn't really have a job anymore, now that my mom wasn't there, but it never occurred to any of us that she should leave. So she stayed and took care of all of us in some unofficial way—cooking sometimes, cleaning sometimes, scolding any of us who needed scolding, helping out at the clinic. Whatever anyone needed.

Camilla got her old job back, partnering with the physician she'd worked with before she'd run. She had said he was her Marjorie Paws, and she was definitely right about that. He put her through the wringer when she went to see him, but he did take her back. She loves her work this time around. She is saving people in bits and pieces instead of putting them back together after explosions and gunfire. The process appeals to her.

Marjorie comes up to visit once a year. She approves of Camilla. She is as brittle as can be, but as near as I can tell she hasn't slowed down one bit. She is doing intensive research on allergies to dander; during her last visit she told me I would soon be reading a paper that would revolutionize the field.

Then she swatted my head—hard—because she thought I wasn't paying enough attention to Rocky, who is not such a great jumper anymore and was meowing like crazy for me to pick him up. In his old age, he sometimes leaps for the bed and doesn't make it, so recently I put a little stepladder by the bedside for him. But he stubbornly refuses to use it. He likes to make Camilla pick him up and put him gently on the bed, which she does quite happily now. He still goes wherever I go. Just not as nimbly.

The rest of the menagerie is still around and going strong. With one addition: Rags has moved in. When his original owner took a job in Atlanta, Camilla asked if we had room for one more. We did.

I remember Anna once asking me why she was the lucky one, the human I'd picked to love. I never had a particularly good answer, although I think I have one now. It was because I found it impossible not to be in love with her.

A year after she'd come back to New York City, I asked Camilla the same question. We were in bed. We'd just made love, which I still found as thrilling as the first time we'd done it in her sublet apartment. We were holding each other; she was still and I was running my hand gently up and down her spine, admiring her bare shoulders. She had the embarrassed naked smile on her face.

"Because we understand each other," she said.

"Really? That's your definition of love? Understanding? That's my definition of a good roommate in a retirement home."

"I think that in a lot of ways, knowledge is love. Here's the thing: You know me so well that you could hurt me with a word or a glance or just a snide comment. You know exactly where I'm vulnerable. The fact that I know you wouldn't ever do that makes me love you every single day."

"And you think you could hurt me the same way?"

"No, not the same way. In completely different ways. I've already hurt you. When I left you, I did the worst thing I could possibly do to you. I'd rather cut off my arm than hurt you like that again."

"Please don't cut off your arm. Especially this left one. It's extremely attractive."

"It's not really knowledge," she said. "That's not love. It's what we do with that knowledge. If we do the right thing, that's love."

She kissed me and buried her face in my chest.

"Do you know the right thing?" I asked.

"When it comes to you, yes."

"Always?"

"Always. Do you? When it comes to me?"

"Yes."

"Well, there you have it," she said.

Then we both fell asleep, and I dreamed only of the future.

From the *New York Daily Herald-Examiner:*

Dr. Robert Heller is one of New York's leading veterinarians. He is the author of three books about taking care of pets, *They Have Nothing but Their Kindness, More Than Human,* and *A Good Place to Start,* and is a regular on the *Today* show with his weekly segment, "The Vetting Zoo." He lives with his wife, Dr. Camilla Hayden, their young son, Gregory Solomon, and their menagerie in Greenwich Village. Dr. Bob takes care of cats, dogs, horses, birds, snakes, turtles, frogs, snails, fish, small pigs, and many varieties of rodents. For nearly fifteen years, he has answered any question you've asked about the animal you love in the tristate area's most popular newspaper. Today's column is his last. At least for the time being.

Dear Readers:

This is just a short note to thank all of you who have written in over the years and who have read my often smart-ass, hopefully helpful comments during the past decade and a half. Fifteen years is a long time to do a column like this, and I'm not sure I have anything else to say. I think it's time for me to learn a bit more about humans, as well as animals, before I resume telling all of you what to do and how to feel.

It's been a privilege serving you. I feel as if you're part of my extended family, and I'm certain that you have taught me way more than I've taught you. If I have any final words of wisdom, here they are: *Don't be afraid of happiness.* Watch your cat when you're gently rubbing his ears. Pay attention to your dog while he fetches the same ball for two and a half hours in the backyard. Savoring happiness is something our pets learn how to do very early on, so I'm not sure why it's such a hard concept for us humans to grasp. But it's worth grasping.

Good luck to all of you. You may not always hear what you want to hear, but may all your questions be answered.

—Dr. Bob

Acknowledgments

I would like to thank Stephen Rubin for his faith and support, John Sterling for his faith and support and annoyingly perfect, meticulous editing, and Esther Newberg for her total *lack* of faith and yet her incredible, never-ending support. This book would not exist without all three of them. I would also like to thank everyone at Random House Studio; they worked extra hard so I could have the time to finish the novel. A very special thank-you to Roman Polanski, who, although I'm sure he doesn't know it, provided the key that opened this book for me.

About the Author

PETER GETHERS is an author, screenwriter, playwright, book publisher, and film and television producer, which is why he's always tired. His previous books include the bestselling trilogy about his extraordinary cat Norton, *The Cat Who Went to Paris, A Cat Abroad,* and *The Cat Who'll Live Forever,* and five internationally bestselling thrillers using the pseudonym Russell Andrews. He is also the co-creator and co-producer of the critically acclaimed off-Broadway hit play *Old Jews Telling Jokes* and one of the co-creators of Rotisserie League Baseball, which begat the fantasy sports craze. He lives in New York City and Sag Harbor, New York.